RECALLED
·· TO ··
LIFE

Also by Reginald Hill

RECALLED
·· TO ··
LIFE

A Dalziel / Pascoe Mystery

Reginald Hill

Delacorte Press

Published by
Delacorte Press
Bantam Doubleday Dell Publishing Group, Inc.
666 Fifth Avenue
New York, New York 10103

(Author's note: All epigraphs in this book come from
Dickens's *A Tale of Two Cities*.)

Library of Congress Cataloging in Publication Data

Hill, Reginald.
   Recalled to life / by Reginald Hill.
     p.   cm.
   ISBN 0-385-30131-6
   I. Title.
  PR6058.I448R4   1992
  823'.914—dc20   92-1380
                                              CIP

Canadian Cataloguing in Publication Data

Hill, Reginald, 1936–
   Recalled to life

ISBN 0-385-30131-6

I. Title.

PR6058.I448R4   1992   823'.914   C92-094097-8

Design by Diane Stevenson / SNAP · HAUS GRAPHICS

Manufactured in the United States of America

Published simultaneously in Canada by Doubleday Canada, Limited,
105 Bond Street, Toronto, Ontario, M5B 1Y3.

October 1992

10 9 8 7 6 5 4 3 2 1

RRH

"You had abandoned all hope of being dug out?"

"Long ago."

"You know that you are recalled to life?"

"They tell me so."

"I hope you care to live?"

"I can't say."

PART
THE FIRST

"Golden Age"

One

"I tell thee that although it is a long time on the road, it is on the road and coming."

It was the best of crimes, it was the worst of crimes; it was born of love, it was spawned by greed; it was completely unplanned, it was coldly premeditated; it was an open-and-shut case, it was a locked-room mystery; it was the act of a guileless girl, it was the work of a scheming scoundrel; it was the end of an era, it was the start of an era; a man with the face of a laughing boy reigned in Washington, a man with the features of a lugubrious hound ruled in Westminster; an ex-marine got a job at a Dallas book repository, an ex-Minister of War lost a job in politics; a group known as the Beatles made their first million, a group known as the Great Train Robbers made their first two million; it was the time when those who had fought to save the world began to surren-der it to those they had fought to save it for; Dixon of Dock Green was giving way to Z-Cars, Bond to Smiley, the Monsignors to the Maha-rishis, Matt Dillon to Bob Dylan, l.s.d. to LSD, as the sunset glow of the old Golden Age imploded into the psychedelic dawn of the new Age of Glitz.

It was the Year of Our Lord nineteen hundred and sixty-three, and it is altogether fitting that this crime of which we speak should have been committed in one of Yorkshire's great country houses, Mickledore Hall, and that its dénoument should have taken place in that most traditional of settings, the Old Library . . .

The library door burst open. A man came running out. For a second he paused. The main doors stood ajar, spilling golden sunlight across the old flagged floor. He took a half step toward the light, a voice called, "Get him!" and he turned and started up the broad sweeping staircase. He was beautifully balanced, with the tapering figure of an athlete, and his long easy stride devoured three treads at a time.

A second man came out of the library now, almost as tall as the other, but dark where he was fair, burly and muscular where he was rangy and loose-limbed. He too glanced at the sunlit doorway for a moment. Then with unhurried pace he began to climb the stairs, taking one at a time, heavy lips pulled back from yellowing teeth in the anticipatory rictus of a hungry bear.

On the first floor landing the fleeing man turned right without hesitation, then right again into the first room he reached. Moments later the burly man arrived in the doorway. The room led through into another, through whose open door a double bed was visible. The fair man made no effort to go any farther but stood defiantly by a huge mahogany wardrobe, his shoulders tensed for battle.

"Nay, Sir Ralph, no more laking. Your fancy woman's waiting. Murder's one thing, but you'll not want to be accused of bad manners too."

"What would a Neanderthal like you know about manners?" sneered the fair man.

"You're dead right. Pig ignorant, that's me. This'd be what you call a dressing room, is it? I'll take your word for it, though a dressing room don't seem right to me without mud on the floor and a pile of old jock straps heaving in the corner."

4

As he spoke the burly man was moving slowly forward. Suddenly reacting to the danger, the other seized a linen basket which stood by the wardrobe and raised it high as if to hurl it. The top came off, spilling items of male clothing over his head and shoulders.

"Trying to make me feel at home, Sir Ralph? That's right good of you," the burly man said with a grin.

This gibe finally broke the other's control. Screaming with rage he flung the wardrobe door open to impede the other's approach and started dragging clothes off their hangers and hurling them like palms before the advancing feet. Chunky tweeds, elegant evening wear, wool, cotton, and finest silk, all alike were crushed beneath that implacable tread till finally the two men stood inches apart.

A hand like a contractor's grab fell upon the fair man's shoulder. Instantly, as if its touch were anesthetic, all life and energy seemed to drain from his limbs and the tense straining body went slack.

"Walkies," said the burly man.

At the foot of the stairs, an older gray-haired man with a lantern jaw was waiting.

"Well done, lad," he said.

"Shall I cuff him, sir?"

"I doubt we'll need to go as far as that, though if he gives any more bother, you can mebbe box his ears."

The burly man laughed. The old jokes were best, especially when your boss made them.

Outside, the sun was low in the sky but still warm. It cast long shadows from the three police cars standing on the white gravel beneath the terrace. In the rearmost car's shady interior the pale face of a woman could be seen, wedged between two women police constables. She looked straight ahead, showing no more animation than a death mask.

The uniformed officers took charge of the fair man and led him down from the terrace into the second car. He turned before he got in and looked back, not at the figures above him, but at the house

5

itself, his gaze moving slowly along the whole facade. Then he let himself be pushed into the rear seat.

On the terrace the man with the jaw spoke a few words to his burly subordinate before running lightly down the steps and getting into the leading car. He held his arm aloft through the open window, like a wagon master preparing his train. Then he let it drop forward, the cars began to crunch gravel, and at the same time their bells started to sound and their lights to flash.

Smiling broadly, the burly man stood on the terrace till he could no longer see the flashing lights nor hear the sounding bells.

Then he turned his back on the sun and slowly reentered the house.

Two

"You can bear a little more light?"

"I must bear it if you let it in."

Lights.

Some hot, harsh, and constant. Others driven at her like snow against a stovepipe, melting soon as touching.

A shallow platform, one step up.

She takes it, pauses, sways, hears the pause and the sway in the watchers' breath.

She thinks: so it must have felt for Mick, that first step onto the scaffold.

A hand steadies her. No executioner's hand, but her savior's, Jay's, cousin Jay Waggs, though she cannot yet think of him as savior. She clutches her old leather-bound Bible to her skinny breast. He smiles at her, a warm smile in a young face, and a memory is touched of faraway times, faraway places. He urges her forward.

There is a chair. She sits. To her left, a pitcher of water with a glass. To her right, a small vase out of which a spray of freesia raises its hand of glory. Before her, a posy of microphones offering some protection from the flashing bulbs and probing gazes but none from the TV cameras covering her every move, like guns on a prison watchtower.

Mr. Jacklin is speaking. Her solicitor. A small gray man who looks so dry that a very little pressure might crumble him to dust. But it is a dryness which kindles to fire at the spark of injustice.

He says, "Let me rehearse the situation in case anyone has strayed in from another planet. My client, Miss Cecily Kohler, was tried for the murder of her employer, Mrs. Pamela Westropp, in 1963. She was found guilty and sentenced to death. The sentence was later commuted to life imprisonment. Almost from the start, doubts were expressed in some quarters about the safeness of the verdict, but circumstances conspired to make a reexamination of the case virtually impossible until two years ago when Miss Kohler's kinsman, Jay Waggs, began to interest himself in the fate of his distant kinswoman, Cissy Kohler. The new evidence he uncovered was first presented to the public in the Ebor television program *Doubt* last spring. Now the Home Secretary has at last accepted that there are serious grounds for believing there may have been a gross miscarriage of justice, and he has issued a release order pending consideration of the new evidence by the Court of Appeal.

"Until the decision of that court is officially made public, I cannot of course comment on the legal implications of what has happened. But I can point out the obvious. My client has spent a longer period in jail than any other woman in the annals of English penology. It goes without saying that she will need a proportional period of readjustment to the rigors of freedom. But being aware of the great public interest in the case, she has accepted the recommendation of her advisers that she should attend this press conference in the hope that thereafter she will be permitted a long breathing space free from the importunities of the media."

"Does that include Jay Waggs and Ebor television?" calls a sharp-faced young woman.

Jay Waggs smiles at her and says, "One question per paper was the agreement. Is that yours, Sally?"

"No! Miss Kohler, I'm Sally Blindcrake, *Daily Sphere*. How did it feel when you heard you were getting out?"

8

Cissy Kohler speaks so softly not even the posy of mikes can pick it up.

"Sorry? I couldn't catch that."

"She says she felt nothing," says Waggs. "Next question."

"Nothing?" insists Blindcrake incredulously. "After all those years you're told you're innocent, and you feel *nothing*?"

Kohler raises her head and speaks again, this time loud enough to be heard.

"I knew it already."

A pause, then laughter, a ripple of applause.

"Next," says Waggs.

"Martin Redditch, BBC television. Miss Kohler, you didn't apply for parole until 1976, though you could have applied earlier. Why was that?"

She frowns and says, "I wasn't ready."

"Ready for what?" shouts someone, but Redditch is pressing on, regardless of the one question limit.

"But you were ready in 1976, right. And it looked like you were getting out, till you attacked and killed officer Daphne Bush in Beddington Prison. At least, you got tried and sentenced for killing her. Or are you claiming to be innocent of that killing too?"

She takes her time, not as if the effort of remembering is painful so much as if the machinery of memory is rusty.

Finally: "I killed her," she says.

Redditch tries to follow up once more but now Waggs cuts him off.

"Okay, Martin, you got two in. We'll call it one for each channel. Next!"

"Norman Proudfoot, *Church Times*. Miss Kohler, the TV program mentioned the Bible your mother gave you as a child. I presume it's that same Bible you're carrying now. Can you tell us what comfort you have drawn from it during your long imprisonment?"

She looks down at the book still clutched tight against her breast.

"It helped me look in at myself. Without it I don't think I'd have survived."

9

This is the longest answer she gives. The questions come thick and fast, some aggressive, some insinuating, some simply inane. All receive the same treatment—a pause followed by a short reply in a soft monotonous voice. Soon Waggs ceases to intervene and relaxes, faintly smiling as the cohorts of the Press dash themselves vainly against the walls of her solitude.

At last the room is silent. Waggs asks, "All done?"

Sally Blindcrake says, "I know I've had my question but it was so long ago I've forgotten what it was. How about me closing the circle?"

"In the interests of balance? Well, that's certainly a novelty in the *Sphere*, Sally. Okay. Last question."

"Miss Kohler. Cecily. Cissy. If you were innocent, why did you confess?"

This time the preliminary pause goes on and on.

Blindcrake says, "Okay, let me rephrase the question. Not only did you confess, but your alleged confession implicated Ralph Mickledore to such an extent that, along with the other evidence against him, it sent him to the gallows. Was he innocent too?"

Waggs says, "Okay, Sally, I should have known better. That does it, folks . . ."

"No! Hold on. I need an answer, Jay. It was your telly program that suggested she was so smashed up by little Emily's drowning that she was fair game for anyone. If she's innocent, then who's guilty? And I don't just mean of the murder. Who was it who twisted her arm till she stuck it up?"

Now Waggs is on his feet drawing Kohler upright too.

Jacklin leans over to the mikes and says, "I cannot allow my client to answer that question outside of a courtroom. We must remember the law of defamation . . ."

"Defamation nothing! You can't defame the dead," yells Blindcrake. "And isn't the guy most likely the late Detective Superintendent Walter Tallantire, then head of Mid-Yorkshire CID?"

Waggs is urging Kohler off the platform. Any discipline the press conference might have had is rapidly disappearing. Cameramen and reporters jostle each other in their efforts to get near the woman. They spill out of the body of the hall and get between her and the door. The air is filled with a blizzard of flash bulbs and a babble of voices.

". . . What about compensation? . . . Will you go back to the States? . . . Are you suing the police? . . . Is it true you've written your memoirs? . . . How much are they paying? . . . Have you heard from James Westropp? . . . What's his son Philip doing now? . . . Did you mean to drown the kid? . . . Is it true you're going into a nunnery? . . . Was Daphne Bush your lover? . . ."

Three uniformed policemen have appeared. They clear a path to the door. One of them flings it open. A camera peers through, momentarily revealing a long corridor in which several men are standing. Then Kohler and Jacklin are through. Waggs turns in the doorway, helping the police to block pursuit. Someone shouts, "Hey, Jay. When they make the movie, how about Schwarzenegger playing you?"

Waggs grins and says, "Thank you for your courtesy, gentlemen, and ladies. That's it. End of story."

He steps back through the door. A policeman pulls it shut behind him.

The scene fades, to be replaced by a close-up of a woman with dead eyes and a mobile lower lip who says, "The rest of our program will be running approximately forty minutes late because of that news conference. We apologize for any inconvenience this may cause to viewers . . ."

Three

"Come on, and have it out in plain

words! You hate the fellow."

Detective Superintendent Andrew Dalziel of Mid-Yorkshire CID stabbed the off-button of the video remote control as if he wanted to drive it through his knee.

"Bastards!" he said. "Bitch!"

"The poor woman," said Maudie Tallantire.

"Poor nowt. She were guilty as hell," said Dalziel. "Three people are dead because of her. I'd have thrown away the key! You save your sympathy for yourself, Maudie. You heard what that newspaper cow said about Wally?"

"Wally's been dead nigh on twenty years," said Maud Tallantire as if explaining something to a simple child. "He's past harm now and who'd want to harm an old woman like me? Oh, I know the times have changed, and I reckon us old 'uns had the best of it, war and all. Everyone knew where they were going then, and in the years after. But it all went wrong somewhere, Andy. But human nature doesn't change. At heart people are still as good as ever they were. They'd rather do you a good turn than a bad one. Look at you, Andy,

12

coming all this way just 'cos you got to worrying about me, and no need at all!"

Dalziel shook his head in affectionate exasperation. Anyone who could cite himself as evidence of the basic goodness of human nature was clearly beyond hope. Maudie was over seventy now, gray-haired, slightly lame, but she hadn't changed in essence from the pretty, amiable, and rather vague woman he'd met more than thirty years ago, and very little, if report were true, from the wide-eyed lass who'd married Wally Tallantire back in the thirties.

"Copper's wife has got to be either tough as old boots to put up with the life, or live in a world of her own so she don't notice," Wally had once confided in him when time and alcohol had matured their relationship. "That's my Maudie. A rare orchid, Andy. She'll need looking out for if anything ever happens to me. You'll do that for me, won't you, lad? Do I have your word on that?"

Dalziel had given his word gladly, but in the event when Tallantire died of a heart attack shortly before he was due to retire, Maudie proved quite capable of looking out for herself. Within a year she'd moved back to her native Skipton and quickly gathered up all the threads of her young life broken when she'd moved from West to Mid-Yorkshire all those years ago.

Dalziel visited regularly for a while, then intermittently, and in recent years hardly at all. But when he saw the Kohler press conference on the telly, he knew the time had come for another visit.

He'd been going to suggest that Maudie might like to think about staying with friends for a couple of days just in case the press came prying, but he wasn't a man to waste breath. Instead he ran his video back a little way, restarted it, and pressed the freeze button when he reached the shot of the corridor through the open door.

"That fellow there remind you of anyone, Maudie?"

"The tall one?" she said looking at the two men touched by his broad forefinger. "He's a bit like Raymond Massey."

"No. Someone you know. And I mean the other one. I know who the tall fellow is. Chap called Sempernel. He came sniffing around at the time. Said he were Home Office but he were a funny bugger, no question. You'd not have seen him. But the other one, the skinny runt, remind you of anyone? And don't say Mickey Rooney, luv!"

"He doesn't look a bit like Mickey Rooney," said the woman, examining the man closely. "He doesn't really look like anybody, but he does look familiar."

"Remember a sergeant called Hiller? Adolf, we used to call him? Wally didn't care for him and got shut of him."

"Vaguely," she said. "But what would Sergeant Hiller be doing there?"

"That's what I'd like to know," said Dalziel grimly. "And he's not a sergeant now. Deputy Chief Constable down south, last I heard. Well, the higher the monkey climbs, the more he shows his behind, eh?"

Maudie Tallantire laughed. "You don't change, do you, Andy? Now how about a cup of tea?"

"Grand. By the way, Maudie, do you still have any of Wally's personal papers? I seem to recall you said you'd put a lot of stuff together when you moved here just in case there were anything important . . ."

"That's right. And you said you'd look through it sometime when you had a moment. But that was donkey's years ago, Andy. And you never had a moment, did you?"

"Sorry," he said guiltily. "You know how it is. But if you've still got it. I might as well take a look now."

"I've probably thrown it out long since," she said. "It were in an old blue suitcase, one of them little ones which was all we used to need once when we went away. Now it takes a cabin trunk! It'll be in the box room if I've still got it, but it's dusty up there and you don't want to spoil that nice suit."

"I'll take care."

She was right about the dust but he spotted the blue case without any difficulty. He picked it up, blew gently, coughed as a dust cloud arose, and went to open the window.

Below in the street, a car drew up. There were two men in it. The one who got out of the driver's side was youngish, dressed in designer casuals, and his elegantly coiffured head moved watchfully this way and that, as though he had debouched in Indian territory rather than suburban Yorkshire.

But it was the other who held Dalziel's attention. Thin faced, bespectacled, dressed in a crumpled black suit a size too large, he stood quite still looking up at the house like a twice repelled rent-collector.

"Bloody hell. It *is* Adolf!" exclaimed Dalziel stepping back from the window. "I should've known that bugger'd move quick."

Shaking the remaining dust from the case he went quickly and quietly downstairs. Just inside the front door was a small cloakroom. He slipped the case under the handbasin, closed the door, and returned to the living room as Maudie came out of the kitchen carrying a laden tray.

"Find what you were looking for, Andy?"

"No, not a sign," he said, removing the video from the recorder and fitting it into a capacious inner pocket. "I reckon you must have chucked it out without noticing. No matter. Are them your Eccles cakes I see? You must've known I was coming. What was it Wally used to say? Never say nowt good ever came out of Lancashire till you've tasted our Maudie's Eccles cakes!"

He seized one, devoured it in a couple of bites, and was on his third when the doorbell rang.

"Who can that be?" said Maudie with the ever fresh surprise of the northern housewife that someone should be at her door.

She went out into the hallway. Dalziel helped himself to another cake and moved to the lounge doorway to catch the conversation.

"Mrs. Tallantire, you may not remember me, but we have met a long time back. Geoffrey Hiller. I was a sergeant up here for a while when your husband was head of CID."

"Hiller? Now isn't that odd? We were just talking about you. Won't you step inside, sergeant? And your friend."

"Thank you. Actually, it's Deputy Chief Constable now, Mrs. Tallantire. Of the South Thames force. And this is Detective Inspector Stubbs."

"Ooh, you have done well. Come on through. Andy, it never

15

rains but it pours. Here's another old friend of Wally's come visiting."

Dalziel, back in his chair, looked up in polite puzzlement as the dark-suited man stopped short in the doorway, like a parson accidentally ushered into a brothel. Then the fat man's face lit up with the joy of a father at the prodigal's return and he said, "Geoff? Is that you? Geoff Hiller, by all that's holy! How are you, lad? What fettle? By God, it's good to see you."

He was on his feet shaking the newcomer's hand like a bushman killing a snake. Hiller had recovered from his shock and was now regarding Dalziel with wary neutrality.

"How are you, er, Andy?" he said.

"I'm grand. And who's your friend?"

"This is Detective Inspector Stubbs. Stubbs, meet Detective Superintendent Dalziel, Head of Mid-Yorkshire CID."

Hiller's tone underlined the title.

Stubbs held out his hand. "Hi. Glad to meet you, supe."

"*Supe?*" echoed Dalziel. "Up here we drink *supe*. Or if it's home made, we chew it. Will you be staying in West Yorkshire long enough to learn our little ways?"

Stubbs glanced at Hiller who said, "Actually, er, Andy, we're on our way to your neck of the woods. This is just in nature of a courtesy call on Mrs. Tallantire in passing."

"I see. In passing Skipton? On your way to Mid-Yorks HQ? From South Thames?"

As he spoke, Dalziel's finger traced two sides of a rectangle in the air, and he smiled an alligator's smile.

"Now that's what I call courtesy! Maudie, isn't it nice of Geoff here to come so far out of his way just for old times' sake? Incidentally, Geoff, I presume you're expected at my shop? I was talking to the Chief yesterday afternoon and he said nowt."

"The Home Office should have phoned Mr. Trimble this morning," said Hiller.

"That explains it. It's my day off which is why I'm here. Social call on an old friend. Mebbe it's your day off too?"

"No," said Hiller. "Not really. I'm afraid there is a business element to my call, Mrs. Tallantire. You may have heard that some question has arisen as to the safety of the verdict in the Mickledore Hall murder case. In fact Cecily Kohler has been released and the Home Office has ordered an inquiry into the affair. Your late husband, Detective Superintendent Tallantire, conducted the original investigation and will naturally figure in the inquiry which I have been instructed to take charge of."

"Now, isn't that funny? Andy and I were only just now talking . . ."

"And you've come to warn Maudie that the press will probably be sniffing around," intervened Dalziel. "Now that is kind. I leave you in good hands, Maudie. Me, I'd best be off. Geoff, I know it's not a nice job you've got, poking around in other buggers' rubbish bins, but where'd we be without the garbage collectors, eh? I promise you, you'll get nowt but cooperation from my department. I'll see you tomorrow, likely."

Hiller tried to look suitably grateful but couldn't get beyond the expression of a postman assured the Rottweiler is just a big softy.

"Actually, er, Andy, we hope to be *in situ* later today."

"You can be up to your necks *in situ* for me, Geoff, but it's my day off, remember? What did you think I was going to do? Head straight back and start shredding the files?"

He laughed, kissed Maudie on the cheek, and said, "Take care, luv. I'll see myself out. See you soon."

He went out, closing the lounge door firmly behind him. As he opened the front door noisily, he reached into the cloakroom, picked up the suitcase, and exited with a slam that shook the stained glass panel.

Separating Maudie's driveway from her neighbor's was a low brick wall. He leaned over and placed the case behind it. As he reached the gate, he heard the front door open behind him. He turned to see Stubbs coming out. He'd always been a distrustful bastard, that Hiller. It was good to know some things didn't change.

"Need something from the car," said Stubbs as he joined him.

"Oh, aye? Hair curlers, is it?" said Dalziel.

As he drove away he saw the inspector return to the house

without opening his car. He drove slowly round the block, parked outside Maudie's neighbor's, and walked briskly up the drive. A window opened as he retrieved the suitcase and he looked up to see a woman viewing him with grave suspicion.

"Yes?" she called sharply.

Dalziel pulled the video out of his pocket, and held it up like a votive offering.

"Are you on line with the Almighty, sister," he intoned. "Are you plugged in to the Lord? I've got a video here that'll turn your telly into the Ark of the Covenant!"

"No, thank you!" she cried in alarm and slammed the window shut.

Shaking his head, he returned to the car.

It was like he'd always thought.

There was no love of religion in West Yorkshire.

Four

"I am not surprised; I knew you were

here . . . if you really don't want to

endanger my existence—go your way

as soon as possible and let me go

mine. I am busy. I am an official."

"**A**n habitual criminal is easy to spot. Ask him, 'Where were you when President Kennedy was shot?' and he'll say, 'I was at home in bed reading a book. I can bring six witnesses to prove it.'"

There was a dutiful titter. Perhaps it's the way I tell them, thought Peter Pascoe.

He looked at the twenty young faces before him. Children of the seventies. Adolescents of the eighties. Lawmen of the nineties. God help them.

He said gently, "Who was President Kennedy?" Pause. A lowering of eyes to avoid catching his. Make the question easier. "What country was he president of?"

An uncertain hand crept up.

"America, sir?"

"That's right. Would that be North or South America?"

The irony of superiors is unfair because it forces you to take it literally.

He went on quickly before anyone could try an answer. "What happened to him? Well, I told you that. He got shot. Does anyone know the year?"

They probably didn't know *this* year! No. That was unfair. He was confusing truth and truism. *Everyone remembers what they were doing when Kennedy died.* Everyone except a few billion who weren't born; or didn't know of his existence, or didn't give a toss that it was over. Everyone in America then? Maybe. Probably their kids had the date and data drummed into them with the Pledge of Allegiance. But this lot, why should they be expected to know anything about other people's myths?

"Was it 1963, sir?"

"Yes. Yes, it was."

He looked at the speaker with disproportionate pleasure. Another hand was waving urgently. Perhaps the floodgates had opened and all his cynical doubts about the ignorance of this generation were going to be washed away. He pointed at the hand waver, nodded, waited to be amazed.

"Sir, it's half past. We're due in the gym with Sergeant Rigg."

He knew Sergeant Rigg. A no-neck Welshman with a black belt and a short way with latecomers.

"You'd better go then."

He looked at his notes. He still had three sides to go. Before she left, Ellie had warned him to go easy on the midnight oil. (Trying to offer a pastoral substitute for scarcer emotional goods?) He pushed the distasteful thought away and concentrated on her words.

"You start by thinking if you speak very slowly you might spin it out for five minutes. You end by gabbling so fast you're incomprehensible, and even then you've still got bucketfuls of pearls left uncast."

He poured them back into his briefcase and followed the cadets from the room.

"Pete, how'd it go?"

It was Jack Bridger, the grizzled Chief Inspector in charge of Mid-Yorkshire cadet training program.

"So-so. I didn't find them very responsive."

Bridger regarded him shrewdly and said, "They're just ordinary lads, not postgrad students. At that age all you think about is fucking and football. Secret is to ask the right questions. Talking of which, sounds like they're going to be asking some funny questions about this Mickledore Hall business."

"They've started. Full inquiry. Fellow called Hiller, Deputy Chief from South Thames, is leading it. Turned up yesterday even though the official announcement of the inquiry hasn't been made yet."

"Hiller? That wouldn't be Adolf Hiller, would it?"

He pronounced the name with a long *A*.

"This one's called Geoffrey, I think. Smallish fellow with crooked teeth. Looks as if he's stolen his suit."

"That's him! Adolf was just his nickname. He were a sergeant here way back, but not for long. Too regimental for old Wally Tallantire. That's how he got his nickname. Some joker started changing his name on notices and lists to *Hitler,* and it soon caught on."

"But he couldn't have been here during the Mickledore Hall case, surely, or he'd not have got this job?"

"No, it was after that. He got moved around like pass the parcel. He were one of those fellows, you couldn't fault his work, but you couldn't thole his company."

Pascoe said, "I never knew Tallantire. What was he like? Cut a few corners, would he?"

"That's the way the wind blows, is it? Well, it figures. Scapegoats are like lawyers. The best 'uns is dead 'uns. As for cutting corners, well, Wally would certainly go the shortest way, once he got a target in his sights. And the Mickledore Hall case was his golden hour by all accounts, the one he reckoned he'd be remembered for. But there's a difference between cutting corners and carving people up."

"So you reckon he was straight?"

"On the whole, I'd say so. I'll tell you one thing, but. Fat Andy won't take kindly to anyone casting aspersions. Wally was his big hero, he took Andy under his wing, and it needed a pretty broad wing, believe me!"

Pascoe grinned and said, "A bit wild, was he?"

"Wild? He's a dormouse to what he were! He'd still be pounding a beat if it weren't for Wally. But Wally was flying high after the Mickledore case, and Andy flew with him."

Pascoe mused on these things as he headed back to headquarters. He tried to imagine Dalziel as a wild young thing in need of protection, but all he could get was Genghis Khan in short pants. The image made him smile. The sky was blue, the sun was shining, he felt good.

He turned a corner. Ahead, rearing out of a rough sea of roof tops, he glimpsed the huge gray front of the cathedral tower. His mouth felt dry. He tried to make spittle and swallow but couldn't. The palms of his hands were sweating so that the wheel felt slimy against them. The tower seemed to be swelling to fill the sky, while the car shrank around him to a biscuit tin. He braked hard, pulled in to the side, felt the wheels hit the curb. His heart was racing like an engine with a stripped gear. His left hand fumbled for the seat belt release, his right for the door handle. His fingers felt weak and unconnected with his mind, more vegetable than flesh, but somehow the door was open, the belt released, and he swung his legs out of the car. An overtaking cyclist had to swerve sharply to avoid collision. She went on her way, swearing over her shoulder. Pascoe paid no heed. He forced his head between his knees and drew in great ragged breaths. After a while he managed to get some rhythm into his breathing. In through the nose, out through the mouth, long, slow inhalations and exhalations. His heart too was slowing, his salivary glands resumed a limited service, and his hands began to feel less like a bunch of radishes bound loosely to his wrists.

When strength returned to his legs, he stood up and walked unsteadily around the car. He forced himself to think about his lecture to the cadets, what he should have told them about criminal investigation, what he shouldn't have wasted time telling them. The sun was pleasantly warm on his skin, the air tasted good. At last he felt able to get back in and drive away. But he didn't let his gaze drift up to the skyline again.

A mile away, a van was backing into Pascoe's spot in the HQ car park. The driver got out and went into the building. Sergeant George Broomfield on the desk said, "Can I help you?"

"Why not? Sergeant Proctor, South Thames. I'm with Mr. Hiller's mob. Got some gear outside in the van. Any chance of a lift?"

His cockney chirpiness grated on Broomfield's ear, which would have surprised Proctor who came from Ruislip.

"Doubt it," he said. "Not for a while, any road. I don't think I've got a body free."

Suddenly Dalziel was there. How a man of his girth could be sudden, Broomfield never knew, but when he wanted he could lurk like a Brazilian striker.

"George, what are you saying? Cooperation's the key word here. Isn't that young Hector I see through there playing with himself? Send him out to help. Fragile stuff, is it, sergeant?"

Proctor, recognizing the weight of authority, said, "Yes, sir. Couple of computers, software, hardware, that sort of thing."

Broomfield was looking alarmed. Not even a cockney deserved PC. Hector who didn't break cups when he washed up, he broke sinks.

"Computers, eh?" said Dalziel. "Then Hector's your man. Strong as an ox. *Hector!* Come on out here!"

He stood by the desk till Proctor and the bewildered-looking constable had gone into the car park. Then he said very seriously to Broomfield, "These people are our guests, George. We've got to take care of them," and set off up the stairs.

He'd reached the first landing when he heard the first crash, and its accompanying cry of anguish followed him all the way up to the second.

He smiled and went on his way to Sergeant Wield's room.

"Don't get up," he said to the sergeant who hadn't moved. "The lad not back yet?"

"No, sir."

"Bloody nuisance. I wish he'd not volunteer all the time for these skives."

Wield who knew very well that it was Dalziel who had volunteered Pascoe for the cadet lecture ("right up your street, being a Master of Ceremonies or whatever it is you are") said nothing.

"Tell him to drop in when he gets back, will you?" Dalziel hesitated at the door, then went on, "Matter of no importance, but how's he been looking to you lately?"

"Bit rough," said Wield. "He's not really been himself since that lass jumped off the cathedral tower. It seemed to knock all the stuffing out of him, somehow."

"Certainly knocked the stuffing out of her," said Dalziel.

He stared hard at Wield's inscrutably craggy features as though challenging him to reprove his callousness, but the sergeant just held his gaze unflinchingly.

"Right," said Dalziel. "Well, keep an eye on him, eh? I know I can rely on your feminine intuition."

He went on to his own office, opened a drawer, and took out the glass of Scotch he'd been drinking when he'd noticed the South Thames van pulling into the car park below his window. He was just finishing it when the door burst open and Hiller came in.

"Well, come on in, Geoff," said Dalziel pleasantly. "Have a seat. Getting settled in, are you?"

Hiller remained standing.

"I think it's time to lay a few ground rules," he said. "First, in front of other officers, I think we should observe protocol. That means 'sir,' not 'Geoff,' okay?"

"Fair enough. No Geoffing around," said Dalziel.

"Secondly, Inspector Stubbs tells me he found you in the room allocated to us by your man Pascoe."

"Just checking you had everything you need, Geoff. Pascoe's a good lad but a bit rough at the edges. He might have overlooked a few of the refinements."

"I found Mr. Pascoe very helpful and obliging," said Hiller. "But I want to make it clear that my inquiry room, especially now I've got my equipment here, is off-limits to all Mid-Yorkshire staff. That includes you, Andy. And especially it includes that moron, Hector. Is he brain-damaged or what?"

"Hector? He's reckoned to be one of our high fliers."

"He'll fly high if he comes within kicking distance of my boot," said Hiller.

A joke, thought Dalziel. Adolf had really come a long way.

"That all, is it?" he inquired politely.

"Just one more thing. While I was talking to Mrs. Tallantire yesterday, she let slip that you'd been asking her about Wally's personal papers."

"Oh, aye? Then she'll have told you that there weren't any," said Dalziel.

"Yes, that's what she said you said," replied Hiller.

"You're not implying I'd try to hide summat as important as that?" said Dalziel indignantly.

"I'm implying nothing. I'm saying loud and clear that if I get any proof that you're attempting to interfere with or obstruct my inquiry in any way, I'll bury you, Andy."

"You'd need to scratch a big hole, Geoff," said Dalziel, his fingers mining his groin as if in illustration.

Hiller smiled thinly.

"I don't do my own digging anymore," he said. "By the way, I've asked Mr. Trimble if your DCI Pascoe can act as liaison between us. Like I said before, he seems a sensible sort of fellow, and I think it's in all our interests to keep things on an even keel."

"Right," said Dalziel. "Pascoe's your man for even keels. Full of ballast. It'll be plain sailing with him."

"Plain sailing's what we all want, isn't it?" said Hiller.

Dalziel showed him out with all the surface regret of a society host losing a favorite guest. He watched him out of sight along the corridor, then he said, "You can come out now."

The door to the storeroom opposite opened and Pascoe emerged.

"Saw you lurking a few minutes back," said Dalziel. "Hear all that, did you?"

"The door was open," said Pascoe defensively.

"Don't apologize. There's three things a good copper never passes up on, and one of 'em's a chance to eavesdrop."

Pascoe didn't care to inquire as to the other two. He followed Dalziel into his room and said, "In this case, eavesdropping hasn't left me much the wiser. I'd appreciate being told what's really going off here."

"You've stopped reading the papers and watching the telly, have you?"

"I've not had much time recently."

"Oh, aye? Family all right, are they?"

Why was it so hard to tell Dalziel anything without getting the sense he knew it already? Pascoe said as casually as he could, "Fine. Well, in fact, Ellie's away visiting her mother for a couple of days. And Rosie too, of course. The old girl's been a bit under the weather. The strain of looking after Ellie's father. He's got Alzheimer's, remember? He's gone totally now, no memory, never speaks, incontinent, the works. So they got him into a home last month and now Ellie's gone down just to check her mum's coping . . ."

He was talking too much.

Dalziel said, "Okay, is she?"

"Yes. I think so. I mean Ellie rang just to say they'd got there okay . . ."

A message on his answering machine. "Peter, we've arrived safely. Rosie sends her love. I'll ring again tomorrow." He hadn't tried to ring back.

"Well, it's an ill wind," said Dalziel. "Lots of time on your hands now to catch up with what's going off. You must've seen that telly program yon Yank, Waggs, made a while back? The one that caused the big stink?"

Pascoe shook his head.

"Well, no great loss. Them TV twats get carried away. Funny angles, fancy music, all film festival stuff without the titties in the sand. I've got a video of it I'll show you sometime, but best for background is this radio thing they did a couple of years back before they started this miscarriage of justice crap. I don't suppose you heard that either?"

He rummaged in a drawer, brought out an audio cassette.

"You listen to that. That was the truth for twenty-five years. Now they're telling us it's a load of lies."

Pascoe took the cassette and said, "I gather you know Mr. Hiller from way back."

"Oh, aye. He got dumped on us but Wally soon saw him off. I reckon that's how he's got on so well. Everyone he worked for'd be so keen to get shot of the bugger, they'd give him a glowing testimonial to get him on his way! Big mistake. You don't get rid of a snake by pushing it into someone else's garden. You keep it close where you can stamp on it."

"It's a nice theory," said Pascoe. "But he must have some ability."

"Too true. The ability to dig up whatever bones the Emmies have buried for him and come running back with them, wagging his tiny tail behind him."

"I'm sorry?" said Pascoe, baffled. "Emmies? I don't quite follow . . ."

"Emmies!" said Dalziel in exasperation. "MI this, MI that. The funny buggers."

"The Security Services, you mean? Come on, sir! Why the hell should Security be interested in Mickledore Hall?"

Dalziel shook his head. "You'd be better off sniffing glue than going to them colleges. Do they teach you nowt? Think about it! There was a government minister there that weekend, Partridge, Lord Partridge now. And the dead woman's husband was one of their own. And there was a Yank, Rampling, he's something important over in the States, and getting more important, by the sound of it. And there was Noddy Stamper, top industrialist, Sir Noddy now, Maggie gave him a knighthood soon as she got in, so you can see what he was made of. Just listen to the tape. It's all there. Well, soon after it happened this long thin fellow, all sweet and pink, like a stick of Edinburgh Rock, turned up. Name of Sempernel, he said. *Osbert*

Sempernel. Pimpernel, we called him, he were so hard to pin down. Said he was from the Home Office but I reckon if I could have snapped him in half, I'd have found dirty tricks printed all the way through. I saw him again this morning when I were watching the Press Conference on the box. Hanging around outside with Adolf. It all made sense."

"Not to me," said Pascoe, skeptically but not overly so. Dalziel's delusions had an X certificate habit of fleshing themselves out into reality. "Are you saying that Hiller will heap all the blame on Wally Tallantire just because this chap Sempernel tells him to?"

"Certainly. He'd hang his own granny if the orders came from high enough, especially if it meant getting up another rung of the ladder."

"Adolf Eichmann rather than Adolf Hitler then?"

"Both," said Dalziel. "And the bugger's taken a fancy to you, so mebbe you should start asking questions about yourself. Any road, you're to act as liaison. Now, you'll get nowt out of Adolf, but yon primped-up fancy pants might start yapping after a couple of port-and-lemons."

"Stubbs? He seems a decent sort of chap."

"SS was full of decent sorts of chap," said Dalziel. "You just keep your ears flapping."

"You mean spy?"

"If that's what you like to call it."

Pascoe wrinkled his face in distaste and said, "At least I should be glad there's not a war on. They shoot spies in wartime, don't they?"

He left, closing the door quietly behind him.

Dalziel reached into the drawer for his whiskey, shaking his head sadly. Under his tutelage, Pascoe had taken long strides toward becoming a good cop, mebbe even a great one.

But if he didn't know there was always a war on, he still had a long way to go.

Five

"I am like one who died young. All

my life might have been."

Cissy Kohler lay on a patchwork quilt and thought, *The way I feel, this ought to make me invisible.* Bits and pieces of past lives, some hers, some not, stitched together in a show of wholeness. Through the chintz curtains she could see the branches of a wych elm swaying in the wind. In the room below she could hear voices but she didn't strain her ears for she knew they couldn't be saying anything that mattered.

"Charming place," said the tall man in the dark suit whose impeccable cut was a foil to a stringy tie which looked as if it had been dropped in a bowl of Brown Windsor and wrung out by hand.

"Yeah, very quaint," said Jay Waggs. "How can I help you, Mr. Sempernel?"

"Belongs to Jacklin, I gather? Decent of him to let you have it."

"I figure it'll be on his bill."

"What? Oh, quite. These solicitors. But it's ideal. Good security. Just the one track down. And that wall behind. Perfect."

He was looking out of the window into the small rear garden.

OUACHITA TECHNICAL COLLEGE

The cottage stood in the U-shaped nook which some peasant who knew his rights had indented in the twelve foot boundary wall of an extensive country estate.

"Perfect," agreed Waggs. "The wall and the guard, they make Cissy feel really at home."

"Ha ha. Droll. Though the guard, as you call him, is of course positioned here to keep the media hounds out, not to keep Miss Kohler in."

"So she's free to come and go?"

"But naturally. Within the limits of our agreement, of course, which I do not doubt that Mr. Jacklin has spelled out in tedious detail. Nevertheless let me recap. Miss Kohler's early release . . ."

"Early!"

"Indeed. HM Government has agreed for humanitarian reasons to anticipate the proper legal process, but not without undertakings on your part. These are principally that Miss Kohler has agreed that neither she nor her advisers will make any public comment, nor publish any form of memoir of this unhappy business without the approval of the authorities. In return for this undertaking, HM Government has indicated it will offer no resistance to any legitimate claim for compensation."

"Big of them."

"I think so. Also Miss Kohler has agreed to remain in this country until the completion of the official inquiry into the circumstances leading up to this unfortunate miscarriage."

"Which could take years!"

"No. I assure you matters are moving fast. Deputy Chief Constable Hiller whom you have met has the business in hand and we anticipate a speedy conclusion. Incidentally, Mr. Hiller tells me that if by chance Miss Kohler had kept any written record of the events at Mickledore Hall, sight of it, on loan of course, might speed matters up and obviate the need of any further interview with her."

Waggs laughed.

"Come on, Sempernel! You know there's no record. You guys went through her cell like pack rats before she got out."

The long man smiled thinly.

"The papers seem to think she may have had some ally through whom such a memoir may have been smuggled out to a place of security."

"Like me you mean? Well, I don't deny that given the chance, I'd have been glad to help. But I wasn't and I didn't."

"I'm happy to accept your word on that, Mr. Waggs," said Sempernel. "There are other possible sources of assistance, of course. She was after all inside for a long time, and could hardly avoid forming relationships. The unfortunate Miss Bush, for instance . . ."

"That was long before my time," said Waggs. "The only memoir I'm aware of is in Cissy's head and I don't know how easy it's going to be to pry that out."

"No? You've met with quite a lot of success so far," murmured Sempernel. "Rest, quiet, and above all time are great healers. They are all at your disposal here. Enjoy them."

He made for the door, stopping to avoid the sagging lintel. Beneath it he paused, looking like Alice in the White Rabbit's house.

"One last thing," he said. "Jacklin has, I hope, made it clear that any grant of a free pardon will be in respect of the Mickledore Hall affair only. In respect of the killing of Daphne Bush, there is no doubt about Miss Kohler's culpability. Her release from that sentence is therefore merely under license which may be revoked in the event of any breach of its terms. You follow me, Mr. Waggs?"

"You mean you've got a string you can twitch whenever you feel like it? I follow."

"Good." Sempernel passed through the doorway and straightened up so that his face was visible only from the long nose down. "I'll say cheerio then."

Protected from the Englishman's watery gaze, Waggs pushed his middle finger into the air as he said, "Yeah. Good-bye."

He watched from the window till he saw the lanky figure negotiate the muddy path, then he picked up the phone and dialed.

"Mr. Jacklin, please. It's Jay Waggs. Jacklin? Hi. How're you doing? We're fine. Yeah, she's resting. Listen, Sempernel's been here. Lots of that slippery Whitehall stuff, but all he's doing is making

31

sure my thick American mind understands the ground rules. Just thought I'd let you know. How are things your end? No change? That's good. Well, keep in touch. Ciao."

He listened for a while longer before putting the receiver down. It might be mere neurosis to imagine he heard significant clicks, but Sempernel struck him as a good man to be neurotic around. And if the phone, then why not everywhere?

He went into the kitchen, blew a kiss at the kettle, and switched it on.

A few moments later he tapped on the bedroom door and entered with a cup of coffee.

Cissy Kohler had sat up on the bed and was reading her Bible.

"Thought you might like this," he said. "It's not home style, but near as I can get. How're you feeling?"

She closed the book, laid it on her lap, and took the cup.

"I'm okay."

"Sempernel was here."

"Who?"

"The one like a straightened-out hairpin. He was just checking we knew the rules."

She drank her coffee with her eyes closed as though taking in visions with the steam. He studied her face and wondered just how much of what was happening she really grasped. At least, if there were listening ears, it made role play that much easier.

He said, "He was asking about your memoirs, Cissy."

She opened her eyes.

"Memoirs?"

"Yeah. There are these stories in the press that you wrote up everything that happened at Mickledore Hall, everything that happened afterward in jail. Somehow you got them smuggled out and they are waiting to be picked up somewhere."

He knew what the answer would be. They'd had this conversation before.

"It's not true," she said without heat. "They're making it up."

"That's what I told him. But if there were any memoirs, Cissy, it'd make things a lot easier for me. The book, the film . . ."

"Which book? Which film?" She regarded him blankly.

"We'll talk about it later," he said gently. "It's early days. We'll talk when you're rested."

"How long will we stay here, Jay?" she asked suddenly. "You said we'd go home soon. You said . . ."

This was dangerous. He cut her off saying, "We will, Cissy, I promise. Just as soon as Mr. Sempernel says it's okay. Don't you like it here?"

She shook her head and said, "Not much."

"Why's that?"

"I don't know. It feels so old . . . so English . . ."

"Yeah. It shouldn't be for long. You rest now, okay?"

Her cup was empty. He took it from her hands and she lay back on the patchwork quilt, with her hands crossed over the old leather Bible on her stomach. Her eyes were still open but he got no impression that they were seeing him. In fact he had a strange feeling that if he stayed here much longer he would stop seeing her.

He turned and left the room.

Six

"Now come and take your place in

the circle, and let us sit quiet, and

hear the echoes about which you have

your theory."

Sod's Law.

How many times on his way home late to a loving family and a hot dinner had he been waylaid by Dalziel and more or less frog-marched down to the Black Bull?

This evening there was no sign of the Fat Man. He met Wield on the stairs and said, "Fancy a quick half?"

"Sorry, it's my karate night."

On the next landing he hesitated, then went down the corridor to the inquiry team's room. A mahogany plaque had been screwed to the door. On it in large black Roman was printed DEPUTY CHIEF CONSTABLE HILLER, with underneath in golden Gothic, *knock and wait.*

Pascoe knocked and waited.

Inspector Stubbs opened the door. Over his *crêpe-de-chine'd* shoulder Pascoe could see the green flicker of computer screens.

"Thought you might like an intro to our local," he said. "The beer's good enough to make the meat pies seem almost edible."

"Love it, but not tonight," said Stubbs regretfully. "Mr. Hiller wants us to get all this stuff into the system before we knock off."

He opened the door wider to reveal Sergeant Proctor surrounded by what Pascoe assumed were the Mickledore Hall files.

"Evening, guv," said the sergeant. "Who does your filing then— a grizzly bear?"

Stubbs frowned, but Pascoe, recalling the state of his own records if ever Dalziel got among them, could not take offense.

"Some other time then," he said.

There was nothing to stop him going to the *Black Bull* alone, but if he was going to be a solitary drinker, he might as well do it in the privacy of his own home.

He heard his phone ringing as he parked the car but it had stopped by the time he got into the house and there was no message on his machine. He checked through his mail in search of Ellie's hand.

Nothing.

He poured himself a beer and sat down to read the paper. Good news was obviously no news. His glass was empty. He went to fill it, opened instead a can of soup, and cut a hunk of bread. This he ate standing at the kitchen table. Then he went into the garden, pulled up a few weeds, wandered back into the house, poured another beer, switched on the television, and watched the end of a documentary on homelessness. Twice he got up to check that the phone was working.

Finally he remembered Dalziel's tape.

He switched off the TV and put the cassette into his tape deck, pressed the start button, and sat back to listen.

An announcer's voice first, blandly BBC.

"And now the last in our series *The Golden Age of Murder* in which crime writer William Stamper has been positing that the Golden Age of crime fiction, usually regarded as artificial, unrealistic, and escapist, may have had closer links with real life than the critics allow.

"So far he has examined crimes from each of the first five decades of the century. Now finally we arrive at the sixties and a case in which we will see that William Stamper has a very special interest. The Mickledore Hall murder."

Now came music, sort of intellectually eerie. Bartók perhaps. Then a male voice, light, dry, with an occasional flattened vowel giving a hint of northern upbringing:

It was the best of crimes, it was the worst of crimes; it was born of love, it was spawned by greed; it was completely unplanned, it was coldly premeditated; it was an open-and-shut case, it was a locked-room mystery; it was the act of a guileless girl, it was the work of a scheming scoundrel; it was the end of an era, it was the start of an era; a man with the face of a laughing boy reigned in Washington, a man with the features of a lugubrious hound ruled in Westminster; an ex-marine got a job at a Dallas book repository, an ex-Minister of War lost a job in politics; a group known as the Beatles made their first million, a group known as the Great Train Robbers made their first two million; it was the time when those who had fought to save the world began to surrender it to those they had fought to save it for; Dixon of Dock Green was giving way to Z-cars, Bond to Smiley, the Monsignors to the Maharishis, Matt Dillon to Bob Dylan, l.s.d. to LSD, as the sunset glow of the old Golden Age imploded into the psychedelic dawn of the new Age of Glitz.

It was the Year of Our Lord nineteen hundred and sixty-three, and it is altogether fitting that this crime of which we speak should have been committed in one of Yorkshire's great country houses, Mickledore Hall, and that its dénouement should have taken place in that most traditional of settings, the Old Library.

If a Hollywood designer were asked to build a set for such a scene in an Agatha Christie film, it would probably turn out something like the library of Mickledore Hall.

Imagine a desk the size of a Ping-Pong table standing on a carpet the size of a badminton court. Scattered around are various chairs, stylistically unrelated except insofar as their upholstery has the faded look of the coat of a very old terrier. One wall is embrasured with three deep window bays hung with dusty velvet curtains, while the other three are lined with towering bureaus behind whose lozenged bars rot a thousand books, untouched by little save time, for the Mickledores were never famed for their intellectuality.

In 1963 the incumbent baronet seemed cast in the traditional mold of Mickledore men, tall, blond, handsome, athletic, with an exuberant manner that might in a lesser man have been called hearty.

Yet there was another side to Ralph Mickledore—Mick to his friends—as evidenced perhaps by his close friendship with that most unhearty of men, James Westropp. At his trial, the defense projected him as the perfect type of English eccentricity, a country squire who ran his estate as if the twentieth century hadn't arrived, with Shire horses pulling his plows, a watermill grinding his grain, and poachers offered the choice of a Mickledore boot up the bum or a Mickledore beak on the Bench.

It was, however, a very different picture that the prosecution inked in. Victorian values might be the order of the day at the Hall, but away from Yorkshire, Sir Ralph came across as a Restoration roué. Nightclubs, casinos, racetracks, the gray area where the haut monde overlapped with the demimonde, here was his urban habitat. The gap between his two lifestyles was presented not as harmless eccentricity but black hypocrisy. And by the end of 1963, juries were very ready to think the worst of their social superiors, though as we shall see it was not this cynicism alone which helped confer on Ralph Mickledore the unenviable distinction of being the last man to hang in Mid-Yorkshire.

The house party assembled on Friday, August the second, for a long weekend taking in the following Monday which was then the now defunct August Bank Holiday. The great and the good were all spilling out of London after the almost unbearable melodrama of the Stephen Ward trial. Though he once provided not the least sensational headlines in this most sensational of years, Dr. Ward may have faded completely from some listeners' minds, so perhaps a little potted history would go down well here as an entrée to the main course.

In March that year, John Profumo, the Minister of War (in those less mealymouthed days we had not yet invented Ministers of Defense) had resigned after it emerged that he had lied to Parliament when *denying allegations of an improper relationship with a young woman named Christine Keeler. The impropriety was more than simply sexual. Miss Keeler was also alleged to have been the mistress of Captain Yuri Ivanov, a Russian naval attaché known by British Security to be an officer of the KGB. Such a link, however tenuous, between a Government Minister and an enemy agent, was clearly undesirable. But it was the lie to his colleagues that broke him.*

The man who had introduced both Profumo and Ivanov to Keeler was a London osteopath and artist, Dr. Stephen Ward, who besides manipulating the bones and painting the portraits of many highly placed people, also it was alleged provided more intimate services. Amidst spiraling rumors of upper-class debauchery on a scale to inspire a new Satyricon, Dr. Ward was finally brought to trial at the end of July on three charges of living on the earnings of prostitution, and two concerned with procuring minors.

On Wednesday, July thirty-first, which seemed likely to be the trial's final day, the court and the nation were shocked to learn that Ward had taken an overdose of sleeping pills the previous night and was critically ill. Despite this news, the judge summed up, the jury deliberated, and in midmorning a verdict was delivered of Guilty on two of the immoral earnings charges, Not Guilty on the rest.

Sentencing was postponed till Dr. Ward should have recovered. When the house party assembled two days later he was still lying unconscious in his hospital bed and it can scarcely be doubted that up and down the country there were many who prayed he would never rise from it.

I am not, of course, suggesting that there were any such among the arrivals at Mickledore Hall that day.

The house party fell some way short of that ideal constitution a fashionable host might have aimed at. Mickledore himself was unmarried, but his only "spare" guest was a man. Children were not usually included in such weekend gatherings, but Mickledore liked kids in the same way he liked dogs and the three couples who made up the guest list mustered eight between them, plus two nannies. And a final oddity; while the tradition admitted of, perhaps even encouraged, the inviting of a token American, this group had no less than three in it, or four if you counted one of the nannies.

But let's get down to details.

The "spare" guest was Scott Rampling, a young U.S. Embassy official, formally attached to the legal department though his subsequent career has been only loosely linked with legality.

The three couples were the Westropps, James and Pamela, plus their infant twins, Philip and Emily, in the care of their nanny, Cecily Kohler; the Partridges, Thomas and Jessica, plus their children Alison (three), Laetitia (seven), Genevieve (nine), and Tommy (twelve), in the care of their nanny, Miss Mavis Marsh; and finally, the Stampers, Arthur and Marilou, plus their nannyless kids, Wendy who was seven, and William who was eight.

That's right. William Stamper, age eight. No coincidence. During that never-to-be-forgotten weekend at Mickledore Hall when the last of the Golden Age murders took place, I was truly there.

From a child's viewpoint, the Hall was paradise. Inside there were attics full of marvelous junk. Outside there were woods, stables, a tennis court, an island with a lake and a couple of canoes, and a haunted folly. And there were only two rules: one, you didn't go canoeing without supervision, and two, you became invisible and inaudible after six o'clock in the evening. Personally, I could have stayed there forever.

For most adults, however, a long weekend was probably quite enough. The atmosphere had something in it of a muscular public school. Nonstop activity was the order of the day, and slacking the unforgivable sin. My father loved it, perhaps because he worshiped the public school ethos with an apostate's fervor. He should have been the perfect type of self-made Yorkshire businessman, forever advertising his humble origins and trumpeting his triumph over privilege and private education. Instead he used his growing wealth to purchase a place in the clubs and councils of the upper crust whose manners and mores he cultivated to the point of parody. Above all things he hated to be reminded that his growing business empire was based on the success of his first venture, Stamper Rubber Goods of Sheffield. I believe that in some areas of South Yorkshire, condoms are still referred to as Stamp-

ers, and of course it was a mixed blessing for him to be awarded the upper-class sobriquet of "Noddy."

My mother was very different. Of the trio of American women present (the others being Pam Westropp and Cecily Kohler), she came from the "best" background, being a Bellmain of Virginia no less, which was the nearest to aristocracy my father dared aim at in his early years. Yet despite her breeding, she remained attractively unsophisticated, a wide-eyed innocent abroad whose unaffected enthusiasms often embarrassed my father, but no one else, for by knowing where her true home was, she was at home anywhere.

A very different type of American was Scott Rampling. Born in the urban sprawl of L.A., he was a young man in a hurry to reach the rosy future he never doubted lay ahead of him. He had got to know Mickledore during one of his frequent visits to the Westropps in Washington and renewed the acquaintance when posted to London in 1961. After the events of that sensational weekend, he vanished from the scene and indeed the country with positively indecent speed, and the infrequency with which his name appeared in newspaper reports of the case and the trial suggests a considerable calling-in of cross-Atlantic favors.

The Partridges were as English as Rampling was American, to the manner and manor born. The family owned a goodly proportion of the North Riding, having preferred acres to earldoms as reward for their loyalty to the Stuart cause in the seventeenth century, and to the anti-Stuart cause in the eighteenth. It was not till Thomas's retirement from active politics that a Partridge finally got a peerage, though as the noble lord says in his lively autobiography In a Pear Tree, he would have preferred land if it had still been on offer. In 1955 he had been elected Conservative member for the seat whose boundaries pretty well coincided with his own. By 1963 he was a junior minister in the War Office, widely tipped for promotion in the next reshuffle. Then the sky fell in. He was too closely associated with his immediate master and long time mentor, John Profumo, for comfort; his name kept coming up in the huge stew of rumors bubbling around Westminister all that spring and summer; and all poor Partridge wanted to do now was keep his head well below the rim of the caldron.

His wife, Jessica, née Herdwick, fifth daughter of the Earl of Millom, was a formidably horsey lady with a great facility for breeding both champion chasers and handsome children. Her fifth (child, that is), was well on its way that weekend.

The Partridge nanny, Miss Mavis Marsh, had every qualification and quality then admired in her profession. In her mid-thirties, she stood about five feet four, but looked taller in her immaculate starched uniform because of her unyielding erectness of posture, a physical trait she extended into her attitude on matters of etiquette, expression, punctuality, probity, and even diet. You never left your crusts when Miss Marsh was at table.

The other nanny, Cecily Kohler, was quite different, more like a big sister than an agent of divine providence. She wore no uniform; indeed she even sometimes appeared in jeans which were then not the universal garment they have since become. When she joined in our water sports, which as an expert canoer she often did, she was likely to end up as wet and tousled as the rest of us. Even her voice was a delight, for in it we heard the authentic accent of all that was most glamorous to our young imaginations. (We had no power to look ahead and see that the sixties were about to start swinging, with our own boring country at the very fulcrum of the mad intoxicating whirl.) We loved her because she loved us, and when I think of her, I still see the flushed and laughing face of a young woman, with russet hair blown across her brow in beautiful confusion. I have no art to link that image with the pallid skin, hollow cheeks, and desperate, dark-ringed eyes of the woman I last saw being pushed into a police car outside Mickledore Hall.

I have deliberately left her employers, the Westropps, to the end because they are the most difficult to characterize. James Westropp must have been, indeed I presume still is, the best connected commoner in the land, a distant cousin of the Queen's and, as a magazine article on him at the time of the tragedy put it, within three deaths of a title whichever way he looked. It might have been expected that such connections would have hauled him up the diplomatic career ladder very quickly, but his apparent lowly status was explained in the same article. Westropp was no career diplomat with his sights on an ambassador's mansion. He worked for the Service that dared not speak its name, which was the coy way they put such things in those days. It could be argued that his sojourn in the States, like perhaps Rampling's in the UK, was a mark of excellence. You only send your best to spy on your friends. His marriage we may assume was a love match. Pamela Westropp was a penniless American widow with a three-year-old son and no rating on the social register. She was very attractive. She was also willful, witty, madcap, moody, impulsive, and obstinate, a mix of qualities which can be fascinating or repellent, depending whether you're buying or selling.

The best man at the Westropp's wedding was Ralph Mickledore, who improved the acquaintance of his friend's new wife during the course of many extended visits over the next four years. By then of course the twins, Philip and Emily, had arrived, and with them, Cecily Kohler. How soon her special relationship with "Mick" Mickledore developed is open to speculation, but some old girlfriend of hers dug up by the papers at the time of the trial recalled she had been adamant when she took the job that she wasn't going to work abroad, so clearly something happened to change her mind.

These then were the actors. Let us move on to the act.

The single great pastime of a Mickledore weekend was shooting things. Male guests could expect to find themselves within minutes of arrival standing up to their ankles in mud destroying whatever the law permitted them to destroy at the time of year, even if it were only rabbits and pigeons.

Female guests were permitted a short settling-in period, after which they were expected to be as keen for the slaughter as their menfolk.

Jessica Partridge was as good a shot as most men and a lot better than my father who suffered some heavy ribbing for his ineptitude. It didn't help that my mother, though not keen on killing things, had done a lot of skeet shooting in her youth and was a pretty fair shot. It was Pam Westropp who was the real dunce. She had no moral objections but very low motor skills, often forgetting to reload or attempting to fire with the safety on. And when she did get it right she rarely hit anything she aimed at.

But not for this was she spared the rigors of the sport. And no one was spared its responsibilities, prime among which was that each guest took care of his or her own weapon, cleaning it after each shoot before replacing it on its chain in the gun room.

At some point after dinner Mickledore would ask in his best Orderly Officer fashion if they'd all done their fatigues. It was no use lying. The last thing he did before going to bed was check the gun room and if he found anything not in order, he did not hesitate to haul the culprit, regardless of sex or standing, out of bed to put matters right.

The gun room was situated at the far eastern end of the guest corridor on the first floor, and was also reachable by a side stair ascending from the old kitchen hall which was used as a gathering and disrobing point for shooting parties, thus keeping muddy boots and dripping oilskins out of the main body of the house.

The same stair continued up to the second floor where the children and their nannies slept.

The gun room was heavily paneled, windowless, and had a double door. Guests were issued with Yale keys for the outer door, while the larger key for the inner mortice lock was concealed on a narrow ledge above the inner door. After cleaning, guests were expected to replace their weapons on the wall rack, and secure them with a self-locking hasp which pivoted to fit just above the trigger guard. Only Mickledore had a key to unlock these hasps. In other words, guests put their guns away but could not take them out again unaided by their host.

The weekend had started early, everyone having contrived to arrive by Friday lunchtime. We had all been to Mickledore Hall before, so no time was wasted by either children or adults in learning the rules. The older children spent most of the afternoon having a super time on the lake with Cissy Kohler while Miss Marsh sat on the bank, knitting and looking after the two infants. The adults too seem to have had a good time if my memory of the atmosphere and Lord Partridge's of the events can be relied on. I should say now that nothing I have read in the lengthy chapter on that weekend in his lordship's memoirs In a Pear Tree is contradicted by my own recollection, though naturally for much of the time we moved in mutually exclusive spheres.

For us children, Saturday started where Friday had left off, only better. But for the adults things had taken a downturn. We felt it in our brief contact with them in the morning and like wise children, we made ourselves scarce. Lord Partridge in his memoirs recalls a sense of fractiousness, of barely repressed irritation, of hidden meanings, with Pamela Westropp at its center. With hindsight he guesses her real anger was aimed at Mickledore, and unable to contain it, she did her best to conceal its object by scattering its manifestations indiscriminately, though, as was to be expected, her husband came in for more than his fair share.

They spent all day at their sport, picnicking by their Land Rovers, dividing and regrouping so that at some stage everyone had spent some time in everyone else's company. Variety did little to improve their spirits. And when they returned to the house in the late afternoon they heard the news that Stephen Ward had died.

The previous night, according to Partridge, as if by mutual agreement no one had mentioned the Profumo affair or the Ward trial. Saturday night was different. Pamela Westropp wouldn't leave the subject. She went on about the hypocrisy of the British Establishment which had hounded him to his death. And she said, "Of course, Mick, you knew him pretty well, didn't you?"

"I suppose I did," said Mickledore unperturbed. "But then so did a lot of us here, I imagine."

He looked around as he spoke. Westropp as usual gave nothing away. My father, I would guess, attempted to look as if he'd been a long time member of the Ward/Cliveden set. Rampling said cheerfully, "Hell, yes, I met the guy, but it was one of your judges that introduced me. I'd have paid more heed if I'd known he was the top people's pimp!" And Partridge himself, who'd met Ward several times but naturally wasn't anxious to advertise the fact in view of recent events, kept quiet and hoped he wasn't being got at.

But clearly it was Mickledore who was Pam's chosen target.

"I suppose you think he deserved everything he got?" she pursued.

"I think he broke the one law of the tribe he wanted to belong to," said Mickledore.

"Which was?"

And Mickledore laid his finger across his lips.

Some time later, it was certainly after eleven for they all remem-ber having heard the stable clock strike, Mickledore made his usual inquiry about "gun fatigues." Pam Westropp said defiantly that no, she hadn't cleaned hers, and was she expected to wash her own dinner dishes too? Nevertheless after another couple of drinks she said she supposed she'd better get it over with, and stood up. Her husband rose too, rather unsteadily, having stuck doggedly on Mickledore's coattails during a wide-ranging tour of the delights of his cellar. It took a hard head and a pair of hollow legs to keep up with Mick when he was in the drinking mood. According to Westropp's later statement, he went upstairs with his wife, offered to help her clean her gun, was told she was quite capable of performing her own menial tasks, staggered into his bedroom, got undressed, fell into bed, and knew no more till awoken by the disturbance later on.

Downstairs, Jessica Partridge was ready for bed too, but her hus-band said he was looking forward to a game of billiards with Mickledore. Warning him not to disturb her, Jessica left accompanied by my mother, Marilou. My father, who liked to claim he needed less sleep than ordinary mortals, said he fancied a stroll around the estate with his pipe, a mode of behavior he probably picked up from the novels of Dornford Yates.

Scott Rampling asked if he could phone the States and Mick told him to use the phone in the study which was in the East Wing. Accord-ing to his statement, confirmed by Mickledore's phone bill, Rampling was in conversation with America for the next hour and a half at least.

Meanwhile my father claimed he had been tempted by the fine moonlit night to walk farther than he intended. He took no heed of time, except that he heard the stable clock strike midnight not too long after he set out on his perambulations. This clock, incidentally, had, presumably still has, the loudest bell I've heard outside Westminster. Mickledore through long usage was untroubled by it, but weekends of haggard faces over the breakfast table had finally persuaded him to fit a device which switched the chimes off between midnight and eight in the morning. So, it wasn't till he got back to the house that my father, who never wore a watch on the grounds that he made time work for him, was able to confirm that it was after one.

He met Mickledore and Partridge coming out of the billiard room. Mickledore, who'd sent Gilchrist, his butler, to bed after dinner, went off to check the house was secure, while the other two went upstairs together.

Outside Partridge's bedroom they paused to finish their conversation. Mickledore appeared at the far end of the same corridor, having ascended the side stairs, and opened the outer door of the gun room. After a few moments, he approached them looking concerned. The key to the inner door was not in its customary place on the ledge. He had his own personal key, of course, but when he tried to use this, it would not go far enough into the hole to turn, and when he peered through the keyhole, he could see another key already in the lock from the inside.

The other two went with him to the gun room to check. Mickledore was right. They could see the key quite clearly. Back along the corridor Jessica Partridge emerged to ask what all the row was, in tones loud enough to rouse my mother. Scott Rampling appeared on his way to bed. Soon they were all gathered outside the gun room, all except the Westropps. Mickledore went and banged on their door but had to go in through the dressing room before he could rouse Westropp. It took some time to penetrate his alcoholic torpor, but when he realized his wife was the only person on the guest floor unaccounted for, he flung himself against the gun room door in vain effort to break it down. But his efforts must at least have loosened the key in the inner lock, for now when he seized Mickledore's key and thrust it into the hole, he was able to turn it and the door swung slowly open . . .

The phone shrilled like an owl in a haunted tower. Pascoe startled, as if he too had been dragged from deep sleep, grabbed it, said, "Hello, this is . . ." and couldn't remember his number.

"Peter, are you all right?" It was Ellie's voice, close and concerned.

"Yes, fine. Hang on." He switched off the tape. "Sorry, I was listening to something. How's things? How's your mum? Your dad? Rosie?"

"Rosie's fine. I tried to ring earlier so she could have a talk to you, but I couldn't be bothered to talk to that bloody machine. She's asleep now. If you ever get home early enough, maybe you could ring . . ."

He could sense the effort not to sound reproving.

He said, "Of course I will, I promise. And your mum, how's she?"

There was a silence. He said, "Hello? You still there?"

"Yes. She's . . . oh, Peter, I'm so worried . . ."

"Why? What's happened?"

"Nothing really . . . except . . . Peter, I'm terrified it's all happening again. I thought it was just physical, you know, the strain of looking after Dad, and she's always had these circulatory problems, and the arthritis, and I thought that once things settled down . . . Well, in herself, physically I mean, she doesn't seem too bad . . . but she's started forgetting things . . . she'd forgotten we were coming though we'd just spoken on the phone that morning . . . and this morning I heard her calling Rosie, Ellie . . ."

"That can happen to anyone," said Pascoe confidently. "I've done it myself. As for forgetting things like phone calls, if I don't make a note of everything instantly, that's it, gone forever."

The silence again, then . . . "I hope you're right. Maybe I'm oversensitive because of Dad."

"That's right. Have you seen him?"

"I went today. I'd forgotten how awful it is, looking into a face you know, being looked at by eyes that don't know you . . . I came out feeling like . . . I don't know . . . like it was all my fault somehow . . ."

"For God's sake! How do you work that out?" demanded Pascoe, dismayed to hear such fragile uncertainty in her voice.

"I don't know . . . using them as an excuse, maybe . . . that's what I've done, isn't it? Saying I thought I should come down here for a few days because I wanted to make sure Mum was coping . . . doing the concerned daughter bit when all I was really looking for was a place to lay low . . . like getting out of something by saying you've got the flu, then really getting the flu like it was a judgment, only far worse . . . not thinking about her at all really . . ."

"Well, let's think about her now, shall we?" said Pascoe sharply.

Again silence, the longest yet. Her voice was calmer when she finally spoke.

"So I'm doing it again, you reckon? Getting in the spotlight instead of sticking to my bit part. Yes, you could be right."

"Forget right," said Pascoe. "Only in this case, maybe you should just go for best-supporting-actress for a while. Look, why not get your mum to come up here for a while? Or I could steal a couple of days leave and come down there."

She thought for a while then said, "No. Mum wouldn't come, I know that. Remember I tried to get her away after Dad went into the home and she wouldn't budge. She knows it's hopeless but she thinks she's got to stay close."

"So, shall I come down?"

"Peter, believe me, I'm tempted, but I don't want to get things all mussed up together. I've used them once as an excuse to get away and I don't want to find I'm using them as an excuse again to step back . . . look, I know I'm putting this badly but we both know we've reached an edge, okay, so it's dangerous, but at least the view is clear . . . God, even my metaphors are . . . what's the opposite of euphemistic? Look, I'd better go now. I can promise Rosie you'll ring early enough to speak to her, can I?"

"Cross my heart and hope to die," said Pascoe. "Take care. Love to your mum. And Rosie. And you."

"Peter, Christ, I'm a selfish cow, this has been all about me and I've not asked anything about you, how you're coping, what you're eating, all the wifely things. You're not living off those dreadful pies at the Black Bull, are you? You'll end up like Fat Andy. Incidentally, I see they've released that poor woman your mob fitted up nearly thirty years ago. Plus ça change and all that."

"Plus ça change," echoed Pascoe. "I'll prepare answers to satisfy your wifely curiosities next time. After I've finished eating this pie. Good night, love."

He put the phone down. His mind was wriggling with thoughts like an angler's bait tin. He poured a long Scotch and took it out into the garden where he watched scallop-edged clouds drift across the evening sky, like thought bubbles in some divine cartoon, but he couldn't read the message.

Old troubles, other people's troubles, were better than this.

He went back inside, ran the cassette back a little, and started listening once more.

Seven

"It is extraordinary to me . . . that

you people cannot take care of

yourselves and your children. One or

the other of you is ever in the way."

. . . *And the door swung slowly open.*

Westropp had clearly feared the worst and the worst was what he found. His wife lay sprawled beside a fallen stool with a gaping hole in her rib cage. In front of her on the table was a shotgun. Properly speaking this table was a workbench, fitted with a vise. Mickledore liked to fill his own cartridges, do his own repairs. The others scarcely had time to register that a loop of wire had been passed through the trigger guard of the gun with its loose ends locked tight in the jaws of the vise before Mickledore had manhandled Westropp out of the room.

"Noddy, get the women out of here. Scott, take care of James. Tom, you come with me."

And drawing Partridge after him, he went back into the gun room and closed the door.

We have a firsthand account of what took place then from Lord Partridge's memoirs, In a Pear Tree, *published last month.*

The dislodged key was lying on the floor. Mickledore stooped to pick it up. Partridge went to the workbench. On it lay a scrap of paper with a note scrawled on it in Pamela Westropp's unmistakable hand.

It read: it's no good—I can't take it—I'd rather destroy everything.

The following exchange then took place.

PARTRIDGE: Oh, God, what a dreadful business.

MICKLEDORE: Yes. Time for maximum discretion, I think. You know what the press can make of an accident like this.

PARTRIDGE: Accident? How can you call it an accident when . . .

MICKLEDORE: (taking the note from him and putting it in his pocket) Because accidents are merely tragic, while suicides are scandalous, and we must protect James and his family, and I mean all of his family, from any hint of scandal.

PARTRIDGE: But I am a Minister of the Crown . . .

MICKLEDORE: Exactly. And you've not been having such a good press lately, have you? Neither your Party nor the Palace will thank you dumping another scandal on their doorstep. Look, I'm not suggesting anything truly illegal, just a little tidying up. You've seen nothing in here except a dead woman, right? Now you push off and do some phoning, you know the right people. Say Pam's been found dead, an accident you think, but you recommend maximum discretion. I'll take care of things in here. Go on. Get a move on. You know it's best.

And off went Partridge. He claims he rang a colleague in London to ask for advice and the advice he received was to contact the police immediately, which was what he did. By the time Detective Superintendent Tallantire arrived, the loop of wire had vanished like the note.

We may never know just how much pressure was put on Tallantire to tread warily. What we do know from his evidence at the trial is that he discounted the accident theory almost immediately. The gun was in perfect working order and it was physically almost impossible to contrive a situation in which Pamela could have fired it by accident as it lay across the workbench with its muzzle pressed against her chest. Then a sharp-eyed forensic man drew his attention to a slight scratch across the trigger and he himself found in the bench drawer a loop of wire with corrugations in its loose ends exactly matching the teeth of the vise.

Now he concentrated all of his attention on Mickledore and Partridge. The others could get away with being vague about what they actually saw in their brief glimpse into the gun room, but these two had been in there for some time.

Tallantire applied pressure and Partridge quickly broke. The recent scandals had not performed the miracle of curing politicians of lying, but they were alert as they'd never been before to the perils of being caught in a lie. So he showed a modest confusion, apologized for an error of judgment, and told the truth. Mickledore showed no confusion, made no apology, but freely admitted his attempts to make the death look accidental and suggested that a patriot and a gentleman could have done no other.

Tallantire ignored the slur and asked for the note. A brief comparison with other examples of her writing convinced him it was in her hand.

A lesser man, faced with a body in a locked room, a suicide note, a device for firing a shotgun with its muzzle pressed against the chest, plus any amount of testimony to the dead woman's unnaturally agitated state of mind that evening, might easily have bowed out at this stage, probably congratulating himself on his skill in so soon detecting an upper-class attempt to close ranks and pervert the course of justice.

But not Tallantire. It is not clear at what point he became genuinely suspicious. Lord Partridge suggests that initially Tallantire's refusal to accept the obvious was due to no more than one of those instant mutual antipathies that spring up between people. He theorizes that Mickledore saw Tallantire as a plodding boor without an original thought in his head, and that the latter regarded the former as an upper-class twit who imagined that his background and breeding put him above the law.

If this theory is right, then Mickledore's was the larger error. And he compounded it by trying to pressurize the police into doing their work with maximum speed and minimum inconvenience to his household and guests.

Only a fool tries to hurry a mule or a Yorkshireman.

Tallantire dug his heels in and insisted on interviewing in detail every adult in the Hall.

The guests, all of whom had rooms along the same corridor, gave him very little. James Westropp, Jessica Partridge, and my mother had all gone quickly to sleep. The two women recollected hearing the midnight chimes, but Westropp had been too fatigued for even that noise to penetrate his slumbers. Downstairs Partridge and Mickledore had played billiards equally undisturbed, while Rampling had been chatting to America and my father had been strolling the grounds.

Tallantire moved up to the second floor. Here, directly above the guests on the first floor, the children and their nannies were housed, while to the rear of the house the Gilchrists, butler and housekeeper, had their flat.

Cissy Kohler was unable to help. Indeed she was in a state of such agitation that she was hardly able to speak without tears starting to her eyes, a condition attributed by most to her closeness to the bereaved twins. By contrast Miss Marsh was her usual calm self. Her nose was badly bruised and when Tallantire opened the interview by commenting upon it, she explained that something had woken her in the night, a noise, and thinking it might be one of the children, she had jumped out of bed in the dark. Unfortunately, in her newly awoken state she had forgotten she wasn't in her room at Haysgarth, the Partridge family home, and walked straight into a wardrobe. As her room was almost directly over the gun room, the time and nature of this noise became important. All she could say was that it was a single, not a continuous or repeated sound, it hadn't originated so far as she could ascertain from the children, and it was not long before the midnight chimes sounded.

The Gilchrists had heard nothing and the butler made it clear that in his opinion things had been better arranged in the old days when no policeman under the rank of Chief Constable would have been allowed in the Hall through the front door.

The other live-in servants, Mrs. Partington, the cook, and Jenny Jones and Elsbeth Lowrie, the two maids, all of whom had their quarters on the top floor, were less superior but just as unhelpful. Jones, a well-starched angular girl, contrived to give the impression that she knew more than she was going to tell, but Tallantire was inclined to put this down to a kind of assexual teasing to make herself interesting.

All this had eaten deep into Sunday. One can imagine the damage-limitation efforts that were going on along the Westminster–Buckingham Palace axis. So far the media had been kept completely in the dark. The Sunday papers were of course full of Stephen Ward's death and didn't miss this chance to rehash the whole sorry story and its attendant rumors. The most sensational of these related to the identities of what had come to be known as The Man in the Mask and The Man with No Head. The former was a figure who, naked except for a leather mask, acted as a waiter at preorgiastic banquets and invited guests to punish him if his service didn't come up to scratch. The latter referred to a photograph of a naked man from which the head had been deleted. Along with most of his colleagues, Thomas Partridge had been posited by the gutter press as a candidate for both roles, and he was very keen to distance himself from this new scandal as soon as possible. So when the police returned on Monday morning, the Partridge family were all packed up and ready to leave.

That would not be possible, Tallantire told him. Not until he had interviewed the children.

Partridge exploded. He was a formidable man when roused and his dressing down of Tallantire was audible all over the Hall. But Tallantire was adamant. He, we now know, had been ordered to wrap this affair up before the Bank Holiday was over, and he wasn't going to let it go till he was sure he'd covered every possible angle.

The row was at its height with the outcome still in doubt when one of Tallantire's minions appeared and whispered something in his master's ear that made the superintendent leave the room with the scantiest of apologies.

His gut feeling that there was more here than met the eye had made Tallantire grasp at straws. Interviewing the children was one of these. Jenny Jones was another. Just in case there was more to her knowingness than the desire of drabness to be colorful, he had sent his most personable young officer to talk to her again.

He had struck gold. Resentment, envy, moral outrage, or just a desire to please, had made Jones reveal that her fellow maid, Elsbeth Lowrie, had had one of the guests in her room that night. Nor was this the first time such a thing had happened, and it wasn't right that she, Jenny, had to do the brunt of the work while Elsbeth was in Mickledore's employ simply because she was no better than she ought to be.

Elsbeth, a shapely blond girl who looked like every wicked squire's vision of a healthy young milkmaid, had seen no reason to tell the police the truth on Sunday, but she saw even less to keep on lying today. She freely admitted that from time to time she entertained some of Mickledore's guests, but only those she fancied, and not for money, that wouldn't be right, though she did acknowledge that her pay packet often contained what she ingenuously described as "a kind of Christmas bonus," a phrase which won her the caption A CHRISTMAS CRACKER in some tabloid photographs.

Her guest on Saturday night had been none other than the Right Honorable Thomas Partridge MP. He had come to her just before midnight (that clock again) and left possibly an hour later, she couldn't be certain.

Like a good politician, Partridge did not deny the undeniable, apologized sweetly for his recent ill temper, and offered full cooperation of himself and his family in return for the exercise of maximum discretion.

Tallantire like a good Yorkshireman said nowt, and instructed his officers to start interviewing the children.

We, as you may imagine, were fascinated by all these comings and goings. My sister Wendy and I had formed a close alliance with the two elder Partridge girls. Their brother, Tommy, newly entangled in the weeds of pubescence, regarded us scornfully as noisy kids, and the other children were of course not yet of an age to enjoy the delights of midnight feasts and doctors-and-nurses. But four children between seven and nine is the nucleus of an intelligence service far more efficient than MI5 and there was little that we missed, though much we couldn't understand.

We four were interviewed by a male detective with a woman police constable by his side. She, I think, would have preferred to see us *one at a time but he was the better psychologist and knew you were likely to get much more out of a relaxed and mutually disputatious group. Also the fact that there were four of us made it easier for him to shut our mothers out, though I doubt if he'd get away with that nowadays.*

I can't remember his name, but his face remains clear, broad and hard, with eyes like rifle sights and a mouth like Moby Dick's. But when he spoke it was very gently. He pulled out a packet of cigarettes, reached them toward me and said, "Smoke?" and I was his forever. I wanted to take one but didn't quite dare and he said, "Later, mebbe. I always fancy a bull's-eye myself this time in the morning." And he took out a huge bag of bull's-eyes and passed these round instead.

After that we were old friends. The girls clearly thought he was wonderful, but it was me he spoke to mainly, very man to man, always glancing at me to confirm anything they said. It was easy to tell him that we hadn't been sleeping as we should have been, but instead had gathered in the room Wendy and I shared for a midnight feast. "And did you hear or see owt?" he asked. By this time I'd have gladly made something up to please him, but as it turned out, the truth was enough. Yes, we'd heard a noise and I'd peeped out through the door, fearing that one of the two nannies was on to us, and at first I thought that my fears were right for I saw Cecily Kohler hurrying down the corridor toward me, but she went right past, presumably to her own room for I heard a door open and shut. Which end of the corridor was she coming from? he wanted to know. The end where the side stairway was, I told him. And how did she look? "Sort of pale and seasick," I remember saying. "Oh, and she had blood on her hands."

I tossed that in almost casually. To an eight-year-old, all adult behavior is in a sense incomprehensible. What are we to make of people who have the power to do anything, yet who spend so little time eating ice cream and going on the Big Dipper? Also nannies were, in our privileged echelon of society, the great clearer-uppers. You wet your bed, you brought up your supper, you grazed your knee, nanny would sort it out. Even I knew this, though presently nannyless because of my father's constitutional inability to keep servants.

So a bloodstained nanny was not necessarily remarkable.

None of the girls had seen her—they'd been cowering out of sight. But I stuck to my story and when they went to Cecily Kohler's room they found confirmation of it in traces of blood in her wash basin and on a towel, blood which was of the same group as Pamela Westropp's.

But of Kohler herself and her young charges, there was no sign.

You should recall that this was still not a murder inquiry. The room had been locked and there was plenty of evidence to support suicide. Up till now, if there had been a crime, no one had an alibi except for Partridge and Mickledore, but now with Elsbeth's testimony that had vanished also. One has the feeling that Tallantire, like some intuitive scientist, had made a mighty leap forward to his results and was now faced with the tedious task of filling in the necessary logical process between.

The superintendent delayed talking to Mickledore till the interviews with the children were done. Then he bluntly accused Sir Ralph of acting as Partridge's pimp, a word I had to look up later in the big dictionary. Mickledore smiled and said that in civilized circles, people were mature enough to make their own decisions and he had merely acted out of loyalty to a friend, a concept he did not expect a policeman to be familiar with.

Tallantire asked him how he spent this time of loyalty while his friend was copulating with the servants (the big dictionary really got some use that day!) and Mickledore replied that he had gone to the library, fetched a book, and sat and read in the billiard room till Partridge reappeared.

It was in the library that Tallantire had established his unofficial HQ which is why I can be so precise about this and other conversations. The deep bay windows with the full-length velvet curtains provided an ideal hiding place for an inquisitive child, though at this remove I can no longer be sure what I heard then and what I have learned subsequently, but in a short space that Monday morning there were several phone calls which produced a variety of reactions in Tallantire from anger to exultation. Presumably among them were the two technical reports which were so fiercely contested during the trial. In the opinion of one pathologist, the path of the wound was slightly downward, not, as would be expected from such a form of suicide, horizontal or slightly upward. And experiments at the police lab suggested that after the first barrel was fired, the shock to the victim plus the gun's recoil would make it unlikely that enough pressure could be maintained to fire the second.

Now at last Tallantire had cause beyond gut-feeling to treat this as a murder inquiry.

"I want Kohler!" he snarled at the hard-faced man. "Why the hell is it taking so long to find her?"

They left the library. Fearful of missing something, Wendy and I followed. Outside we could see policemen everywhere. Tallantire started to talk to a uniformed inspector while our friend with the bull's-eyes walked out to the end of the rickety old jetty projecting into the lake. He seemed to be staring out at the little island in the middle of the waters. It was covered with willows whose trailing branches formed a natural screen around its banks. Cissy Kohler had called it Treasure Island and we had enjoyed a marvelous game out there with her on Saturday while Miss Marsh had sat in a chair on the lawn and looked after the younger kids.

Now I walked a little way along the jetty and stared out toward the island too. I saw it first. Under the screen of willows was the shallow crescent of a canoe. I hurried forward eager to gain kudos from my new friend, but he must have spotted it himself.

He put his hands to his mouth to form a megaphone and in the loudest voice I ever heard issue from human lips he bellowed, "Miss Kohler!"

At that cry every bird within half a mile seemed to rise squawking into the air. Then just as quickly everything went still. All the human figures round the margin of the lake froze. Even the very wind in the trees died away. And slowly as if summoned by the call rather than propelled by human hand, the prow of the canoe swung out from under the willows. We could see quite clearly the outline of the woman though the children were not visible.

Then the hard-faced man shouted again.

"Come in! Your time is up!"

I began to laugh because that was what the man called at the boating pond in the park near where we lived. But what happened next wasn't funny, though no two witnesses seemed to see the same thing. Some said Cissy Kohler tried to swing back under the willows. Others said she drove the paddle into the water in an effort at flight to the farther bank. Still others claimed that she deliberately flipped the canoe over as if opting for death by water rather than the risk of it by rope. To my young eyes she just seemed to get entangled in the trailing branches, then capsized.

The man at the end of the jetty let out a very rude word my mother would not let me say, kicked off his shoes, hurled himself into the water, and headed out to the island at a tremendous crawl. Out by the canoe we could see only one head, Kohler's. Then it vanished as she dived. Up she came with something in her arms. She tried to right the canoe with one hand, but couldn't manage it and when the police-man reached her, he found her clinging to the hull with what turned out to be the child, Philip, in her arms. Now the policeman dived and dived, while his colleagues ran to the boathouse and launched the other canoe and an old duck punt. By the time they'd got to the island, he'd brought up the little girl, Emily. But it was too late.

They were all rushed to the nearest hospital some fifteen miles away. There it was confirmed. The little boy would be all right. But Emily was dead.

At the trial the defense lawyer tried to suggest that Superinten-dent Tallantire acted with brutal insensitivity in forcing Cissy Kohler to leave the hospital and return to Mickledore Hall to be interrogated, but there were plenty of witnesses to prove that the young American refused to let herself be hospitalized, and this left only a choice of the Hall or a police interview room. And as in the public's eyes the ques-tion was simply whether Cissy Kohler had killed the child by selfish carelessness or incidentally in an attempt at self-destruction, there was little sympathy to be whipped up for her.

She was driven back to Mickledore Hall early that Bank Holiday afternoon, allowed time to change from the hospital robe into clothes of her own, then Tallantire, despite some protests from my mother, went to start the interrogation.

From start to finish, it took the best part of five hours. Soon that room became the atmospheric center of the house. A woman police officer was summoned, but for long periods she stood on duty at the door while Tallantire remained alone with the woman. Food was sent in, but came out untouched. From time to time the superintendent emerged but Kohler never. The first time he appeared, he looked exultant as if he were making rapid progress, but thereafter his mood changed. Sometimes his voice would be heard raised in anger and sometimes a woman's sobbing was clearly audible through the closed door. At no time did Kohler have a solicitor present, though the woman officer confirmed that she was given the opportunity. Tallantire spent most of his time out of the room making or taking telephone calls. Alas, despite my best endeavors, I couldn't get in a position to overhear any of these, but after his final conversation, about five o'clock, he looked as if a great load had been lifted from his mind. He went back into the bedroom and finally emerged about fifty minutes later looking weary but triumphant, like a man who has brought his argosy through heavy seas into a safe haven.

His relief made him for once ignore my lurking presence.

"That's it," he said to the hard-faced man. "She's coughed. We're home and dry."

We can only guess at what stage all the detailed information which provided Mickledore's motive came into Tallantire's possession, but I suspect much of it must have been confirmed during that last phone call. The details of course provided the press with enough columns to refurbish the Parthenon, but briefly the facts were these.

Pamela Westropp and Cecily Kohler, employer and employee, were equal in one respect. They both loved Mickledore with an obsessive passion, the former to the point where she would bear no rival near the throne, let alone on it, the latter to the point where she would do anything for him.

Mickledore in his man-about-town mode had run up huge gambling debts against the security of the estate. In his country squire mode, he had wooed and won the daughter of the Laird of Malstrath, a first generation title purchased along with several thousand acres of grouse moor by George MacFee, a second generation whisky millionaire. Mick's motive was simple. He anticipated that her portion would pay off his debts and save the estate. But there was a problem. Despite

George MacFee's alcoholic background and social aspirations, he was a devout member of one of the stricter Scottish sects whose reaction to news of his prospective son-in-law's sexual and economic excesses was as predeterminable as if it had been written in the Good Book.

The engagement was to be made public the following weekend at Malstrath Keep, the castle which went with the lairdship. Pamela had to be told. Presumably Mickledore hoped that he could persuade her that this marriage of convenience need not interfere with their affair. But he knew enough about women in general and Pam in particular to recognize that Pam had hopes that went deeper than this. True, the fact that the Westropps were Roman Catholic made divorce difficult, but she was working on it. So the ever practical Mickledore prepared a contingency plan.

Perhaps the pleasant atmosphere of that first day gave him hope that all might yet be well. At some point, probably just before they all went off to bed, he got Pam alone and broke the news.

I doubt if her immediate reaction was encouraging. But all hope vanished the next day when he got a note from her. We only know for certain the few words that survived, but Superintendent Tallantire's reconstruction must surely be pretty close.

Mick, I've thought about it all night and it's no good—I can't take it—I'd rather destroy everything—if you go ahead with this I'll make sure George MacFee knows all about us—and about your debts—believe me—I'll do it—let's talk again I beg you—

Her behavior during the day got more and more eccentric. Mickledore knew he had no time to lose. And he also saw that with a little bit of editing, Pam had put a very useful suicide note into his hand.

But now, in the best Golden Age tradition, he made his one mistake. It is hard to understand why a man desperate to rid himself of one troublesome woman should do so by putting himself at the mercy of another. Perhaps he let himself be swayed by his certainty, confirmed by Cissy's own admission, that she resented his affair with Pam far more than she did the prospect of his loveless marriage to the Scottish heiress.

Whatever the reason, he invoked her help, not foreseeing that the bloody reality of the deed, plus the drowning of Emily Westropp, would so demoralize her as to make her putty in the hands of a ruthless and determined man like Walter Tallantire.

"What now, sir?" said the hard-faced man. "Back to the station with both on 'em?"

But Tallantire smiled and said, "Not yet. He likes to play at being a real throwback, so let's do things properly in the old style. Tell Sir Ralph and his guests that I'd like to see them all in the library in half an hour."

So there it is. Because of Tallantire's active dislike of Mickledore plus a mordant sense of irony, the last of the Golden Age murders was to end in proper Golden Age style, with the suspects assembled in the library for the final dénouement.

In fact there was no lengthy unknotting. Oh, yes, I was there too. With such advance notice it was easy for me to collect Wendy and get ourselves well hidden in the folds of those musty-smelling velvet curtains across the deep bay.

Tallantire was straight to the point, speaking with the ponderous certainty of a man who has destroyed doubt.

"I regret to tell you that Mrs. Westropp's death was neither accident nor self-slaughter. I believe she was murdered."

I heard the gasps. I could feel the shock. Then someone, I believe it was Partridge, said, "But the room was locked from the inside!"

"I don't think so. True, a key was left on the inside, but not inserted so far that it interfered with the turning of a key on the outside."

"But it wouldn't turn," I heard my father say. "I tried the thing myself. The keyhole was blocked till we shook the inside key loose."

"I don't think so," repeated Tallantire. "I've tried to turn a key on the outside with the inner key fully inserted, and you're right, sir, it won't turn. On the other hand, I bounced myself as hard as I could against that door for a quarter of an hour and I never managed to shake the inside key loose. Conclusion? The inside key was never fully inserted."

"But dammit, how do you explain that we couldn't turn the key?" demanded my father.

"Simple," said Tallantire. "It must have been the wrong key. One near enough the original to deceive the casual glance, but with a little bit filed off a couple of teeth perhaps, that's all it would take."

"But when Westropp tried it . . ."

"He was given the right key," said Tallantire.

And now the full implication of what he was saying must have dawned. There was a moment of complete silence.

Then Tallantire said, "Perhaps I should tell you that this has gone beyond speculation. We have a full and detailed confession from one of the perpetrators of this terrible crime . . ."

He paused for breath or effect, then went on, "Miss Cecily Kohler. She has cooperated fully and we are now taking her into town for further questioning. Sir Ralph, I must ask you to accompany us as I believe you also may be able to help us in our inquiries."

If it was Tallantire's intention to provoke a guilty reaction in the best tradition, he must have been overwhelmed by his own success.

Mickledore said, "What? You say that Cissy . . . ? But she . . . oh, Christ, this is crazy!"

And then he was running.

There was so much noise and confusion that I risked a peep. Mickledore was through the library door, Tallantire was shouting, "Stop him!" The bull's-eye policeman went in pursuit, there was the noise of receding footsteps, then some other kind of noise upstairs. Then silence.

Tallantire said, "Ladies, gentlemen, I assume you will be leaving the house shortly. Please make sure that you leave your contact address with one of my officers before you do so, as there may be other questions I need to put to you. Thank you for your cooperation. Good day."

And so he left. Wendy and I were by this time both very excited and very frightened. Though not fully understanding everything, we knew that this had been one of those strange adult occasions at which our presence was strictly forbidden, so we did not dare move yet. There was utter silence in the library but it was the silence of shock, not the *silence of emptiness. Through the window we could see three police cars parked before the house. At the rear window of the third car I spotted a pale pale face which I thought I recognized as Miss Kohler's. Then after a while Mickledore came out of the main door between two policemen who led him to the second car. He half turned before he got in, as if to take a last look at the Hall. Then he was pushed into the car. Finally Tallantire appeared and got in the front passenger seat of the leading vehicle.*

Now the grim procession set off. There was no obstacle they could have anticipated for several miles, but perhaps as a last gesture of triumph over a way of life and a set of people I'm sure he despised, Superintendent Tallantire switched on the flashing lights and warning bells. I watched them glide away down the long drive, lost sight but not sound of them as they dropped down to the tree-lined river, glimpsed the lights once more as they climbed the winding road up the far hillside. Then they passed over the crest and soon the bell notes were buried deep in the next valley glades and it was as quiet outside the Hall as within.

Thus ended my direct involvement with the Mickledore Hall murder case. As I said at the beginning, it was the best of crimes, it was the worst of crimes; the best because, though perhaps Cissy Kohler wanted her rival out of the way, it was not this that made her join the murder plot but a deep, altruistic and ultimately destructive love for a worthless man; and the worst, because Mickledore's only motive was cold, calculating, selfish greed. Perhaps you don't think best is a superlative to apply to murder whatever the motive. But remember this. Cissy Kohler was young and she was foolish and though she helped take a life, in a very real way she has given her own life in exchange. I only knew her briefly as a nanny before she turned into a murderess, but it was long enough to recognize that she loved us too, the children, and we all thought she was marvelous. That's what I remember now— her love. Children need it in abundance, and where it is given abundantly, we never forget, and should always be ready to forgive.

Sir Ralph Mickledore was hanged on January 14, 1964. The following year the death penalty for murder was completely abolished, but even a few more months, with a Labor Government back in power, would probably have saved him. Cecily Kohler's death sentence was commuted to life imprisonment. In 1976, within sight of being released on parole, she killed a prison wardress with whom it was alleged she had been having a lesbian relationship. Once again found guilty of murder, she is still in prison having served the longest continuous period of imprisonment recorded for a woman in the annals of British legal history.

So ends this series, The Golden Age of Murder. Raymond Chandler said that Hammett took murder and gave it back to the people it really belonged to. But he deliberately missed the point that the class-ridden world of the British Golden Age is based on a reality at least as strong as his mean streets. The Golden Age crime novel to me makes the snobbery of British society laughable, while the hard-boiled thriller makes the violence of American society enjoyable. In which case, who then can claim the moral high ground?

But philosophical debate has not been my aim in these programs. What I have wanted to show is that the society which produced the kind of complex, artificial, snobbish detective fiction known as Golden Age produced real-life murders to match, carefully planned and cunningly executed by men and women who knew that by taking the lives of others, they were putting their own at risk.

Do I sound almost nostalgic? If so, for what? For 1963? Perhaps. It is an occupational hazard of amateur historians to see watersheds everywhere, but it seems to me not unfitting that a year which saw the death of the last romantic U.S. president and the destruction of a British government for trying to evade its own moral responsibilities, should also have housed the Mickledore Hall murder case.

After this, to catch the public imagination crime had to be extremely bestial or involve a great deal of money. As events later the same year showed, it was soon to be possible to steal two million pounds and become a folk hero even if you bludgeoned someone to death in the process. Up to 1963 it was still possible for thinking men to believe in progress. A just war had been fought and won, and this time the result would be, if not a land fit for heroes, at least a society fit for humans. We who grew up in the sixties and seventies and came to *our maturity in the dreadful eighties have seen the destruction of that dream without ever having had the joy of dreaming it.*

So, is it surprising that I should be nostalgic for an age that still had hope? And is it reprehensible if my nostalgia should even embrace what was surely the last great murder mystery of the Golden Age?

Eight

"The things you see here are things to

be seen, and not spoken of."

When the tape finished Pascoe went out into the garden and looked at the emergent stars. He'd been wrong about other people's troubles. They weren't a diversion, merely an addition.

How long the phone rang before it pierced his dullness he didn't know. He rushed back inside and snatched it up.

"You took your time. Not in bed already, are you?" said Dalziel.

"No. I've been listening to that tape."

"Oh, aye? What do you think?"

"You never told me you were personally involved."

"What makes you say that? Stamper never mentioned my name."

"You got described. Once seen, never forgotten."

"Ha ha. I wish you had been in bed."

"Why's that?"

"Then you'd have had to get up. I want you down here straight away."

"Why?" said Pascoe. "I'm not a dog, comes when you whistle . . . shit!"

The phone was dead. In any case his aggression was unconvincing. What was the alternative? A couple more hours of his own company till he felt tired enough to risk the waking horrors of sleep? He went out almost cheerfully.

As he got out of his car in the HQ car park, he was surprised to see that Dalziel's space was empty and even more surprised when the Fat Man detached himself from the shadow of a parked van. There was something almost furtive about the movement and furtiveness sat uneasily on that bulk. He beckoned Pascoe toward the entrance.

"Evening, sir," said Pascoe. "Any particular reason why we're going on like a couple of burglars rather than the city's finest?"

"Funny you should say that," said Dalziel.

He led the way in, pausing as if to check there was no one about before starting up the stairs. On the first landing he once more checked that the corridor was empty before moving swiftly along it and stopping before the door upon which Hiller's mahogany name plaque hung. Pascoe's curiosity turned to concern as Dalziel inserted a key.

"Hang on a sec," he said.

"Belt up and get yourself in quick," hissed Dalziel.

He was pushed into the room and the door closed quietly behind him. It was pitch dark. He took a tentative step forward and caught his shin against a chair.

"Stand still," ordered Dalziel and next moment a small desk lamp came on, its light reflected in three computer screens with the greening pallor of a three-day corpse.

Pascoe said with quiet vehemence, "Now hold on, sir, I said I'd keep a friendly eye on Mr. Hiller, but that stops well short of breaking and entering."

"Who's broke owt?" demanded Dalziel. "And what's the world coming to if the head of CID can't enter any room he likes in his own station?"

"Fair enough. But I don't see why a man who can enter anything he likes should need any assistance from an ordinary mortal like me."

"Don't get cheeky, lad," said Dalziel sternly. "And give me some credit. If it were just desk drawers or a filing cabinet I wanted into, you could be lying all alone in your pit, feeling sorry for yourself. No, it's them bloody things I need help with."

He banged his fist in frustration on the keyboard of one of the computers. Pascoe winced.

"You know all about these things, don't you? You went on that course and you're always shooting your mouth off about us not using them enough. Right, here's your chance to give me a practical demo of how useful they'd be."

"At the right time in the right place, I'll be glad to," said Pascoe. "At this time the right place for me is bed. Good night, sir."

He turned toward the door. And froze.

He could hear footsteps in the corridor. They reached the door. And passed on.

Dalziel, as if he'd heard nothing, said, "All right, lad, I'll not beg. You bugger off home and I'll see what I can do meself. Man who can play the bagpipes shouldn't have much trouble with one of these jobs."

He flexed his huge fingers over a keyboard, like a plumber about to start an eye operation with a wrench. Pascoe groaned, knowing, and knowing that Dalziel knew too, that any attempt at interference by a noninitiate would be unconcealable.

"Move over," he said.

Hope that Hiller might have made access difficult was soon dashed. The man obviously believed that a good lock and his name on a door were security enough. The poor sod had been away from Dalziel too long.

"What do you want to know?" asked Pascoe.

"Everything yon bugger knows."

Pascoe sighed and said, "This isn't an old-fashioned interrogation. I can't just thump it and ask it to cough up the lot. And even if I could, God knows how long it'd take to spew it all out, and you've only got me for five minutes, and that's not negotiable."

"All right," said Dalziel. "Main thing I'd like to know is where Kohler's shacked up now."

The implications of this were too frightening for discussion. Pascoe hit the keys, half hoping it might prove impossible to access Hiller's program, but addresses were clearly not classified as restricted information.

"There you are," he said tearing off the printout. "Now let's go."

"You said five minutes," objected Dalziel. "Let's have every bugger's address, all them as were at Mickledore Hall that weekend."

"Why should they be in here?"

"I know Adolf."

He was right. The printer spewed out address after address, balking only at James Westropp.

"This is grand," said Dalziel watching the printouts roll off. "Fit one of these in the station bog and think of the saving. Now what about . . . ?"

"What about nothing. This is the end."

Pascoe set about tidying up. There was a chance this illicit access might go unnoticed and he wanted to maximize it.

"Stick that stuff under your jacket for God's sake!" he told Dalziel who was clearly prepared to wander round the station trailing clouds of printout paper.

Their roles were now reversed. It was Pascoe made furtive by fear who checked the corridor was empty.

"Right, let's go," he said.

Dalziel seemed to take forever locking the door and Pascoe was in an agony of impatience lest they should be discovered at this final moment.

"Right," said the Fat Man finally. "Let's get out of here before you faint. You're as nervous as a curate on his first choirboy."

Pascoe didn't reply. He was looking aghast at the mahogany plaque. Through the first "l" of Hiller's name ran a crossbar turning it to Hitler.

"I might have known!" he cried. "It was you!"

He licked his finger and rubbed at the bar but the ink was indelible.

Dalziel drew him gently away, saying, "Can't have Adolf think-ing we'd lost our sense of humor. You eaten tonight? You've got to look after yourself even though the cook's away. Tell you what. I'll treat you to a fish supper and we can eat it at my place while we talk about what to do next. We'll go in your car. I didn't bring mine. Less evidence I've been here tonight, the better."

"Whereas I don't count?"

"Nay, lad. Your great advantage is, you're beneath suspicion!"

They stopped at a chippie a few streets from Dalziel's house. He was obviously well known here, raising two fingers as he went through the door and being served immediately over the head of a thickset youth who said more in puzzlement than complaint, "Who the hell are you?"

"Doctor," said Dalziel. "It's an emergency. I've got a fish dia-betic in the car."

When they got to Dalziel's house they found it had been bur-gled.

It was the usual job. Kitchen window smashed, drawers ran-sacked.

"Portable radio, brass carriage clock, gold cuff links, ten quid in loose change," said Dalziel after a quick scout round. "Draw that curtain to keep out the draft and let's get stuck into our haddock afore it gets cold."

He deposited a ketchup bottle and two cans of beer on the kitchen table, sat down, and began to unwrap his fish and chips.

"Aren't you going to . . . ?"

"What? Ring the station and drag half the squad round here to scatter dust over me haddock and chips? You know the score, lad. Five percent clear up on your normal opportunist break-ins, so what's the odds on this?"

Pascoe slowly unwrapped the newspaper round his fish. It was the local *Evening Post* and he found himself looking at the weekly Crime Roundup column where the trivia of brawls and burglaries enjoyed a mayfly's exposure. Here was an explanation of Dalziel's cynicism. But not of its phrasing.

He chewed a chip and said, "Why should the odds be any worse on clearing up *this* job?"

"Cos it weren't opportunist and it weren't a break-in," said Dalziel promptly. "Probably came in through the front door, smashed that window as an afterthought on the way out."

Pascoe went to the window and examined it, went through into the entrance hall and looked at the front door.

"What makes you say that?" he asked, returning to his seat in the kitchen. "I can't see anything."

"Me neither. You've got to give credit where it's due. Are you not going to eat that haddock?"

"If it wasn't just a straight break-in, what were they after?" insisted Pascoe.

Dalziel who had rapidly devoured his own fish broke a bit off Pascoe's and put it in his mouth.

"Wally Tallantire's papers, I'd guess," he said chewily.

"What? But Mrs. Tallantire said there weren't any. Didn't she?"

"Adolf's not the trusting type," said Dalziel sadly.

"But I don't believe he's the burgling type either."

"No, he'd not do owt as chancy as that. But he'd mebbe pass on his thoughts to them as would."

"You mean this security connection you've dreamt up?" Pascoe laughed incredulously. "You're telling me they'd set up a break-in just to have a look for some nonexistent papers?"

"Who said they were nonexistent?"

"You mean you have got them? This gets worse. Just what hell are you playing at?"

"Playing at? Don't know what you mean," said Dalziel helping himself to more fish.

"Concealing evidence. Stealing computer files. For Christ's sake, what are you dragging me into?"

"You make everything sound so sodding sinister! All I'm trying to do is protect a mate's reputation. You'd do the same, wouldn't you?"

"If it was worth protecting, maybe," said Pascoe savagely.

"Oh, aye? How about if I said your Ellie's a mixed-up cow who's finally found an excuse to run off to her mam? Whoops, watch it, lad. You wouldn't hit a man who's left you some haddock, would you?"

Pascoe found he was standing with his fists balled. He tried to unclench them, found he couldn't.

"What was that in aid of?" he said softly.

"Just showing that sticking up for a mate's got nowt to do with truth. Even if Wally turns out as guilty as hell, I'll still smack any bugger that says so."

Pascoe's hands relaxed.

"All right, Socrates," he said. "But it's not as simple as that."

"Never is, not in life, but law's different. 'Guilty or not guilty?' 'Please, m'lud, it's not as simple as that.' Christ, the judge would hit the ceiling then cling on up there so he could shit on you from a great height! No, our Adolf won't be perhapsing around with this one, not when there's no bugger to answer back."

"There's you."

"Aye, there is, isn't there? Story of my life, answering back."

"Perhaps you'd better start answering me," said Pascoe resuming his seat.

"Sure you want to know? Ignorance might be your best defense."

"It never has been with you," said Pascoe.

"True. You're much better off knowing and lying," said Dalziel. "So ask away."

Pascoe chewed on a cold chip. Dalziel had lied about leaving him some haddock. And what else?

He said, "It's back to basics. That tape's filled me in on the authorized version, but I need to be brought up to date on the revised version too. I missed the telly program and didn't pay much heed to the newspaper reports. So what happened to make the powers-that-be admit an error?"

"Jay Waggs happened for starters. He's a bit of a chancer by the sound of it. Media man, try his hand at anything but always on the lookout for the shortcut to the big time. He claims to be a distant relative of Kohler's and says he was brought up on these stories of cousin Cissy who disgraced the family and was locked up in the

Tower of London. He researched the case, came over here, got permission to visit her, and, according to him, became convinced there'd been a miscarriage of justice. He got some backing from Ebor Television because of the Yorkshire connection and made a program about the case. I've got it on video."

Dalziel rose and put a cassette into his video machine.

"Dead giveaway that," he said as he pressed the start button. "First thing any self-respecting burglar nicks nowadays is your VTR. Another beer?"

"Why not?" said Pascoe resignedly.

He caught the can Dalziel tossed him and pulled the ring opener as the screen bloomed into color.

It was a slick, well-made program. Its pluses were Mickledore Hall, now a National Trust property with its decoration and furnishing virtually unchanged from 1963, and Waggs himself, who came across with a uniquely American combination of brashness, sincerity, and charm. Its big minus was the almost total absence of direct contribution from those present during the fatal weekend. To compensate, Lord Partridge's memoirs were extensively quoted; there was a distant glimpse of Elsbeth Lowrie, now a buxom farmer's wife, feeding hens, and in a rather grisly interview, Percy Pollock, the public hangman, now a frail white-haired septuagenarian, testified that Ralph Mickledore had gone to the scaffold protesting his innocence.

"He would, wouldn't he?" interposed Dalziel.

"Shh," said Pascoe for at last, after assertion and argument, it looked as if they were getting down to evidence.

This took the form of an interview with the one Mickledore Hall guest willing or able to appear. It was Mavis Marsh, the Partridges' nanny. Far from the stiff and starchy figure of William Stamper's recollection, the woman who appeared on the screen was an elegantly dressed and attractive woman relaxing very much at her ease in a luxurious armchair in a room which looked like an illustration from an interior decorator's brochure.

In voice-over Jay Waggs said, "I met Mavis Marsh in her Harrogate apartment and asked her to tell me what she recalled of that night."

Miss Marsh spoke in a light clear voice with a genteel Morningside accent.

"I was on the second floor, and my bedroom was directly above the gun room. I went to bed early and fell asleep almost at once. I don't know exactly how long I'd been asleep when something woke me up . . ."

"What was it?" interrupted Waggs.

"I don't know. A sort of crash . . ."

"Could it have been a gunshot?"

"Possibly, though of course I didn't think of that at the time."

"Was any attempt made later to reproduce the sound? I mean, for instance, did the police experiment by firing a shot in the gun room to test your reaction?"

"No. There was some talk of it, I recollect, but it never came to anything."

"Why was that?"

"I suppose they'd got Cecily Kohler's confession by then so thought it would be a waste of time."

"Okay. So you heard a noise. What then?"

"My first thought was naturally of the children, and I jumped out of bed very quickly. I suppose I forgot where I was and headed for where the door would have been in my room at home, I mean at Haysgarth, the Partridge family seat. The result was, I walked into a wardrobe and banged my nose."

"What did you do then?"

She looked amused and said, "I did what any normal person would have done. I yelled out and sat down on the bed. My nose felt as if it were broken and it was certainly bleeding. I staunched it with some tissues from my bedside table, then I went to the door."

"You found it all right this time?"

"I rarely repeat a mistake," she said with a sudden acidity that gave a glimpse of the stern nanny beneath the sophisticated surface. "And besides, I'd switched on the light by now. I went into the corridor and I saw Miss Kohler."

"Cissy? What was she doing?"

"She was standing outside her room."

"As if she'd just come out, you mean? Like maybe she'd been disturbed by the same noise as you?"

"Possibly. In fact, very probably. But when she saw me she came straight to me. I must have looked a ghastly sight. My nosebleeds always produce a disproportionate amount of blood. She made me go back to my room and lie on the bed while she cleaned me up. She was very efficient I recollect, which is what I would expect from a trained nanny. She assured me no bones were broken and told me to lie on my back with a cold compress on my nose till the bleeding had completely stopped. Then she left me to rest."

"So when William Stamper saw her in the corridor with blood on her hands, it was probably your blood?"

"It would seem very likely, yes."

"Did you tell this to Superintendent Tallantire?"

"I can't honestly remember but I would assume so."

"It doesn't appear in your signed statement."

"I naturally left it to the police to decide what was and what was not relevant."

"But later, didn't you feel you ought to speak out . . . ?"

Miss Marsh fixed Waggs with a gaze that would have stopped apples falling.

"Speak out about what, pray? A murder had been committed. Miss Kohler had confessed to being Sir Ralph's accomplice in its commission. We were all in a state of considerable shock. I had told the police all that I knew."

"But when it became apparent at the trial that the prosecution were making such a lot of Miss Kohler's appearance in the corridor with blood on her hands, blood of the same group as Pamela Westropp, Group B, which is of course your group too, didn't you then feel some unease?"

"Had I known of this, I might have done, though the fact of her confession must have still told heavily against her. But at the time of the trial I was in Antigua. Lord Partridge, Mr. Partridge as he was then, took his family out there to his cousin's estate to avoid media harassment almost immediately after leaving Mickledore Hall. He had to return because of his parliamentary duties of course, but his wife and I and the younger children remained abroad till January."

"Didn't you follow the trial on the radio or in the newspapers?"

"No we did not. What had happened at Mickledore Hall was not a topic Lady Partridge cared to discuss. Total abstention seemed the best course."

"And the defense made no attempt to talk with you?"

"There was a letter from some lawyers. I took advice from my employers and replied that I was unable to add anything to my statement."

"But now you know all the facts of the trial, all the details of evidence, how do you feel about things, Miss Marsh?"

The camera closed in on the nanny till her face filled the screen. Her complexion stood up very well to the close scrutiny and the eyes that focused unblinkingly on the lens were clear and hard as diamonds.

"If the verdict depended at all on the evidence of the blood, then clearly it was in error and ought to be set aside."

"And the confession?"

She made an impatient gesture.

"She was young, possibly immature. Anyone who has had to deal with children professionally will know that their propensity for denying obvious truths is matched only by their readiness to admit to obvious falsehoods. They do it out of misunderstanding sometimes, and sometimes they do it out of a desire to please. But most often they do it out of simple irrational fear."

"But she didn't retract."

"Of course not. Why, having chosen what clearly seemed to her the lesser of two terrors, should she now once more put herself in the way of the greater? If you can't see that, young man, then clearly you yourself are obtuse enough to make a policeman!"

"My God," breathed Dalziel. "I'd love for her to have the changing of my nappies."

The program finished a few moments later with a passionate

plea from Waggs for the case to be reexamined and justice to be done at last. Dalziel looked at Pascoe and said, "Well?"

"Why didn't you do a gun test?"

"We did. But we did it while the stable clock was chiming. You couldn't hear a bloody thing outside the room."

"But the noise that awoke Miss Marsh . . . ?"

"Probably was the kids. Or she dreamt it. Wally weren't worried about it."

"Why?" asked Pascoe, then answered his own question. "Because it was too early. Because Mickledore was still downstairs with Stamper getting ready for his stroll and Partridge for his gallop. Because if he had planned the murder, he would know the ideal time to commit it was while the stable clock was chiming. So he wasn't interested in Marsh's accident because its timing was wrong. Understandable, I suppose. But how the hell could he justify ignoring the explanation of Kohler and the blood?"

"She didn't tell him," said Dalziel. "Don't ask me why, but she never mentioned Kohler."

"How can you be so sure?"

"Because I'm sure Wally would've done something about it!" snarled Dalziel.

"All right. But if he decided that Mickledore used the clock as cover for the gunshots, then how do you tie in Kohler wandering around upstairs with bloodstained hands before midnight?"

"Who said it was before midnight? There were four kids larking about upstairs. Stamper said it was before the chimes struck that he saw Kohler, true. But one of the girls said the chimes were actually striking and the other two said they'd struck already. Can't trust kids' evidence."

"Not unless it suits you," said Pascoe.

"Ha ha. Forget the kids. What do you reckon to what you've seen as reason for letting Kohler loose?"

"Not a lot," admitted Pascoe. "With the Appeal Court, the longer it takes, the harder it gets. I reckon the Hartlepool monkey would be hard put to get a pardon now."

"So?"

"So there's probably more than we've heard about. Maybe something the 'Powers That Be' prefer to keep out of the public gaze."

"And what kind of thing might that be?"

Pascoe was beginning to feel like a circus horse being put through hoops.

"Something to do with security, sex, the Royals, or anything that would lose votes," he said shortly.

"Well done," said Dalziel approvingly. "And if you cast your mind back to Mickledore Hall in 1963, what do we find? Partridge, a randy workmate of Profumo's whose son and heir coincidentally happens to be a Home Office minister in the current mob; Westropp, a second cousin of the Queen's who is some kind of spook; Rampling, a Yankee who's in the same line of business; Stamper, a businessman who's got the Tory license to print money so long as he prints plenty for them; and Mickledore, their jovial host who borrows from anything with a wallet and bangs anything with a purse. Plenty there to explain why yon bugger Pimpernel came oozing out of the Smoke, I'd say."

"You'll need to say it a bit more plainly, Andy," said Pascoe, using the familiarity to underline how off-the-record this conversation was.

"Look, if I knew precisely what were going off, don't you think I'd tell you?" said Dalziel in an injured tone. "All I'm saying is, I'm not going to sit back and let them make out Wally got it wrong."

"So what are you going to do about it?"

"Dig a few old bodies up. Talk to them."

"And how do you propose getting them to talk back? By holding a seance?"

"Sarky! Nay, lad, you're the clever bugger. Yon foreign fellow who went drifting around the Med after the Trojan War, what was his name?"

"Odysseus? Or Aeneas?"

"The one who went down to hell to talk to the dead. Remind me, how did he manage to get them to talk back?"

"I think they both went," said Pascoe. "And if I recollect right, they both used a similar method. To get the ghosts to speak, they had to dig a trench and fill it with blood."

"I knew I could rely on you, lad," said Andrew Dalziel. "That'll do very nicely."

PART
THE SECOND

"Golden Bough"

Nine

"Oh father, I should so like to be a

Resurrection-Man when I'm quite

growed up!"

"**I** am," said Miss Marsh, "what you might call a bleeder. Not fully hemophiliac in the Romanoff sense, you understand, but once I start, I take a deal of staunching."

Not just blood either, thought Pascoe who had anticipated a frosty welcome from the ex-nanny but instead found himself drinking Earl Grey and listening to nursery reminiscences which stretched forever like childhood summers. At one point without interrupting her flow she had arisen, gone over to an ornate escritoire which looked as if it would fetch a bob or two at Sothebys, and taken from a drawer a well-filled photograph album. Thereafter her lecture was illustrated, and for the first time Pascoe truly appreciated the Shandyan dilemma that present becomes past at a rate faster than past can be retrieved into the present.

Then just as he despaired of ever introducing his proposed line of questioning, she gave him an entrée with an anecdote about the sanguinary consequences of little Tommy Partridge's cute way with a pin.

"That's why you bled so much at Mickledore Hall when you walked into the wardrobe door?" he interposed.

"Indeed yes. If I'd guessed that my little accident was even a scruple in the scales of justice, I would of course have spoken up years ago. But I never knew. As I was saying to your Mr. Hiller only yesterday afternoon, I still do not understand how your Mr. Tallantire came to ignore the true explanation of the girl's bloodstained hands."

Pascoe couldn't understand it either, but there were many things beyond his understanding, what he was doing here being one of them.

"I want to know everything Adolf knows," Dalziel had said. "So first thing tomorrow you bugger off and talk to Marsh and Partridge."

Now was the moment when Pascoe, who had no recollection of volunteering his services at all, should have contested the principle instead of weakly raising objections to the practice.

"No use seeing them till Mr. Hiller's been, is it?" he said cunningly.

"Naturally. And as he went to see them this afternoon, you'll be okay."

"How the hell do you know that?" Pascoe had cried.

"I had a look in Adolf's desk diary afore you came tonight," said Dalziel, waggling his great fingers. "Computers may bother me but I were brought up on drawers."

"But I can't just take a morning off . . ."

"I'll cover for you," said the fat man impatiently. "I'd ring Partridge and make an appointment. Lords like protocol, it makes 'em feel important. Nannies get lonely and prefer surprise visits."

Not even sociology lecturers uttered their truisms with such authority as Dalziel, perhaps because his were more likely to be true.

Pascoe glanced at the Bamberg clock which looked genuine as did many other of her elegant ornaments, if he could trust an eye sharpened by long acquaintance with stolen property lists. She was clearly a collector, or perhaps the rich and powerful showered such gifts upon those who sheltered them from the more nauseating aspects of child rearing. The clock's gilded hands warned him that the rich and powerful were wont to shower something quite different on those who kept them waiting.

He said, "And this noise that woke you, was any other explanation found for it, apart from the possibility of its being the fatal shot?"

"Not that I know of. I am sure it must have come from either the room below which was the gun room, or the room adjacent which was my girls' room, or the room above which was the maid, Lowrie's room."

Perhaps after all it was Partridge banging away! Pascoe frowned to hide the thought from Miss Marsh's Presbyterian eye.

"I should not of course have been in that room. As the senior nanny I should have had the proper nursery room farther down the corridor but as Kohler had her infant twins to care for, I did not insist on precedence."

"And the other children?"

"Opposite my room and next to the twins was my Tommy. And opposite Kohler and next to my girls were the Stamper children."

"Who didn't have a nanny?"

"No." She pursed her lips. "The worst of combinations for proper child rearing, I'm afraid. An American and 'trade.' Sir Arthur, as he is now, had his heart in the right place, but without the background, he was quite unable to distinguish between a kitchen skivvy and a valued family aide. Mrs. Stamper in her democratic American way was equally unable to draw a line between mutual respect and overfamiliar interference. Thus they had great difficulty in keeping nursery staff. I am no snob, Mr. Pascoe, but there are some things it is necessary to be born to."

Like murder? wondered Pascoe.

He said, "Do you think Sir Ralph could have killed Pamela Westropp?"

"Certainly," she said. "He could have done anything."

"You sound as if you approve?"

"My approval doesn't come into it. People like Sir Ralph are beyond the judgments of the commonalty, Mr. Pascoe. We do not disapprove of an eagle for killing a lamb, or a panther for pulling down a goat."

"You do if you're a farmer," said Pascoe. "So you think he was guilty?"

"I didn't say that. On the whole, I suspect he wasn't."

"Because of the doubts about Miss Kohler's confession, you mean?"

"Of course not. What has that to do with anything? No, I just feel that if someone like Sir Ralph Mickledore set out to commit a crime, he would not be so incompetent as to let that blundering ox of a policeman come within a thousand miles of him."

"You didn't find Mr. Tallantire very sympathetic then?"

"No I did not," she said sternly. "He had the manners and the prejudices of a union agitator. It comes as little surprise to learn that he bullied a confession out of that American child and falsified evidence to destroy a man whose simple existence must have filled his soul with envy and resentment."

She spoke with great passion and Pascoe thought glumly how delighted Hiller must have been to hear such a positive condemnation of his prey.

He said, "Thank you for your time, Miss Marsh," and rose.

"But I haven't shown you all my albums," she said, gesturing to the escritoire drawer which looked crammed with enough material for a Holroyd biography. "Of course I realize how tedious an old woman's memories must be . . ."

"Oh, no, no," he assured her, and paid for his politeness with a conducted tour of the photo-lined hall on his way out. She didn't actually say, "There's my last Duke on the wall," but got pretty close.

"Now this is one of my favorites," she cried as he managed to get his hand on the doorknob. "Some of my young gentlemen and myself when I was at Beddington."

"Beddington?" he said in astonishment.

"Yes. I went as housemother there after I left the Partridge employ. I fancied a little change."

By now his mind had made the adjustment from Beddington, the women's prison, to Beddington College, the public school. He looked at the photo just to make sure. Miss Marsh sitting at a garden table surrounded by half a dozen young lads. Before she could start on a life history of each, he said rapidly, "Wasn't it Beddington Prison that Kohler served the first part of her sentence in?"

"Was it? How strange. The college is, naturally, at a considerable remove from the prison though by an interesting coincidence, it was the same distinguished architect who designed both buildings. There is a significant pattern in such things if we look for it, don't you agree, Mr. Pascoe?"

He nodded vigorously and opened the door. He would have agreed with anything to get out of there.

In the street he stood and looked up at the elegant Georgian town house so tastefully converted into six elegant flats that only the multiple bell push showed it was no longer the home of some rich Harrogate gentleman. Nannying must be a profitable business—unless of course the apartment too was a grace and favor perk from her grateful employers.

Perhaps he was in the wrong business. He tried to imagine himself and Dalziel in starched blouses pushing prams together through the park. But instead of bringing a smile to his face, it brought a picture of Rosie into his mind and with it a heart-constricting certainty that he was never going to see her again. He could feel all the symptoms of panic starting. He tried to recall the techniques for controlling them but instead found himself running drunkenly down the street toward a distant phone box. He had to ring, had to hear her voice; his sanity, his very life depended on it. But by the time he reached the box, it was passing. He still wanted to talk to his daughter, but knew now that he mustn't, that he could not trust himself not to let his terror trickle down the line and infect her.

But the temptation was still strong and to block it he picked up the receiver and dialed the Mid-Yorkshire number.

"CID," he said. "Hello. That you, Wieldy? Peter Pascoe here."

"Oh," said Wield's voice without much enthusiasm. "Where are you?"

"Harrogate. Look, do me a favor. There's a Mavis Marsh lives in a flat here. Find out how much rent she pays, and how much she should. No, not urgent. Just idle curiosity."

And an excuse for ringing. He gave the address once. With Sergeant Wield you never had to repeat yourself.

"You going to be long?" wondered Wield.

"Rest of the morning certainly."

"Anything I should know about?"

"Hasn't Him Upstairs told you?" fenced Pascoe, uncertain what form Dalziel's "cover" might have taken.

"Haven't seen him. Seems he rang in first thing and said his grandmother had been taken ill and he had to go and see her."

"His *what*?"

"That's what I thought. If he ever had a granny, which I doubt, she must be seriously dead by now."

"And he left no message for me?"

"Not for you. About you. Said you'd rung him in the night with a bad toothache and you might be a bit late as you'd likely need an emergency dental appointment. Your dentist in Harrogate, is he?"

So much for the promised cover. It was pathetic, except that to a man who could use a sick granny as grounds for bunking off, a dental appointment might shine like the brightest heaven of invention.

He glanced at his watch. He was going to be late for a lord, adding discourtesy to deception. Pulling the wool over a garrulous nanny's eyes was one thing, but this was really going naked into the conference chamber. Dalziel's rather surprising dip into the epic past came to his mind. What was it Aeneas carried to get him into, and out of, the nether regions? A golden bough, that was it.

"You still there?" demanded Wield's voice in his ear.

"Yes, but I shouldn't be," said Pascoe. "See you later."

He stepped out of the box. The street, though it was called something Grove, was quite devoid of trees. But he could see a sign saying THE GROVE BOOKSHOP. He had read somewhere that if you approached a writer with his grandmother's head in one hand and his latest book in the other, you were sure of a genial welcome.

In the shop they said, yes, they had a copy of *In a Pear Tree*, it was twelve pounds ninety-five, and no, the paperback hadn't been published yet, there'd been an unexplained delay.

Groaning with the natural pain felt by most educated Englishmen at parting with money for books when the libraries are full of them, Pascoe paid.

Ten

"Is your hand steady enough to write?"

"It was when you came in."

Two hundred and fifty miles to the south, Detective Superintendent Andrew Dalziel was also confronting the high cost of literature.

He rarely read crime novels, but bookstall advertising had left a subliminal impression that the genre had more Queens than Solomon, so when he rang the bell of William Stamper's St. John's Wood flat, he anticipated the epicene, and would not have been dismayed by drag.

Instead the door was opened by a burly man in a balding woollen dressing gown, his unshaven face pouched and pallid with what Dalziel's expert eye identified as the effect of a serious hangover.

"Morning, lad. Like a ciggy, or do you still prefer bull's-eyes?"

"I'm sorry . . ." said Stamper, blinking hard. His reopened eyes looked at air. Somewhere behind him Dalziel's voice said, "If this is what writing does to you, I'd give it up and get a real job. Kitchen in here? You look like you need a coffee almost as much as me. Ever travel Intercity? Every time you lift your cup, they hit a bump so's you throw the stuff over your shoulder. Best place for it, I reckon."

"Who the hell are you?" demanded Stamper.

"You've forgotten me already?" said Dalziel, amazed. He paused in his task of spooning large quantities of instant coffee into half pint mugs to produce his warrant card. "Detective Superintendent Dalziel. But you can call me Uncle Andy."

"Good God! The bull's-eyes. It's you . . . only there's a lot more of you."

"Aye, well like they say, the merrier, the more. You've not stayed still yourself. I'd not have known you from yon skinny little kid. Is there owt to put in this?"

"Milk, you mean?"

Dalziel frowned and said, "I'd not advise milk to a man in your condition. It curdles the stomach. Me, I'm all for this homosexual medicine."

Stamper stared, then said, "Homeopathic, you mean?"

"Aye, that's the lad. Hair of the dog. It's all right, I see it."

If he did, it was with some strange Celtic third eye for he now strolled into the living room and set the mugs on a pile of typescript on a desk, one of whose drawers he opened to reveal a half-filled bottle of Teacher's. He poured a carefully judged measure into each mug.

"Enough to taste but not to waste," he said. "Well, how have you been, young William?"

Stamper drank and shook his head, not negatively but in search of clear thought.

He said slowly, "Hold on. I stopped being young William God knows when, and you were never Uncle Andy. So let's get things in their right perspective. What the hell do you want, Superintendent?"

"Not sure. I got off at Kings Cross, wanted somewhere for a coffee and a crap, and you were handiest."

"How did you happen to have my address?"

Dalziel said, "Have you not been getting my Christmas cards then? No, seriously, that program you did on the murder, it were good. Only, you were still accepting the verdicts then. Now Cissy Kohler's gone free."

"So?"

"So, did it surprise you? I mean, you must've done a lot of research on the case. Did you turn up anything that made you think, hello, that's funny?"

Stamper shook his head, winced, and said, "No, but it was a retrospective, not an investigation."

"Oh, aye? Well, now you know you missed summat. That must nark you a bit."

"Not a lot," said Stamper. "Okay, when Waggs contacted me, I admit I did wonder if I'd missed an opportunity for a bit of media glory, but I couldn't honestly make out a case for getting the scent first."

"So you talked to Waggs? I didn't see you on his telly show."

"No point," said Stamper. "There was nothing I had to contribute."

"Little lad hiding behind a curtain and nebbing on the moldy oldies? Same little lad who spotted Kohler wandering around with blood dripping from her hands? Come on! With credentials like that, these telly people would likely have paid good money to hear you fart! How's your dad, by the way?"

"What?"

"Arthur Stamper. *Sir* Arthur, I beg his pardon. One of Maggie's knights. Service to industry, weren't it?"

"Service to self," snarled Stamper. "As to how he is, I wouldn't know. I haven't seen him since . . . for a long time."

"No? Aye, well, that figures, hating his guts like you do . . ."

"Now, hold on. . . ."

"No need to be coy," said Dalziel. "If you want to keep a secret, you shouldn't take advertising space on the airwaves."

Stamper drank again and said, "It showed that much?"

"Not so a deaf man in a smithy would have noticed," comforted Dalziel. "What did he ever do to you?"

"Fed me, clothed me, paid for my education, gave me all the advantages he lacked, and never forgave me for not becoming in fact what he was in fantasy. I could have been an utter wastrel as long as I did it in the right way—sacked from Eton, rusticated from Oxford, cashiered from the Guards, that sort of thing. Then he'd have been delighted with me. Instead I moped at boarding school and went into such a decline that the staff were glad when my mother took me away. I was frightened of horses, hated hunting, cried if I saw anything being shot, and hid behind my mother's skirts whenever he came near me. So he took it out on her instead. If I hate him, it's for her sake as much as my own. But I hope I stop some way short of hatred. Let's call it a vigorous contempt." He laughed. "God knows why I'm telling you all this."

"Father figure," said Dalziel complacently. "You're hoping I'll give you a cuddle and a bull's-eye. And your mam? How's she?"

"She divorced him, as I guess you know, and moved back to the States," said Stamper shortly.

"When was that?"

"Middle of the seventies."

"Oh, aye. Saw her little Willie through college, did she? Then took off."

"Something like that. She's a very remarkable woman. What the hell is all this about, Mr. Dalziel? I know they've released Kohler. Does that mean they reckon Mickledore was innocent too and the case is being reopened?"

"I wouldn't know owt about that," said Dalziel. "Like I said, I'm just off the train, and had a bit of time to kill, and thought I'd renew an old acquaintance seeing you were so handy. Now I'd best be on my way. How do I get to Essex from here?"

"Essex?"

"Aye. It's near London, isn't it? Can I get a bus?"

"Essex is a large county," he began to explain. "It depends which . . ."

His voice trailed off in face of Dalziel's expression of bucolic astonishment at the extent of his wisdom.

"I think you can find your own way to Essex, Superintendent," he said.

"Nay, lad, I thought you were building up to offering me a lift. You've got a car, I daresay."

"Right. But not a taxi."

"I weren't thinking of paying. Still, if you aren't coming, I'd best be off. No telling how long she'll be at this address. Got any message for her? From what you said in your talk, you seemed quite struck."

Stamper said quietly, "Who is it you're going to see, Mr. Dalziel?"

"Didn't I say? Cissy, of course. Cissy Kohler."

Stamper rubbed his hand over his stubble.

"I'll need to shave and shower," he said.

"Aye, it'd be best, especially if it's a small car. No mad rush. We're not expected."

He picked up his coffee mug, noticing that it had left a brown ring on the typescript. From the other side of the wall, he heard a shower start up. Immediately he started opening drawers in the writing desk. An address book held his attention for a while. He made a couple of notes then dug deeper till he found a bundle of letters all in the same gracefully flowing hand.

He picked one out at random. Like most of the others it was headed *Golden Grove,* and it bore the date January 3, 1977.

Dear Will, it was such a joy to get your Christmas card and letter. If you knew how much I look forward to hearing from you, I know you'd write more often, but at least now I can feel sure it's just natural laziness that keeps you from writing, not as I feared resentment. I wish you'd come to see us. I know that, even if there was just the teeniest bit of resentment there, once you saw how truly happy I am, it would vanish right away . . .

The shower stopped. Dalziel skipped to the end.

. . . So do try to come. And if you see Wendy give her my love. I write of course, but she was never a good correspondent and since I married again last summer, she hasn't written at all. There's no repairing the past, is there? But that shouldn't stop us spinning a better future. Do I sound folksy? Well, what do you expect? We're both content to sit in our rockers out on the porch for the next thirty years (God spare us) and watch the tourists go by! Take care and write soon. A very happy New Year to you from your loving momma.

He heard the bathroom door open.

When Stamper came back into the room, Dalziel was leaning back in the office chair with his feet on the desk, studying the coffee-stained typescript.

"You don't write this stuff under your own name, do you?" he asked.

"I could get to seriously dislike you, Dalziel," said Stamper.

"Only joking," said Dalziel. "It's quite interesting. This is the Chester Races case, isn't it? The one that ended with Lord Emtitrope hanging himself in his stables? You're not still on this Golden Age of Murder thing, are you?"

"My agent got me a commission to turn the series into a book," said Stamper, taking the script from Dalziel and looking angrily at the coffee stain.

"Is that right? Nice," said Dalziel. "All the work done and paid for by the BBC and now you're going to get paid for it all over again."

"It makes up for all the times you work for nothing," said Stamper.

"It also explains why you'd not be so keen to help Waggs." Dalziel grinned. "I mean you'd done all the graft, why hand everything you'd got over to a gabby Yank?"

"He was welcome to it," said Stamper. "As you know, if you heard the program, I found nothing which made me doubt the verdict."

Dalziel thought, people told you things by the way they didn't tell you things.

He said, "You got warned off, didn't you? Don't talk to Waggs."

"What? Why do you say that?" demanded Stamper with a force that didn't quite come over as indignation.

"Because the Chester Races case happened in 1961," said Dalziel. "It's your new last Golden Age murder case, isn't it? They've leaned on you to drop Mickledore Hall from your book too."

He knew he was right and knew too why Stamper had proved so ready to join him on his hunt for Cissy Kohler. A man who feels he's behaved shabbily will often then behave irrationally in an effort to get right with himself.

"Rubbish," said Stamper. "My publisher merely felt that with all the current uncertainty, the Mickledore case was best left out."

Another thing Dalziel knew was when to let a man save his face and when to kick him in it.

He said, "Ever hear of Ongar?" syllabling the word skeptically as if in doubt such an outlandish sounding spot could really exist.

"Of course. Is that where she is?"

The Fat Man grinned and said, "Little boys should be seen and not heard. Just you drive, sunshine, and leave the thinking to your Uncle Andy!"

Eleven

"We have lost many privileges, a new philosophy has become the mode and the assertion of our station in these days might . . . cause us real inconvenience."

One of the real privileges of wealth is that you don't have to keep people standing on your doorstep to show them what you think of them.

You can direct them to another door. Or you can admit them and choose which of your many rooms makes the appropriate statement.

Peter Pascoe on arrival at Haysgarth had been shown by an androidal retainer into a small twilit chamber which he, as a chronic paronomasiac, soon characterized as an antiroom.

It was antiheat, antilight, anti anything that might have leavened the load of a man who had dared to be late for a lord.

Perched on the edge of a chair which made the thought of a

misericord seem like a dream of Dunlopillo, he tried to distract his mind usefully by researching Partridge, or at least culling what he could about him from the dust jacket of *In a Pear Tree*.

From what he read, he was soon (he hoped) to be in the presence of a paragon. His glittering if untimely curtailed political career apart, he had innumerable other claims to distinction: in agriculture he led the list of great landowners who had moved over to organic farming; in the arts, he was patron of the Yorkshire Chamber Music Festival, sponsor of the Haysgarth Poetry Prize, collector and exhibitor of modern British painting (himself an accomplished watercolorist), as well as being an active director of Centipede Publishing and a member of the management board of Northern Opera; in charity, he was patron and codirector of the Carlake Trust for Handicapped Children; in sport he was on the British Winter Olympics committee, the Board of Sport for the Handicapped, the subcommittee on Natal Qualification for Yorkshire Cricket . . .

Pascoe gave up, surfeited with worthiness. Where did these sods get the time? His own corresponding entry would read something like: he worked so hard he hardly had time to neglect his family.

Shying back from the tempting darkness of introspection, he flipped through the pages till he hit the chapter on the events at Mickledore Hall.

It made interesting if rather florid reading. Somehow the impression was given that with a nobility outside the job description of one not yet elevated to the Lords, Partridge had sacrificed his own reputation rather than obstructing justice by providing Mickledore with a false alibi.

His description of the whole weekend was coated in the same golden varnish. The theme was the fall of innocence, the breaking up of the Round Table, and it was played through all its variations. The Hall itself became a symbol of that Merrie England so beloved of Tory elegiasts, where everyone was happy in that estate whether council or country, ordered for them by God and a benevolent government. The description of the shooting party that first afternoon was pure pastoral, though with the "Glorious Twelfth" still more than a week away, there hadn't been much to destroy but a few pigeons, crows, and rabbits. Yet Partridge cast an autumnal glow over the proceedings, with the bronze harvest rippling through the fields, the sighing trees heavy with fruit, the shot birds tumbling through the air in balletic slow motion. And beneath it all, like thunder distantly heard on a clear day, rolled the note of approaching doom.

Dinner that first night came across as a Golden Age Last Supper. "I felt," wrote Partridge, "as if around this table we had everything necessary to take us forward from the high plateau we had reached after the trauma of war to that still distant but clearly visible peak of socioeconomic harmony we had all been struggling for. There was Stamper, the rising industrialist, representing the ordinary people and showing them how far they could go. There was Westropp, the diplomat, a member of that marvelous family which is the jewel in our constitutional crown, yet free from any taint of living off the public purse. There was Scott Rampling, young, forceful, an embodiment of all that marvelous energy with which John F. Kennedy was revitalizing American society. There was Mickledore himself, our host, a man with all the talents, a man who showed by his universal popularity that far from being the divisive thing the Left would claim, our British class system is harmonious and unifying so long as each man accepts his place unselfconsciously and with dignity. And there was myself. I too was sure in those days that I had something to offer, more than I had yet been called upon to display. No more of that.

"And, of course, there were the ladies. How readily there came into my mind as I glanced around that room the old saw, that behind the rise of every great man you will usually find a woman. How little I then recalled the second part of the saying—and behind the fall of most great men you will usually find another woman!"

I wonder if Ellie had read this, thought Pascoe. He tried to recall any recent screams of outrage and loud thumps as heavy volumes hit the wall and decided she probably hadn't. There'd been a review in *The Guardian*, however, which had made her laugh. She'd showed it to him (hadn't it been by William Stamper?) and he'd laughed too. The piece had been headed ANOTHER LOST LEADER? and it had gone on to suggest that if all the lost leaders of postwar politics were put in Trafalgar Square they probably couldn't find their way to Nelson's Column.

He went on to read how Partridge, before he went to bed that first night, smoked a cigar on the terrace overlooking the park and the lake, in the company of Rampling and Mickledore.

"I said, 'This is what it's all about, the struggle, the labor and the wounds, isn't it? Men of goodwill, at one with nature, while over there, where those cottage lights are twinkling, ordinary decent families can go to sleep, safe in the knowledge that their future is in good hands.' I believed it then. I believe it now. But as events were soon to remind me, life isn't a two-handed game. There are snipers lurking in the dedans eager to interrupt the play and careless whether they hit the players in their rackets or in their balls."

Pascoe laughed out loud. Stamper (it *had* been Stamper) had qualified his mockery by saying that beneath the old buffery lurked a sharp mind and a certain tongue-in-cheek humor.

The door burst open and in strode the noble author himself, looking older, grayer, and a great deal more irritated than his dustjacket facsimile.

Pascoe, keen to gain the kudos which seemed implicit in being discovered plunged in the man's book, rose and held the volume before him like a talisman.

It certainly caused a change in Partridge's expression as irritation darkened into wrath.

"What the hell's that you're waving at me?" he snarled.

Perhaps after all it was the silver threads of granny's head that were the true writer's golden bough.

"It's your book, sir. I was hoping perhaps you'd sign it . . ."

"Sign something for the police? Oh, yes, you're very good at getting people to sign things, aren't you? That's your blasted forte, I'd say."

So it was moral indignation on behalf of Cissy Kohler that was dulling the sunset glow of his lordship's features to a cyclonic luridness. Pascoe could admire that. He said soothingly, "Yes, sir, it's a tragic business, and naturally we're all very keen to see that justice is properly done now and all due reparation made . . ."

"Reparation? What possible reparation can you people make? God, you can't even be consistent in your errors! That's twice you've buggered me about. Not satisfied with ruining my career, now you wait till I've published my memoirs so you can make a silly arse of me all over again! Thank God I was able to hold back the paperback when I first got wind of this farce. I'm going to have to rewrite a whole chapter, do you realize that?"

And Pascoe recalled that whatever order being a lord and a writer and a human being came in, Thomas Partridge was a politician first, foremost, and forever. And a disappointed one, the most dangerous sport of the species.

You don't feed hungry lions with organic yogurt. Confucius? Or Dalziel?

He said insinuatingly, "If I were you, sir, I'd maybe hold back on the rewrite a bit longer."

The wrath cleared from Partridge's face like an April squall.

"Now why do you say that?" he wondered. "Fellow who came yesterday seemed to think it was all cut and dried. Police cock-up, bad apple, *mea culpa*, won't happen again sort of thing. Odd dried up kind of fellow. Me, I prefer bad apples to wizened prunes, I must say. What're you doing in this morgue? This is where we put the bailiffs and local party officials. Come through here."

He led the way into a light, airy, and infinitely more comfortable room. There was a tray on a small table bearing a jug, a couple of mugs, and a bottle of rum.

"Sit down. Have some cocoa. Mustn't have coffee anymore, it fouls up the system or so the quack says. Rum?"

Pascoe shook his head.

"Suit yourself," said Partridge lacing his own mug liberally. "Now tell me, young man, what exactly are you doing here?"

It was time for a drop of honesty, but not too much. Even rum-pickled politicians had been known to choke on that heady brew.

"In fact, as you may have guessed," said Pascoe flatteringly, "I'm only sort of semiofficial. It's just that when a Force comes under investigation, we like to protect our backs, if you follow me."

"I can understand that," said Partridge. "But this is old news. You'd be a mere boy, there's no way your back needs protecting."

"It's, I don't know, a matter of honor, I suppose," tried Pascoe.

Partridge smiled and said, "Honor, eh?"

He took a crested spoon out of the sugar bowl, studied it carefully, then said, "One; and counting."

Pascoe said, "All right. Friendship then. Superintendent Tallantire had friends. If, as has been alleged, there has already been one fitting-up, they don't want to see it compounded with another."

"If? The Kohler girl's roaming free, isn't she?"

"Yes."

"So are you suggesting that perhaps she is really guilty after all?"

"No. I mean, look, to be quite honest, sir, as you so rightly point out, it was all well before my time. I'm merely trying to help out . . ." He put on his boyish appealing face, the one Ellie said set old ladies reaching for the biscuit barrel.

"Help a friend who's one of these friends who're bothered about Tallantire, is that it? I suppose it does you credit. Tallantire's dead, isn't he?"

"His widow isn't," said Pascoe sternly.

"Spare me the indignation, young man. All I meant was, he can't sue. Mickledore neither. So the ideal solution would be to find that Mickledore was in fact guilty as charged and that Superintendent Tallantire in his eagerness to make the charge stick, interrogated Kohler overzealously and browbeat an admission of complicity out of her."

"Ideal for the Home Office perhaps."

"Whereas if Mickledore were innocent also, and Tallantire was misled rather than a misleader, then that means there was a frame-up perpetrated presumably by the real killer. So tell me, Mr. Pascoe, is it as a witness or a suspect you now want to talk to me?"

He sat back in his chair and sipped his rummy cocoa and smiled benignly. Stamper had been right in detecting the sharp mind beneath the flummery.

"From my reading of the case, you had a fairly . . . substantial . . . alibi."

Partridge laughed.

"Young Elsbeth you mean? Yes, she was certainly substantial. But as Tallantire pointed out at the time, not without a hint of satire, her estimate of my performance time and my own didn't quite gel. Curious thing, sex. At the age when you want to spin it out forever, often you can't control it. Then later when you'd love a bit of the old explosiveness, it takes so long you sometimes fall asleep. Hello, my dear. Come in and meet another of our wonderful bobbies."

A woman had entered the room. She was dressed for riding and if, as Pascoe guessed, she was Lady Jessica, clearly the pursuit of foxes was less aging than the pursuit of fame. Her face flushed and her eyes bright from her exercise, she looked twenty years younger than her husband though in truth she was sixty-three to his seventy. Behind her Pascoe could see a man of about forty, also wearing riding gear. Pascoe recognized him from the papers. This was Tommy Partridge, MP, Minister of State in the Home Office, and a coming man. He was also a going man. Deterred either at the prospect of being nice to a copper or by the glance his mother shot at him, he turned and clattered away.

"You're a small improvement on the last one," said Lady Jessica running a cold eye over him. "But I hope this isn't going to become a habit."

Pascoe had long grown used to discourtesy but this took him by surprise. Partridge with the ready oil of an old politician said, "Mr. Pascoe's come in person rather than phoning just so that he can get my autograph on his book, wasn't that good of him? I'm most flattered. What's your first name, Mr. Pascoe?"

He took the book and opened it at the title page, pen poised.

"Peter." Pascoe thought that Dalziel would probably have gone on asking questions about Partridge's night with Elsbeth Lowrie despite or perhaps because of Lady Jessica's presence, but every man has his own weapon. He said, "You were out of the country during the trial, I believe, Lady Partridge. But presumably you followed it via the media?"

"I don't think we had media in those days, did we, dear?" joked Partridge, but his wife replied grimly, "Why do you presume that?"

"Because of your personal involvement," said Pascoe. "A friend was murdered. Another friend accused. It would be natural for you to follow it in the papers. Or if not, surely you and your husband would refer to the trial when you corresponded?"

"He was no friend of mine. Nor was she," said the woman. "Is there a point to this catechism?"

"I was merely wondering if you, or you, Lord Partridge, felt any doubts about the verdict or had any reservations about the conduct of the investigation at the time?"

Partridge's mouth opened, but his wife was quicker off the mark.

"No. I thought the police behaved with great propriety if not to say delicacy. Policemen still knew their place in those days. As for the verdicts, I saw no reason to question them then any more than I do now. Mickledore was a wastrel, the girl was clearly unstable."

"Come come, my dear, *de mortuis* . . ."

"The Kohler creature is not dead, Thomas, but roaming free, because of gutlessness in high places!"

Pascoe was fascinated enough to risk a provocation.

He said, "You mean you disapprove the Home Office decision?"

She glowered at him and said, "I presume you are unsubtly referring to my son's recent promotion. Don't worry, his time will come. But meanwhile this gang of grocer's assistants and board school boys have to be allowed to overreach themselves so that decent people can see them for the third raters they are. Then perhaps we'll see our flag raised high again, instead of wrapped round the balls of cretinous *untermensch* rioting outside football grounds!"

Pascoe pressed on, "But the new evidence offered by Miss Marsh . . ."

"Marsh? What has she to do with anything?"

"It was her evidence about the blood which helped persuade the Home Secretary to release Kohler," said Pascoe. "When I talked to her earlier, she implied that if she'd been aware of the importance of this at the time of the trial she would have spoken up then. Now it's understandable that, immersed in her duties and a thousand miles away, she did not keep abreast of events. But you, ma'am, and you, sir . . ."

There was a crack like a gunshot. It turned out to be Jessica Partridge slapping her boot with a riding crop, a gesture Pascoe had never encountered outside of a bodice-ripping movie.

"I've got better things to do than stand here and be quizzed about the oddities of domestics, particularly that Marsh woman," she cried.

"She remembers your family with great affection," said Pascoe.

"Indeed? I find that surprising as the last time I spoke to her was to dismiss her for inefficiency and insubordination," said Lady Partridge. "Thomas, I shall shower before lunch. Mr. Pascoe, good-bye. I don't expect I shall see you again."

She walked out, splay-footed in her riding boots, her jodhpured haunches swaying centaurishly. Pascoe regarded Partridge blankly, waiting to see if he intended to follow his wife down this patrician road or whether the politician would still hold sway.

"Some more cocoa, Mr. Pascoe? No? I think I will."

The rum bottle gurgled. He drank deep, sighed with pleasure.

"Good stuff. My family has old West Indian connections. I spent a long period out there in my youth. This was one of the better habits I picked up."

"You took your family out to Antigua after the Mickledore affair, didn't you, sir?"

"You have been doing your homework. Good. I approve. That's right. I had come to accept the kind of assault on privacy that government service opens one up to, but I saw no reason why my family should have to put up with it."

It was nobly spoken but with a sufficient hint of self-mockery to make Pascoe risk a familiarity.

"And it must have been easier to speak with one voice when there was only one voice speaking?"

"What? Oh, yes. I get you. My wife is an understanding woman,

Mr. Pascoe. But a private understanding is not the same as a public complacency. No way I could trot Jessica out as the loyal little wife like so many of them did. No, those were dangerous days, desperate days. The press had been after us all of course ever since Jack Profumo talked himself into a corner. There was a new rumor a day; headless men, men in masks, congas of copulating ministers stretching from Whitehall to Westminster! I came in for my fair share of attention, being young and sociable. But once the word got out about me and Elsbeth, I was everyone's favorite fucker. God, the indignities I had to undergo to prove that at least I didn't figure in anyone's snapshots. Looking back I sometimes think it was all a mistake. Did you ever see the photo of the Headless Man? He was hung like a Hereford bull. If, instead of driving myself to distraction proving I was basically a good family man who occasionally erred, I'd said, yes, that's me all right, and pleaded guilty to every excess laid at my door, I would probably have swept the country before me and been Prime Minister for the last twenty years!"

He laughed and Pascoe joined in, partly from policy and partly because of the disarming charm of the man's racy self-mockery, whose very openness invited his own.

"So tell me, young man," continued Partridge, more serious now. "Did I sacrifice a career merely to help an innocent man onto the gallows?"

"Couldn't say, sir. Like I said, my only concern is to see that Mr. Tallantire gets a fair crack of the whip."

"Oh, yes. Did you know him?"

"No."

"I did. I remember him as a bang-'em-up-and-throw-away-the-key cop of the old school. Not the kind of chap I'd expect an educated yonker like yourself to get sentimental over. You're unofficial, you say? Which means you're vulnerable. Perhaps you ought to ask yourself, is the reputation of an old cop you didn't know and probably wouldn't have liked worth risking your career for?"

"So what can they do to me?" said Pascoe with an indifference not altogether assumed. "Turn me into a civilian and make me earn a living that doesn't keep me awake at nights?"

Partridge pursed his lips, then said, "Word of advice, young man. Not giving a damn's only a strength if your enemies *do* give a damn. So how far have you got? You've talked to Nanny Marsh, you say? Last I heard she was matron at Beddington College. I think I gave her a reference."

"Even though your wife fired her?" said Pascoe.

"Oh, that," said Partridge dismissively. "Some silly domestic tiff. Fact was we'd run out of kids for her to nanny and Jessica was clearly past farrowing. Was she any help?"

"Not really. Wanted to talk about the past but not necessarily the parts of the past I wanted to talk about."

"That's what age does to you, Mr. Pascoe," said Partridge, rising. "More the future shrinks, the more time you spend contemplating your backside."

Clearly the interview was over. Only Andy Dalziel would have had the brass neck to go on sitting as if it weren't. He let himself be ushered toward the door.

"Anything comes to my mind, I'll give you a ring," continued Partridge. "I've still got connections. I'll see what I can find out about Home Office thinking on this one."

"That's kind of you," said Pascoe.

He must have let his skepticism show for Partridge laughed and said, "Quite right, young man. There's no such thing as a free cocoa, in or out of Westminster. Remember, I've got a personal stake in this. Did I, or did I not, help put an innocent man's neck in a noose? So I'd expect you to keep me updated on anything you unearth. Swops?"

Man shouldn't make promises he can't keep, but it's okay for a cop to make promises he's no intention of keeping. The Gospel according to St. Andrew.

"Swops," said Pascoe. "One thing you maybe could tell me, just out of curiosity. What happened to Westropp after all this?"

"Sank right out of sight as far as I know. It must have hit him tremendously hard, wife, daughter, all in a couple of days. He resigned from the Diplomatic . . . went abroad. I believe there were family business interests in South Africa. Or was it South America?"

"And the boy, Philip?"

"Now there I did hear something. Got sent back to school here. Only natural. Abroad's all right for the sun and *la dolce vita,* but you can't let the blighters educate your kids, can you? It's been nice meeting you, Mr. Pascoe."

He offered his hand. Pascoe took it. When he tried to withdraw it after a brief shake, Partridge held on.

"Aren't you forgetting something?" he said.

He wants perhaps that I should kiss his ring and swear fealty? wondered Pascoe.

He said, "Sorry?"

"The book," said Partridge holding up *In a Pear Tree* which he held in his other hand. "After all, that was the main purpose of your visit, wasn't it? To get it signed."

"Of course." Pascoe smiled. "Thanks a lot. An autographed first edition. That must be worth something."

"Never believe it," said Partridge dryly. "An unautographed second edition is much rarer. All I've done is stop you taking it back for a refund."

Pascoe opened the book and read the inscription.

For Peter Pascoe, good luck with your assays of bias, from Partridge (an attendant lord).

"Oh, no," he said. "I think this is very valuable indeed."

And had the pleasure, rare as sex in a submarine, of seeing a flicker of self-doubt pass over a politician's face.

Twelve

"He told me that he was traveling on business of a delicate and difficult nature, which might get people into trouble, and that he was therefore traveling under an assumed name."

Getting out of London was like getting out of long johns. It took forever.

Dalziel, who liked to be able to step quickly away from both his cities and his underwear, said, "You're not a spare time taxi driver, are you?"

"What?"

"Nowt. Just that you seem to be going all round the houses which doesn't make sense unless you've got a meter running."

"You know a better route, you take it," retorted Stamper.

"Don't get your knickers in a twist," said Dalziel. "It's these bloody streets. And all these cars. Wasn't like this when I were a lad."

"No?" Stamper laughed. "All ponies and traps then, I suppose."

"You still saw horses pulling carts," agreed Dalziel. "Better for the roses, and better for the rest of us too, I reckon."

"You say so? I'd not have put you down for the nostalgic type," said Stamper.

"You're a fine one to talk," said Dalziel. "That radio thing you did, it were fuller of nostalgia than an Old Boys' dinner."

"That was what the producer wanted, I suppose," said Stamper.

"Sounded like you meant it to me."

"Perhaps. I was looking back to a time when I was only eight, before I found out what a pain life really is. That must have colored things."

"Your dad's oddities didn't bother you then?"

"I don't suppose he'd give up on me then."

Dalziel nodded his understanding, then said, "Funny how things get to look different. Your dad must've been the same kind of jumped-up twat then as you reckon he is now. Me, I didn't notice. You were all just a load of silly sods pissing about in yon bloody great house like you were living inside a film. But the other guests must've known what he was. And if they knew, then I ask myself, how come Mickledore and his mates got so friendly with a prat like your dad?"

He watched Stamper keenly in search of a defensive reaction, but the man simply considered the question seriously.

"Money's the answer, of course," he said. "Making it was his single great talent. Mickledore needed a nonstop supply by the sound of it. And Tory Party funds too. But there was another attraction for Partridge, I'd guess. My father had invested in TV when the franchises came up for grabs and I think it was about then he got his first local paper, so Partridge would see him as a potential manipulator of the masses."

"*First* local paper?" said Dalziel. "He's got a lot then?"

Stamper grimaced and said, "A lot of everything. Inkerstamm, that's his conglomerate, have got their grubby fingers in all kinds of pies."

"Inkerstamm? Their head office is near Sheffield, isn't it? At least he's stuck close to his roots."

"Oh, sure. But just so that every time he looks out of his window, he'll be reminded how far he's traveled!"

This sounded a bit metaphysical to Dalziel. He said, "How about Westropp? What was he after, money or manipulation?"

Stamper said, "I think he was probably just Mickledore's guest, too well bred to check his host's guest list."

He sounded oddly defensive, especially about a man whose profession probably trained him to check bathwater for sharks.

Dalziel said, "And of course there was your mam."

"What the hell does that mean?" demanded Stamper.

"She struck me as a very nice lady, that's all, the kind of lass anyone would be pleased to have to stay."

"I'm sorry," said Stamper. "Yes, you're quite right. She's something else. Everyone loved her. I took it for granted as a kid. It was only later I got to realize how much rarer a talent that is than mere capacity for getting rich."

"Everyone loved her? But she chose your father."

"Why not? When you don't have to work at being loved, perhaps you don't need to develop powers of judgment."

Dalziel yawned and said, "So, to put it short, your mam and dad got asked out because he had the chinks and she had the charm. But she saw through him in the end."

"Oh, yes. She may be judgmental, but she is neither insensitive nor stupid. Unfortunately by the time she realized her mistake, she'd had my sister Wendy and myself."

"Now, that were real bad luck," said Dalziel dryly.

"I mean, she was trapped."

"Why? Women usually get custody. Any road, she were a Yank. Once she'd got you over there, he'd not have got you back in a hurry."

"My mother's mind didn't work like that. Also my father kept such a tight rein on her and on us that it would have taken an SAS operation to break us free."

"Probably've got you shot too. What's young Wendy doing now?"

"She's in PR," said Stamper shortly.

Something in his tone alerted that inner ear which stops good cops from buying time-shares.

"She doesn't work for Inkerstamm, does she?"

"So what if she does?" demanded Stamper.

"Nowt, except I thought you and her would be on the same wavelength."

Stamper shrugged in an effort at unconcern and said, "In the end, daughters get from their fathers whatever they want. It's sons who have to make do with what their fathers want."

They were moving much faster now and Dalziel realized that they had got onto a motorway. It must be the M11. He reached into his inside pocket and took out the large-scale OS sheet he had bought on his way to Stamper's flat. As far as he could make out, the cottage where he hoped to find Kohler was close up against the boundary wall of something called the Ongar Estate, and well off the beaten track. When Stamper turned off the motorway onto the main road leading to the town of Ongar, he said, "Slow down, it gets a bit complicated soon."

He gave directions in clear unambiguous terms with plenty of time for Stamper to adjust. After a series of twists and turns onto progressively narrower roads, Dalziel said, "All right, pull over."

Stamper obeyed, bringing the car to a halt on a grass verge. He got out and looked over the hedge across empty fields.

"Lost, are we?" he said.

"No. We passed it a quarter mile back."

"So what the hell are we doing here?"

"There's a lane down to this cottage. I could see the roof of a car halfway down."

"So she's got a car."

"Mebbe. But it looked a funny place to park a car to me. More likely they've got a minder."

Stamper said disbelievingly, "But you're a police superintendent."

"That's no reason to throw my weight around," said Dalziel rebukingly. "Besides the walk'll do us good. I reckon if we stroll across this field and through yon wood, we'll hit the wall of the

Ongar estate that Kohler's cottage is up against. Then we'll just have to follow the wall round till we get there."

As a broad outline, it proved correct. What it omitted was all reference to brambles and briar, bog and barbed wire. Both men bore the marks of their presence by the time they reached the high boundary wall, though surprisingly Dalziel's technique of plowing straight ahead regardless of obstacles had resulted in rather less damage than Stamper's attempts at circumnavigation.

Finally Dalziel said, "There we are, sunshine. What did I tell you?"

The wall curved inward in a deep U at the center of which stood a small cottage. Dalziel didn't make for it straightaway but instead seemed more interested in a pair of holly trees growing against the wall to form a rough archway. In the darkness beneath it was a narrow gate set in the wall. Its flaky rusty bars didn't look as if they had been opened in years but his nose had caught the heavy smell of oil amid the sweet perfume of hawthorn and wild rose. He stooped beneath the hollies and touched the gate. It swung open without a sound.

"Interesting," he said, turning back to the cottage. "Let's see if there's anyone at home."

He walked across the neglected patch of garden to the rear door and tried it. It was locked. Then he walked round the building peering through windows.

"Why don't we just knock?" demanded Stamper. "There's someone in. I can hear a radio."

"Aye, you're right," said Dalziel with heavy sarcasm. "Must be someone in if there's a radio on. That's the first thing they teach burglars."

"Are you saying they've gone? I mean really gone? Couldn't they just be out for a walk somewhere?"

"You reckon? Not very inventive for a writer, are you?"

"All right! Just stand where you are!"

The words came from behind them. Dalziel turned. A large young man in baggy slacks and a crumpled linen jacket was staring at them aggressively.

"Morning," said Dalziel. "If you want the folk in the cottage, they seem to be out."

"Out?" echoed the man in puzzlement. Then reverting to aggression he demanded, "Who the hell are you?"

Dalziel flushed indignantly and said, "I'm Lord Ongar's estate manager and this is his lordship, and he doesn't care to hear language like that. Who are you, anyway? Don't you know this is private property?"

The man began to look uncertain and said, "I'm sorry, but I've got to ask . . ."

"Oh, you're official, are you?" said Dalziel. "Mr. Sempernel said there'd be someone here taking care of things. We'd better just have a glimpse of your authority to be on the safe side."

The man pulled a wallet from his inner pocket and showed the fat man an identity card.

"Right," said Dalziel. "Fair enough. Perhaps we should have given notice, but we were just out inspecting the estate and his lordship took a fancy to step through the wall and take a look at our famous neighbor."

"Through the wall . . . ?"

"Aye. Through the gate," said Dalziel pointing.

The gate clearly came as a shock to the young man. He tried it as Dalziel had done, then went to the back door of the house and, as Dalziel hadn't done, started to beat on it.

"No use," said Dalziel. "They're out. But they can't have gone far. They left the wireless on."

"Oh, shit," said the young man. Then remembering Dalziel's reproof he flashed an apologetic smile at Stamper, said, "Excuse me," and hurried away up the lane.

"What's all this Lord Ongar crap?" asked Stamper. "Was he a cop? Where's he gone? And where are Kohler and Waggs?"

"Sort of cop but not the sort you ask the time of," said Dalziel shepherding Stamper rapidly back the way they'd come. "He's gone to radio in. I daresay when he mentions us, he'll get told to move his arse back to the house and finger our collars."

"What for?"

"Personation for a start. You could be in big trouble."

"Me? I did nothing."

"You personated a lord, I only pretended to be an estate man-ager. Not to worry. He'll go chasing after us through yon little gate. We'll be long gone by the time he realizes he's wrong."

"And Cissy Kohler? Where's she gone?"

Dalziel shook his head at the man's obtuseness.

"Where'd you want to go if you'd been banged up for all them years? Unless we've set the dogs on her trail too soon, I'd say that Cissy Kohler's well on her way home."

Thirteen

"What is it?"

"News from the other world!"

Within two minutes of driving out of the Partridge estate, Peter Pascoe suspected he was lost. The clincher was a small village pub called the Pear Tree, which he was sure he hadn't passed on his outward journey. A good cop noticed such things.

He stopped before it to examine his map, glanced at his watch, groaned at how late it was, and decided that this might be his best chance of getting a bite to eat before evening.

The pub was empty except for a solitary drinker who looked like he could be on his way to a *Wizard of Oz* party as the Scarecrow.

"Morning," said Pascoe as he went to the bar. There was no one serving so after a while he tapped a coin on an ashtray and said "Hello?" in that tiny tentative voice used by well-brought-up Englishmen to draw attention to themselves without actually drawing attention to themselves.

Nothing happened.

"TURD!"

The thunderous bellow came from behind. He spun round in

time to see the scarecrow's mouth closing. What unwitting offense had he committed to merit this abuse? Pascoe wondered.

"What's this bloody din then?"

He spun back to the bar. A large red-faced man was standing there as if he'd been standing there all along. He was glowering angrily at Pascoe. Even for rural north Yorkshire, this was unwelcoming.

"Man wants a drink, turd." No, not turd; *Ted*, with the vowel stretched and given a West Country or perhaps Welsh openness.

"You take care of thy own business, Vince Tranter, and I'll take care of me customers. What'll it be, sir?"

The man's tone became if not polite at least politic as he addressed Pascoe direct.

"Half of best," said Pascoe. "Do you do any food?"

"Pasties," said Ted.

The scarecrow sneezed into his beer. It was a sound as nonphonemic as a sound can get, yet it conveyed derision and warning clear as a Party Political Broadcast.

"I'll just have a packet of peanuts," said Pascoe. "The Pear Tree. Interesting name. Because of the Partridge connection, is it?"

It was partly polite conversation, but also an instinctive reaction to a potential source of relevant information.

"Likely," said the landlord. "That'll be eighty-two pence."

"I've just been up at the house," said Pascoe as he paid.

"Is that right?"

"Yes. Matter of business. It was a sad loss to the country when he gave up his seat. Thank God that his son was cast in the same mold, that's what I say."

"He does well enough," said the man. This came close to being a thaw and Pascoe, hoping that a very little more pressure would crack the ice, went on. "We got to talking about the old days. By coincidence I happen to be a friend of the old nanny, Miss Marsh. You'll likely remember her if you've been around some time."

It was like the touch of the Snow Queen's finger.

"Never heard of her," snapped the man. "You want owt else?"

"I don't think so," said Pascoe.

117

"Grand. I'll get back to me dinner."

He sent a scowl at the scarecrow which included Pascoe in its penumbra and left.

"Used to be the Green Man," said the scarecrow.

"I'm sorry."

"The pub. He changed it few years back. Said he didn't want a name that had anything to do with them Greens. All long-haired antibloods wanting to stop a man doing what he liked with his own property, that's what he said. Asked his lordship's permission to change it to the Partridge Arms."

"And his lordship said no?"

"Sharp, that one." There was definitely a Welshness there. "Knew it would make him look bloody ridiculous, grubby little drinking hole like this called the Partridge Arms, so he suggested the Pear Tree."

"And the landlord agreed?"

The scarecrow sneezed again.

"Ted? He'd have called it the Bare Behind if his lordship had told him to. You'll get nothing about the big house out of Ted, nor any of the others round here. These locals know who butters their parsnips!"

Pascoe picked up his drink and nuts and went across to the man's table. On closer examination, the scarecrow proved to be a man of about sixty whose unkempt appearance was due to sartorial eclecticism rather than simple scruffiness. Taken separately, his dress shirt, tartan muffler, brocaded waistcoat, striped blazer, moleskin trousers, and military forage hat were all of the highest quality and, though antique, scrupulously clean.

"You're not local then?" said Pascoe.

"Don't be silly!"

"How long have you been in these parts?"

"Oh, thirty years and a bit more."

Pascoe laughed. "How long do you have to stay before you become local?"

"There's people born here who aren't local," said the man earnestly. "It's a burden inflicted on only the select few, thank God."

"If you rate them so low, how come you decided to stay around?"

"Man with one eye travels the world till he finds a spot where most of the people are blind."

"So what do you do?"

"This and that. Anything the locals can't manage, which is quite a lot."

"And you don't think I'll manage to find one who can give me any information about the Partridges and their nanny?"

"No way. Bribes are no use either. They don't understand them, see? Offer them a pint and they'd take it and lie to you. Offer them a pony and you'd scare them off."

"Whereas you . . . ?"

"I'll lie for nothing. But for a pony you'll get gospel."

Pascoe looked at him dubiously.

"Twenty-five quid's a lot for a pig in a poke," he said.

"Bargain basement," retorted the scarecrow. "I'm only offering you that price because you're British. It cost the Yank fifty."

"The Yank?"

"Him who got the other nanny out. I saw him on telly."

"Waggs, you mean? You spoke with Waggs? When was that?"

"Couple of years back," said the man vaguely. "Taking inflation into account, you'll see I'm offering a real bargain."

"So what are you selling?" asked Pascoe.

"What are you paying?" replied the man.

He produced his wallet and counted out twenty-five pounds. He meant to wave it seductively in front of the man but somehow the notes were pulled from his fingers without his feeling the friction.

"Nanny Marsh left the Partridge house about twenty years ago."

"Yes, I know. Under a cloud."

The scarecrow laughed.

"Oh, she'd been under something right enough, but it was a bit more substantial than a cloud."

He patted his stomach significantly.

"Good lord," said Pascoe. "But who . . . ?"

"Well, I wasn't actually present at the coupling, but if you put a

119

heifer in a field with a randy old bull, you don't need to look far when she drops a calf, do you?"

"Partridge, you mean?" said Pascoe who liked to have things clear, especially when dealing with a Celt.

"Who said that? Not me. You may be a libel lawyer for all I know. But take a stroll round the village and after a while you get used to seeing the same little round faces peering at you."

"So what happened to Miss Marsh?"

"Off to a clinic somewhere, was the word. Quick clear-out, large severance payment so to speak, impeccable references, carries on her career elsewhere."

It made a good old-fashioned bodice-ripping yarn. Except it was hard to imagine Mavis Marsh letting anyone rip her bodice without administering a sharp slap round the ear and a decree of banishment to bed without any supper.

"Is that it then?" he asked. "Not much for twenty-five quid."

"Depends what you do with it, I'd say. Mr. Waggs seems to have done all right. When they make the film, I wonder if I'll be in it?"

"Which film?"

"Bound to be a film, isn't there, boy? Haven't you noticed? There's nothing the Yanks do, from making love to making war, that doesn't end in a film. Must be written into their constitution. Pity Burton's gone, he'd have done me nicely I reckon. Now we've got the bribing out of the way, I can let you buy me a pint with a clear conscience."

Pascoe looked at his watch.

"Sorry," he said rising. "No time. I've got to dash."

"Another time," said the scarecrow.

"Perhaps. One thing you could help me with before I go. Just idle curiosity, but how come you're dressed with such . . . variety?"

"Souvenirs," said the man smiling. "Also advertising."

"Advertising what?"

"One of my little lines of business. I am as it were a living *memento mori*. I do most of the undertaking round here. And when they put on their garments of immortality, I get first choice of their garments of mortality, see? Drowning man sees his whole life pass in front of him, they say. We're a long way from the sea here, so they have to make do with me instead!"

On his way back to town, Pascoe thought of many things, of randy lords and pregnant nannies, of the way in which Welshmen were somehow normal in their eccentricities and Yorkshiremen extraordinary in their normalities, of his empty stomach, his fragile marriage, and whether Dalziel would reimburse him the twenty-five pounds he'd paid the scarecrow plus the twelve ninety-five he'd paid for the book.

He found himself whistling "We're off to see the Wizard." But when he finally entered the Emerald City, he found the Wiz was still not back.

Sergeant Wield was waiting for him. There was no art to read emotion in the sergeant's moraine of a face, but his body language was eloquent of reproach.

"I'm sorry, Wieldy. Has anything being happening?"

"Nowt I haven't been able to keep on top of with threats, promises, and a few downright lies," said Wield. "Only good things that's happened is Jack at the *Black Bull* gave me extra chips when I told him you and Mr. Dalziel wouldn't be in."

"You got some lunch then? Lucky you," said Pascoe.

"It were business. *Your* business," said Wield producing his notebook.

"What? Oh, the Harrogate business. Did you get anything?"

The sergeant consulted his notebook.

"I got three pints, a steak and kidney pie, and two helpings of Black Forest. Who do I claim off?"

"Don't be so mercenary," reproved Pascoe hypocritically. "Who was the glutton anyway?"

"Friend of mine from the town hall. He's got a friend in Harrogate."

Wield's eyes had fallen on the copy of *In a Pear Tree* which Pascoe had laid on his desk. He flicked it open delicately and read the inscription.

"Mate of yours, is he? Didn't know you kept such rich company."

There was a note of irritation in his voice and Pascoe heard himself responding in kind. "You've got some objection?"

"It's your business."

"But you reckon because he's a Tory lord, he's someone to be steered clear of? I'd have thought you'd be suspicious of knee-jerk prejudices like that, Wieldy."

It was a low blow, but Wield shrugged it off with a show of indifference.

"What do I know? It's another world."

"Come on, it's our world too, he's a public figure," said Pascoe, finding himself forced into a defense of Partridge by his guilt at his own irritability. "He does a lot of good."

"Charity, you mean. Aye, I heard him making a radio appeal for them handicapped kids' homes, the Carlake Trust, is it? I even sent something. But it's not exactly Mother Teresa stuff, taping a five-minute chat, is it?"

"He does rather more than that," said Pascoe with dust-jacket expertise. "He's codirector. And the royalties from his book go to the Trust."

"Likely he can afford it," said Wield. "I mean, a man who can hand out leases on two fifty quid a week flats can't be short of a bob or two."

Suddenly Pascoe was diverted from seeking the cause of his own irritation to understanding Wield's.

"What's that you say?"

"That flat you asked about. There's a management company runs the house, and behind them there's a property company called Millgarth Estates. And you know who the principal shareholder is? That's right. Your favorite author, Lord Partridge."

"You said, hand out leases . . . ?"

"Aye. This woman lives there, free and clear of all rent, ground rent, management charges, the lot. Who is she, anyway? His bit of stuff?"

It dawned on Pascoe that they had a common source of irritation. Wield's was at being kept in the dark, his was at having to work in the dark.

He said, "No, she is his old family nanny."

Wield whistled and said, "Nice work if you can get it. What's it got to do with us?"

It was a good question. Better perhaps was, what's it got to do with Ralph Mickledore? With Pam Westropp? With Cissy Kohler?

He said wearily, "God knows, Wieldy. And He's not in today."

Sometimes the dark was the safest place to be.

Fourteen

"For gracious sake, don't talk about

Liberty; we have quite enough of that!"

It wasn't till she stepped aboard the Boeing 747 at Heathrow that Cissy Kohler realized she had missed the space age.

Television, books, newspapers, they all fed you information fricasseed with fiction, so that Apollo 11 became indistinguishable from *Star Wars.* Prison was a time capsule. The events in the brief period since her release had passed in a kind of decelerating blur. It was as if she'd stepped straight out of Mickledore Hall into this huge machine with stairs to an upper deck and more seats than a cinema.

They were in first class. She relaxed in her broad and comfortable seat and peered out of the window. A memory stirred of the first time she had seen this airport thirty years ago. Then a voice said, "Mr. Waggs." And she looked up to see Osbert Sempernel's distinguished gray head stooping over Jay.

He wore the same or an identical Savile Row suit, the same or an identical discolored tie, and definitely the same expression of superior unconcern.

Jay Waggs said, "Hi."

"I wonder if I could have a word."

"As many as you like. If you've got a ticket, you can have a whole bookful."

"It would be better back in the terminal," murmured Sempernel. "More private."

"Hell, we couldn't hold up all the other good people on this plane."

"There are plenty of other flights. It would just be a matter of tying up a few loose ends."

Waggs glanced at his watch and said, "I make it you've got seven minutes to do the tying, Mr. Sempernel."

"I could have you both taken off," said Sempernel mildly.

"Well, you could, but I'd make a lot of noise, believe me. And our solicitor's back there in the terminal and he'd make a lot of noise too. And just imagine the noise the media would make if this little lady you've had illegally locked up for half her lifetime was dragged screaming from the plane that was taking her home. Papers are all in order too. Mr. Jacklin saw to that."

"A very thorough man, your Mr. Jacklin," said Sempernel.

"That's right, but he's not perfect," said Jay Waggs. "I reckon he forgot to mention that little gate in the wall and the key he had to the lock."

"We had an agreement, Mr. Waggs," said Sempernel.

"Still have," reassured the American. "All that's changed is that Cissy here couldn't wait to get home."

Sempernel stood in silence for a moment. Then he said, "In that case all that remains is to wish you bon voyage."

"And you too, Mr. Sempernel, wherever you're going."

He straightened up and left.

Cissy said, "Is there a problem, Jay?"

"No problem, Ciss." He smiled.

"Good." She knew there was a problem, would be many more. But for the moment she wanted to surrender herself to her sense of wonder at being in the bowels of this huge machine. She felt an almost sexual shudder run through her body as the jets began to roar, and the climax came when the monster did the impossible and lifted itself clear of the speeding runway into the skies. She watched the ragged coastline fall away, then they were above the clouds, and all sense of movement faded, and with it her sense of wonder too. Now they were simply sealed tight in a narrow metal-lined room. This was familiar territory.

Food was served. It was good. She refused wine. She'd had a glass of champagne her first night in the cottage. It made her head swim. There were plenty of sources of confusion in this brash new world without admitting more through her mouth.

"Okay, Cissy?"

"Fine, Jay."

She gave him the half smile which was still the best her face muscles could manage. Men were like alcohol, to be treated with caution till you were sure that you'd got their measure. You thought you could use people, then you found they were using you. Like Daphne Bush. She saw her stretched out on the cell floor, eyes wide, seeing nothing . . . or seeing everything . . . She forced her thoughts back to Jay. For twenty-seven years the men she saw had all been defined purely in terms of function . . . chaplain, doctor, solicitor . . . then came Jay. He said he was kin, but that wasn't a function. Finally she had got a label on his cell. He was some kind of crusader. She knew a bit about the crusades. Alfred Duggan's novels in the prison library had stimulated an interest, and in the time capsule, an interest was something you nursed tenderly.

She knew that after the crusaders achieved their aim and liberated the Holy City, their minds switched from the sacred to the profane, from divine justice to plunder and fiefdoms.

Time to take a little step back to the world she'd been out of.

"Jay, who's paying for this?"

She wasn't really interested but the only other thing she wanted to talk about wasn't a subject to be aired in a crowded plane.

"No need to worry about that," he said. "What's mine is yours till we get the big payoff you're due."

The crusader's personal pennant breaking out alongside the red cross banner over the liberated city.

"You think the Brits will still pay the compensation they promised now we've skipped?"

"Sure they will. What are they going to say? We did a deal to keep her quiet? Okay, they might drag their feet a bit now we've jumped the gun. But they know what this is worth on the open market. This is Prisoner of Chillon stuff, the Count of Monte Cristo, Doctor Manette. Your memoirs . . ."

"I've told you, there are no memoirs, Jay."

"So you write them. Or get someone else to write them. One way or another you can be rich, Ciss."

She turned her wide unblinking gaze on him. Sometimes the impression it gave was simple candor; other times it was as blank and unrevealing as a pair of sunglasses.

"I don't want to be rich, Jay, I've told you that all along. All I want from you is one thing. After that I'll settle for peace and quiet and no one bothering me."

"Yeah? That's about the most expensive commodity on this planet."

"You mean, I need to sell myself publicly to afford to live privately?"

"Something like that. You can't turn back the clock, Ciss, but with the right money, you sure as hell can slow it down."

"Who needs money?" she said. "Prison does that for free."

She turned away from him and out of her capacious handbag she took the old Bible. For a while she sat with it open on her lap, her lips moving soundlessly as her eyes moved over the columns of words. Finally she closed the book and her eyes together and, settling back in her seat, slipped back into the time capsule with an expertise learned over long years, stepping out instantly into the memory stirred earlier as she looked out at the airport.

She was coming down the steps from a BOAC Comet IV, a young woman in her early twenties, blooming with excitement as she set foot for the first time on European soil.

In her arms was little Pip, still sobbing from the earpopping descent. In front of her were James Westropp and his wife, Pam, who was carrying Emily, Pip's twin, also crying lustily. There'd been some debate as to whether John, Pam's son by her first marriage, should accompany them, but it had been decided that, aged six and newly started at school, it would be unfair to uproot him till James got his next foreign posting. So he'd stayed in the care of his aunt, Pam's sister, much to Cissy's relief. She got on well with the boy, but his resentment of his stepfather made him a real handful and she had problems of her own which made two bawling infants quite enough to cope with in this new land.

"This is no way for English children to greet their native land," said Westropp as they walked across the tarmac.

"English? Come on! They're at least half American," protested Pam.

"Of course. And that's the half that's wailing. I thought I recognized the accent."

Often they wisecracked this way like they were in a movie comedy, but Cissy's sensitive ear detected something sharper than wit in their exchanges.

In the terminal building she saw a sign dividing native sheep from alien goats and said to Pam, "I think I should join this line. I guess you'll be okay because you're married to an Englishman, so could you take Pip too?"

"What are you talking about, Cissy?" said her employer. "You don't think James is going to hang about while some clerk decides whether you've come to steal the Crown Jewels, do you?"

Westropp was talking to a man wearing a peaked cap white enough to serve Pam's morning croissants off.

He led them out of the main flow of arrivals into a palatial lounge where they were offered drinks while the brief formalities were gone through. As they prepared to move on, a voice cried, "There you are! I wish they treated me like this. Pam, you look gorgeous. Jimmy, you look as if you've just been expelled for conduct unbecoming. Pip and Em, you are at last distinguishable one end from the other. And Cissy, the fairest nanny in the land!"

And Ralph Mickledore, six foot tall, broad-shouldered, tow-headed, with an infectious laugh and more energy than any other man Cissy had met, was upon them. Each greeting was punctuated with a kiss, leaving Pam smiling, Westropp grimacing, the twins bawling, and Cissy blushing.

"What on earth are you doing here, Mick?" asked Westropp.

Dark, slightly built, with a thin intelligent face and watchful eyes, he was as unlike his friend as possible. It must have been an attraction of opposites. And why not? Cissy knew all about such attractions.

"Welcoming my dearest friends home, of course, what else? I need to go back to Yorkshire tomorrow, so I thought this would be the best way to see you before you were hit by the dreaded jet lag."

"Now isn't that just too thoughtful of you," said Pam. "Here, you can carry your goddaughter for your pains."

"No pain. Pure pleasure," said Mickledore taking the child. "Welcome, young Em, to your true home. You too, Pip. And Cissy, this is your first time in God's Own Country, isn't it? That deserves another kiss. May your stay be long and happy."

Well, it had been long anyway. And at first marvelously happy, though not without its surprises.

During the time she'd worked for the Westropps, she'd imagined she'd got to know them pretty well. She could have written a program of their social life, a catalog of their tastes in music, books, and cuisine. But soon she came to realize that a true understanding of foreign fauna only comes with seeing them in their native habitat.

She had assumed wealth, but it was soon clear that by the standards of many in their circle, James Westropp was rather poor. Mickledore for instance spent money at a rate which made her blink. But Westropp's relative poverty didn't seem to matter. His friendship was obviously a currency stronger than mere dollars. Nor was it a matter of simple English class snobbery. Among their close acquaintance were people whom even Cissy's limited knowledge of London society classified as odd. And once when she overheard James say, "God, she's such a common little woman, isn't she?" Cissy was puzzled to discover it wasn't some nouveau riche climber he was referring to, but one of his own relatives a couple of dozen places, not to mention a religion, nearer the throne.

"Mick" Mickledore was proving an enigma too. After his first couple of visits to New York she had felt confident she knew him inside out. What you saw was what you got, always supposing your luck held. Now she began to realize there were depths to his character in every sense. The first time they went to stay at Mickledore Hall it was like meeting a new man. It was all a question of the way he focused his limitless energy, she decided. He wasted none of it on regrets or anticipations. In town the pleasures and pursuits of urban life occupied him wholly so that you'd never have believed this man could be content spending long periods working his Yorkshire estate. And in the country he gave the impression of a man who would prefer walking a mile in a blizzard to strolling a few yards along Piccadilly.

It wasn't surprising to find that his great sexual energy obeyed the same rules. He took his pleasure wherever he was. This did not mean he was incapable of true loyalty and affection, however. A woman might have to turn a blind eye for the best part of their life together, but a woman who was willing to do this stood a chance of making a successful long-term relationship with Mickledore. So Cissy assured herself and it was on this slender thread that she hung most of her hopes of lasting happiness.

But that was for the future. For the present she was content to snatch what joy she could and never hint of the dreams which filled her sleeping of a life in which all her lover's smiles were for her alone and where no rival survived to threaten her joyous peace.

She dreamed now, and as so often, the dream went beneath its own perfection into the imperfections on which it was based and she saw again the staring eyes, the streaming blood . . .

She cried out and burst into consciousness with a force that sat her upright.

But it was all wrong. She wasn't in the Westropp's Kensington apartment with Pip and Emily in the tiny nursery next door. And she wasn't in the narrow bed in the prison cell which had been her home for so many many years . . .

She looked with terror at the stranger by her side, flinching from the touch of his fingers on her arm.

He said, "Cissy, you okay? Sorry to wake you, but we're beginning our descent. You'll need to fasten your belt."

She turned her head away from him, looked out of the window. Far below like an effect in a child's pop-up book, she saw a prickle of skyscrapers.

"There it is, Ciss," said Jay Waggs. "The land of the brave, the home of the free."

"I hope they'll let me in," said Cissy Kohler.

Fifteen

"I am anxious to have your opinion

. . . on a very curious case . . ."

At six that evening with still no sign of Dalziel, Pascoe went home.

As soon as he got into the house, he picked up the phone and dialed his mother-in-law's number.

Ellie answered almost immediately.

"How's it going?" he asked.

"I found her standing in the kitchen this morning looking into the recess where the central heating boiler is. She looked completely confused."

"So she'd heard the boiler make a funny noise. They all do!"

"No! She was close to being terrified, Peter. Then I remembered. When I was a kid before they got the old kitchen extended, that used to be the larder. She had a milk jug in her hand. She'd gone to the larder to get a bottle of milk."

"Conditioning's hard to alter. I still switch the wipers on every time I want to turn right, and I've had this car for three years."

"You're as helpful as the doctor," snapped Ellie.

"You've spoken to her doctor?"

"This afternoon. Complete waste of time. Old Doc Myers retired soon after they put Dad in the Home. Now there's this thing that looks like a schoolgirl and talks like she's addressing a class of infants."

"Oh, dear," said Pascoe. "And what did she say?"

"She said that I must expect a certain degree of vagueness in the old, adding in passing that Mum must have left it pretty late to have me, as if any problem with her health was likely to be my fault. She told me Mum was being treated for various specific physical conditions none of which were immediately life threatening, but that at present, as my experience with Dad should have taught me, senile dementia was untreatable. In other words, *tough*."

"Perhaps it's just that she'd prefer to make her own diagnosis," suggested Pascoe.

"You were there? Funny, I didn't notice."

It was time to move on.

"Is Rosie there?" he asked.

"I'll get her."

It was a joy to hear his daughter's voice say, "Hello, Daddy," and a relief to detect nothing but delight at the novelty of staying in her grandmother's house. When Ellie came back on, he said, "Sounds as if she's enjoying herself."

"That's what grannies are for. How are you?"

"Oh, I'm fine. Andy's been away today, so I wasn't force-fed any meat pies. I'm just about to treat myself to one of your vegetable casseroles from the freezer."

"What a good boy you are," said Ellie. "Where's our fat friend at then?"

Pascoe hesitated. He doubted if Ellie would approve Dalziel's quest to prove that Wally Tallantire was in the right, and he was certain she would think him crazy both personally and professionally for his complicity. The doorbell rang.

"Hang on," he said. "Someone's at the door."

"No, I'll ring off," said Ellie. "I'd better get Rosie to bed. We'll talk tomorrow, okay?"

"Fine. Good night then."

He put the phone down. It was like two fighters relieved to accept a draw. Except that the guilt he was already feeling at his relief left him well behind on points.

The bell was ringing again, a long impatient peal, and he knew before he opened the door whose great finger was trying to drill the bell push through the jamb.

"Evening," said Dalziel. He was carrying an old blue suitcase and looked like the kind of brush salesman even a medieval stylite might have found it hard to deny. "I rang the zoo and they said you'd escaped early."

"Early?" Pascoe heard himself almost screaming. "And where the hell have you been all day?"

"Christ, Peter, you remind me what it was like being married. You need a drink."

They were in the lounge now with Dalziel taking a bottle of Scotch out of the sideboard and pouring two sturdy stoupfuls.

"That's better," he said as he emptied one of the glasses. "You need to take out a small mortgage for a glass this size down among the Cockneys. How'd it go this morning?"

Recriminations were wasted breath. Pascoe described his morning, while Dalziel listened intently, at the same time absentmindedly drinking the second Scotch.

"Well, well," he said when Pascoe finished. "The more I hear of Nanny Marsh, the more I like her. Screwed by the lord, sacked by the lady, does she end up in a workhouse for fallen women? No way! She parks her fanny in a luxury flat, rent free, in Harrogate! How'd she strike you, lad?"

"Like a little old retired nanny most of the time, except that now and then I got a sense of someone else peeping out and having a not very friendly laugh at me. There's something not quite right in all this . . ."

"You're never satisfied, are you? Have another whiskey."

"I've not had one yet," said Pascoe. "Perhaps I should pour while you tell me about your day?"

134

He decanted two decent measures while Dalziel started to describe his adventures in darkest Essex.

"So what do you make of that, sunshine?" he asked when he'd done.

"This fellow in the car was security, you say?" asked Pascoe.

"He had one of them identification cards that tell you nowt," agreed Dalziel.

"Then this means this is even more serious than we thought!"

"Not than I thought," said Dalziel grimly. "Way I see it is, Waggs dug up summat that gave him the leverage to get Kohler out . . ."

"Something that provoked her to want to get out," interjected Pascoe. "She'd shown precious little enthusiasm before."

"Aye, you're right. So a deal's done, part of which is that she stays put here, so they set a watch on her, only she does a runner . . ."

"There has to be a time factor," said Pascoe. "They couldn't be planning to sit on her forever."

"Right again," said Dalziel with almost paternal pride. "Go on."

"Go on where? I need ten times more information to make the next jump. Look, I can offer you hypotheses which put Tallantire in the clear and hypotheses which paint him black as a miner's snotrag, and I can probably do you most points in between. Okay, there's definitely something odd going on, but it may not be the kind of oddness you're looking for. Have you thought of that?"

Dalziel poured more whiskey.

"Be a good little hostess," he said, "and fetch my case in from the hall."

Pascoe had been trying to forget about the case.

"What's in it?" he asked uneasily.

Dalziel laughed and said, "You're scared mebbe I've come to spend the night! Calm down, your reputation's safe. It's Wally's papers. I stowed them in the left luggage and I've just picked them up now when I came off my train."

Not bothering to hide his relief, Pascoe got the case.

Dalziel opened it and arranged its contents in three untidy piles on the floor.

"I did a quick sort out before I stashed it," he said. "Wally was a bugger for order on the job, but when it came to his own stuff, he kept things in a right tip."

"Reminds me of someone," murmured Pascoe.

"Aye, there's some mucky buggers about," agreed Dalziel. "This lot here's letters, bills, that kind of stuff. Nowt there for us. This pile's some stuff he was putting together on his old cases. He were thinking of writing his memoirs when he retired. Well, he never made it."

"What happened exactly?" asked Pascoe.

"The usual," said Dalziel. "Heart attack. He carried far too much weight, I were always on at him about it. He'd been down to London, died in the train back. He were in a carriage by himself and went on to Newcastle before anyone noticed. I thought of him today as I traveled back."

Amusement at the idea of Dalziel warning anyone about the dangers of obesity mingled with sympathy at the note of genuine regret.

"I'm sorry," he said.

"No need to be," said Dalziel briskly. "Well, not much. Wally would have hated retirement. Writing his memoirs was just his way of trying to spin things out a bit longer, I reckon. I doubt it would have come to owt."

"Anything much on the Mickledore case?"

"Aye, some interesting stuff. One thing I don't have is his notebook. He was a great scribbler on the job, was Wally. Used to say his own notebook was the only bedside reading he ever wanted. Man who noted everything could solve everything. I hope Adolf and his vultures didn't get their claws on it, else it'll be long gone. But this is what Adolf would give his left bollock to get hold of."

He handed Pascoe a handwritten sheet.

I am Cecily Kohler from Harrisburg, Pennsylvania. For the past two and a half years I have been working as nanny to the Westropp family. On the night of August 3, 1963, I went into the gun room at

Mickledore Hall where Mrs. Pam Westropp was cleaning a shotgun. Something happened, I don't know what, but it went off accidentally and killed her.

It was unsigned.

"Whose writing is this?" asked Pascoe.

"Wally's. This too," said Dalziel passing another sheet.

I am Cecily Kohler from Harrisburg, Pennsylvania. I am an American citizen employed by the Westropps to look after their children. I liked my job except that I didn't much care for Pam Westropp who was always picking on me. We had a fight about something in the gun room and a gun went off, killing her.

"What the hell is all this?" demanded Pascoe.

Dalziel passed another sheet.

I am Cecily Kohler from Harrisburg, Pennsylvania. Mr. James Westropp is very nice but his wife was funny, always up and down and the children never knew where they were with her. So in the end for their sake I decided to kill her in the gun room and fix things so it would look like an accident.

"And this," said Dalziel.

I am Cecily Kohler from Harrisburg, Pennsylvania. I hated my employer because she was always up and down, like she was on drugs, and neglected the children. Also she slept around. So I decided to kill her and arrange things so it would look like suicide.

"Just one more," said Dalziel.

This one was different, not an original but a photocopy and written in a different, much less precise hand.

I am Cecily Kohler from Harrisburg, Pennsylvania. For the past two and a half years I have been working as nanny to the Westropp family. It was through my job that I met Ralph Mickledore when he visited the Westropps in the States. We became lovers and because of this, though I'd never planned to work abroad, I decided to accompany the family when they returned to England. I liked my job except that I didn't much care for Pam Westropp. Her husband is very nice but she was up and down, like she was on drugs or something. Sometimes she'd not come near the children for days, then she'd be all over them, interfering with my work, and close to smothering them with hugs and kisses, but soon as one of them needed a diaper changed or brought their feed back, she'd get tired of them and push them back at me, like it was my fault. Also she slept around. I knew that Ralph had been with her, I think she threw herself at him, and when she found out he was going to get married, she threatened to tell everyone about everything, and it would have ruined everything, for me as well as Ralph, so I suggested we should kill her. It was my idea. I would have done it myself only I needed his help to make it look like suicide. She really deserved it and the only thing I'm sorry for is little Emily. I took the children out in the canoe so I could drop the key in the lake, I mean the key Mick had fixed so it wouldn't open the gun room door. Then I thought I'd hide because I was frightened of talking to the police again. I wasn't thinking straight after what I'd done, the longer I stayed under the willows, the more confused I got, the light on the water, the wind in the trees all seemed to get in my mind somehow. I'll never forgive myself for what happened to Em. There's no punishment they can give me to get me right for that.
Signed: Cecily Kohler, August 5, 1963.

"This is her actual confession?" said Pascoe. "Written by herself? So what about the others, in Tallantire's hand?"

"You're the clever cunt. What do you make of them?"

"I know what Mr. Hiller would make of them. Tallantire drafting confession after confession, using them to beat away at the girl till it didn't seem a matter of whether she would confess, but merely of which version she would choose. And all the time using her guilt at the kid's death to turn the screw. In the end when he's got her word perfect, he says, okay, write it and sign it. It's like filming Monroe. When she got it right, it was a take, sod everything else!"

"I don't like the way your mind's running on lasses with big knockers," said Dalziel reprovingly. "So that's how you see it, eh? Good. Now you know why I didn't want Adolf getting his hand on this lot."

"Look, sir," said Pascoe unhappily. "I know I said I'd help, but if something comes up suggesting there may have been irregularities . . ."

"You can put that tender conscience back in the pickle jar," growled Dalziel. "I'll tell you why Wally took so long getting Kohler to cough. It weren't because he was grilling the lass till she didn't know her arse from her elbow. No, the trouble was she were ready to sign anything from the start! So long as it didn't incriminate Mickledore, that is. That's all that Wally wanted, to stop her protecting her lover. Her guilt was never in doubt, but she couldn't have done it by herself . . ."

"Of course she felt guilty," interrupted Pascoe. "The little girl had drowned . . ."

"You mean, she'd drowned the little girl," said Dalziel. "Oh, you can wrap it up as accident or whatever you like, but I was there, remember? I came up with that kid's corpse in my arms and I saw Kohler's face closer than I see yours. And she knew she'd killed her, believe me. She knew!"

He sank a cleansing drench of Scotch, then went on in more measured tones. "At the trial, most people agreed with her when she said there was no punishment bad enough. There were plenty who reckoned she should have hung alongside Mickledore, or even instead of Mickledore."

"I can vaguely recall people talking about her like she was some kind of monster," said Pascoe. "Then in the mid-sixties the Moors case came along, and once the public learned what Ian Brady and

Myra Hindley had done to those kids they tortured and murdered, that changed all the definitions. So what you're saying is Tallantire suspected she was protecting Mickledore and used these drafts to edge her in deeper and deeper till he got the admission he wanted? But what put him on to Mickledore in the first place?"

"Instinct, lad. He told me, the minute he set eyes on the bugger, he thought, *That's my man!* What's that sour face for?"

"There is a school of thought which prefers the evidence to lead to the man."

"Don't give me that crap. You know as well as I do, most times you've got your perpetrator long afore you can prove it. First thing Wally did when he got called in was contact the Yard and ask them to dig out anything they could on Mickledore's town life, particularly any rumors of naughties with Pam Westropp."

"And when did they come through? Stamper on the radio seemed to think it wasn't till Monday afternoon?"

"That's right. Not a dickie from London all day Sunday or Monday morning. It was Bank Holiday, of course, so everybody who was anybody would be warming their backsides on the beach. Except Sempernel, this fellow from the funny buggers. Well, he were younger then, probably drew the short straw, so he got dragged off his lilo and sent up here to make sure no one really important was inconvenienced by the nasty northern police."

"And what did he do?"

"Nowt really. Just drifted around like a wanked-out waiter, always moving off if you caught his eye. But I reckon when he saw that Wally meant business, he rang his bosses, and they decided that once the press got onto it, them shit-stirrers would waste no time dropping hints about Mickledore's gambling debts and stirring Pamela's porridge and mebbe even his liaison with the whiskey lass. So if Wally were going to read about it on Tuesday morning, he might as well be told on Monday afternoon, so's he could get the whole thing sewn up."

"But all that provided was motive. He still had no real evidence against Mickledore till he squeezed this confession out of Kohler!"

"Means, motive, opportunity, plus Kohler's confession. What the fuck else do you want?" demanded Dalziel.

"What about this key? The one Mickledore fixed so it wouldn't open the door, the one Kohler says she threw in the lake? Did they find it?"

"They sent the divers down, naturally. But it's a big lake. The jury seemed happy to do without it."

"And that's okay?" Pascoe laughed. "Who was it said, juries are like thimblerig, the trick is working out which bum is sitting on the brain. Wasn't it . . . you? Sorry. What happened in court anyway?"

"Kohler condemned herself. She pleaded guilty, didn't give evidence, just sat there looking like she thought the whole thing were a waste of time. Came across like Lady Macbeth."

We loved her because she loved us. William Stamper's words in his radio program. How could such a change come about?

"And Mickledore?"

"Pleaded innocence and ignorance. Did his honest country squire act like he were at an audition. He were so open you could've parked buses in him. I began to think he might get away with it. But one way and another the prosecution managed to get the other side of his life into the picture. And there was always the sight of Kohler sitting there, like something he'd rather have kept in his attic. Funny thing when the verdict came in. From all accounts he still thought he'd get off, but he didn't turn a hair when the foreman said, 'Guilty.' Raised his eyebrows a bit, like he'd been dealt a club when he'd have preferred a diamond. And when he was asked if he'd owt to say before sentence, he said loud and clear, 'As you at least must know, my lord, I am totally innocent of this crime and do not doubt that eventually I shall be proved so.' Kohler, on the other hand, who'd pleaded guilty, collapsed and had to be hospitalized. Mental and physical breakdown. She spent the first six months of her sentence in hospital."

"And Mickledore. Did he appeal?"

"In a manner of speaking. He didn't get official leave, but he asked to see Wally. Hang on, here it is."

He dug around in the case notes pile and came up with a thick-ish sheaf of typed pages stapled together.

"What's this?" said Pascoe.

"I told you Wally were thinking of writing his memoirs. He got as far as doing an outline. Here we are. This is the bit about the Mickledore case."

Pascoe took it and read.

"After the trial, Mickledore asked to see me. Said he assumed I was an honest man. If so, I wouldn't want doubts, but I must have them, the way things had gone so easily. I told him get on with it. He said he'd hoped it wouldn't come to this, but now he had to tell the truth. It was James Westropp who'd killed his wife. He'd kept quiet out of loyalty, hoping all through trial for acquittal. I said, what about Kohler? He said she was Westropp's mistress, so besotted by him, she'd do anything, especially after causing his daughter's death. I said, where's the proof? He said that was my job. All he knew was that Westropp was getting protection because of who he was. Claimed he himself had been given to understand he'd be okay if he just kept quiet, but he'd never expected things to go this far. Now he was getting worried. Desperate, I said, to come up with such a story. He said, for Christ's sake, Tallantire, don't turn out a crook like the rest of them. All I ask is that you double check everything. In the end, I promised. Checked. Nothing. Mickledore trying it on. N.B. Westropp not available then. Might be interesting now all dust has settled to check where he is and get his reaction to Mickledore's attempts to incriminate him."

"He talked to you about this?"

"He mentioned his visit to the jail."

"How hard would he check? I mean from what you say, he was certain from the start that Mickledore was his man. Also he got a lot of kudos out of the case, didn't he? High point of his career, that sort of thing."

"That'd make him check all the harder," said Dalziel aggressively.

142

It was, thought Pascoe, time to change the subject.

He said, "These memoirs. You don't know if Wally got as far as trying to find a publisher?"

"Not that I know of. Why do you ask?"

"There are quite a few penciled corrections, they look professional, as if maybe some editor had read the outline. It comes automatically to these people. They couldn't read a shopping list without correcting it."

Pascoe spoke with the expertise of a man who'd seen the returned scripts of his wife's novel.

"Let's have a look. Aye, you're right. That's not Wally's hand. But why'd he send summat like this to a publisher?"

"To give an idea of the kind of book he proposed, in the hope of getting some money up front before he started the job proper."

"Aye, that'd be Wally's way," agreed Dalziel. "Let's have a look."

He scattered the pile of correspondence over the floor, then cried triumphantly, "Here we are. By God, he got a tickle. Cagey old sod!"

The letter was headed TREEBY AND BRACKEN with a WC1 address. It read, *Dear Mr. Tallantire, Thank you for the outline which I now return. I've taken a copy for my own reference as I think it certainly has potential, particularly if you can get the emphasis right. I've starred the chapters which look most interesting to me. If you are coming to London in the near future, why don't we have lunch and discuss how we might proceed? Looking forward to hearing from you. Yours sincerely, Paul Farmer (Editor)*

Underneath in Tallantire's hand was scribbled 12:30, March 22.

Pascoe flipped through the outline. There were asterisks by a few of the chapter headings, mainly one, sometimes two. The Mickledore Hall case alone had three. He started pointing this out to Dalziel but the Fat Man was staring at the date.

"Bloody hell," he said. "That's the day Wally died. On his way back from the Smoke."

Suddenly Pascoe felt cold.

Dalziel went down on his knee and started doing a loaves-and-fishes on the correspondence file, apparently creating as he distributed. Soon most of the carpet had vanished beneath a sea of litter.

"Nowt else," he said.

"Perhaps they heard he'd died," said Pascoe. "Or it could be they decided there was nothing in it for them after all."

"You don't buy a man lunch to turn him down," growled Dalziel. "What do you know about this Treeby and Bracken outfit anyway?"

"Hang on," said Pascoe. Ellie's literary ambitions had added a *Writers' and Artists' Yearbook* to their library. He flipped through the pages. "Not a lot of help. No longer exists as an independent imprint. Got gobbled up by Centipede a few years back. But hang on. There's a list of Centipede's current directors here and there's a Paul Farmer among them. Could be the same."

"Right. Give him a bell in the morning, see if he remembers owt."

"Why me?"

"Right up your street, talking to poncy sods like publishers. Right. On your feet. Have you had your supper?"

"No, but look, I'd really rather . . ."

"Come on, lad. Not going mean on me, are you?"

"Mean?"

"Aye. I treated you last night. Your turn tonight. Fair do's."

Pascoe thought of his vegetable casserole, two hundred calories tops.

He said, "I'm definitely not going to the Black Bull."

"That's handy, 'cos I'm not either."

In the doorway Pascoe paused to look back. The lounge looked like a field after a pop festival.

"Hurry up," said Dalziel. "We're late."

"For what?" said Pascoe, suddenly alarmed at the prospect of something worse than a leap in his cholesterol level. "I'm not doing any more burgling."

"What are you on about? There's someone I want you to meet, that's all. Someone every good cop ought to meet at least once."

"Who's that then?"

"Old Percy Pollock, that's who."

"Pollock? Good God, you don't mean Pollock the hangman?"

"That's the boy. Good company is old Percy. But he's a stickler for punctuality, so get your finger out. I suppose in his line of business he never cared to be kept hanging around!"

Sixteen

"What a night it has been! Almost a night . . . to bring the dead out of their graves."

A storm broke over the city as they drove to their rendezvous. This was the pathetic fallacy at work, thought Pascoe, a fancy compounded by his realization that they were heading for a pub called the Blind Sailor. Now was the time when a genuine golden bough would come in most useful, for weren't they going to meet the ferryman himself, whose strong muscles had floated many a poor wretch across to the farther shore? It was a fancy he did not share with Dalziel.

At first sight, Percy Pollock was a disappointment. White-haired and frail, he leaned on a knotted oak stick as he rose to greet them, bowing his head gravely as he was introduced. But he did not offer his hand till Pascoe proffered his.

They sat at an old cast-iron table with a raised brass rail in the shadowy snug of which they were the sole inhabitants. Dalziel ordered drinks, and even paid for them, the while chatting about the weather, the price of tea, and the progress of various members of the Pollock family. It still amazed Pascoe how much the Fat Man knew about everyone. Perhaps it explained his cavalier attitude to records. Pollock's replies were slow and courteous, and gradually a sense of the man's powerful presence stole over Pascoe. It derived from a kind of inner stillness, a steady undramatic self-assurance. Perhaps this is what you got from a career spent seeing men not afraid of God afraid of you.

At last, the formalities finished, Dalziel bought another round, settled himself comfortably, and said, "Now, Percy, what I'd really like is a bit of a chat about Ralph Mickledore."

"Mad Mick? Aye, I thought it might be about him," said Pollock.

"Why Mad Mick?" asked Pascoe.

"It's what the warders called him. Not to his face. It was always Sir Ralph to his face. Does that surprise you, Mr. Pascoe? Like I say, courtesy costs nothing, and besides he were very well liked inside."

Dalziel said, "Percy took his job very seriously. When he knew he had a client in the offing, he opened a file, talked to the fellows looking after him, found out what made him tick, isn't that right, Percy?"

"That's right," said Pollock. "There's more to hanging a man than knowing his build and weight. No two men will take it the same way. Be prepared was always my motto. And besides, no matter what he may have done, no man deserves to be taken off by a stranger."

"So you'd start your homework soon as the verdict came in?" said Dalziel.

"Oh, yes. No waiting for appeals or ought of that," said Pollock. "I never like to feel rushed. Often it meant it was wasted effort, of course. Sentence commuted. Happened more and more often after the war. Well, I never grudged the time. But with Sir Ralph, I knew it wouldn't be wasted, almost from the start I knew."

"Oh, aye," said Dalziel. "And how was that?"

The old man turned his candid blue-eyed gaze on the detective and said, "I can't rightly tell you that, Mr. Dalziel. Things were said. After a while I knew. This one wasn't for reprieve. Short of a voice from Heaven, and maybe not even then, this one was for the drop."

Dalziel shot Pascoe a glance. Signifying what?

"But why did the warders call him Mad Mick?" persisted Pascoe.

"Because he made them laugh," said Pollock unexpectedly. "He just acted like he was at home most of the time. Mr. Hawkins, the chief officer, would be walking past and Sir Ralph would bellow 'Hawkins, pop out and get me an *Evening Post,* there's a good chap.' He called them all by their surnames, no misters, but no one took offense because he didn't do it to give offense. And he was just the same with the governor. 'Nugent,' he would say, 'the food in here's appalling. I'm having a few brace of pheasant sent from the estate for the chaps on my wing. Hope the cook's up to it. Perhaps you'd care to join us?' And he'd mean it, you see. He wasn't taking the piss, if you'll excuse the expression."

It was at moments like this that Pascoe knew why the English had never gone in for a socialist revolution. You can't expect flagellants to throw away their whips.

"When they weren't lost in admiration, did his guards reckon he was guilty?" he asked abruptly.

The old man regarded him mildly and said, "Those of us who work for the prison service can't afford such speculations, Mr. Pascoe. You can't sit with a man the night before he hangs if you think he's innocent. And you certainly can't put a rope around his neck."

"Aye, but did he ever say owt about the murder, Percy?" said Dalziel.

"I suppose he'd talk about it to the police and his solicitor when they came a-visiting, but according to Mr. Hawkins, he acted like he was innocent, or at least he acted like he didn't believe he'd hang, right up to the end. Week before, he even asked one of his guards to put a fiver on a horse for him. Said he knew the trainer and it was due a win. The man went straight to Mr. Hawkins."

"Because it was against the rules?" said Pascoe puzzled.

"Because the race wasn't scheduled till two days after the execution date," said Percy Pollock.

This gave them all pause for a few moments. Dalziel was the first to break the silence.

"And you yourself, Percy, when you finally made direct contact, how did he strike you? What did he say?"

Across Pascoe's mind flickered a black and white image of Miles Malleson in *Kind Hearts and Coronets* asking the condemned duke for permission to read the ode he had composed to mark the occasion.

Difficult to top that, but Percy came close.

"He said good-bye to everyone. Then he cupped his ear like he was listening and said, 'Hush!' We all hushed, and listened. Nothing. Then he laughed and said, 'Sorry, I thought I heard a galloping horse. Cheer up, Nugent . . .'—the governor was looking as upset as ever I've seen him—'It looks as if it's going to be a far far better thing after all. Thank you, Mr. Pollock. At your convenience.' And that was it, gentlemen. Forty-five seconds later, Sir Ralph was dead."

"You're very precise," said Pascoe.

"Yes, sir. This was by way of being a record. Usually I reckon on between fifty and eighty from the time I take them out of the cell, depending on how they move. But he stepped out so sprightly it was all done in forty-five. And he was my last, my very last, so it'll stand forever, I suppose."

There was a note of melancholy nostalgia in his voice that revolted Pascoe but before he could speak, Dalziel said, "You had your contacts at the women's jail at Beddington too, I expect, Percy."

"Oh, yes. It's a long time since I had to take off a lady, a long long time. But I had my contacts."

"Anyone who would have been working there when Kohler topped the wardress?"

Pollock thought a moment then said, "There's Mrs. Friedman. She retired the year after, I think. She was there."

"And where is she now?"

"She lives locally, I believe. Would you like me to check, Mr. Dalziel?"

"I'd appreciate it, Percy. Now will you have another drink?"

"No, thank you," he said standing up. "Time I was home to my supper. Good-bye, Mr. Pascoe. A pleasure to meet you."

He offered his hand. Presumably his initial hesitation had been conditioned by the reluctance of some people to shake the hand that had slipped the noose over so many necks. Pascoe felt this reluctance more now than he had on first encounter, and to cover his slowness in responding, he said lightly, "The bet Mickledore wanted placed, what happened?"

"Oh, it was put on. In fact, when word got around, so many officers, not to mention the inmates and their families, backed the horse that its odds shortened from twenties to fives."

"Oh, aye?" said Dalziel. "And did it win?"

Percy Pollock smiled sadly.

"I'm afraid not. It fell at the last fence and broke its neck."

They sat in silence for a while after Pollock had left, Dalziel because he was eating a steak and kidney pie with double chips, Pascoe because he felt deeply depressed.

"Have a chip if you want," said Dalziel. "Not up to Black Bull standards, but they'll do."

"No, thanks. Like I said, I'm not hungry."

"You'll waste away to nowt. Man who doesn't take care of his belly won't take care of much else."

Pascoe felt this as a reproof and said, "I do my job, full or empty."

"Oh, aye? Then do it. What do you make of old Percy?"

"Not a lot. If anything, I suppose he came down on the side of Mickledore being innocent."

"What makes you say that?" asked Dalziel studying a piece of kidney with the distrust of a police pathologist.

"That business about there being no chance of reprieve for him. That sounds like a fit-up."

"Rumor. Ancient rumor at that," said Dalziel, deciding to risk the kidney.

"What about Mickledore's demeanor? He acted as if he expected to be reprieved."

"So what? He doesn't sound the type to collapse and kick his legs in the air. Stiff upper something, it's what they learn 'em at these pubic schools."

"But if you take what he said at the end. 'Looks like it's going to be a far far better thing after all.' Now the implication of that . . ."

"Yes, yes, I get the implication," said Dalziel impatiently. "I'm not totally ignorant. I go to the pictures too. And I'll tell you this for nowt, I can't see Mad Mick as Carter the martyr."

"Carton," said Pascoe. "Who incidentally didn't look very likely material for Carter the martyr either. But isn't the point that Mickledore didn't want to be a martyr anyway? His kind of code says you do everything you can to cover up for a chum in trouble, no matter what he's done. Look at the way Lord Lucan's mates closed ranks when he vanished. But I doubt if any of them would have been willing to hang for him."

"That's the choice they'd have got from me if I'd been running the case," said Dalziel. "So you're saying that when push came to shove, Mick said, sod this for a lark, and sent for Wally to tell him the truth, viz, that Westropp dunnit after all? So what about Westropp then? This famous Lucan code says it's okay if you're the guilty party to let your best mate swing for you?"

"There may have been other considerations. He more or less vanished, didn't he? Perhaps the funny buggers locked him up in a dungeon at Windsor till it was all over so he couldn't drag the family name through the mud. Perhaps he simply bottled out. Perhaps he reckoned that if his best mate had been stuffing his wife, then hanging was what he deserved. Or perhaps he didn't do it after all, but Mickledore got the wrong end of the stick and thought he did, which would mean that Westropp could have believed Mickledore really was guilty."

Dalziel shook his head in admiration.

He said, "If ever Dan Trimble catches me banging his missus, I want you along to offer ten good reasons why he shouldn't believe his eyes. All right, you've got Mickledore sorted. He thinks he's doing a favor for a mate, then finds too late he's been thoroughly stitched up. Me, I don't believe a word of it, but just for the sake of argument, how does little Miss Kohler fit in? I mean, isn't she even less likely to let her lover hang for something he didn't do than something he did?"

Pascoe thought, if Kohler got driven half mad by the death of Emily, then pushed the whole way by Tallantire browbeating a confession out of her, she doesn't need a motive.

He said, "You'll need to ask her that yourself. But I suspect it'll take more than a dead granny or a dental appointment to get you where she is."

"We'll see," said Dalziel. "Meanwhile here's what we do tomorrow . . ."

"I'm not doing any more interviews," said Pascoe firmly.

"Nay, I'd not send a pup to snap at Sir Arthur Stamper, that's work for a full-grown hound," said Dalziel ungraciously. "You just ring that publisher fellow, see what you can find about Wally's memoirs. You can manage that, can you? You've got a lovely telephone voice."

He returned his attention to his plate and disinterred another sliver of the suspect kidney. Holding it up for inspection on the end of his fork he said, "You didn't notice a barber's next door, did you?"

Seventeen

"Will you tell me who denounced him?"

"It is against the rule."

Pascoe had never phoned a publisher before and in his inexperience first dialed the number at 9:15 A.M.

At his third attempt, at 9:40, he made contact with a woman whose voice vibrated with a mix of suspicion and disorientation such as he hadn't heard since his last dawn-knock raid.

His request to be put through to Paul Farmer perked her up, perhaps because its very naivety revealed she was in touch with a lesser breed outside the metropolitan time zone. He was invited to try again at 10:30.

At 10:29 he rang once more. This time he was put through to Mr. Farmer's secretary who asked him if he were a writer in a voice which suggested she was about to blow a whistle down the phone if he said yes. He summoned up his best Dalzielesque orotundity and gave her the full majesty of his rank. She seemed unimpressed but a moment later a male voice, light and pleasant, said, "Farmer here. How can I help you, Mr. Pascoe?"

Pascoe explained, adding that he realized it was all a long time ago.

"That's all right," said Farmer, laughing. "My long-term memory's a lot better than my short-term these days. I find I can't remember who won Booker two days after the ceremony."

"I thought that was a condition of entry," said Pascoe. "But you do recollect Superintendent Tallantire?"

"I do indeed. Interesting chap. Lots of good stories. I couldn't see the great reading public being much interested in his life and hard times in urban Yorkshire, but you do seem to have rather a good class of crime up there and I could see great potential in a memoir of the big cases he'd been mixed up in, with the strictly autobiographical stuff kept down to a minimum."

"So you had lunch? How did you feel after you'd actually talked to him?"

"I felt I was right. There was a real money spinner here, prepublication extracts in one of the popular Sundays, a bit of TV exposure on the chat shows, I think we could have turned your Mr. Tallantire into a mini-star. That's what made it all the more annoying, not to mention embarrassing."

"That he died, you mean?" said Pascoe thinking this was a touch insensitive.

"What? Don't be silly. That I had to turn him down."

"You were going to reject his idea? Yet you still took him out for lunch?"

"That was the trouble. I'd brought him up at our last editorial meeting and got the go-ahead to set up a meeting. Then on the morning of the day we were having a lunch, word came down from above, police memoirs were no longer our cup of tea. Too late to cancel, so I had to go through with it, knowing the poor chap was to be elbowed."

"Did you tell him?"

"I didn't intend to. Chickenheartedly I thought I'd just play along, then write to him in a few days saying, sorry, on mature consideration et cetera. But in the end after I'd listened to him for a bit, I found I was getting so keen, I just had to come clean. At least I felt able to suggest another couple of houses I was pretty certain would jump at him, and we parted on good terms. I kept an eye open but never saw anything. He died, you said? Was that soon after we met? Before he had a chance to shop around?"

"Yes. Quite soon," said Pascoe. "Tell me, Mr. Farmer, why did you think your firm decided to turn the memoirs down? Whose decision would that be?"

"Someone like me, as I am now, I mean. *Then* I was simply an editor, coal-face stuff, dealing direct with writers and their writings. Now I suppose I'm a publisher. The kind of meeting I attend, and one of which I shall shortly be late for, decides on broad policies and wider strategies."

"Yes, but weren't you surprised?"

"Not really. Sort of thing happens all the time, and especially after a change of management."

"You mean internally? Or as a result of a takeover?"

"Both. Publishing houses are like third world countries, constantly under threat both from foreign invasion and civil war. God, the changes I've been through. Treeby and Bracken were a nice little independent publisher when I joined them. Then they were bought by the Glaser magazine group which wasn't so bad. At least it was still about the printed word. Then Glaser got gobbled up by Harvey Inkermann, the investment people, and suddenly it was all about finance and returns and investment. Even then we laughed when we heard about the Centipede takeover. Lots of jokes about free condoms with every book! But we laughed too soon. Centipede was clearly just another bargaining counter in the discussions between Stampers and Inkermann . . ."

"Hold on," said Pascoe in whose mind a diaspora of information was coming together. "This Stamper, he'd be the Sheffield Stamper . . ."

"That's right. The dreaded Sir Arthur."

"And his company amalgamated with Harvey Inkermann to form . . ."

"Inkerstamm. You must have heard the story that when they

joined up, Sir Arthur wanted top billing in the new conglomerate name, but the best they could come up with was Stinker!"

"Very droll," said Pascoe. "And who was it that owned you when you were dealing with Superintendent Tallantire?"

"As I was trying to tell you, we'd just been subsumed by Inkerstamm and forced into a shotgun marriage with Centipede. New brooms were being flourished, and in those circumstances, much that is good always gets swept away with the dross, just to establish who's in charge. Your Mr. Tallantire was, I fear, a victim."

Perhaps a victim indeed. But it was all so farfetched. Treeby and Bracken would hardly register on Stamper's mind except as a line in a balance sheet. So, a new senior editor flexing his muscles. And an aging bobby after a career full of hard drinking, irregular eating, and sleepless nights, has a heart attack. Nothing odd there.

"Just one more thing," he said. "I don't suppose you can recall if Mr. Tallantire referred to a notebook during your lunch?"

"Oh, yes indeed. Several times. I recall joking that perhaps he should forget about his memoirs and just publish the notebook, and he smiled and said it was better to have ten bob to spend than a quid to bequeath. The phrase struck me."

"Shit," said Pascoe as he replaced the phone. He didn't need to rescan the list he'd dug out of coroners' records, but he did anyway. When people die in public places, a careful inventory is made of their possessions, very careful indeed when the dead man's a copper. Nowhere in the list of what was found on Tallantire's person or in his briefcase was there a mention of a notebook.

Pascoe knew all about detectives' notebooks. Some cops recorded no more the minimum that regulations required. Others wrote copiously. And a third group kept two notebooks, one officially recording the case in hand, the other omnivorous, devouring every fact or fancy that touched upon the case, no matter how distantly.

From all accounts, Tallantire had belonged to this group. If Dalziel's judgment of the man was correct, he wouldn't have hushed up any information, no matter how delicate, that had a direct bearing on the Mickledore Hall killing. But in an affair like this, involving a royal, a cabinet minister, an American diplomat, and God knows who else, at a time when British public life was going through the greatest turmoil since the trial of Queen Caroline, what peripheral details, recorded conversations, gossip, hints, innuendoes, plain theorizing, might have found its way into the missing notebook?

Tallantire's own comment, recalled by Farmer, that publishing the notebook might bring him money to bequeath rather than spend, hinted that it contained just this kind of material.

And next thing he's dead on a train. Coming back from a visit to a publisher. And the notebook has vanished.

At what point does subsequence become consequence? Later, to a rationalist thinker. Sooner, to a working cop. Pascoe, philosophically and professionally, tried to tread a middle way. As he did in most things, he thought with bitter self-mockery.

Middle of the road's grand, unless it's the M6 on a Bank Holiday.

The Gospel according to St. Andrew Dalziel. Who else?

And with each passing hour Pascoe could feel the traffic building up.

Eighteen

"I have less need to make myself agreeable than you have, being more independent in circumstances."

There was a time when *Sheffield* in a word association test would have provoked either *steel* or *Wednesday*. Now it was likely to be *snooker*.

Despite this sad falling away, Dalziel still liked the place. It had the vibrant energy of a frontier town. For any true born Yorkshireman, after Sheffield it was Africa. All right, there was the *cordon sanitaire* of the White Peak whose open acres might cushion the shock for a while, but in no time at all you were unmistakably into that nowhere called the Midlands through whose squeezed-out diphthongs the Cockney cacophony could be clearly heard.

The huge Inkerstamm building had risen from the eastern wasteland of the city and was a dominating presence as you drove down the M1, though reaching it once you left the motorway proved problematical. And actually getting inside looked likely to prove impossible.

Dalziel came to a stop at a security barrier painted like a barber's pole. For a while nothing happened, then out of the cabin at the pole's end strolled a guard built on the same lines as the building ahead. He was dressed like an American highway patrolman, and from his belt dangled a truncheon carved from a bough of oak and polished till it reflected the sun which vanished behind him as he stooped to the window with the complacent smile of a man used to complete physical domination.

"Got yourself lost, luv?" he inquired.

Dalziel, who knew that the farther south you got in the county, the more unisex "luv" became, felt neither insulted nor invited, but he had to admit to a feeling that came close to intimidation.

He produced his warrant card with his most fearsome scowl and said, "I'm here to see Sir Arthur Stamper."

The guard's smile broadened.

"Just you sit there awhile, Mr. Dalziel," he said, mispronouncing the name, "and I'll see if there's anyone home."

He strolled back to his cabin, spoke into a phone, listened, wrote something down, and ambled back out.

"Your lucky day," he said. "You're expected. Wear this at all times."

He handed over a plastic lapel badge with Dalziel's name and arrival time printed on it in indelible ink.

"I'm not a bloody parcel," snarled Dalziel.

"Take that off and you could end up being wrapped and delivered like one." The guard laughed as he raised the barrier with one finger. Even allowing for the counterweight, it was an impressive performance.

Dalziel was checked again twice, once in the car park, once at the main entrance, and his irritation kept him from wondering how he came to be expected when no one knew he was coming.

His second interlocutor said, "You'll be met in the atrium," as he opened the door.

"What's one of them when it's at home?" demanded Dalziel, but he received no answer and would probably have heard none as he stepped with incredulous awe into what had to be the largest urinal in the world which even provided trees for visiting dogs.

It took him only a moment to grasp that the tinkling came from a series of central fountains and the figures niched round the walls were statues, but the green and white tiles remained unadjustably lavatorial and the trees, though thin and etiolated, were undoubtedly trees.

Threading her way through this ectopic boscage came a woman, high heels clicking on the tessellated floor.

"Superintendent Dalziel?" she said, getting the pronounciation right. "You're early. Come this way."

Dalziel might have asked, "Early for what?" if a more pressing question had not been occupying his mind.

Was William Stamper after all a Queen of Crime? How else to explain his appearance here in a fetching white blouse and gray pencil skirt?

All answers came together.

"I'm Wendy Stamper," said the woman. "By the way, I thought it was a Mr. Hiller who had the appointment to see my father?"

"My colleague," said Dalziel. "He'll be along shortly."

But not too bloody shortly, he hoped as she led him into a lift which ascended at a knee-trembling speed that made him think nostalgically of his hot youth.

He said, "I were talking to your brother yesterday. He didn't remember me at first sight either."

"Either?"

"Aye. We met at Mickledore Hall. I were just a young bobby then, the one who gave you the bull's-eyes."

The lift stopped and they stepped out into a discreetly lit, plushly carpeted corridor. The woman looked at him frowningly.

"Sorry," she said. "It was a long time ago. I was only a child."

"Your brother's memory was very good once he got going."

"My brother makes a living out of fictions," she replied. "Would you like some coffee?"

They had moved into what might have been an elegant drawing

room were it not for the computer terminal alongside the rosewood desk.

"No, thanks," said Dalziel gingerly settling onto a chair with that expensive antique look which in his experience often meant woodworm. It sighed but held. "I could mebbe manage a Scotch, but."

A lesser woman might have glanced at her watch. Wendy Stamper went without hesitation to a cabinet and from a decanter poured him a measure which had the twin merits of being generous and a malt of great quality and strength.

He rolled it round his mouth, failed to identify it, and asked, "What's this then?"

"Glencora," she said. He'd never heard of it and she added, "It's a very small company, and most of its output goes for export."

Which explained the strength. He'd read somewhere that the Yanks liked their liquor stronger because they preferred their drinks in mixtures, which in the case of Glencora was like using fresh salmon to make fish fingers.

He said, "You don't get on with your brother then?"

"Did he say that?"

"No, but it stands to reason. You working here and him having nowt to do with your dad."

"You can agree to differ without falling out," she said.

"Oh, aye? Even when he reckons your dad's a jumped up nowt who tret his wife like shit?"

She didn't let herself be provoked, even managed a slight smile.

"I think I do recall you now. I assume it's the Mickledore Hall business you want to talk to him about? Because that woman has been let off?"

"You didn't like Cissy Kohler then?" he said.

She thought, then said grudgingly, "Yes, I suppose I liked her well enough."

But you don't want to like her, thought Dalziel.

He said, "Do you still think she did it?"

She replied, "Who else?" but it came out as a real question rather than the rhetorical affirmation she probably intended.

A buzzer sounded on her desk. She picked up a phone, listened, said, "Right," and put it down.

"He'll see you now," she said to Dalziel. "Come this way."

If the daughter's office was Regency lady's drawing room, the father's was Victorian gentleman's study. Stamper rose from behind a huge desk and came to meet him, hand outstretched.

"Come in, Mr. Dalziel. It's been a long time since we met. You were only a constable. You've come a long way since then. Congratulations."

"You've not done so bad yourself, Sir Arthur," said Dalziel slightly taken aback by this easy recognition. But why not? Stamper himself was little changed except for a deeper channel in his grayer hair. And if there had been any rough edges to his social act all those years ago, they had long since been polished away.

"Drink?" he said. "I've got a whiskey I'd be glad of your opinion on . . ."

"Glencora, you mean? I've tried it and I'll not say not to the other half."

He sank into a leather sofa big enough for a small orgy and said, "By gum, you've got some nice stuff in here."

It was a test. Gentlemen didn't boast about their possessions. Self-made Yorkshiremen gave you provenance and price.

"Have I? I suppose I have," said Stamper with a faint note of surprise at finding himself judged a man of taste. He handed Dalziel a crystal tumbler full of the pale nectar and sat behind his desk.

"One tends to accumulate things," he said, "but I'm not what you'd call a collector. Except for the desk. I collected that. Recognize it?"

"Any reason I should?" asked Dalziel.

"It's from the library at Mickledore Hall! They sold off some of the furniture before the National Trust got their claws on the place."

"I see. You wanted a souvenir? Present from Blackpool sort of thing?"

"I wouldn't quite put it like that. But it was undeniably a memorable weekend. None of us came out of it unchanged."

"Lady Pamela didn't, that's true," said Dalziel. "And Westropp neither. And Partridge's career went up the spout too. But I can't see how it affected you, Sir Arthur."

"No?" Stamper sounded faintly surprised. "Ah, well. I suppose what you're here for is to find out if I had any doubts about the verdict. Well, I can put your mind at rest. I had none, nor did I find anything reprehensible in the way that Superintendent Tallantire conducted the case."

"But now that Kohler's been set loose . . ."

"Administrative incompetence," said Stamper shortly.

"You mean, like someone left the door open and she just walked out?" said Dalziel.

"I mean that the woman should either have been paroled years ago or if, as is reported, she refused to apply for parole, this should have been judged *prima facie* evidence of mental derangement and she should have been returned to the psychiatric hospital she started her sentence in."

"But if she's innocent—and that's what the Home Secretary reckons, isn't it . . . ?"

"Yes, yes," said Stamper testily. "So perhaps she didn't help Mickledore directly, but at the very least she probably knew what he was up to and afterward felt guilty enough to associate herself with the crime. Silly notions these lovesick girls get, don't they?"

"I wouldn't know, sir," said Dalziel stolidly. "Must have been a nasty shock for you too, being such a close friend of Sir Ralph's."

"We weren't all that close."

"Close enough for him to borrow money, but?"

"To borrow a tenner some degree of closeness may be necessary," said Stamper. "For larger sums, a commercial arrangement is enough."

"You got your money back, did you, sir?"

"I got what I wanted. Money's not everything, Dalziel. But perhaps you find that hard to understand."

"Job satisfaction, you mean? Oh, I think I understand that."

"Then perhaps you'll understand what a joy it was to be a British businessman in those days. The fifties and early sixties. We'd won the war from '39 to '45, but we nearly lost it again from '45 to '51. Cleaning up after those socialists was a frightful chore, but we did it, by God we did it! And we got our reward."

"Oh, aye. I remember. You'd never had it so good."

"And Macmillan was right! And we'd have had it even better if it hadn't been for that stupid tart! Sixteen years we lost because of her."

"I always heard Mr. Profumo had sommut to do with it as well," said Dalziel with a mild attack of feminism. "Any road, the good days came round again for you and your mates."

"Indeed they did. But it never felt the same. In those days we were set fair to get back on top of the heap again. Now, we've got to struggle to keep up with the French, for God's sake!"

He glanced at his watch. End of interview? thought Dalziel. Instead Stamper plucked the glass from his hand and said, "Refill."

"As much as you like. It's grand stuff."

"I'm glad of your approval. I always take expert advice before an investment."

"Investment? You mean . . . ?"

Sir Arthur smiled. "Come, come. Can't have senior police officers mixed up in insider dealing, can we?"

"I suppose not. Getting back to Sir Ralph, did he strike you as the kind of man who'd sacrifice himself for a mate?"

"What?" Stamper considered. "Yes, it's possible. Certain kinds of breeding develop a sense of loyalty incomprehensible to outsiders."

"Like in pedigree dogs, you mean? I've never thought of it like that," said Dalziel, his face aglow with innocent interest.

A line of loathing momentarily creased Sir Arthur's mask. A phone squeaked on the huge desk. He picked it up, listened, and said, "No, that's fine. Send him up."

Replacing the receiver and his good-natured smile, he said, "How's your drink, Mr. Dalziel?"

So once again, all was made clear.

It was Hiller who'd arrived, Dalziel had little doubt of that, and even less that this clever bastard had known all along his own visit was unofficial, keeping him talking to engineer a head-on collision with Adolf.

Sooner or later such a confrontation was inevitable. Dalziel wasn't frightened of it, but he'd rather it had been later, and he didn't care at all to be maneuvered into it. He could lie about their discussion of course, but it occurred to him that the sly bastard probably had a tape running in his desk. On the other hand, it had been Stamper who set the reminiscence ball rolling by recognizing him . . .

He said, "Well, it's been nice talking about old times, Sir Arthur, but I really must get down to business. Private security forces. There's been a lot of concern expressed lately about the use of private security groups, the way they're recruited and trained, and the limits of their authority. We've got an inquiry team operating in Mid-Yorkshire and I'm going round neighboring police authorities gathering facts. Now, here at Inkerstamm you've got your own organization and there's been some disquiet expressed about them . . . ."

Stamper was looking surprised, a genuine dropped-jaw surprise, not an upper-class raised-eyebrow imitation. But the voice was holding out.

"I'm sorry? What on earth are you talking about?"

Suddenly Dalziel was on his feet, leaning over the desk, his mouth almost touching Stamper's face so that though his whispered words would be beyond reach of even a sensitive microphone, they would reverberate thunderously in the man's ear.

"I'm talking about puffed-up noddy merchants who keep private armies so no one can get close enough to tell 'em what pathetic little pricks they really are."

"Now, just tha' hold on, Dalziel! No bugger talks to me that way!"

It was there, the old Yorkshire accent, loud and sweet.

Dalziel stood back and said, "Ee bah gum, Art. It's grand to have thee back wi' real folk again."

There was a tap at the door which opened almost simultaneously to reveal Deputy Chief Constable Hiller.

"What fettle, Geoff—sorry—Sir?" cried Dalziel. "Sir Arthur and I are just this moment finished. Thanks for your cooperation. I'll see myself out."

Pausing only to make sure his glass was empty, he pushed between the lowering-faced Hiller and the puzzled-faced Wendy Stamper, and went quickly across the hallway into the woman's office.

There was an outside phone on the desk. He picked it up, dialed. A voice said, "South Yorkshire police, can I help you?"

"CID. Mr. Monkhouse, please. That you, Des? Andy Dalziel here . . . I'm grand. Listen, you know that private security review we set up in the county? Well, I'm taking a personal interest and I'd like your okay to me asking a few questions round your patch . . . Thanks. Oh, and I'd like it yesterday, if that's okay . . . Aye, I'll tell you about it some time. Thanks a lot. I owe you a pint. All right, two. Cheers."

He put the phone down as Wendy Stamper came back into the room.

"Just checking the time," he said.

She said, "That man Hiller seemed surprised to find you were here."

"Adolf? I shouldn't worry. His short-term memory's going. Anything surprises him that happened later than 1963. That's why he's on this inquiry."

"And why are you on it, Mr. Dalziel?"

She hadn't, he decided, been in on her father's little trick, but she had worked out for herself that something fishy was going on.

"Justice," he said sternly.

"Justice? You mean that because the innocent have suffered once, you want to make them suffer again?"

He didn't think she was talking about Mickledore and Kohler. He said, "See much of your mother, do you, Miss Stamper?"

"No."

"Because she's in America, you mean?" probed Dalziel. "Jet-setter like you, that should be no problem."

"I don't see that this is any of your business. Can I have your pass, please?"

He handed it over, she filled in a time, signed it, and handed it back.

"That'll get you through the gate if you show it in the next fifteen minutes."

"You count 'em in and you count 'em out? That's tight security."

"You object?"

He smiled and fixed the label back in his lapel.

"Of course not. How come your brother blames your dad while you lay it all on your mam? She stuck around till you were old enough to look after yourselves, didn't she?"

"I was old enough to see what was going on a long time before that," she said. "Girls mature a lot earlier than boys."

"Is that right? My experience is, kids see a lot but don't understand the half of it, not even lasses."

"Then you must have had a very easy time of it," she flared.

He scratched his chin reflectively and said, "Didn't have to suffer a lot of country house weekends, that's for sure."

"I'm sorry. I shouldn't make comments about other people's lives. What do any of us know about each other?" She was back in control. "Look, you'd better be on your way, Superintendent, or I'll have to do your pass again."

"Right. Mebbe we'll meet again. Thanks for the drink. Nice drop of pop, that Glencora. Could do really well with the right management, don't you think?"

Her face smoothed into an android blank as she answered, "I wouldn't know about that, Mr. Dalziel. Good-bye."

He pondered on this and other matters as he drove back to the gate. The barrier was down, the jovial giant was leaning against its center, one huge hand negligently raised. Dalziel slowed to a crawl but he kept going. The giant's complacent smile remained till the car got within a couple of feet. Now he frowned his disapproval and leaned forward to slap the bonnet commandingly.

Dalziel looked puzzled and kept on coming. The bumper made contact with the guard's shins, nudging them back till they could go no farther and he came sprawling across the bonnet, his buttocks wedged tight against the barrier and his eyes popping with anger and shock.

Now Dalziel put the brake on, climbed out of his seat, walked slowly forward, and unhooked the man's long truncheon from his belt.

Holding it vertically he said softly, "Some people might say this was an offensive weapon, friend. Me, I reckon it's just a spare backbone. And unless you'd like me to fit it personally, I suggest you raise that barrier without opening your mouth. Not even to smile. Especially not to smile."

He strolled to the rear of the car, laid the golden truncheon under the back wheel across a slight unevenness in the surface, climbed into his seat, and reversed slowly. There was a satisfying crunch.

The giant straightened up. Dalziel smiled at him through the windscreen and laid a finger across his lips. The man turned away and raised the barrier. It seemed to take more effort than it had before.

Dalziel drove away. There was another nice crunch which he enjoyed. Not a bad morning's work, he thought. But he did not deceive himself. There was trouble approaching. But so what? It was going one way, he was going the other, and soon it'd be behind him with all the other trouble that littered his past. Clear horizons were for boring holidays on the Costa Brava. Hell, which he didn't believe in, would be sun, sand, and a tideless sea.

And heaven? (Which he didn't believe in either.)

Good whiskey in your belly. Satisfaction in a job well done. Anticipation of a struggle ahead. And a mate or two you could rely on. In fact, the status quo. The conclusion took him by surprise. Was he really in heaven after all, sitting in a stuffy car on a crowded motorway? Perhaps he was. And perhaps knowing it made it hell after all.

He shook his head in irritation. He was thinking too much, like the boy, Pascoe, and look how miserable it made that poor sod.

He leaned all his considerable weight onto the accelerator and slipped into the endless line of cars doing no more than twenty mph over the legal limit heading north in the outside lane.

Nineteen

"My way out of this is to put you all

in the wrong."

The explosion came at two o'clock that afternoon.

There was still no sign of Dalziel when Pascoe returned from lunch, but there was an urgent message requesting their immediate attendance upon the Chief Constable.

The atmosphere in the Chief's office was like a First World War court-martial. Trimble's face was stern though relatively neutral, but Hiller, occupying a chair ambiguously placed to one side of the Chief's desk as though to give him a buttock on both the seat of judgment and the prosecution bench, wore the expression of a vengeful hamster.

"Mr. Dalziel?" said Trimble.

"Not back yet, sir."

"Back from where?" demanded Hiller.

It was a wife-beating question, inviting him to admit complicity, claim ignorance, or essay deceit.

He said, "From lunch, sir."

Hiller looked ready to assault him but Trimble intervened.

"I think we can leave Mr. Dalziel to answer for himself. Mr. Pascoe, I understand you have been detailed to act as liaison officer between Mr. Hiller's inquiry team and CID."

"Yes, sir."

"I ask because it may be that it was some rather broad interpretation of this duty that took you to Haysgarth to interview Lord Partridge about the Mickledore Hall case yesterday morning."

It was a tenuous line of defense but probably the only one possible that Trimble was offering him. Yet all that Pascoe could think was how wrong he'd been to even dream that he could trust a lord.

"Yes, Mr. Pascoe?" prompted Trimble.

Oh, sod it, thought Pascoe. What was the point of all this boxing clever when down the road they were already drawing lots to see who got the firing squad detail?

"No, sir," he said.

"No, what?"

"No, it wasn't any such misinterpretation of my liaison role that took me to Haysgarth."

"All right," said Trimble, patience at end. "Then what?"

Pascoe drew in a deep breath and with it, or so it seemed, the office door, which swung slowly open to reveal Dalziel.

"Got a message asking me to drop by, sir," he said, making it sound like an invitation to afternoon tea.

Had he been listening at the door? wondered Pascoe, as perhaps did Trimble for he said, "Excellent timing, Andy. As always. I was just asking Mr. Pascoe here why he interviewed Lord Partridge yesterday."

"Oh, that. Don't be too hard on the lad, sir. I admit I were a bit narked myself when I heard what a cock-up he made, but after my experience this morning, I've got a lot more sympathy."

He shook his head ruefully. Pascoe groaned inwardly, Hiller's lips, already tight, faded to a pale line, and Trimble sat back in his chair and looked as if he were trying to think of England.

"Explain," he said gently.

"It's this private security firm inquiry you're so keen on, sir. Lord Partridge since he came out of politics doesn't get any official protection but he does have a firm called SecTec who keep an eye on things. So I thought his lordship would be just the man to give us a customer's eye view of the private sector. Only it seems Peter, Chief Inspector Pascoe that is, let himself be lured into some idle chitchat about the Mickledore business. Personally, I wouldn't be surprised if his lordship weren't trying to pump the lad, you know how these politicians' minds work. Any road, her ladyship came in, got her knickers in a twist, and Mr. Pascoe, being a well-bred sort of chap, thought it best to beat a retreat."

Hiller could contain himself no longer.

"And I suppose coincidentally that's what happened to you this morning when you spoke with Sir Arthur Stamper?"

"Aye, that's right," said Dalziel beaming with pleasure at Hiller's perspicuity.

"Perhaps I should warn you that Sir Arthur taped your conversation."

"Grand! Then if you listen to it, you'll hear it was him that recognized me from way back and set off talking about Mickledore. I had a hell of a job getting him back on course. Then you turned up, Geoff, and steam had to give way to sail."

If Hiller *had* grown a Hitler mustache, he would have swallowed it by now.

Trimble said almost indifferently, "I suppose you had cleared yourself with South before going to Sheffield?"

"Oh, aye. Des Monkhouse'll have it on record."

"I don't doubt it," snarled Hiller. "Called in one of the famous Dalziel favors, did you? And what about your *lad* here visiting Mavis Marsh? I suppose that was about private security firms as well? I warned you what would happen if you got in my way, Dalziel . . ."

"Mr. Hiller." Trimble spoke quietly but his voice was like a gunshot across a saloon brawl. He let the ensuing silence confirm itself then went on, "I think I'd like a private word with Mr. Dalziel now. I'm sure you have a great deal of work on your plate, and I assure you it will proceed without any impediment. Mr. Pascoe, thank you for . . . coming," he concluded.

As they descended the stairs together, Hiller said without looking at him, "I'm disappointed in you, Mr. Pascoe. I'd heard good things, but I see now that bad habits are not easily avoided if you keep bad company."

"I'm sorry, sir. But if loyalty's a bad habit, then you're right. That's all that's motivating Mr. Dalziel, loyalty to his old boss. Okay, so he acts . . . erratically sometimes, but the only thing personal in it is that sense of loyalty. That can't be altogether bad, can it?"

He spoke with a passion born more of uncertainty than conviction and now Hiller looked at him.

"I believe in loyalty too, Mr. Pascoe," he said with something not unlike sympathy in his thin voice. "Loyalty to a common cause. Anything else is just personality cult. But there are other habits you might care to pick up from Andy Dalziel. For instance he prides himself on not letting himself be used. Now there's a quality worthy of emulation by all of us, wouldn't you say?"

They parted. Pascoe went back to his office and tried to settle to some work but his head was overcrowded with Hiller's words and speculation about what was being said up in the Chief Constable's office. At last he heard the approaching beat of Dalziel's step accompanied by a bravura humming of "Colonel Bogey." Sometimes he came at you like Queen Mab and sometimes like the band of the Coldstream Guards.

"There you are then," cried the Fat Man as he came through the door. "Come on. I'll need you around when I clear up so you can see where things are."

"Clear up . . . ?"

"Aye, lad. It's your chance to shine. You'll be looking after the shop while I'm away. On your feet, get a move on, jildi!"

Pascoe hurried along behind the retreating figure, catching up with him only when he halted at his own desk.

"Right. Where to start? Let's see. Good Scotch in this drawer, best at the back of yon cabinet. I've marked the levels and tested the specific gravity. That apart, I don't think there's owt else to say. You'll find everything in order."

"What's happened? Have you been suspended?" demanded Pascoe.

"Don't be daft! Two things Desperate Dan doesn't like. One is twats like Adolf shouting the odds at him, t'other is spooky sods in the Smoke trying to pull his strings. When you're my size, you can afford to be flexible, bend with the wind. But a little chap like Dan needs to show he's the boss."

"So you've not been suspended?"

"There's them as would like to see it. Some twat—he didn't mention names, but it'll be yon bugger Sempernel likely—rang up and went on about this fellow turning up at Kohler's hideout. Big fat sod with an uncouth northern accent, he'd said, so Dan could see it were no use trying to pin it on me. Anyway, the long and short of it is, he asked me if I had some leave coming, suggested I might like to take it. You don't look happy, lad? Not feel up to the job, is that it?"

Pascoe was recalling the last time Dalziel's embarrassing presence had been removed by "leave." All his absence had meant was that he popped up at even more unexpected times and places than normal.

He said, without much hope, "Will you actually be going away? I mean, far away?"

"Eh?" Dalziel laughed. "Oh, I see what's bothering you. No. I've learned my lesson. You won't find me hanging around here, getting under your feet. I'm going to put myself as far as I can get from all this crap."

"Oh, yes? And where's that?" said Pascoe hesitating to experience relief.

"Hang on," said Dalziel who had picked up his phone and dialed.

"Hello! Mr. Foley, please . . . Come on, luv, bank managers aren't busy with clients at this time of day, they're busy putting on their British warms afore they head off to treat other bank managers to expensive grub at my expense. Tell him it's Andy Dalziel . . . Jim, lad! What fettle? Look, two things, first off I want to buy some shares. Glencora Distillery . . . I don't give a toss if you've never heard of it, you didn't know they'd privatized water till it started running green . . . How many? All I can afford and a few more besides. And don't hang about. Second, I want some traveler's checks. U.S. dollars. That's right, American. You've heard of America? Well, I'm going there the day after tomorrow . . . Very droll . . . I'll be in later on then . . . cheers."

He put the phone down and contemplated Pascoe's dropped jaw with undisguised glee.

"America?" said Pascoe. "You're not going after . . . oh, shit! Look, sir, do you think it's wise? Do you think it's *possible*? It's a long way, and bloody expensive, and I doubt if you'd even get a flight at such short notice."

"All fixed," said Dalziel producing an airline ticket. "Heathrow to New York. Sorted it out on my way back from Inkerstamm."

"But you didn't know then that the chief would suggest . . ."

Pascoe let his words fade to nothingness. He thought of mind and matter, will and law, and then of Hiller's warning against letting himself be used. But why listen to warnings from a man incapable of following his own precept?

"What was all that about shares?" he asked.

"Stamper gave me a tip."

"Why'd he do that, for God's sake?"

"Didn't mean to, but you know these self-made buggers, can't resist showing off. Hello!"

The phone had rung and Dalziel had scooped up the receiver at first ping with the speed of an Australian slip fielder.

"Percy, how are they hanging? No, you're dead right, not funny. Sorry . . . Right, I see. Look I'm going to be away for a few days, so why don't you give Mr. Pascoe a ring when she gets back? Aye, he'll talk to her. Full authority. That's grand. Take care of yourself."

The phone went down.

"That was Percy Pollock," said Dalziel. "Mrs. Friedman, her who worked at Beddington Jail, she's away on holiday just now, but expected back shortly. I said you'd deal with it, okay?"

"I suppose so," said Pascoe unenthusiastically. "What am I supposed to do with her?"

"You'll think of something, lad," said Dalziel. "Now I'd best go out and buy myself a phrase book, unless there's owt else you want to say?"

Pascoe shook his head.

"Nothing," he said. "Except bon voyage. And God Save America."

PART THE THIRD

"Golden Apple"

Twenty

"Unsettled weather, a long journey,

uncertain means of traveling, a

disorganized country, a city that may

not be even safe for you."

The Immigration queue snaked before him like an Alpine pass with its head almost hidden in the clouds.

Dalziel took a pull from a half-empty flask of duty-free malt.

"How long do you reckon, luv?" he asked the woman he'd been sitting beside since Heathrow. Her name was Stephanie Keane. She was in her thirties, comfortably but elegantly dressed in a loose-fitting organdy blouse and skirt, quite pretty in an anorectic kind of way. Her first response to Dalziel's conversational gambits had been frosty, but once she caught on that he was a tyro at this kind of trip, she'd thawed and let herself be elected Beatrice to his lost soul. She was, he had learned, co-owner of a Midlands antiques firm, and a frequent transatlantic traveler in pursuit of her profession.

Now she cast her expert eye over the queue.

"Three hours minimum," she said.

"You're joking," said Dalziel incredulously. "I'd not queue that long to watch England stuff Wales."

She gave him the look of amused condescension with which liberated woman views the futile muscle-flexing of prehistoric man.

"So what are you going to do about it?" she inquired satirically.

Pensively Dalziel took another drink. Then he screwed the cap back on and slipped the bottle into his shoulder bag.

"Sorry about this, luv," he said.

And, stooping down behind her, he put his right hand between her legs, grasped the front hem of her skirt, and jerked it up hard against her crotch, at the same time twisting her left arm behind her back.

"Right, sunshine," he said, "consider yourself nicked."

Stephanie Keane screamed and tried to swing at him with the briefcase in her free hand but she might as well have whipped a bull with daisies. Jerking her skirt tighter so that she was on tiptoe, he forced her forward through the ranks of passengers who scattered before them like sheep in a meadow, till finally their way was barred by an armed and uniformed man.

"What's the trouble here?" he asked.

"No trouble," said Dalziel. "I'm a cop, and this's here's a smuggler. Why don't we have a word with your boss before you do summat daft like ruining your career?"

Five minutes and several more uniforms later, he finally reached a gray business suit. In it was a fortyish black man with a boxer's scarred and flattened face and teeth perfect enough to please a monumental mason. He gently removed the furious woman from Dalziel's grip, handed her over to a couple of uniforms, invited her to accompany them to a nearby room where she would be taken care of, then ushered Dalziel into a carpeted office, presumably to take care of him.

"Passport, please," he said.

"Help yourself. You pronounce it Dee-Ell."

"How else?" said the man. "I'm David Thatcher, by the way."

"Oh, aye? I think I knew your auntie."

The man smiled and said, "So how can I help you, superintendent?"

"Depends what you are."

"I guess I'm a sort of superintendent too, though I don't know if it means the same on your side of the pond."

"It means I can do owt I like, so long as I don't let them catch me."

"Then for once our common language unites us. This woman you say is a smuggler, have you had her under surveillance long?"

"Just since I got sat next to her at Heathrow. Never saw her before that."

"Oh. So how come you think she's a crook?"

"I've been talking to her for six hours," said Dalziel. "She were very helpful, very laid-back about everything, Immigration was tedious but no hassle, Customs were a doddle as long as you weren't wearing ragged jeans or a turban. She knew it all."

"So?"

"So it was herself she was reassuring," said Dalziel grimly.

"Did you tell her you were a cop?" asked the black man.

"Don't be daft. I said I were a publican on a visit to my daughter who'd married a Yankee airman."

Thatcher regarded him steadily then said, "Okay. Wrongful arrest suits can be very expensive over here, Mr. Dalziel, but we'll take a close look at this lady. Anything I can get you while you wait?"

Dalziel delved into his flight bag and produced his bottle of Scotch.

"Glass mebbe. Two if they'll not let you stay for the strip search."

Thatcher grinned broadly and went out.

In the event Dalziel probably spent almost as much time in the room as he would have done in the queue, but at least he was sitting comfortably drinking from the glass one of Thatcher's men brought him. Finally the black man himself appeared, carrying another glass and a big bag of something called pretzels.

"Any luck?" said Dalziel.

Thatcher shrugged and said, "These things take time. You said something about some Scotch?"

They sat and talked in an apparently desultory fashion, but Dalziel soon realized he was being interrogated by an expert. He didn't mind. It made a change being on the receiving end. His first instinct was to throw up a smoke screen but after a while he found himself telling quite a lot of the truth.

"So Kohler's back home, but you think she really was guilty and they're going to do a shit job on your old boss, right?"

"That's how it looks to me."

"So what's your game plan, Andy?"

"To catch up with Kohler and have a little chat. Also to talk with the rest of the American connection, see what I can squeeze out of them. Oh, aye, there's plenty for me to do."

He spoke confidently. Thatcher grinned, sipped his Scotch, and said, "That's what Stephanie Keane sounded like, I guess."

"You what?"

"Talking laid-back to reassure herself. Andy, to coin a phrase, this is a big country. How the hell are you going to find Kohler for a start? And what's the rest of this American connection you mentioned?"

"Well, there's Marilou Stamper, she's a Yank. Got a divorce so likely she's living here somewhere. And there's Rampling, he was at the U.S. Embassy back then, and now he's something important, at least I've seen his name in our papers so I shouldn't have any problem tracing him . . ."

He was whistling in the dark, but it didn't bother him. He'd been in the dark before and if you whistled loud enough, something usually came snuffling along to see what all the noise was.

Thatcher said, "Rampling? You don't mean Scott Rampling?"

"Aye, yon's the bugger. Stocky blond lad, could have been another young Kennedy, leastways that's how he looked twenty-seven years ago."

"That's not how he looks now. You're right, you'll have no problem tracing him, but I doubt you'll find it easy to see him. In fact I'm not sure it would even be wise to try."

"Why's that?"

"The reason you've read about him is he's in line to be Deputy Director of the CIA which is an appointment that needs clearance from the Senate. He knows where all the bodies are buried which means he's got a lot of friends, or, put it another way, he's got a lot of smiling enemies who wouldn't be sorry to see something nice and dirty dug up in his background. It wouldn't take much—politically we're a neurotic society—so even if Scott Rampling's pure as the driven snow, he might not take kindly to an unofficial English cop linking him with an ancient murder case."

"He can please himself," said Dalziel indifferently.

He finished his drink, screwed the top back on the now almost empty bottle, and stood up.

"Well, I'd best be on my way. Enjoyed our chat."

"Hold on," said Thatcher. "What makes you think we're finished?"

"Come on, lad! You'd not be chewing the fat with me so relaxed if you hadn't got yon cow in the bag. I bet you told her I was a cop and we'd been following her for days, and now she's busy dropping everyone she can in the shit. I know the type. What was it? Antiques? A big scam, only she got greedy and decided to mix in a bit of private enterprise?"

"You may turn out to be a marvel," said Thatcher. "At first she was very tight-lipped, even when I said you'd been following her for weeks. So finally I showed her my law degree and ran a few sentences before her, maybe I exaggerated a tad, but the thought of five years in the slammer concentrated her mind wonderfully. She's over here to oversee the unpacking of a shipment of antiques all properly documented from your side, only a lot of the documentation itself is a work of art. Seems there's stuff there which would never have got an export license even if it hadn't been stolen in the first place. She's done this before a couple of times, gets well paid, but not enough. So this time when this pair of very hot eighteenth-century miniatures turned up in her shop, she chatted to a mate in Boston, got a good offer, and simply wrapped them in her underwear. 'Repro samples' was going to be her story if they got spotted, but as no one had ever bothered her before, she wasn't too much worried."

"They never are till they see the whites of your eyes," said Dalziel. "So that's that. How do I get out of here?"

"Back to the Immigration line, you mean?" said Thatcher.

"Nay, lad. You wouldn't?" said Dalziel in alarm.

"Believe me, if Keane had come out clean, you'd be so far back in the line, you'd be up to your knees in water," said Thatcher evenly. "But then I wouldn't be drinking your Scotch, would I? So let me show you the express route through the formalities. Here's my card by the way. Anything I can do, call me. I owe you."

"Thanks," said Dalziel. "I may just do that."

"And take care of yourself, Andy. You're a long way from home and the house rules are different over here."

"I'll be so quiet, you'll scarcely notice I'm here," promised Dalziel.

The Manhattan skyline made a dramatic frieze against the evening sky as Dalziel's taxi crossed the East River, but the Fat Man was in no state to appreciate it. He hadn't been so terrified since Mad Jack Dutot had pressed a double-barreled shotgun against his balls and invited him to choose left or right.

Deposited outside his hotel on Seventh Avenue, Dalziel carefully counted out the exact fare. The driver looked at him expectantly.

"You want a tip?" inquired Dalziel.

The man pursed his lips in an expression that was acquiescent without being eleemosynary.

"All right, here's one, take up skydiving. You'll live longer and so will your passengers."

He went into the hotel followed by a cry of, "Up yours, fatso!"

It wasn't a great hotel but it wasn't a flea pit either. It was the early hours of the morning, home-time. He dumped his case in his room and went down to the coffee shop on the first floor where he made a hearty supper of hamburgers and fries. Back in his room it was still too early American-time to go to bed, but his body disagreed, so he compromised by removing his shoes, finishing off his duty-free Scotch, and stretching out on the bed.

Four hours later he awoke from a dream of Mad Jack Dutot and the shotgun. It was bad but not a nightmare. It had been the reality that was the nightmare till Wally Tallantire walked in and assured Dutot that whichever barrel he used to scatter Dalziel's family jewels, the other was going straight up Mad Jack's own arse.

Dutot who, despite his sobriquet was a not unreasonable young man save on the subjects of bank robbery and Sheffield Wednesday, said, "Sod it. It's not loaded anyway," in proof of which assertion he pointed the weapon at his own foot and squeezed the trigger.

The resultant explosion, smoke, pedal dispersion, and loud screaming gave Dalziel cover under which he was able to go outside and clean himself up. When he'd tried to thank Tallantire, the superintendent said, "Word of advice, lad. Next time you want to be a hero, wear plastic pants or a brown suit."

Dalziel rolled off the bed, stripped, went into the bathroom, and stood under a searingly hot shower till British time, both past and present, had been sloughed out of his system. Toweling his crotch vigorously, he came out of the bathroom, feeling at last he was one hundred percent in New York and got instant confirmation in the shape of a pallid young man going through his suitcase.

If anything, the youngster looked the more shocked of the two, but this was small consolation as he instantly pulled a small handgun out of his waistband and screamed, "Hold it right there!"

"Nay, lad, I'll hold it anywhere you like," said Dalziel reassuringly. "Do I look like I'm going to give you trouble?"

He was quite sincere. His reading of the British tabloids had taught him that New York was full of drug-crazed muggers with Saturday night specials that went off if you farted. Suddenly he felt a strong nostalgia for Mad Jack Dutot.

He glanced at his watch. Eight hours in this sodding country and he'd been mixed up with an art smuggler, a homicidal cab driver, and a nervous mugger. He must be on *Candid Camera*! If so, it occurred to him that the mugger was having trouble remembering his lines.

Time for a prompt before the inarticulate young man decided that guns spoke louder than words.

"Don't you want my watch then? It's a good 'un, stands up to God knows how many atmospheric pressures, though what a man would want with knowing the time when his eyeballs have gone pop, I've never been able to fathom."

As he spoke he took a step forward, pulled the watch off, tossed it on to the bed, saw the man's eyes follow its flight, draped the huge towel over the handgun, pirouetted to one side with the deceptive speed of an angry bear, and as the weapon went off, hit the youngster behind the ear with a fist like a steam hammer.

Then he got dressed. A shot in the night was clearly not regarded as a summons for room service in New York, so after he'd buttoned his shirt, he picked up the phone and got the desk.

"Room 709," he said. "Can I have Security up here, please. Oh, and while you're at it, you might let the housekeeper know I'll need a new bath towel."

Twenty-one

"I am a doctor . . . let me examine it."

"I do not want it examined . . . let it

be."

"**D**on't your colleagues ever warn you about smoking?" said Peter Pascoe as Dr. Pottle lit another cigarette from the dog end between his lips.

"I tell them if they keep out of my lungs, I'll keep out of their heads," said Pottle.

He was head of the psychiatry unit at the Central Hospital. Pascoe, despite Dalziel's skepticism, had been using him as a consultant on police matters for years. That was why he was here today, he assured himself, an assurance he'd have found more convincing if the particular case he'd presented for Pottle's scrutiny hadn't been the Mickledore Hall murder. With Dalziel's departure, he had made, and meant, a fervent promise that there'd be no more meddling in the inquiry. After an initial euphoria at Dalziel's absence, however, he found himself strangely unable to enjoy the freedom he now had to shape CID more in his own image. Ellie was still away, her telephone conversation was evenly divided between concern for her mother and contumely for her mother's doctor, and Pascoe did not feel able to break the tacit truce which had evolved around their own personal battle. He'd come to the Central to talk about security after a man with a record of sex offenses had been caught hiding in a toilet near the children's ward. His business finished, he had found himself diverting without forethought to Pottle's office. And when the man had said, "Yes, amazingly, I do have a moment. How can I help you?" all that had come into his mind was the Mickledore Hall affair.

Finally the discussion had run out of steam. There was nothing to do but leave. Instead he heard himself making the crack about smoking.

"I'm sorry," he said. "None of my business."

"That's okay. Nice to have someone concerned about my health. What about you, Peter? Back to full strength?"

Pascoe noted the *Peter*. They weren't exactly friends. Perhaps men whose professions created such instant wariness never could be. But they'd reached a stage of affectionate mutual respect. He tried to remember Pottle's first name.

"Yes, fine. I'm looking after myself for a few days. Ellie and Rose are away. It's her mother; my father-in-law's ill, Alzheimer's, I may have mentioned it to you, he's in a Home now, but the strain on my mother-in-law . . ." He was explaining too much. He tried a light finish. "Anyway, if you're any good at washing up and ironing, I could do with some help."

"I'd like to help you all I can, Peter," said Pottle quietly. "Just precisely what is it you want?"

Perhaps after all the cigarette smoke was functional, thought Pascoe, providing a screen which pushed the crumpled face with the big Einstein mustache back to a confessional distance.

He took a deep breath of secondary carcinogens and said, "I want to be happy again."

"Again?"

"Like I used to be."

"You mean in some personal Golden Age when the summers were long and hot and felt like they would never end?"

"No, not childhood. It's adult happiness I'm talking about."

Pottle looked dubious.

"You know what Johnson used to say about anyone claiming to be happy? Pure cant. The dog knows he is miserable all the time."

"If the best you can do for me is tell me everyone's in the same boat, maybe I understand why you're smoking yourself to death."

"Hoity toity," said Pottle. "Tell me what form your unhappiness takes?"

"Lying awake at night worrying about *everything*. Not being able to see the point of *anything*. Panic attacks. How am I doing? Still running with the pack?"

"And what do you think might be the cause of these conditions, or any one of them?"

"I've got to do my own analysis too? Is this because I don't have private health insurance?"

"What are you so angry about?" asked Pottle mildly.

"I'm not angry!" exclaimed Pascoe. "I'm just irritated . . . look, I'm pretty busy at the moment, couldn't we . . . Oh, shit. All right. Here we go. Why am I angry? Well, it's better than being . . . It's all about control, isn't it? And I'm not in control. At first it was externals, things happen in relationships, like me and Ellie. We're apart, I don't just mean physically, that's just a step toward admission, but for a long time we've been drifting farther away. We've both tried, at least I know I've tried, no, that's not fair, she's tried too; and there we are, two intelligent people trying to do something they both want desperately, but not being able to pull it together because . . . because why? Because what?"

"You tell me," said Pottle.

"I think she blames me for her friend, you know, that suicide, the woman who jumped from the cathedral. She says she doesn't but I think she does."

"And you? Do you blame yourself?"

"I did. I blamed myself. I blamed everyone. Then I thought I didn't, I thought I'd got it under control, that it was a choice, and

189

what right had any of us to interfere with that choice, so where was the guilt?"

"That sounds reasonable."

"*Reasonable?*" said Pascoe bitterly. "I remember *reasonable*. Just. Reason means control, right? Me, I've lost control of relationships, I've lost control of events, and finally I've lost control of myself. I wake up in the night and the most trivial of worries comes at me like a mad rottweiler. Or worse, I'm going about my business in the full light of day, and suddenly I'm terrified, the whole physical world becomes a threat, I can't even control my own muscles, for God's sake!"

"Have you seen your doctor?"

"Don't be silly. Do you think he'd pass me fit for work if I spoke to him like I've spoken to you?"

"Perhaps not. Do you think you *are* fit for work?"

"Fit?" said Pascoe slowly. "I don't know about fit. But I know I need it. Your lot invented occupational therapy, didn't you?"

"No. Like your lot, we don't invent, we observe. And another rule we have in common is, never dismiss the simple explanation. Could be there's a physical origin for at least some of your symptoms. Talk to your doctor. Mention me so that he can refer you back. That way you'll get me on the NHS. Might as well use it while you can, like finishing your pudding on the *Titanic*."

Pascoe laughed. It felt good. He rose to leave.

"Thanks," he said. "And thanks for listening to me about the Mickledore case. Even if it was a cover, it was useful hearing your comments."

"There you go again, dismissing the simple," said Pottle. "It wasn't just a cover. You could have asked me about this intruder, couldn't you? In fact, that was your obvious excuse for calling on me. No, you chose the Mickledore case because this inquiry genuinely concerns you. And it interests me too. The woman's state of mind in particular. You know, after all that time inside, it was probably harder to leave jail than stay in. The miracle with Lazarus was not that Jesus brought him back to life, but that he bothered to come."

"So we should be asking why?"

"Indeed. And while you're at it, there are two other people with dodgy motivations. This fellow Waggs, and our own dear friend, Andrew Dalziel. You might do worse than ask yourself what makes them run, Inspector."

"*Chief Inspector*, if we're getting formal again," said Pascoe.

"It's mixing relationships that messes them up," said Pottle. "Coming in here, you may sometimes be a patient, but leaving you're always a cop. Take care."

As he drove away, Pascoe felt better than he had done for weeks. It was probably just the illogical euphoria of getting out of the dentist's, even though you had another appointment next week. So what? Don't knock. Relax and enjoy!

His radio crackled his call number. He acknowledged and the operator said, "Message from Sergeant Wield. Ring him as soon as you can."

He stopped at a phone box and rang HQ.

Wield said, "I tried to get you at the hospital security office but they said you'd left."

"I'm sorry. I got diverted. What's up?"

"Nothing, just a message for you, and as I'd no idea if you were coming straight back here or not, I thought I'd better put out a call."

The reproachful note again. Pascoe had meant to fill the sergeant in after Dalziel's departure, but having washed his own hands of the business, it hadn't seemed important.

"So what's the message, Wieldy?"

"A Mr. Pollock called. Said to tell you Mrs. Friedman was back from holiday and would be taking a drink with him in the Blind Sailor this lunchtime. I thought it might be urgent."

A querying note this time.

"Not really," said Pascoe. "But thanks all the same. See you soon."

Percy Pollock. He heard the soft melancholy voice in his imagination and shuddered. Thank God he'd washed his hands of all that. Yet as he drove into the town center, he found Pottle's comments about Kohler and Waggs, and Dalziel too, buzzing round his mind like an invisible fly in a hotel bedroom.

He glanced at his watch. Just after midday. Trimble and Hiller couldn't expect him not to eat. And if you can't sleep, chasing flies with a rolled up newspaper is better than despair.

He switched lanes and headed for the Blind Sailor.

Twenty-two

"No, you wicked foreign woman, I am

your match."

Dalziel's first full day in the New World was buzzed in by his bedside phone.

"Hello," he yawned.

"Mr. Dalziel? Sorry to trouble you, sir, but there're a lot of reporters down here at the desk would like to talk with you."

"Reporters? What the hell do reporters want with me?"

He found out when he got up. Someone had pushed a tabloid paper under his door. He looked at it in disbelief. There was his photograph occupying half of the front page with the banner headline, CROCODILE DALZIEL!

He recalled now that a reporter had turned up with the police last night, probably alerted by their radio. *Hotel guest mugged* would have rated no interest but *Brit tourist socks hotel mugger* was worth a couple of lines on a quiet night. Unfortunately the story had rung a bell with someone who'd picked up the news of the airport arrest earlier, and the two stories together had added up to this silly season splash.

He knew how to nip such journalistic nonsense in the bud. You confronted its perpetrator with a menacing jocularity and suggested that life, liberty, and the pursuit of Pulitzers required his presence elsewhere.

Ten minutes later he entered the hotel lobby with the confident tread of a lion who knows that one roar will clear him a space at the water hole.

Five minutes after that it occurred to him he must still be jet-lagged. Quite simply, he'd forgotten where he was. What was menace in Mid-Yorkshire was just good copy over here, and once they realized they'd got themselves a genuine original, the more he roared, the more they encouraged his roaring. He heard himself resorting to pleading.

"Now, listen, lads, all I want is a bacon buttie and a mug of tea, then I'll get down to some serious sight-seeing . . ."

"A bacon what? A what of tea? What sights are you planning to see, Mr. Dalziel? You got any advice on cleaning up the subway? What about a midnight stroll through Central Park? Would you say you look for action or does it just happen around you naturally?"

He'd identified the guy who'd started the trouble and was seriously wondering how he'd look with a concave nose when a soft voice in his ear said, "You must be starving. I know where to get the best bacon in New York."

He felt a gentle pressure on his arm, let himself be guided by it, and next moment found himself spinning through a revolving door onto a crowded sidewalk. His pilot turned out to be a beautiful young black woman with a brilliant smile which showed rather more teeth than was the norm in Yorkshire. She led him into what he would have categorized as a transport caff except that the counter was crowded with men and women in smart business suits buying something called coffee-to-go which went in the kind of brown paper bag he associated with illicit sex material. His guide steered him into a booth with a table so narrow there was no way for them to sit opposite each other without their legs interlocking. It felt like a good time to relax and think of England.

"See anything you fancy?" the woman asked. Her voice was

deep and throaty, purring through full, slightly moist lips behind which the teeth gleamed like a chain saw cutting through a mango.

He said, "Eh?"

"Do you see anything you fancy for breakfast?"

He dropped his gaze to a menu as large and obscure as the Rosetta Stone.

"I like to know who I'm eating with when I've not brought my taster," he said.

"I'm Linda Steele," she said.

"Aye, but *what* are you? A journalist?"

"A writer. Free-lance. I do anything I can get to do, features, reportage, research. I get pieces published once in a while, help other people with their projects. I've got a few TV credits, did you ever see that documentary Columbia did on the Washington riots . . . ?"

"Missus, it's no use trying to impress me with telly. Back home I'm so far behind with *Dallas*, there's people not born yet who are dead. So what do you want with me, Linda Steele?"

"I want to buy you breakfast."

"I'll not quarrel with that. Can I get bacon and eggs? I don't suppose they do black pudding?"

"Black . . . what?"

"Never mind. I like me bacon crisp enough to shave with, and me eggs like a parrot's eye."

Linda Steele translated the order into American and the waitress replied in kind.

"She wants to know if you want syrup."

"No, thanks. Marmalade."

"With your eggs?"

"With my toast! Bloody hell, you'll be offering me kippers and custard next. Right, luv. What's a journalist expect in return for a breakfast over here?"

"How about an exclusive?" she said smiling.

"Nay, lass, I don't come cheap as that, not even for syrup. Any road, that daft paper you've got there tells you all there is to know."

She had a copy of the Crocodile Dalziel tabloid sticking out of her bag.

"Not really," she said pulling it out and spreading it before her. "I don't see anything in here about Cissy Kohler."

Dalziel whistled a long E flat, inserted his left hand under the table, and began to scratch his knee. The vibrations communicated themselves to the woman's contingent thigh but she kept on smiling.

"You wouldn't know a fellow called Thatcher, would you?" asked Dalziel finally.

"He said you were sharp," she laughed. "Yes, I know Dave. He mentioned you to me, said he thought there might be a story in it. Only, by the time I got to you, you'd managed to create your own news."

"That's right, luv. So what do I need with a free-lance?"

"A lot. The way I see it, all you've got so far is publicity which doesn't get you any closer to Cissy but could get her a lot farther from you."

"Oh, aye? And how do you make that out?"

"She sees the story, recognizes the picture. A Yorkshire cop in New York. If she's not paying heed, Jay Waggs certainly is. They don't want to be bothered so they take off."

The breakfast arrived. It crowded the plate and smelt good. Dalziel shoveled his mouth full of bacon and said crisply, "So they're in New York then?"

"Maybe."

He tested a yolk with his fork. It was to his satisfaction.

"How come you've got their address?" he asked.

"Dave Thatcher felt he owed you so he got some of his contacts to check around. They dug it out."

"Oh, aye? Then why not give it direct to me?"

She smiled and gave a little mammary shiver.

"Perhaps he felt he owed me too. This way he kills two birds with one stone."

Dalziel tried not to let himself be diverted by speculation about the nature of Thatcher's debt to the woman. He said, "So what do I have to do to get it from you?"

"The address you mean?" she said raising her eyebrows. "Just give me exclusive rights on any story that comes out of all this."

He thought, chewed, nodded.

"All right. But I'll need more than the address. Let's talk money?"

"Money?"

"Aye. Cash. Spondulicks. Dollars."

"I thought you were doing this out of loyalty to a dead buddy?"

"What makes you think loyalty comes cheaper than disloyalty? I'm only a poor British cop. Even our bribes have dropped way behind inflation. If this takes more than another couple of days, I'll be spent up."

Their gazes met, his wide-eyed, candid, appealing; hers narrow and assessing.

"Okay," she said. "I reckon I can swing expenses."

"Ah," he said. "So you're not just doing this on spec. You've got a market fixed up already."

For a second she looked annoyed, then she laughed.

"I can see I'm going to have to watch you, Andy," she said. "Yeah, I gave a buddy in the business a ring, let him have a vague outline, and got him really interested. So there's a budget, but it's not bottomless."

"My needs are simple," said Dalziel sweeping a roll around his plate. "So what's the address?"

She gave it to him. It meant nothing. She produced a city street map and marked it in.

"This is what they call the Upper West Side. It's an apartment building. Very pricey."

"I didn't get the impression Waggs was stinking rich."

"It's not his. Dave's contacts reckon it belongs to his backers."

"Backers?"

"Yeah. Waggs is a guy who puts deals together, you know, the kind who's always selling more than he's really got? For him to get this Kohler thing rolling, he sold the idea to a West Coast finance group called Hesperides. They've been behind a lot of pretty successful film and TV stuff in recent years. All very respectable."

197

"But?"

"But way back where the money starts . . ." She shrugged. "Back home you've probably got the same kind of linkup between respectable big business and crooks."

"Oh, aye. We call it privatization. So what are you saying?"

"That getting close to Waggs and the woman may not be all that easy. First off, these apartment buildings are purposely built to keep unwanted visitors out. Second, Hesperides won't be too keen on seeing someone getting between them and their investment."

"I was wondering why you hadn't just gone rushing round there yourself," said Dalziel. "I didn't bank on rough stuff. Maybe we should renegotiate."

"Later maybe," she said, squeezing his leg between hers. "I guess there comes a time when us poor defenseless girls need a big tough man."

"In that case," said Dalziel, "I'd better have another couple of rashers of bacon!"

Twenty-three

"Papers and precious matters were

brought to us . . . by the strangest

bearers you can imagine."

"**M**r. Pascoe," said Percy Pollock. "Allow me to present Mrs. Friedman."

The woman sitting next to him in the snug of the Blind Sailor was small and gray-haired. She had cherry cheeks, wore wire-rimmed spectacles, and looked more like an advertiser's image of a favorite granny than a retired prison officer. The image fragmented slightly when in reply to Pascoe's, "Same again?" she pushed her glass at him and said, "Large gin. Nothing in it."

Pascoe got straight down to business.

"Mr. Pollock tells me you were working at Beddington Jail when your colleague, Daphne Bush, died?"

"When Cissy Kohler killed her, you mean?" Her voice was sharp, incisive, used to command. "That's right."

"So you knew them both. Were you on close terms?"

"With Daphne? Pretty close."

"And with Kohler?"

"You don't get close to prisoners. At least, I didn't. But I knew her well enough."

"What did you make of her?"

"She lived inside herself, know what I mean? A lot of them do, those that are in for the duration. We shut them in, and they survive by shutting us out."

"Disturbed, you mean?"

"No. Well, not *disturbing* anyway. She did what she was told, no fuss. But she wasn't creepy with it like some of them. The other prisoners respected her, but she didn't have any special friends."

"Except Daphne Bush?"

"Oh, yes. Daphne." The woman sipped her gin. She didn't look so cutely grannyish now. Nor so old. Only mid-sixties, Pascoe guessed. And a match for anyone.

"Was . . . *is* Kohler lesbian?"

"I'd have said not. But inside that means nothing."

"I'm sorry?"

She said, "Everyone needs affection. If you're inside for the duration, you've got to make do, haven't you? Needn't even be physical, but that's where most of the trouble starts, not because of lousy conditions, but because X's best friend is playing too much Ping-Pong with Y."

"But Kohler didn't have any special friends, you say?"

"No. Daphne was the first person to break through."

"How did that happen? Did Bush make the running?"

"Well, she certainly took a fancy to Kohler, I could see that. And when Daphne wanted something, she knew how to make herself very attractive. Bright, entertaining, full of sympathy. Oh, yes, she could really turn it on."

There was an unmistakable note of personal bitterness here.

"And when she turned it off, what was she like?"

"Immature, selfish, insensitive," said Friedman promptly. "It didn't matter how close you felt you were, she could still say or do things which showed she hadn't got the faintest idea what made you tick. Being nasty with people is one thing, we can all manage that.

But not knowing how nasty you're being is really dangerous. As she probably found out, poor cow."

"How far did their relationship go?"

"Did they screw, you mean? I don't know. If they didn't, it wouldn't be for want of Daphne trying, though I got the impression that she was willing to hold her horses in the expectation of a real fling when Kohler got her parole."

"Did Kohler apply for parole because of her relationship with Bush, do you think?"

"Daphne certainly thought so," said the woman. "Me, I'm not so sure. She'd certainly shown no interest before, though she'd been qualified to apply for ages. Perhaps she thought there was too much feeling outside against her, because of the little girl's death. But this was no sadistic child killing; she was no Hindley, was she? I doubt if more than a handful of people would even have remembered her name after all those years."

"Any other possible reason why things changed?"

The woman thought and said, "There was her visitor."

"What visitor?"

"It was in the summer. The same year. 1976. She never had visitors, not in all the time I knew her. So I noticed this one."

"Can you recall the name? Or what he looked like?"

She returned his gaze blankly but it wasn't a blank of ignorance.

Shit! He'd sounded too eager. Whatever he imagined he was doing, this woman was negotiating and he'd just bumped up her price. Best to back away from the identity of the visitor for the time being.

He said, "So after this visit, Kohler started getting friendly with Bush and showing an interest in parole?"

"Yes, but in what order I couldn't say. Except I sometimes wondered if Kohler couldn't have been using Daphne while letting Daph think it was her making all the running."

"Using her for what?"

Mrs. Friedman shrugged. Pascoe again got the feeling of a tactical reservation rather than a refusal. He changed tack.

"So she and Bush were good friends and the parole board were on the point of letting her loose. What happened?"

"It was a Thursday afternoon, I remember. Free association time. Kohler was alone in her cell. Daphne went in for one of their little heart to hearts. Next thing there's a lot of shouting, then screaming, then a sharp crack, then silence. I was one of the first in. Daphne was lying on the floor, eyes wide open, staring at nothing. There was blood everywhere. Her head had hit the angle of the wall by the door. Or been smashed against it by someone holding her hair which showed signs of being pulled out at the roots . . ."

"What about Kohler?"

"She just stood there. She said, *I've killed her.* Later when she was asked if she did it on purpose, all she said was, *How can you kill someone and it not be on purpose?* That was it. Another life sentence. When a con kills a screw, she needs the Archangel Gabriel as witness for the defense to get away with it, and maybe not then. Quite right too."

Pascoe ignored the implication and asked, "So what do you think caused the quarrel?"

"An educated guess? I'd say that Daphne started fantasizing about the future and Kohler finally made it clear that once she was out, that was that, all Daphne was getting from her was a nice card every Christmas. So Daphne turned nasty and started throwing dirt at her, only being Daphne, she had no idea of just how hurtful whatever weapon she'd got would be to Kohler. She flipped and hit out."

"With intent to kill?"

The woman shrugged and said, "Like I say, it doesn't matter."

"What was she like after the trial?"

"I only saw her once. They soon transferred her from Beddington, naturally. But I got the impression she'd gone back inside herself, like this time she wanted to bury herself so deep, no one would ever get to her again."

"But someone or something did," said Pascoe. "She's finally out."

"Yes. I thought about it when I heard. And I thought, well,

something did get to her once, no reason why that something shouldn't have got to her again. And I doubt it has much to do with any television do-gooder."

"I'd be interested to hear your theories, Mrs. Friedman," Pascoe said.

She tapped her empty glass significantly on the table. Pascoe reached for it but she slid it away from him toward Pollock. He took it, rose, and made for the bar.

Now she leaned across the table toward Pascoe. Behind the granny specs her eyes were black as coal and twice as hard. It was haggle time and she didn't want any witnesses.

She said, "I gather from Mr. Pollock this is by way of being private business rather than strictly speaking an official police matter."

"Dual status, you might say," said Pascoe carefully. "Why do you ask?"

"Information's like medicine, Mr. Pascoe," she said. "Private costs more than National Health. In fact if you wait for National Health, it can sometimes take so long, it's hardly worth the bother."

He said, "What are we talking about, Mrs. Friedman?"

She said, "Suppose Kohler had used Daph as a post box so she could write to someone outside without anyone inside knowing officially."

"I'm supposing," said Pascoe.

"Suppose someone wrote back care of Daph. And suppose someone knew where to lay hands on that letter. What would you think that might be worth, Mr. Pascoe?"

Pascoe smiled. Now he knew he was haggling, he wasn't going to fall into the error of overeagerness again.

"Not a lot," he said. "A fifteen-year-old letter? Can't have been all that valuable else it would have been sold off long ago."

"Perhaps it got saved up for a rainy day."

"That's possible," admitted Pascoe. "But look at it this way. For a long while now, ever since that Yank, Waggs, started stirring things, there's been a lot of media interest in Kohler. If this letter had any real value, whoever's got it would have flogged it to telly or the tabloids for about a hundred times more than a poor off-duty cop could afford." He finished his half pint of bitter and said, "I'd better be off. Another half hour and I'll be back on duty and I don't want to be around here then, do I, Mrs. Friedman, in case I get a whiff of something not quite kosher."

Percy Pollock spotting a lull in conversation came across and put her gin in front of her. She drank without looking at him and he retreated to the bar. Pascoe watched her face. She gave nothing away there, but she didn't need to. He'd sat at too many interview tables not to follow the thought process without a visual aid.

He said, very sympathetically, "You've tried the media, haven't you? But you got a dusty answer. Only you don't want to admit it, because you reckon that would knock my offer right down into the basement. Am I right?"

She smiled now, more like dressed-up wolf than granny.

"You're not daft," she said. "But you're not quite right. Yes, I rang the *Sphere* some time back, when the interest in Kohler started. I didn't mention the letter, though. Just wondered if they'd be interested in paying for an old prison officer's reminiscences, no names, no pack drill. We set up a meeting."

"And?"

"And the next day I got a phone call from a man who said he was in the Home Office Department dealing with pensions. It was nothing he said, just an inquiry about length of qualifying service. But when we got that sorted he chatted on, all very friendly, about how he was sure I knew I was still bound by the Secrets Act and that any breach of confidentiality would certainly mean loss of pension rights and possible prosecution."

Pascoe whistled. "So you forgot about the tabloids? Very wise. Someone at the Home Office must have big ears."

"And big muscles," she said grimly. "The Pension Department don't have that kind of clout, I tell you. And I've been thinking ever since, if they were putting the screws on at that sort of level just on account of a few reminiscences, then that letter must be really valuable."

"In which case you should think yourself lucky they don't know about it," said Pascoe who was beginning to suspect it was something he didn't really want to know about either. "So you reckon it's really valuable? Except that you haven't got anyone you dare try to sell it to, which makes it worthless."

"I've got you," she said.

"Maybe. How much are you asking?"

She looked at him like a pork butcher in a meat market.

"Five hundred," she said.

"Come on! Who do you think I am?"

"Mebbe you should speak to your Mr. Dalziel. You're only his rep, Percy tells me."

"Does he?" said Pascoe. "Then perhaps he's also told you that if Mr. Dalziel had come himself, by now he'd not only have had that letter in his pocket, he'd likely have had your pension too!"

From her reaction, it appeared that at the very least Pollock had suggested he would be a much softer option for she said immediately, "All right. Four hundred."

"One," said Pascoe.

"Three."

"One fifty."

"Two fifty. And I'll tell you what. You can see the letter and if you don't think it's any interest, give me it back with a tenner for my trouble and we'll forget the whole thing."

It was an offer hard to refuse, though his heart sank at the bill of expenses he was going to present Dalziel with.

He said, "I'll need chapter and verse. What I mean is, I want to know the lot, how you got hold of it, everything you know about the circumstances surrounding it."

She thought, nodded.

"Deal," she said.

"Right," he said. "For a start, this visitor Kohler had. What was his name?"

"Not his. Her," she said.

"Her?"

"That's right. Her name was Marsh. Mavis Marsh."

205

Twenty-four

"We all have our various ways of gaining a livelihood. Some of us have damp ways, and some of us have dry ways."

For her first twenty-four hours in New York, Cissy Kohler had not left the apartment. Most of the time she lay on her bed, blowing skeins of smoke at the ceiling. Jay raised no objection. He spent most of the time on the telephone.

The morning of the second day passed in much the same way except that this time when she heard Jay's voice talking in the next room, she picked up the bedside phone, covered the mouthpiece, and listened.

"Look, I tell you, she hasn't written any memoirs, I've checked her stuff."

"Couldn't she have smuggled them out?" A man's voice, deep, almost growling.

"Maybe. I doubt it. It's no problem. I know guys, give 'em a

206

couple of facts and a week, can write stuff so authentic she won't know she didn't do it herself."

"Okay. So long as we don't find something showing up somewhere else. Exclusivity is what we put our money in. Feeling here is we want to go with this soon as we can. We've been getting a bit of pressure from some strong people, nothing we can't cope with yet, but the sooner we get this in the public domain, the better."

"Say anything too soon and you'll have wall-to-wall reporters. This has got to be private."

"So why not take her round to the clinic now, get it over with before he snuffs it?"

"I've told you, he'll go home to die, I know that for sure. She can get to Bellmain at home, but she wouldn't get past first base at the Allerdale. It's like the Pentagon. My way is best, believe me."

"When I stop believing you, you'll know. Believe *me*. Keep in touch."

She was lying on her back reading her Bible when Jay came in. He said flatly, "You were listening."

"Yes."

"Shit. Listen, Cissy, I've got to talk to these guys like that."

"Who are they, Jay?"

"Hesperides. It's a finance corporation. They back a lot of media enterprises. They've invested a lot of money in you, Cissy."

"Don't you mean, they've invested a lot of money in you, Jay?"

"I suppose. But I needed that money to get you out."

"So you made promises? And to Sempernel too? You're pretty free with promises, Jay. What about those you made to me?"

"You'll get what I promised, Ciss. Listen, I'll be up-front with you, I owe these guys. They backed another project I set up, only it didn't work out. Now I've got to keep them sweet, or else . . ."

"Or else they'll want their money back? Give it to them. Tell them we'll pay them off when I get my compensation."

"They don't just want their money back, Ciss. They want it back times a couple of million. And they're very concerned about their corporate image. By which I mean, they think that anyone who jerks them around and stays healthy is a bad advertisement."

She thought about this, then shook her head.

"I'm sorry, but I don't see there's anything I can do. I don't even know yet if I'm grateful to you. Most of the time I doubt it. After you've done what you promised, maybe I'll have room in my mind to think things through. Meanwhile, don't let these people near me, for I won't lie. The best I can give is silence."

"That's all I want," he said, smiling. Their gazes locked for a moment, then he pulled back his focus to take in the whole of her face.

"Cissy, you look terrible!" he said. "You mustn't stay stuck in here all the time. We've got to get you out in the fresh air."

"In New York? Has some kind of miracle happened since I was last here?"

"Come on," he said.

She didn't want to go but had no will to resist. The buildings loomed menacingly, the traffic and people rushed by in a torrent that threatened to sweep her away. It was a relief to reach the park a couple of blocks to the east. They walked in silence for half an hour and then, because he'd observed how unsettling she found the streets, they took a cab home.

The next morning they went out again, and again in the afternoon. She realized to her mild surprise that she was enjoying the park. Here at least there'd been little change and from time to time some small thing, like a kid's kite bucking against the wind, or the World Series intensity of a softball game, would join the lacerated edges of her torn-apart life. Such healings were fragile as spans of snow across a dark and fathomless crevasse, but they brought a life and color to her cheeks which, though quickly fading, did not completely fade.

At breakfast on the fourth day, Jay announced he had to go out and might not be back in time for their morning walk.

"So I'll go by myself," she said.

He looked at her assessingly, then smiled.

"Why not?"

She watched from the window till he emerged five storys below and climbed into the driving seat of the blue Lincoln which had been waiting for him at the airport. His backers obviously liked to keep up appearances at both ends of a bargain.

The Lincoln pulled away. She turned and picked up the first volume of the telephone directory and looked up The Allerdale Clinic. It was on East Sixty-eighth between Madison and Park. She looked out at the gray skies, put on her raincoat, and went to the elevator.

She'd chosen right. Rain was already pocking the sidewalk. A cab came by, hesitating before going on to pull up in front of the next building. While she debated whether to pursue it, another pulled in before her and a young black woman got out. Two cabs in New York on a wet morning! It had to be a good omen. She climbed in.

East Sixty-eighth Street was a narrow canyon of big handsome houses.

The clinic was so discreet she hardly knew it was there even when she was dropped right in front of it. She entered what could have been the vestibule of a very expensive, very old money apartment house. Jay had said a quiet life came expensive these days. Obviously a quiet death didn't come cheap either.

An elegant receptionist looked up from a computer keyboard and asked if she could be of assistance.

"I'd like to see one of your patients," said Cissy. "Mr. Bellmain."

The girl touched a couple of keys and said, "Your name is . . . ?"

"Waggs," said Cissy. "Mrs. Waggs."

"Thank you. Would you take a seat?"

She sat down, riffled the pages of a glossy magazine unseeingly. The girl murmured into a phone. A door opened and a woman came toward her. She was middle-aged, dressed in a smart black business suit. She said, "Mrs. Waggs? I'm Mrs. Amalfi, the clinic's Executive Officer. How may we help you?"

"I'd like to see Mr. Bellmain. I'm an old friend. I was in the area so I thought, why not call?"

"I understand. Unfortunately we have strict rules at the Allerdale, Mrs. Waggs. In the interests of our patients, visitors are restricted to a list prepared by the family. I'm sure if you are an old friend you'll have no difficulty getting your name added to the Bell-main list."

"Yes, of course, but as I'm here anyway . . ."

"I'm sorry," said Mrs. Amalfi, standing to one side so that Cissy could rise. There was no contact but she felt herself drawn up and urged out. She was long accustomed to obedience to people with such authority. Only once during those slow years had she lost the control which let them keep theirs. Only once, and a woman had lain there dead.

The rain had slackened off though the lowering sky promised only a temporary relief. She set off walking without any attempt to choose a direction. When a cab came toward her after four blocks, she hailed it, meaning to direct it back to the apartment. But she found she wasn't ready yet to step back into that particular cell and instead said, "Macy's."

"You always walk away from where you're heading?" inquired the driver.

"If I can manage it," she said.

Her acquaintance with New York was restricted to half a dozen shortish visits with the Westropps, but Macy's was what she remembered best. For a while as she stepped once more into that world of hustling, bustling commercial color, she felt the years between slip away. But soon she began to feel fatigued and confused. Finally she took refuge in the coffee shop, sat down thankfully, and lit a cigarette. She didn't have time to inhale before two women at the next table told her she was in a nonsmoking zone. It wasn't done with any of the diffident politeness she'd have expected thirty years ago, but with a mordant savagery, as though she were committing an act of public indecency.

She dunked her cigarette in her coffee and left.

Outside the rain was now bouncing off the tarmac and suddenly cabs were rarer than unicorns. She started walking up Broadway, old memory struggling against new panic. There had been changes here, new buildings for old, old vices dressed up as new. She struggled to keep her observation at an assessing, objective level, but darkness kept washing in on the flurries of rain turning the Great White Way into a tunnel of night along which the untimely car headlamps smeared light like the spoor of snails.

She tried a trick she had learned in prison. When you can't fight your fears anymore, run with them, steering them into ever more gothic regions of your subconscious till finally you tumble over into such grotesqueries that even blind panic has to pause and smile.

She was Snow White in the storm, she told herself, with malicious laughter screeching from the foul black air, skeletal arms stretching to trip her, evil eyes watching for her to stumble. But beneath it all she sought the assurance that it was only the harmless owl gliding through the storm-tossed trees under which sheltered a myriad tiny creatures, all as frightened as she.

It might have worked in a forest. But here were no trees, only concrete and glass, and the bright-eyed creatures sheltering in these doorways looked far from harmless.

She was moving faster and faster. Now she was running, crashing into other pedestrians with force enough to draw attention even in rainy New York. At an intersection the DON'T WALK sign lit as she approached. She saw it but her mind was beyond obedience and she would have plunged straight into the speeding traffic if a hand had not grasped at her arm.

She spun round, ready to strike out, to scream.

She found herself looking at an elderly man wearing the black clothes, broad-brimmed hat, and benevolent smile of an old-fashioned preacher.

"Lady, you want to die?" he said.

"It's the best offer I've had all morning," she gasped hysterically.

"Business that bad, huh?" He examined her sympathetically. "Lady, you sure are wet. How much you charge for fucking you dry?"

He thought she was a hooker. Somehow this snapped her self-control back into place.

She said, "Twenty-seven."

"Dollars?" he said in surprise.

"Years," she said. "I don't think you can afford it."

She walked all the way back to the apartment, driving her limbs at a pace which created enough heat to drive out the damp from her flesh if not from her clothes. She felt a tremor of something like triumph as she approached the entrance to the building. She hadn't achieved anything concrete but she'd ventured out alone, taken risks, and was returning unscathed, ready to fight another day.

As she pushed open the street door a hand grasped her elbow, a touch light as a feather, tight as a vice.

"Well, Cissy Kohler! Here's a stroke of luck! I were just on my way to see you."

She felt herself guided across the vestibule, past the questing gaze of the concierge, up to the elevator. Its doors only opened if the man at the desk pressed a switch. The grip on her arm relaxed. She looked up into a face she had only seen this close once before in her life. Then too her hair had been dripping water down her brow and her cheeks. The man had not been smiling then as he was now, but his eyes had been the same.

He said, "Smile nicely at the man, Cissy. Then we'll go up and have a little chat about the old days."

All she had to do was shout. She looked into those hard condemning eyes.

Then she turned toward the concierge and smiled.

Twenty-five

"What do you make, madame?"

"Many things."

"For instance—"

"For instance . . . shrouds."

Dalziel hadn't made a conscious decision to dump Linda Steele. What happened was, it started raining as they came out of the deli. Steele waved at a cab which came to a halt some fifteen yards beyond them. A young man in a business suit immediately jumped in and the cab pulled away.

"Cheeky sod!" exclaimed Dalziel.

"Happens all the time," said the woman philosophically.

"Not to me."

He saw the cab was balked by the lights at the next intersection. Suddenly he was off running. The jails of Mid-Yorkshire were full of people who'd been surprised to discover how fast a man of his bulk could move if properly motivated. He reached the cab, wrenched open the door, and fell in.

"What the hell!" exclaimed the passenger angrily.

Dalziel, too out of breath to speak, put his huge mouth close to the man's ear and bellowed, "Aaarrgh!" Terrified, the man opened the other door and fell out onto the damp tarmac.

"Hey, what the fuck's happening back there?" demanded the driver.

"You've just been hijacked, sunshine," gasped Dalziel.

The lights changed. The traffic started to move. He looked back and saw Linda Steele, slow in her high heels, coming gamely up behind them.

"So where to?" said the driver, beginning to edge forward with the traffic.

"Libya," said Dalziel, smiling apologetically out of the rear window. "But there's somewhere I'd like you to stop off first."

Perhaps eager to be rid of his unexpected passenger, the driver drove in a manner which made the trip from the airport seem like a cortege. It turned out to be counterproductive. As he started to pull up outside the apartment building Dalziel said, "No. The next one."

"Jesus. Make up your mind, fella!"

Dalziel wasn't listening. He was watching Cissy Kohler standing on the sidewalk. For an uncharacteristic moment he vacillated. Confront her now, or watch and follow?

Then the decision was taken out of his hands. Another cab pulled in, Linda Steele got out, and Kohler got in. It would have been easy to hail Steele but this time Dalziel did make a conscious decision.

"Right, Ben Hur," he said. "Follow that cab!"

Half an hour later his problem had increased by fifty percent. He could still either confront or follow. But he could also go into the building she'd just come out of and try to find out what she'd been doing there. He could, of course, come back here later, but by then it would be a cold trail. Following by cab wasn't an easy option in city traffic. They'd been lucky to keep in touch this far. As for confronting her, he wanted somewhere quiet and private for that.

Or perhaps he was just rationalizing his own unacknowledged reluctance to speak directly with this woman.

Christalmighty, that was how the lad Pascoe talked!

He made up his mind. Cissy Kohler was walking away through the rain. Let her go. He knew where her lair was now.

"What do I owe you?" he said to the cab driver. "Apart from my life, I mean?"

A small very discreet plaque above the door said ALLERDALE CLINIC. He went through and found himself in a swish vestibule. Over a counter a receptionist smiled welcomingly at him. Like Linda Steele she seemed to suffer from an excess of teeth, long rows of perfectly white obelisks, gleaming, symmetrical, like a military grave-yard after a bad war. He returned her smile, wondering whether to opt for deception or bribery.

"Can I help you, sir?" she asked.

"Aye. Mebbe. Not me exactly. The wife," he extemporized, plumping for deceit on the grounds that with dental work like that, bribery was likely to be too rich for his constabulary pocket.

"Has she been suffering long?" said the woman sympathetically.

Dalziel, who had not seen his wife for nigh on twenty years, certainly hoped so.

"Long enough," he said vaguely. "This place were recommended by a friend. Miss Kohler. In fact she said she might be calling in today. You've not seen her, have you?"

"I'm sorry," said the woman. "The name doesn't ring a bell. Would you take a seat, Mr. . . . ?"

"Dalziel." He examined her face and could find no sign of de-ceit, but that meant nowt except mebbe she was better at it than he was. Either way, deceitful or genuinely ignorant, she clearly wasn't going to help him.

He took the suggested seat and thumbed through the glossies. They were all the latest editions, not the dog-eared relics of yester-year strewn around your normal English waiting rooms. The whole place smelt of money. This must be where rich Yanks came to have their corns removed or their faces lifted. He toyed with the idea of returning to Yorkshire with a face lift and a hair transplant. That'd make the buggers sit up! He felt a sudden pang of nostalgia for "the buggers." To distract himself he filled in a magazine questionnaire to test his assertiveness rating and discovered to his mild surprise that he was almost clinically shy. Pondering this, he doodled idly, blacking out the teeth of makeup models. This turned his thoughts to Linda Steele. He felt a little guilty at having slipped her leash, not so much for her sake as for Thatcher's. The man had done him a kindness and might misinterpret his reactions if Steele reported back to him.

He took Thatcher's card out of his pocket and looked round for a phone. There was one on the receptionist's desk. The girl herself had vanished. Dalziel rose, went to the desk, and picked up the phone.

"Mr. Thatcher's office. Can I help you?"

"I'd like to speak to Dave, please."

"Mr. Thatcher's busy just now . . ."

"Tell him it's Andy Dalziel."

All over Yorkshire that was sufficient to make a lot of important people put down their business papers, their soup spoons, even their mistresses, and head for the phone. No reason why it should be Open Sesame here, but no reason not to try either.

"Hello? Thatcher."

"Dave, just to say thanks for pushing Linda at me. We've sort of got separated, but I'll make sure she doesn't take it out on you . . ."

"Look, I'm kind of busy right now. Maybe we can talk some other time. I hope things work out."

The tone was distant, the line went dead. He'd been cut off in every sense. Thatcher clearly thought all debts had been paid.

"Up yours too, sunshine!" he barked into the mouthpiece before replacing it. He turned to find the receptionist watching him fearfully.

"Wrong number," he said. "How things going?"

"Mrs. Amalfi, our executive officer, will see you now," she said.

She led him from the reception area into an airy office with a carpet like quicksand. You could feel it sucking the money out of your pocket. Behind a rosewood desk stood a middle-aged woman wearing a smart black business suit. The paleness of her features was accentuated by jet black hair so tightly drawn back from her brow that it looked like it had been painted on. Her eyebrows had been plucked to baldness and her lips were set so tight, it was difficult to see if she had any teeth at all which made a change.

"Jancine Amalfi," she said, offering her hand. "I'm sorry you've been kept waiting. Please have a seat. I believe you are making inquiries about the possibility of transferring your wife to the Allerdale?"

"That's right. What I'd really like . . ."

"A few details first, Mr. Dalziel," she said fixing him with a gaze which seemed to burn through to his slim wallet of traveler's checks. "Forgive me if I'm direct, but we do not deal in false hope here at the Allerdale, only in facts. We shall of course need sight of your wife's full medical record, but an outline picture now would be most helpful, if you feel able to talk about it."

"No problem," said Dalziel.

"Good. So tell me, where is the carcinoma located?"

"You what? Carcinoma? That's cancer, isn't it?"

"That's right."

"No," said Dalziel emphatically. "The lass out there must've picked me up wrong. It's not cancer."

It was one thing to wish a fair dollop of discomfort on his ex-wife, but even his unforgiving nature balked superstitiously at pretending cancer.

"Not cancer? What then?"

"Piles," said Dalziel. "Ingrowing piles. They can be very serious."

"Indeed they can," said Mrs. Amalfi. "But I'm afraid it is you who have got things wrong, Mr. Dalziel. The Allerdale Clinic is a cancer treatment center, with a reputation second to none, I am glad to say."

She was clearly puzzled that he could have made such an error, like someone behind a bank counter being asked for a beer.

He said, "I'm sorry. It was this friend, well more acquaintance really, Miss Kohler. I heard her talking about the place and must've picked it up wrong. You'll know her likely. Smallish lass. Very thin face, grayish hair. I think she might've been in a bit earlier."

217

Subtle stuff; might have worked with a backward toddler; all it got him from Mrs. Amalfi was a long cool look.

"The name doesn't ring a bell," she said rising. As resistant to authority as Cissy Kohler was conditioned to it, he still found himself being shepherded through the door, into the vestibule, and toward the exit.

But before Mrs. Amalfi could bounce him into the street, the doors swung open and Scott Rampling came in.

Dalziel recognized him instantly. Not that Thatcher hadn't been right. This balding, bulky, cold-eyed middle-aged man was a million miles from the fresh-faced, blond-haired all-American boy of Mickledore Hall. But Dalziel had sat by that boy, and watched that fresh face as he answered Tallantire's questions, and such impressions to an ambitious young detective were as indelible as those of first love to a romantic poet.

Interestingly, he saw the recognition was mutual. And unwelcome. But showing Dalziel he was unwelcome was like shooing a hungry dog with a rib of beef.

"I'll go to the foot of our stairs!" he exclaimed in delight. "Mr. Rampling, isn't it? By gum, what a coincidence. Must be how long? Twenty-seven? Aye. It must be twenty-seven years since we met."

He pumped Rampling's hand and waited with interest for his response.

To do him justice, it was high quality.

"How're you doing, Mr. Dalziel?" he said. "I saw your picture in the paper this morning and thought, I wonder, could that be the same? Lot of water under the bridge, huh? We were both a lot younger then. You over here on business or pleasure?"

"Pleasure mainly, I hope," said Dalziel. "Not *here*, of course. I mean you don't come to these places for pleasure, do you? No, I'm just paying a quick visit here."

He caught a momentary shift of the eyes toward Mrs. Amalfi and in the plate glass door he saw her minute shake of the head. Also through the door he spotted a couple of wedge-shaped men staring at him like Dobermans and remembered that Rampling was a very important person.

"I'm sorry I don't have more time to talk now, Mr. Dalziel," said Rampling. "I'm visiting a sick colleague, then I've got a couple of meetings. But it would be good to talk to you about old times. Tell you what, why don't I give you a ring if I can see my way clear to having a quiet drink with you before I head back to Washington?"

"That'd be grand," said Dalziel with maximum effusion. "I hear you're up for a top job. Congratulations."

"That's kind of you. Good-bye for now, Mr. Dalziel."

He made for the door leading to the clinic's interior. Mrs. Amalfi followed, pausing to glance back at Dalziel who stood at the exit door buttoning up his coat in preparation for the pelting rain. He smiled and waved.

"Bye-bye, Missus. And thanks." Then he went out. Satisfied, she followed Rampling.

Dalziel came back in.

"Sorry," he said to the receptionist. "Something I forgot to say to Scott, to Mr. Rampling. How long will he be staying, do you know?"

He didn't doubt that once the fearsome Mrs. Amalfi had a word with her, he'd be Public Enemy Number One, but for the moment he was banking on being sanitized in her eyes by his evident familiarity with someone like Rampling.

"It shouldn't be too long," said the woman. "Mr. Bellmain's on a fifteen minute visit cycle."

"Bad as that?" said Dalziel. "Poor sod. Get a lot of visits, does he? Family? Friends?"

It was a clumsy try. She said coolly, "Would you like to leave a message for Mr. Rampling?"

"Aye. Tell him he forgot to ask the name of my hotel."

He wrote it down. It was he suspected surplus to requirements. He went out again, passing the two protectors who looked at him with grave suspicion.

"Tums in, chests out, lads," he said. "You never know who's watching."

A cab pulled up and a rather dumpy woman got out, her face well concealed behind dark glasses and a turned-up Cossack collar.

Dalziel was too busy making sure he got into the cab to pay her much heed, but a certain familiarity nagged at him as she walked past the two men with a nod. An old film star perhaps?

He gave the address of Waggs's apartment.

"And drive like I'm a flask of nitroglycerin," he said.

"Hey?" said the man incomprehendingly.

Dalziel looked at the name on the identity card. It had about fifty letters, most of them consonants.

He said, "Please yourself, sunshine."

When he got out at his destination, he felt as happy as a round-the-world sailor to feel solid land beneath his feet. He half expected to find Linda Steele lurking, but if she was, she was making a good job of it. What he did see was Cissy Kohler striding along the pavement, trailing more spray than a water-skier.

He hesitated only a moment before deciding what to do. A crook out on license was still a crook, and a cop off on leave was still a cop. Not even cars driving on the wrong side of the street altered that relationship, though they did remind him he ought to tread a little more lightly than on the sidewalks of Mid-Yorkshire. So he slapped his hand on her shoulder with only enough force to bruise her collarbone, not to break it.

He was surprised that she put up no resistance. Like Rampling, she clearly recognized him but that was no reason. On the contrary, he'd have thought.

Perhaps she knew that Waggs and a couple of Hesperides heavies were waiting in the flat? But there was no sound as they entered and it felt empty.

She turned to face him and he saw her clearly for the first time. Prison had pared her to the bone. His glimpse of her on television hadn't conveyed to him the full extent of the change. It wasn't just a question of three decades of aging, there was simply nothing left of the young woman whose world had come to an end in 1963. Except perhaps for the eyes. They were regarding him now with the same empty blankness, like windows in a derelict house, that he recalled as he'd burst to the surface with the lifeless body of Westropp's daughter in his arms.

There'd been water running down her face then and there was water running there now, dripping from her cheeks and chin onto the expensive carpet.

"Get yourself dried," he said harshly. "I can't abide a wet woman."

"It's a matter of taste," she said enigmatically.

But she headed for the bathroom. He heard the door being locked, then the shower started up. This suited him nicely. He did a quick turn round the living room and found nothing of interest. He pushed open a door. A bedroom. In the wardrobe male clothes only. So she and Waggs weren't kissing cousins. In fact, from the way she'd clutched her Bible at the press conference, he guessed she'd sublimated all that stuff, and any notion of guilt along with it most likely.

Waggs traveled light or was a very careful man. He passed on to the other bedroom. It looked even barer with little that was feminine in sight, but the Bible on the counterpane told him it was Kohler's. Searching was easy because there was next to nothing to search.

He heard the bathroom door open but he didn't move. He had no objection to her finding him in here. In fact it was probably a good thing to establish their relationship from the start. Cop and criminal. Not all the religion in the world was going to change that.

There were footsteps behind him. He didn't turn, waited for her indignant protest, readied himself for his crushing response.

Then it occurred to him that he could still hear the distant shower. No louder, still running.

It hadn't been the bathroom door.

The thought dead-heated with the blow, which was either very expert or very lucky as it caught him at precisely the right point on the stem of his neck to switch off all the juice running between his mind and his muscles. He fell heavily across the bed, still conscious in the way that a man who has drunk a couple of bottles of Scotch might still be conscious. His senses struggled to maintain a limited service. Touch had gone completely; he could feel nothing. Smell, taste, and sight were occupied by the counterpane up against which his nose and mouth were pressed, giving his eyes about an inch of

221

focus which wasn't enough. Hearing was faint and intermittent, like a patrol radio in a dead area.

Two voices. A man's. A woman's.

Hers: . . . what . . . hell . . . you done . . .

His: . . . found . . . here . . . thought . . . burg . . .

Hers: . . . in papers . . . at Hall . . . waiting . . . I . . . to clinic . . .

His: . . . Almighty . . . why . . . told you . . . what . . .

Hers: . . . n't let . . . your name . . . no diff . . . thought . . . said . . .

His: . . . yeah . . . Ciss . . . ruined . . . thing . . . back . . . tell . . . William . . . afternoon . . .

Hers: . . . sure . . . home . . . day . . .

His: . . . sure . . . grab . . . quick . . . way . . . burg . . . wakes . . .

Hers: . . . all right . . . doc . . .

His: . . . fine . . . side . . . barn . . . move . . . of here . . .

Reception was fading. Perhaps all it required was a slight adjustment of aerial direction. He tried to move his head and straightaway went spiraling into a darkness where the only signals were meaningless bleeps from long dead stars and, beyond them, silence.

Twenty-six

"Not a theory; it was a fancy."

Peter Pascoe read the letter for the tenth time.

It was unheaded except for the date, September 3, 1976.

Dear Miss Kohler,

Your letter has reached me, reviving memories of a pain I would rather have forgotten. My first instinct was to ignore completely what you had written, it smacked so much of a mind driven to desperate self-delusion by all those years in prison. But in case silence should be interpreted however insanely as affirmation, I will make this one effort at communication.

Your craziest insinuations I refuse to dignify with a rebuttal, but your suggestion that I must bear some of the responsibility for Emily's death I find so repugnant that I must throw it back at you with scorn. She was in your care and it was because of the failure of that care that she died. Until you are willing to accept fully the burden of your guilt, you will hardly be fit to return to the world at large.

Yet you tell me you are hoping to return in the near future. If this is the decision of the authorities, so be it. I offer no comment except to

223

say I will brook no further attempt to communicate with me. I have recently remarried and have even taken on a new name, so attempts to harass me will be in vain. My lawyer has been instructed to open all letters addressed care of his office and to destroy any from you.

To wish you luck in the future would seem merely ironic. All I will wish is that you may find a way of forgetting the events of that terrible weekend, or at least the strength to desist from trying to force them back into the minds of others.

Yours sincerely,
James Westropp

Someone tapped the window of his car.

He turned his head, saw the uniform, and said, "Oh, shit."

Opening the door he climbed out.

"Excuse me, sir," said the young constable, "but could I see your driving license?"

"Forget that," said Pascoe. "Take a look at this."

He produced his warrant card.

The young man studied it uneasily.

"I'm sorry, sir, but is this official? I mean, should we have been informed?"

"Don't worry," said Pascoe. "You haven't blown a stakeout. I'm in Harrogate on private business, visiting an . . . acquaintance in those flats. She isn't in, so I was waiting. I take it someone rang in to report a strange man loitering with intent?"

"That's right. A Mrs. Wright."

Pascoe looked up, saw the figure watching from a window which he gauged was in the flat next to Miss Marsh's.

"I'm sorry, sir, I'll still have to check this out," said the constable.

"Of course you will. I may have forged it with my Toytown printing kit. Look, so you don't have to hang around while they buzz through to my patch, see if you can get Mr. Dekker to the communications room."

DCI "Duck" Dekker was an old sparring partner. His sarcasms

were infinitely preferable to the risk of alerting Hiller he was back on forbidden territory.

He was in luck.

A short while later a familiar grating voice said, "Detective Chief Inspector Dekker here. What's this all about, Tomkin?"

Pascoe leaned forward to speak into the mike.

"Duck? Peter Pascoe. Constable Tomkin, who has been most courteous and efficient, needs to know I am what I say I am."

"Does he now? Mebbe I need to know what it is you say you're doing afore I say what you are."

"Just visiting, Duck. Private business."

"Oh, aye? Well, I suppose it's better not crapping on your own doorstep, eh?" said Dekker with scant regard for the fact that he was blackening Pascoe's reputation on an open airwave. "You're a sly one but! Tomkin, you there? Let Mr. Pascoe go with a stiff warning as to his future behavior. Out."

Pascoe sighed, looked at the young man's face, saw doubt there, said, "Joke. Look, why don't we go in and reassure Mrs. Wright together?"

And perhaps at the same time get some indication of Mavis Marsh's whereabouts.

Mrs. Wright, a plump, middle-aged, twinset-and-pearls kind of woman was glad to be reassured, but not herself very reassuring.

"Miss Marsh? Oh, she's in. Of course I'm sure. I can hear her radio in my bathroom. She never leaves anything plugged in when she goes out. Terrified of fire, you see."

"When did you last actually see her?" asked Pascoe.

"This morning. Well, heard her actually. I was going out and I heard a man's voice, then Miss Marsh's saying, 'Please come in,' and I looked, and I saw a man stepping into her flat."

"What did he look like?" asked Pascoe.

"Oh, a very respectable kind of man. I mean, not a plumber or meter reader, nothing like that. Tallish, wearing one of those nice short overcoats that army gentlemen used to wear. I only saw him from behind for a second, but he looked rather distinguished."

It could of course simply be that Miss Marsh did not wish to receive any other visitor that day but Pascoe was growing concerned.

He said to Tomkin, "Perhaps you ought to try her."

"Me?"

"It's your patch," reminded Pascoe. "I'm just visiting."

They went together and rang the bell, then rapped on the door. Pascoe called, "Miss Marsh? Miss Marsh? Are you all right?"

Nothing.

He looked at the constable who said, "Mebbe there's a spare key?"

They both looked at Mrs. Wright who had silently followed them.

"I don't have one. Probably the managing agents do," she said doubtfully.

Tomkin reached for his personal radio. Pascoe stayed his hand.

"I think it'd be wise not to delay," he said.

"You reckon? Okay, if you say so, sir."

The youngster took a step back. This time Pascoe interposed his whole body.

"It looks a very solid door," he said.

"And she'll have the security chain on," said Mrs. Wright. "If she's in, she always has it on."

Pascoe turned to the door. Screening his actions from the woman he used his Swiss Army knife to remove a small section of the jamb, then inserted the narrow strip of tapered plastic which Dalziel called his Access card.

When he felt it catch the tongue, he pushed. The door swung open. It wasn't on its chain.

He went across the narrow photo-lined hallway and opened the lounge door. It was the same well-ordered temple of opulence he recalled from his previous visit, and Miss Marsh was sitting in the same deep armchair. The only difference was that this time she was dead.

The lolling head, staring eyes, and sagging mouth were evidence enough but he confirmed it at her wrist. There was no sign of violence. The *Telegraph* she had been reading lay on the floor a few inches below her dangling hand. Beside her chair stood an elegant wine table on which rested a half-empty cup of tea and a plate with a currant scone on it. The radio was tuned to Radio 4.

"Is she dead?"

He turned to see Mrs. Wright in the doorway alongside PC Tomkin.

"Yes. Tomkin, perhaps you'd escort Mrs. Wright back to her flat and ask if you can use her phone. I'd get Mr. Dekker down here if I were you."

He waited till they had gone, then using a handkerchief, he quickly checked the other rooms. Bedroom and bathroom were as tidy as you'd expect in a first-class hotel. Only the kitchen showed signs of occupation. There was a baking tray with two scones still in it on top of the oven and, poignantly, the sweet evocative scent of baking still in the air.

Nowhere could he see any sign of intrusion, struggle, or search.

Tomkin returned.

"Mr. Dekker's on his way," he said. "Sir . . ."

"Yes?"

"This is my first . . ."

Pascoe took pity on him. It wasn't fair having a senior officer of uncertain standing muddying the waters.

"It's your case," he said. "I'm just a witness. Have you checked she's dead?"

"No, sir. I mean, you . . ."

"You'll need to for your report. Wrist and neck. Fine. Resuscitation?"

"Do you think we should try? I mean, she's cold, there's nothing . . ."

"I agree. But you'll need to put down that you thought of it and your reason for not trying. First because it was clearly far too late, and second because you wanted to cause as little disturbance till the scene-of-crime officer got here. Those were your reasons, right?"

"Yes, sir. That's right."

"Then you asked me to make sure no one came in while you escorted Mrs. Wright back to her flat and reported in. Now you're asking me to wait outside with you. I've not noticed you using your notebook. Do it now. When Mr. Dekker starts asking you questions, you'll be amazed at how much you'll instantly forget!"

They went out. Pascoe paused in the hallway. *If you want to see my life, look around you.* But these photos hadn't been the woman's life, only part of it. Had she been content with her comforts or had the crying of her lost child disturbed her dreams? And why the hell had she gone to visit Cissy Kohler?

Ten minutes later Duck Dekker arrived with a scene-of-the-crime team. He was a craggily angular man who had played for Yorkshire seconds in his teens till six consecutive ducks had reconstructed both his career and his name. He ignored Pascoe till he had got his team to work, then with a jerk of his head, he invited him to stroll to the far end of the corridor.

"This going to embarrass you with your missus, Pete?" he asked.

"For God's sake!" said Pascoe indignantly. "You've seen Marsh. She was in her sixties!"

"Aye, well, that'd make it *bloody* embarrassing, wouldn't it?" said Dekker. "So what's the tale?"

Pascoe told him briefly, concluding, "So in a way, you're right, Duck. This *is* going to be embarrassing, but not for the reason you thought."

"I see that, my boy. You're in deep crap. Best hope is you can come up with sixpence."

Half an hour later that seemed a vain hope.

"Sorry," said Dekker. "This mysterious visitor were probably the insurance man. She saw him off, baked some scones, made herself a cuppa, sat down, and snuffed it. Our quack found her quack's number and rang him. Seems she had some kind of heart trouble. So looks like you're guilty of the worst crime in the book, my son. Bad timing."

"Shit," said Pascoe.

"Can't keep you out of it, I'm afraid. I'll need a statement. You're a witness."

"Okay. But I'd better make sure Dan Trimble hears about this from me first."

"Bit of advice," said Dekker. "You'll get more sympathy from the umpire if the bowlers parted your hair."

"Hiller doesn't bowl bouncers. He bowls rotten eggs. Hit or miss, you're in a mess."

But he took the advice and, using Mrs. Wright's phone, he rang Hiller first.

His initial response was coldly professional.

"Anything to suggest foul play?"

"Not yet, sir. But I've got a feeling. The way I see it is . . ."

"I'm as capable of constructing theories as you, Mr. Pascoe," said Hiller, his words soft and cold as snowflakes. "You'll have talked to Mr. Trimble?"

"No, sir. Not yet. I rang you first."

"Ah." The snow melted a little into surprise. "Tell Chief Inspector Dekker I'd appreciate a copy of his report and the postmortem findings at his earliest convenience."

That was it. No rockets, no explosions.

He rang Trimble with a lighter heart and a few moments later was reeling from the full blast of the little Cornishman's anger.

"What I really want to say to you, Mr. Pascoe, I'll say to your face!" he climaxed. "Be in my office at nine-thirty tomorrow morning!"

The phone went down with a crash which probably disconnected it.

He wandered slowly back to Marsh's flat, empty now except for Dekker.

"How'd it go?"

"There's always emigration."

"Well, don't go to America. If Andy Dalziel's over there, Yorkshire will have been blacklisted by now! Come on. As you're a mate, I'll seal this place up like a crime's been committed, but it's odds on natural causes."

"Hold on," said Pascoe. Someone had been through the escritoire and left the drawer ajar. "Why have you removed the albums?"

"Albums?"

"Yes. Last time I was here, there were at least two thick photo albums in that drawer."

"So everything's got to stay the same when you're not around? She could have put them somewhere else or even thrown them out!"

"No. Far too precious. Mind if I look around?"

They weren't anywhere else.

Dekker, impatient, said, "Okay, if someone wanted to steal the albums, it must've been because of the photos, right? Then why not take them pictures in the hall too?"

Pascoe examined the walls.

"Too heavy," he suggested. "You could slip the albums in a brief-case. Also going through the albums would take an age whereas you could check these photos one by one very quickly to see if . . ."

His words tailed off. He approached within six inches of the wall and moved slowly along it.

"Have you ever thought of specs, Pete?" said Dekker.

"I'm looking for . . . here it is! Look, there's a pinhole here where a hook has been removed."

"So there's a pinhole. But there's no space where a picture's been removed, is there?"

"Yes, there is! Look here. The photos on this row have been rearranged to hide the space, but the gaps between these three aren't quite right and, look, you can see a faint mark on the paintwork, there was a slightly longer photo here."

And as he reached this conclusion he remembered what it had been, Miss Marsh and a group of her young gentlemen at Beddington College. The photo she had singled out for his special attention as he left.

He told Dekker who said, "Grasping at straws now, is it?"

"Not straws," said Pascoe, returning to the kitchen. "But scones maybe. Look at that tray. How many scones would you say she baked? From the position of these two and the marks on the tray, I'd say at least six. One on her plate half-eaten. That leaves three to account for."

"So she had a good appetite."

"Maybe. Or maybe she sat down with her visitor, offered him a cup of tea . . . The tea pot! Let's have a look."

Pascoe picked up the pot, removed the lid, fished inside.

"Three tea bags," he said triumphantly. "She made a full pot. And it's almost empty. She gave her visitor tea and scones!"

"So what?"

"So what kind of man when his hostess has a heart attack, reacts by washing up his cup and his plate and sloping off with a briefcase full of photos? What he can't manage, of course, is to put the chain on behind him as Miss Marsh would certainly have done."

Dekker shook his head.

"Pete, I can think of a dozen simple explanations."

"Me too," admitted Pascoe. "All I'm asking is, dig deep on this one. Make sure the pm's a really searching suspicious-circs job, not just a quick natural. For a start, ask 'em to check exactly how many scones she'd had. Tell 'em to count the currants." He crumbled one of the remaining scones in his fingers. "See. Six . . . seven . . . eight . . . I bet she kept a steady average! Will you do that?"

"Why not?" said Dekker. "I've nowt but a couple of thousand better things to do. You'll be off home now to a hot supper? Lucky bugger!"

Pascoe was able to smile, but his investigatory euphoria quickly faded as he drove east. He tried to revive it by stopping off at a nice little country pub he knew for a pint and a steak, but the last time he'd been here had been with Ellie, and he left both his meal and his drink half-finished.

It was still fairly early when he got home. There was no mail, nothing on his answer machine. He didn't give himself time for thought, fearful of where thought might lead him, but washed two sleeping tablets down with a tumblerful of whiskey and went straight to bed.

Twenty-seven

". . . you know there really is so much

too much of you!"

Dalziel awoke.

He had a pain, not in his neck where he'd been struck, but more frighteningly in his chest.

Was this it? The fat man's last farewell?

He began to move cautiously; thought, sod this for a lark, if I've got to go, let's get it over with! and pushed himself violently upright.

The pain vanished. He looked down at the bed and saw the cause. Religion, always a pain in the arse, was also a pain in the chest. He had been lying on top of a Bible.

Now his head began to ache. He looked at his watch. He'd been out for about fifteen minutes. All around were signs of hasty departure.

He went into the living room and was glad to discover they'd moved too quickly to take the booze. A three-inch gargle of bourbon made him sit down rather suddenly, but another inch and a half brought him back to life and his feet.

He found a note pad by the telephone and started scribbling

down everything he could recall of the half-heard conversation. Then he did a thorough search of the flat in case their haste had made them overlook something important.

It hadn't, perhaps because they'd brought so little with them. The only personal relic was Kohler's Bible. He picked it up, opened it, and read the inscription on the fly leaf.

To Cecily. "The Lord shall preserve thee from all evil: he shall preserve thy soul." From your loving mother. Christmas 1951.

The Lord hadn't done such a great job so far, thought Dalziel as he riffled through the pages to make sure there was nothing interleaved. There wasn't. He tossed it back on the bed and made for the door.

And stopped.

He went back to the bed, picked up the Bible again, and opened it at the first chapter of *Genesis*.

He'd been right. There were marks on the page.

At first it was an underlining of whole words *God . . . void . . . darkness . . . face . . . waters . . .* As if in despair the woman had started seeking divine comfort and found instead (it can't have been hard) some crazy cipher through which God sent his special condemnation. But gradually this underlining stopped to be replaced from Chapter Twelve by small dots under individual letters.

Now the Lord had sa̱id unto Abram, Get thee out of the coun-
try, and from thy kindred, and from thy father's house, unto a land
that I w̱ill s̱hew thee: And I̱ w̱ill make of tẖee a gṟeat nation, aṉd I
will blȩss thee, ạṉd make thy name great; and thou shalt be a bless-
ing: And I w̱ill bless ṯheṃ that bless thee, and curse hịm that çur-
seth thee: ạṉd in tẖee shall all faṃilies of the earth be blessed.

I wish I were dead with Mic and Em

She had moved from trying to get a divine message out to putting her own in.

He flicked through the pages. The dots proliferated. By *First*

Samuel they were appearing both under and over letters, and he worked out this meant she was no longer bound by strict sequence, but could move back and forward on the same line which was much more economical. By *Ecclesiastes* there was a system of annotation almost musical and he guessed that this form of writing had become as natural to her as typing to a trained secretary.

It would take some deciphering, but he guessed that here were those memoirs, that journal of her life and thoughts, which the tabloid scavengers would give their best friends' balls to get their hands on. Waggs would probably kick his own if he knew what his panicky haste had made Kohler leave behind. And Kohler herself? How was she going to feel when it dawned on her what had happened?

For the first time in twenty-seven years Dalziel felt almost sorry for the woman.

He heard the apartment door open.

This time he wasn't going to be caught unprepared. He moved silently behind the bedroom door. Footsteps approached cautiously. Paused. Then someone stepped into the room. The second the figure registered on his sight, he moved, launching himself in the kind of tackle which had once turned fleet-footed halfbacks into stretcher cases. Fortunately time had slowed his impetus, and place offered a soft bed for landing on rather than a solid patch of earth. Even so there was no strength for resistance left in the limp body crushed into the mattress beneath his bulk.

Nevertheless he raised his hand threateningly, and at the same time recognized that not only the threat but the tackle itself had been unnecessary.

Beneath him Linda Steele opened her eyes and gasped, "Okay, Dalziel. What the hell are you going to do? Rape me or preach me a sermon?"

And he realized that his upraised hand was clutching Kohler's Bible.

"How the hell did you get in here?" he demanded, slipping the book into his jacket pocket.

"Power of the press. I looked all over for you, finally came back here, and the guy downstairs said someone that sounded like you had gone up with Kohler, then Waggs came back, and not long after the two of them left like they'd conjured up the devil. Talking of whom, I realize now that you're just glad to see me, but could you be glad vertically for a while?"

"Eh? Oh. Sorry."

He pushed himself off the bed. She'd not been altogether wrong, he realized. There had been a certain element of pleasure creeping into their contact and not the sort he'd ever experienced on a rugby field.

Standing upright brought pain to join the pleasure. He put his hand to the back of his head and winced.

"You okay?" said Linda Steele, sharp-eyed.

"I will be. Someone slugged me. Waggs, I think."

"Jee-sus. How bad is it?" she said, touchingly solicitous. "You need a doctor?"

"Nay, lass. I've heard what them buggers charge over here. It's you who can provide all I need."

"What do you have in mind?" she asked uneasily.

He smiled and said, "Just look at the time. It's hours since you bought me breakfast and my belly thinks me throat's been cut!"

Dalziel hadn't made his mind up how much to tell Linda Steele but his instinct advised very little. She was after all not only a woman but a journalist, neither of whose need-to-know ratings occupied much space in Dalziel's scheme of things. A woman's started at how to boil an egg, then got debatable. A journalist's stopped at how to breathe in.

On the other hand, as well as giving him his only lead, she was picking up his expenses, which aroused his curiosity as much as his gratitude. There's no such thing as a free journalist.

Also she was strangely attractive, even dentally speaking. He got a warm glow from the memory of their legs interlocking beneath the breakfast table.

She took him to what she claimed was the best deli in town. They sat side by side, which limited opportunities for patellar interlock but was a great promoter of gluteal frottage.

Interestingly she seemed happy to accept his sketchy account of how he'd spotted Kohler coming out of the apartment house, followed her round town for an hour or so, then accosted her when she was about to reenter.

"So you've no idea where they've bolted? Or why?" she said.

"Wish I had," he said. "Don't bother with the menu, luv, I'll have some of that."

He pointed at a neighbor's overcrowded plate. But when the waitress came, he heard Steele order him a sandwich and scowled at her meanness, till a piled high plate was put before him.

"This is a sandwich?" he asked in amazement.

"Something wrong?" said Linda Steele.

"Nay, lass. This looks like the best thing that's happened to me since I got here!"

"That's hard to believe, Andy," she said. "I'd have thought a well-set-up guy like you would have struck lucky, no problem."

As she spoke she regarded him sultrily and ran her prehensile tongue round the Grand Prix circuit of her lips.

Dalziel regarded her thoughtfully over a sheaf-sized forkful of corned beef. Okay, so he had to admit he fancied her. But that didn't entitle her to jerk him around just because she felt safe in company. Time to get this thing on the table, so to speak.

He forked another bale of beef to his lips and clamped his free hand round her upper thigh.

"You lost something, Andy?" she asked.

"I were just wondering what's for afters?"

"Anything particular you fancy?"

"We could go back to my hotel room and try room service," he said.

He thought that was pretty smooth. In Barnsley it would probably have won an award for smoothness. But this unsophisticated woman threw her head back and howled with laughter.

"That's what they call it in England these days, is it? Well, why not? There must be worse ways of spending a wet afternoon."

Whatever her motive, she gave with unstinting hand and everything else. He was happy to find himself entirely free from jet-sag or whatever they called it. In fact the only trouble was that, as any demolition man knows, if you place a stick of aging gelignite too close to a source of heat, it may explode spontaneously.

"Come on, Dalziel!" she protested. "You got another date or something?"

"Thought that was how it were done over here," he said with an uncharacteristic effort at insouciance. "Sort of American Express."

"Stick to what you know," she advised. "Meantime, I think we'd better take some time out. You got anything to drink?"

They lay together drinking whiskey and talking. She was almost as good as Dave Thatcher in the subtle art of casual interrogation, and he saw no reason not to tell her as much about his quest as he'd told the airport man. But still she probed his mind as her assessing fingers probed his body. Mebbe this was how all American journalists worked. In which case he was lucky he hadn't got those guys who shopped Nixon!

Finally he tired of being quizzed, but he'd found out the hard way not to be rude to a lass who'd got her hand where Linda had hers, so he said, "What about you, luv? You a native New Yorker?"

"Do I sound like I am?" she asked almost indignantly.

"Nay, you all sound alike to me," he said. "There's differences, is there?"

"You're joking? No, you're not joking! Well, let me tell you, I'm from Ohio. I came to the Big Apple about five years back to make my fortune. I'm still working at it."

"Could be your luck's turned today," said Dalziel complacently. "By the by, I've often wondered, what's all this Big Apple stuff? More like Big Anthill from what I've seen so far."

"Careful who you say that to, they're very sensitive, these New Yorkers," warned Linda. "I've heard all kinds of explanations. One I like best is that to you European folk, America was like those legendary islands way out west, you know, where the sun always shone and there were golden apples growing on the trees. New York being the first landfall for most people got the name, Big Apple."

"Oh, aye, I remember summat of that at school. Weren't there some nymphs used to run around naked, guarding the apples?"

237

"That's why you remember, is it?" She laughed. "Yeah, I think you're right. And funny thing, now I come to think of it, you know what those guardian nymphs were called. The Hesperides. That's right. Like Jay Waggs's backers."

"That's all right then. I were worried when I thought they might be a bunch of gangsters, but naked nymphs are right up my street."

"You say so? Well let's see. But none of this American Express this time, Andy. Let's try for a bit of English reserve, huh?"

He took a deep breath, thought of England, the Dunkirk spirit, once more unto the breach, rule Britannia . . .

"Andy, they should use you to pay off the National Debt," said Linda Steele. "Okay if I take a shower?"

"Help yourself," he said.

He lay on the bed and listened to the water running. Then he rose quietly and went through her handbag. There was nothing of any interest except a journalist's card and more spare condoms than a nice girl ought to carry. Condoms made him think of Arthur "Noddy" Stamper. Of William Stamper, crime writer and broad-caster. Of his voice on the *Golden Age of Murder* program . . . *my mother was . . . a Bellmain of Virginia no less* . . . Of the receptionist at the clinic . . . *Mr. Bellmain's on a fifteen minute visit cycle.*

Kohler had gone to a clinic where a patient called Bellmain was being visited by Scott Rampling.

It didn't make much sense. Normally he was a patient man. Everything made sense if you gave it time. Even perhaps life. But time in this mad scrambling place was a much scarcer commodity than it was back in Mid-Yorkshire. There, he had often mocked the boy Pascoe's tendency to go scampering round a case, dropping hypotheses like crap from a dysenteric duck, but he wouldn't have minded that muddying flow here and now. Perhaps he'd ring him later.

Linda Steele came out of the shower, glowing darkly, like charcoal on a barbecue.

Perhaps, thought Dalziel, I'll ring Pascoe much later.

"I left the shower on for you," she said. "If you'd come in to rub my back, think of the water we'd have saved."

"Nay, lass. Likely we'd have been in there yet," he said reaching out. She slipped out of his grasp like a Welsh fly half, got behind him, and pushed him showerward.

"I gotta run," she said. "You've fucked up my schedule."

"That's what I'm here for," he said. But he didn't resist too much. It would have been demeaning to find his eyes were greedier than his belly and besides, when you weren't sure what people wanted, best thing was to let 'em have their own way.

He got into the shower, started caroling one of the rugby songs of his muddy youth, and after a while he lowered the volume and moved back to the door which was slightly ajar.

Through the crack he saw Linda Steele bending over his suit-case. She was still naked and the view convinced him he needn't have worried about his appetite. Now she closed the case and picked up his jacket from the scatter of clothes about the floor. Christ, the Bible, and the notes on Waggs's and Kohler's half-heard conversation were still in his pocket! He turned his head away and called, "Hey, luv. Pour us a drink, will you? I hate being wet out and dry in."

"Okay," she called. She still gave herself time for a quick shufti through his wallet, but she dropped everything pretty quick when he turned off the shower, and she had her pants on and a glass in her hand as he emerged swathed in a towel.

"Service is lousy here," he said.

"See the management," she said.

That depends who they are, he thought as he sipped and watched her finish dressing.

He said, "Where do we go from here?"

"I'm all for long engagements," she said. "Or are you talking about Kohler? You're the cop."

"Not here," he said. "Like I said before, I just came over on impulse. I don't know what I'd have done with her even if Waggs hadn't thumped me."

He took a long pull at his bourbon and watched her through the bottom of his glass. She ought to have been looking disappointed at the revelation that he was just another dumb cop with no ideas outside his nightstick. She was merely looking thoughtful.

She was also looking at her watch.

"Shit. Andy, I gotta run. Listen, why don't we both poke around some more? I'll see if I can get some kind of trace on Kohler through my contacts. She may still be in the city. We'll meet tomorrow and cross-check, okay?"

"Fine. Where? When?"

"There's a bar next to the deli where we ate. Stroke of noon. Last there pays. See you."

After she'd gone he opened the wardrobe door and studied himself in the full-length mirror inside.

"What makes you so fucking irresistible?" he asked.

The mirror didn't reply. Or perhaps it did.

As he got dressed he studied his notes on the half-heard conversation. Filling in the blanks was easy enough to start with, but became problematical halfway through.

KOHLER: *Jay, what the hell have you done?*

WAGGS: *I found him poking around in here. I thought he was a burglar.*

KOHLER: *It's that cop who was in the papers. He was at the Hall that weekend. He was waiting for me when I got back. I went to the clinic.*

WAGGS: *Christ Almighty! Why did you do that? I told you not to. What happened?*

KOHLER: *They wouldn't let me in. I gave your name. It made no difference. I thought you said . . .*

WAGGS: *Yeah yeah. Listen, Ciss, you could've ruined everything. I came back to tell you I'm seeing William in town this afternoon.*

KOHLER: *You're sure he'll be at home today?*

WAGGS: *Sure I'm sure. Grab some stuff quick. I want to be away when this burglar awakes.*

KOHLER: *Will he be all right? Shouldn't we call a doc?*

WAGGS: *He'll be fine. He's built like the side of a stone barn. So move it. Let's get out of here!*

He didn't like the middle much. Who the hell was William? The only William he'd come across in the case so far was Stamper and what would he be doing over here? Unless he'd come to see his mother . . . or this mysterious male Bellmain who was terminally ill in the Allerdale Clinic. *A Bellmain of Virginia*. Where the hell was Virginia anyway? For all he knew, New York was in Virginia. He should've paid more attention in Geography instead of letting himself be distracted by little Lettie Lovegrove whose thirteen-year-old tits stuck out like a pair of rugby balls under her sweater.

He'd noticed a travel desk in the hotel foyer. They ought to know.

He went down. A young woman with sinus block smiled gamely through her pain and said reedily, "Can I help you, sir?"

"Mebbe. Where's Virginia?"

"You mean generally? Here, let me show you." She produced a map. "This is New York. And down here's Virginia."

His heart sank. There looked a lot of it and by British standards it looked a long way away.

"Well-populated, is it?" he asked, thinking that maybe it was mainly desert or something and the first village post office you went into, they'd point you to the Bellmain residence straightaway.

"All the space you'd want, sir, but with plenty of big cities too. Is it business or holiday you're thinking of?"

"If there's that much of it, it's academic," he said.

"Academic? In that case what you're probably interested in is historic Virginia. There's so much to see. Mount Vernon, Fredericksburg, Jamestown, Williamsburg, Appomattox . . ."

"Hold on," said Dalziel. "That last but one, Williamsburg, was it? There's a place called Williamsburg down there?"

"Yes, sir. Very famous, it's where . . ."

"Aye, aye," he said impatiently. "I had a friend, name of Bellmain. Marilou Bellmain. I think she came from Williamsburg. House called Golden Grove. How could I set about finding if she were still down there?"

The woman said, "One moment," turned to a phone behind her, dialed, and began a murmured conversation.

Dalziel took his notes out of his pocket and studied them.

The woman wrote something down on a pad, said, "Thanks a lot," turned back to him, and pushed the pad toward him.

"Would this be your friend, sir? It's a very good address, if you're thinking of paying a visit. Right in the historic area. We'd be happy to make all your travel arrangements . . ."

Dalziel wasn't listening. He was hearing different words.

Cissy, you could've ruined everything. I came back to tell you they're moving him to Williamsburg this afternoon.

You're sure? He's going home today?

Sure I'm sure. Grab some stuff quick. I want to be halfway to Williamsburg when this guy wakes.

"Sir, sir," said the woman, a note of impatience at last creeping into her voice. "Would you like our assistance or not?"

"Of course I would, missus," said Dalziel in an injured tone. "What else do you think I'm here for?"

Twenty-eight

"All here is so unprecedented, so

changed, so sudden and unfair, that

I am absolutely lost."

Pascoe awoke.

There was sunlight across the bed and for a moment, as he opened to its touch like the lesser celandine, he felt as he'd felt in childhood when sleep swept away all yesterday's woes and each new morning's prospect was bright and serene.

Then he saw the clock and flower turned to flesh.

It was five to nine and he was due in Trimble's office at 9:30.

He walked through a cold shower and shivered into his clothes in two minutes flat. He noticed there were a couple of messages on his answering machine, recorded while he lay senseless under his pall of pills and booze. He listened to them as he drank coffee and ate a crust of dry bread dunked in the marmalade jar.

The first was from Ellie, timed at a quarter to ten the previous night.

"Hi, where are you? Walking the mean streets protecting us all?

Or out on the bash with the other top guns? Sorry. I know you'd ring if you could. Anyway, Rose is fine and I'm fine and Mum is . . . well, I think it's worse than I imagined, only, after what she went through with Dad, she doesn't want to know, so she hides it from herself by hiding it from me. I noticed she was going to bed later and later, and when I nagged her into talking about it, it came out that often when she wakes up in the morning, she doesn't know where she is or even who she is, and that's making her scared to go to sleep. I tried talking to that adolescent doctor again but all I got was a shrug of her skinny shoulders, so in the end I went along to the hospital and asked to see the geriatric consultant. Christ, you'd have thought I was an Irishman trying to deliver a package to the Home Secretary, they got so defensive! In the end I lost all patience . . . Okay, I mean I started shouting at them! Well, there was this bloody staff nurse . . . for God's sake, I've stood on picket lines to get them more pay! I'm sorry. You're probably getting the message that diplomacy failed. So here's what I've decided to do. I'm booking Mum in for a full-scale check at the Lincolnshire Independent Hospital. Yes, that's right, I'm going private, and you know what I feel about that, but I've got to be sure everything that can be done is getting done. She was surprisingly easy to persuade once she heard the magic word *Private*. First time I've ever been pleased about her middle-class conditioning! In a way I'm glad you're not in, Peter. It means you'll have time to practice a completely neutral tone of voice because I swear that if I get even the ghost of a whiff of ho-ho-ho-I-told-you-so from you . . . Anyway, I know that all I'm probably doing is postponing the admission that she's irreversibly on the same route as Dad, but I've got to try. All my principles for a moment of time, eh? Peter, ring me. And ignore what I said about the ho-ho-ho. I could do with a good laugh with you, even if it's on me. Bye."

Shit shit shit! He looked at his watch. He was going to need St. Christopher on his side already. No time for the second message even if it were the voice of God . . . Oh, Christ, it was! He paused in the doorway and listened.

"Where're you at, you dirty stop-out? Listen, I'm off to a place called Williamsburg in Virginia tomorrow. I'll be staying at The Plantation Hotel, don't know the number but you can easy find it. Give us a ring and let's know what's going off. If you see Dan Trimble give him a big wet kiss from me. And if you see Adolf, try a quick goose step up his backside. Cheers!"

He switched off and went out of the house at a run.

St. Christopher and the green god of traffic lights conspired to get him into Trimble's office only eight minutes late, but in any case the chief was sitting behind his desk with the defeated look of a man to whom time and space had come to mean very little.

In front of him on his desk was a tabloid newspaper.

"Sorry, sir, but the traffic was jammed solid," lied Pascoe ungratefully.

"What? Oh, yes. We'll need to . . ." He took a deep breath, then said, "What the hell do I care about traffic? My daughter's been on a trip to the States, Mr. Pascoe. She got back home last night. She brought me a liter of very old cognac which didn't get much older, as she also brought me this."

He turned the tabloid round and pushed it across the desk. Pascoe saw the headline CROCODILE DALZIEL. Uninvited, he sat down to read the rest. It didn't take long. It was the kind of paper which assumed in its readers the attention span of a lively four-year-old.

"Is it really that bad, sir?" he said in the bright tone of a ship's surgeon asking Lord Nelson what a man with only one arm wanted with two eyes anyway. "If anything, it reflects rather well on Mid-Yorkshire."

Trimble said, "If you work it out, you'll see this has all taken place in his first twelve hours on American soil. What will he do in a week?"

"End organized crime by the sound of it," said Pascoe. "They may want to keep him."

Trimble smiled wistfully, then composed his face to an official coldness as he said, "You may be wondering why I'm not ordering your instant reduction to the ranks. The first reason is that my daughter's thoughtful gesture has reminded me that you are still the lesser of two evils. The second is that Mr. Hiller seems to feel that he may not have made it as clear as he should have done that he did not require your assistance. This I find puzzling, having heard him in my presence address you on the subject in terms so pellucid that a backward sports commentator could have understood him. But it does give me an excuse, if not a reason, for letting you yet again off the hook."

"I'm sorry," said Pascoe.

"No, you're not. Not yet. But you will be if you disobey instructions once more. *My* instructions, whose clarity is not in doubt. You will not make contact, in person, by phone, by proxy, or by any other means, with anyone connected with Mr. Hiller's inquiry. If any such person should contact you, you will immediately refer them to Mr. Hiller. Do I make myself clear?"

"Yes," said Pascoe. "And no."

"I'm sorry?"

"Yes, you make yourself clear, sir," said Pascoe. "But no, I can't undertake to follow these instructions."

Trimble passed a hand over his face.

"Did I really hear you say that?" he asked wonderingly.

"What I mean is, I need reassurances. When all this started, I admit I was out of line. Because of loyalty—misplaced loyalty you might say—to Mr. Dalziel, I bent the rules. I was probably wrong, I was certainly professionally wrong because I didn't have any good professional reasons. But now it's different. To put it starkly, I think there's a chance that Mavis Marsh's death was arranged because of her connection with the Mickledore Hall affair. Before I can agree to follow instructions to stay away from the case, I need to feel sure that it's going to be properly investigated. If you can give me that assurance, sir, and the same assurance about all aspects of this business, and that all relevant findings will be published, then fine, I'll get back to bringing CID records up to date, and very glad about it too."

"Oh, dear," said Trimble, looking down at the American tabloid. "I may have got you and Andy Dalziel in the wrong order after all. Let me, without prejudice to my right to throw you out of here and suspend you without pay, make a couple of points. One is, Marsh's death *is* being treated as suspicious by our colleagues in West Yorkshire, mainly I gather at your instigation. The other is that I, as a man as well as a policeman, resent your implication that I would let myself or anyone under my command be diverted from the strictest observation of proper legal procedures."

Pascoe felt reproved but unrepentant. No point in changing your mind once you'd dived off the high board.

"I'm sorry, sir. I didn't mean to imply you would. But I do wonder, just how much is Mr. Hiller under your command?"

For a moment he thought he'd gone too far but after a long silence Trimble said mildly, "That you must judge for yourself. In fact, in the whole of this business, judging for yourself might not be such a bad thing." There was a knock at the door. "That will be him now. Come in!"

Hiller entered. He seemed to have shrunk even farther into his suit. Adolf after a week in the bunker, thought Pascoe unkindly, then recalled a little guiltily that in this business at least, Hiller had not yet given him cause for unkindness.

Trimble said, "I've just been talking to Mr. Pascoe about his involvement in the Marsh case. Do we know any more yet?"

Hiller sat down heavily and said, "DCI Dekker rang me ten minutes ago. He'd got the pathologist's report."

"And what's the verdict?" prompted Trimble.

"Indeterminate. She suffered from arrhythmia, some kind of fibrillation, that's when the heart beats too fast, and she was taking a digitalis-derived drug. An overdose of this, or even a build-up through taking prescribed doses, can evidently lead to heart block. That means the heart rate drops too low to feed the required amount of blood to the brain, inducing dizziness and fainting. Sometimes the heart stops altogether for a few seconds. Sometimes, without outside aid, it won't start again. And, of course, during such an attack it would not be difficult to make sure it didn't start again."

"Are you saying this is what happened?" demanded Trimble.

"I'm saying that evidently it could have happened," said Hiller irritatedly. "There is no evidence either way. Unless we take as evidence the fact that the pathologist found only five currants in her stomach?"

"I'm sorry?" said Trimble.

"I gather Mr. Pascoe can explain."

Pascoe explained. He kept on explaining. He wasn't yet sure how they were going to react, but at least he would know that they knew everything there was to know. He laid out the facts without comment until Trimble, with the reluctance of a hypochondriac asking his doctor to tell him the worst, said, "And what is your interpretation of these facts?"

"When Marsh went to see Kohler in June 1976 she told her something that made her want to get out. Thereafter she applied for parole and began to accept Daphne Bush's overtures of friendship because she needed a private channel to the outside world. Bush became her letter box. I don't know if she wrote to anyone else but she certainly wrote to James Westropp. And in that letter she accused him of being the real killer of his wife. When Bush brought Westropp's reply to her cell, the two women fell out—it may have been because of the letter, there may have been some other reason —they had a fight, and Daphne Bush got killed."

"Hold on," said Hiller. "I've read all the evidence. There was nothing about a letter being found in the cell."

"I think Mrs. Friedman removed it, along with anything else that might have suggested there was anything going on between Bush and Kohler. Partly to protect a colleague's reputation, partly because in her eyes there's no such thing as mitigating circumstance when a con kills a screw."

"She admitted this?"

"She admitted nothing. She's a very careful lady. How much she really knows, I wouldn't like to say. Not all that much is my bet. I think she got really pissed off when her chum started going gooey-eyed over Kohler and they had a row. It wasn't just a general principle that made her keep her mouth shut when Kohler was on trial, it was a particular hatred. She was delighted to do her bit to see that Kohler got another life sentence."

"But why would Miss Marsh go to see Kohler in the first place?" asked Trimble. "Were they friends? Or was it just some purely altruistic motive?"

"I doubt it," said Pascoe. "She struck me as a lady with a keen eye for the main chance."

"What makes you say that?" said Hiller.

"Just look at her! Living at her ease in that posh flat by dint of putting the squeeze on Partridge because he'd fathered a child on her!" exclaimed Pascoe. "I've just told you all about that."

"Yes, you did," said Hiller. "It's been puzzling me. You say the source of your information is some old Welshman who lives on an estate village?"

"That's right."

"Put not your trust in Welshmen, Mr. Pascoe," said Hiller almost facetiously. "One other thing Mr. Dekker told me the pathologist said. Miss Marsh was not a virgin, certainly. But equally certainly, she'd never had a child."

Pascoe was taken aback, and before he could recover, Trimble pressed home, "Perhaps Marsh went to see Kohler to talk about the blood evidence. Perhaps she offered at that time to give testimony and that's what sparked Kohler's interest in getting out."

"Why wait so long?" demanded Pascoe.

"Perhaps it had been nagging her conscience for years but she'd persuaded herself it made no real difference. Then the coincidence of her being at Beddington College while Kohler was five miles away in Beddington Jail brought it to the surface. But when Kohler killed Bush, that just confirmed to her that she'd been rightly condemned in the first place."

It made some sense, certainly more than his own theories.

Trimble concluded, "When the basis of your conclusions proves wrong, change your conclusions. Basic rule of detection, Mr. Pascoe."

In his head Pascoe heard another voice, "When you're sure of where you're at, lad, who gives a fuck if you started from the wrong place?"

Hiller was standing up. Trimble said in a nonauthoritarian voice, "Do you want a chat, Geoff?"

Looking gray and weary, the DCC shook his head. "I think it better not. In the circumstances. Mr. Pascoe, thank you."

He left.

Trimble said, "Well, Peter, it looks like the same angel that's covered Andy Dalziel's tracks all these years has taken you under his wing. But be warned. There are people out there ready and able to blast angels out of the sky if they feel the need."

It was an odd thing to say. But Pascoe wasn't really listening.

He was looking at the door which had just closed behind Hiller and wondering why he had the sense of having just witnessed a man destroying his own career.

Twenty-nine

"One, two, three, four, five, six, seven,

eight, nine, ten, eleven, twelve. Hush!"

Dalziel liked trains, especially he liked trains when the alternative was driving on the wrong side of a road more crowded with maniacs than the corridors of Bedlam. The girl on the travel desk had tried to persuade him that New York was unique and if he let her rent him a car at very reasonable rates, he'd find things much different on the turnpike. But Dalziel cocked an ear to Seventh Avenue in full throat outside and said, "I'd rather sup lager and lime."

She booked him a seat on something called the Colonial and a room at a hotel called the Plantation, all of which sounded too folksy for comfort. Nor was he much impressed by her assurance that the hotel was on the edge of this "historic area" she was so reverential about. But he comforted himself with the thought that over here "historic" probably meant something built before the Korean war.

He left a note for Linda at the desk, explaining where he'd gone. He reckoned she'd come round breathing fire when he stood her up at lunch time, and a bit of checkbook journalism would soon loosen

251

the travel girl's tongue, so he might as well tell the truth and keep himself qualified (he hoped) both for her favors and his expenses.

Once he'd made up his mind to head south, professional courtesy took him along to the police in case they needed him in connection with the man he'd caught in his hotel room.

It was like walking into a TV series. He found himself sitting in a room as crowded as the Black Bull on a Saturday night with a detective who managed to look harassed and laid-back at the same time. After checking through some papers the man said, "That's okay. You won't be needed."

"Now? Or ever?" wondered Dalziel.

"Or ever," said the man laconically.

"You don't bother with witnesses at your trials then?" said Dalziel with real interest in this highly desirable state of affairs.

"Shit, the trial's done. He went into night court, a year suspended. He's long gone."

"Attempted robbery? A year suspended? Good job he had a gun else you'd likely have had to pay him pocket money," said Dalziel incredulously.

"His lawyer did a deal. He said he walked into your room by accident and panicked. He had a license for the gun and no record. Listen, Mr. Dalziel, with the lawyer this guy's got, think yourself lucky he's not suing you for felonious assault!"

"This brief, I mean lawyer. Did the court have to appoint him?"

"No. He came running. Rich family probably. We're deep into democracy over here. Can't tell a punk by his clothes anymore."

Dalziel left, deeply dissatisfied. If he'd known the bugger were going to walk free, he'd have hit him harder. Perhaps things would be more normal once he got out of New York.

At Penn Station, though pleased by the absence of horses, he was rather disappointed to find that the Colonial belied its name and looked nothing like the huge locomotives he recalled from childhood Westerns. But Hollywood reasserted itself when a portly black conductor appeared in the doorway above him and said with the easy freemasonry of girth, "Now let me help you there, Mr. Mostel. Am I glad to see you! They told me you were dead."

Dalziel, confused by the assonance, was slow to catch on.

"What's your problem, sunshine?" he asked.

"Well, pardon me, you mean you ain't Zero Mostel?" said the man with affected embarrassment. "I'm so sorry. Let me show you to your seat, sir. Better still, let me show you to two seats."

"You cheeky bugger," said Dalziel. "Move over before we get wedged."

He'd just got himself comfortable when there was a tapping at the window. He looked up to see Dave Thatcher gesturing him urgently toward the door. Sighing he rose and returned to the platform.

"How do, Dave?" he said, coldly. "Didn't think I'd see you again."

"I couldn't talk on the phone," said Thatcher. "I called your hotel this morning and they said you were catching the Colonial. Listen, you said something about a woman called Linda. Tell me about her."

Dalziel, who'd been speculating that Thatcher might be here in the role of jealous boyfriend having got a whiff of the previous afternoon's bonking, was taken by surprise.

"Linda Steele. Black lass, journalist. Says you put her on to me."

"Why should I do that?"

"Pay a favor. Get yourself on her short list. She's a fancy lass."

"You mean you fancy her?" Thatcher smiled. "You want to watch yourself, Andy. I've never heard of her. And I don't sic journalists on cops I owe favors to."

"She gave me Waggs's address in New York. Kohler was with him."

"She did?" Thatcher took some sheets of paper out of his inside pocket and studied them. "That clinches it. I thought she might just be some free-lance on the make, but if she's got info like that, she's on the inside track."

"Dave," said Dalziel patiently. "I've got a train to catch. How about telling me what's going off here?"

"Okay. Listen. After you left the airport, I made a couple of calls. I felt I owed you, so I chucked the names Waggs and Kohler at a few people. I've got good contacts. Couple of hours later this guy strolls into my office. I know him vaguely but not half as well as he seems to know me, not a quarter so well as he wants to know you."

"Me? He wasn't one of your contacts then?"

"No, he wasn't. I couldn't see any way your little problem could involve national security."

"Ah," said Dalziel. "I've got you. A funny bugger."

"I'm sorry?"

"We've got 'em too. Funny buggers, I call the lot on 'em. So what's his sport?"

"These guys don't advertise job descriptions. But ultimately, and this may just be a coincidence, his boss could be Scott Rampling."

"Stuff me," said Dalziel. "So what'd he want to know about me?"

"Everything I could tell him. Which, before you ask, is exactly what I told him. I could see no reason not to."

"Oh, aye? So what's this? A follow-up visit?"

"Yeah. Real subtle, ain't I? In fact, he suggested if you got in touch again, I should be nice to you and see if I could get a line on what you were doing. Which, as well as being surrounded by ears I wasn't sure of, was another reason I choked you off when you rang."

"So what *are* you doing here, Dave?" wondered Dalziel.

"Putting the record straight. I don't like being jerked about by these what-did-you-call-em? funny buggers. Especially I don't like the idea of people latching on to you under pretense of being friends of mine. This woman, apart from giving you Waggs's address, what else has she done for you?"

Dalziel scratched his groin reminiscently.

"Oh, odd things," he said. "She had a good poke around my room, that's for sure."

"That seems to be the in-game. Wasn't there something in the papers about you catching a hotel thief?" said Thatcher.

"Aye. So what . . . hell's bells, you don't reckon he was one of 'em too? Mebbe that would explain . . ."

"What?"

254

"They slapped his wrist, told him to be a good boy in future, and let him go."

Behind him doors were slamming. The conductor leaned out and said, "You coming or not, Mr. Mostel?"

Dalziel climbed aboard. It would have been good to spend more time talking to Thatcher but he had the feeling that the important place to be was Williamsburg.

"Mr. Mostel?" said Thatcher.

"A joke. This country of yours is full of jokers."

"Maybe. But jokes can turn nasty. You take care, Andy. Men like Rampling have got long arms and sharp teeth."

"I'd best buy some bananas then," said Dalziel.

The train was moving. Thatcher walked alongside it.

"You might as well have this," he said, passing his sheets of paper through the window. "It's all on Waggs. Kohler's a blank, completely off the record."

"Thanks," said Dalziel. "You've not asked what I'm doing on this train."

"What I don't know, I can't be accused of withholding." Thatcher smiled. "Ring me if you need an interpreter. Bye!"

As the train picked up speed, Dalziel returned thoughtfully to his seat. He had an unfamiliar sense of things getting out of control. He'd laughed off Thatcher's warning, but now, slipping ever deeper into this strange, huge country, it felt less like a laughing matter. Back home in Yorkshire, bearding lions in their dens was run-of-the-mill work for an old white hunter. But here, though he might be worth a headline as Crocodile Dalziel, basically he was nowt more than a fat old tourist with a million quids' worth of medical insurance which a good kicking would probably absorb in a long weekend.

"Ticket, sir," boomed a voice in his ear.

"What? Sorry, I were miles away."

"That's what you're paying for," said the conductor as he examined the ticket. "You'll need to keep your strength up. Buffet's three cars down."

"I hope the grub's better than the jokes," said Dalziel rising.

It was. He got himself a couple of monumental sandwiches and a matching bourbon. It wasn't the Caledonian cream, of course, but it certainly made your teeth tingle.

Then, the inner man refreshed, he turned his attention to the papers Thatcher had given him.

A quick examination revealed that what he had here was the life and hard times of Jay Waggs as told to a computer. Or rather, a whole family of computers. Some chum of Thatcher's must have accessed all the data storage systems by which the modern pilgrim's progress is charted. Tax, health, education, credit rating, the law, God knows what else. At a glance the picture seemed complete, but a second glance revealed what Thatcher must have spotted on the platform, that none of these mighty memory banks had recorded Waggs's last known address. It had taken Miss Linda Steele to put him on that trail, presumably at the instigation of Scott Rampling.

He shelved speculation as to Rampling's motives and concentrated on Waggs's life. First thing that caught his attention was that the man used two names, but not necessarily for criminal purposes. Born 1957, christened John, the only son of Mr. and Mrs. Paul Petersen of New York City, he had been orphaned when six and brought up thereafter by his aunt, Mrs. Tess Heffernan.

Mrs. Heffernan got divorced two years later (cause and effect? wondered Dalziel) and in 1966 married John Waggs of Ann Arbor, Michigan. The couple formally adopted the boy, changing his surname to Waggs, and it was presumably now that he also became Jay to differentiate him from his adoptive father. His recorded life now ran smoothly till he got to college age. He enrolled in a business studies course under his former name of Petersen, switched after a short time to a filmmaking course, stayed with that rather longer, then completed his formal education with a spell at drama school. Armed with this variety of experience but without any formal qualifications, he now launched himself on the entertainment industry, ready to be anything in the expectation of being rich, wheeling and dealing and picking up flotsam and jetsam along the foreshore of illegality, and only occasionally getting his feet wet.

All this Dalziel was able to decode, not because he knew much about the media world, but because he was long acquainted with the life patterns of those who exist on the shadowy edges of things. A good pointer was the degree to which Waggs clearly found it useful to have some legal entitlement to two names. He moved between them with great facility though generally favoring Petersen till about three years earlier.

His bank balance was low, though his credit rating was okay. He'd had an appendectomy, some expensive dental work (what was it with these people and their teeth?), wasn't HIV positive, was a registered Democrat, had one conviction for attempted fraud (selling an option he didn't own—fine and suspended sentence), several outstanding traffic violations, and a security rating which seemed incredibly low for a man who hadn't actually tried to booby-trap the President's private bog. He was unmarried.

So what did it all add up to? Not a lot, thought Dalziel gloomily.

Sodding useless things computers! The only vague glimmer of light was that security rating, and not all glimmers were equally welcome, as the condemned man said just before dawn.

He shoved the paper in his pocket and took out instead Kohler's Bible. He'd looked at it the previous night but it was slow tedious work following this trail of minute dots, especially when all you got out of it was the introspective ramblings of a woman at the edge of reason. If she had tucked any amazing confessions away in here, it was going to need a steady analytical mind to mine them out. Someone like Wield. He had the patience. Or mebbe the boy Pascoe. He could probably get a computer to do it. But as for himself . . . he groaned as he checked the size of the task ahead.

"Lordy, lordy, you *are* full of surprises!" It was the conductor again. "That's a good book you've got there. A really good book."

"Oh, aye? I suppose you've read it from cover to cover?" growled Dalziel.

"On my mammy's knee. But don't you worry. I won't spoil it for you by telling how it comes out."

"Thanks," said Dalziel. "Hold on, sunshine, before you run off, you know so much about the Bible, what's your favorite bit?"

"Now there's a question. Now let me see. Psalms, I love the

psalms. One three seven, that's my favorite. By the waters of Babylon, there we sat down, yea, we wept, when we remembered Zion."

"Thanks," said Dalziel, riffling through the pages till he reached
the psalms. The dots were crowding thick here as Kohler refined her
system and it was easy to get lost, but he persevered and after a while
a smile spread across his face. When systems fail, ride your luck.
When women stop weeping, they start giving you their life story.

"Thanks a lot," said Dalziel.

Shaking his head at these Anglo-Saxon oddities, the conductor
went on his way, leaving the smiling man to his task. But the smile
did not last long.

> *Midnight I heard the youngest Partridge child cry. I looked in then
> went to tell Marsh. She wasn't in her room. I thought I heard a
> noise from the next door where Tommy was sleeping. Like a cry or
> gasp of pain. Opened door quietly and looked in. Saw but at first
> could not believe. Boy naked on bed, kneeling astride him naked
> woman, his cock in her mouth. She saw me, got off, came to me,
> spoke. Didn't recognize her till then. It was Marsh. Smiling, her
> mouth wet. I hit her. Blood from her nose spurted over my hand.
> Ran from room back to my room, washed hands.*

" 'Jesus wept,' " murmured Dalziel. Tommy Partridge, now the
Right Honorable Thomas Partridge, MP, Minister of State in the
Home Office, then the twelve-year-old son and heir of Thomas Partridge Senior, MP, Minister of State in the War Office. Had Kohler
told her story then to anyone? Certainly not to Tallantire. Wally was
a bastard when it came to harming kids. Little Emily Westropp's
death had removed any sympathy he might have had for Kohler. But
if she'd told him about Marsh, he'd have jumped on the scots nanny
from such a height, she'd have made a new tartan.

He read haltingly on.

> *I sat on my bed in a daze, I don't know how long. It was the
> stable clock starting to strike midnight that roused me. Had to talk
> to someone. Ran down side stairs to guest floor. Don't know why but*

it seemed important I got there while chimes still sounding. Turned corner by gun room as last stroke rang out. The door opened and Mick appeared. Looked terrible, clothes disarrayed, face shocked till he saw it was me. Thank God it's you, he said, something awful's happened. I tried to push by and he held me, but I could see her, Pam, covered with blood.

Someone took the seat next to him. He looked up in surprise and irritation. There was plenty of room in the carriage without squeezing alongside the broadest bum in transit. But his irritation turned to surprise and suspicion when he recognized the man next to him. Well-groomed now and smartly dressed in a gray business suit, he was still unmistakably the young hotel mugger who'd slipped so easily out of police custody.

Before he could speak, a hand tapped his shoulder and a familiar voice said, "Hi, Andy. Running out on me, huh?"

He twisted round to see Linda Steele leaning over the seat behind him. At the same time he felt the Bible pulled from beneath his fingers and the young mugger was on his feet and moving swiftly away down the aisle. As Dalziel rose to give chase, Linda Steele slipped into the vacated seat and barred his passage with her lissome body.

"Why bother?" she asked. "It's not worth it, believe me."

He watched the gray suit vanish into the next coach, shrugged, and subsided. It was, in any case, picky work, translating those dots, and he didn't much like what he'd been reading either.

"Next time I get yon bugger within reach, I'll break bones first and ask questions after," he said, subsiding. "So you're a funny bugger too. Never slept with one of them before, not as I know of. If you were taking pictures, will you send me a set of prints?"

She laughed joyously, then became serious and said, "Andy, I don't sleep around with anyone. It's not in my job description. I really took a shine to you."

"Don't worry about bruising my ego, luv," he said. "Nowt wrong with mixing business and pleasure. I doubt if there's been a fuck since the world began that hasn't been paid for eventually, one way or another."

She studied his face so closely he felt her warm breath.

"I have hurt you, haven't I?"

"I can thole a lot of that kind of pain," he said. "If anything, I'm relieved I can't be accused of bedding a reporter. That'd really knacker my reputation back home."

"I'm sorry to disappoint you, Andy, but I really am a journalist. I just happen to be working for the government too."

"Oh, it's the government, is it? They're the buggers who're sending people to rob me? Threaten me? Search my luggage? I thought that was why folk came to America, so's they could get away from places where officials robbed and threatened them?"

"I don't follow. Who's threatened you?"

"Your young mate back there, he was the guy who came into my room with a gun, or didn't you know that?"

"No. Truly. He's just a guy I was told to work with."

She looked genuinely perturbed but Dalziel reminded himself that they probably wouldn't be talking like this if she hadn't spotted him with Dave Thatcher on the platform and guessed her cover was blown.

"So what are you doing, luv? Just following orders?" he said.

"That's right. But don't worry, Andy. If anyone starts telling me to push people into a gas chamber, I'll tell them to take a hike."

"Glad to hear it. And next time you're in England and someone robs you in broad daylight on a train, you be sure to give me a ring. Better still, call round in person and we'll continue this full frank and fearless discussion over a hot mattress mebbe."

She said very seriously, "I'll remember that, Andy. Believe me, I'm new to this kind of work and there are a lot of things about it I question."

"Glad to hear it," he said again. "And here's another question you might like to bend your mind to. Where exactly do I send my expenses claim to?"

For a second she looked blank, then she laughed again, joyously, toothily. "I really do love you, Andy. You take care of yourself, hear?"

Still laughing, she flowed away down the aisle.

Dalziel watched her go. Funny thing about these Yanks, he thought. They took you serious when you were joking and they fell about laughing when you were dead serious.

Sighing at the problems of foreign travel, he made his way to the buffet.

The rest of the journey passed swiftly, punctuated by large sandwiches, and long drinks. They passed through Washington and he thought he glimpsed the mugger on the platform. He also thought he glimpsed the Capitol but it might just have been someone's summerhouse.

From time to time, he thought about the passage he'd translated from Kohler's memoirs. He tried to make sense of it but didn't like some of the sense he was making. Marsh ending up being kept in comfort by the man whose son she had abused . . . well, he could fit that into the scheme of things easy enough. But Kohler running into Mickledore by accident *after* the killing, Kohler guilty of nothing more than helping him cover up the crime . . .

Perhaps the real question was how much reliance he could place on the ciphered ramblings of an incarcerated woman desperately trying to reassemble the scattered jigsaw of her life? He liked that. Scattered jigsaw. Sort of thing the boy Pascoe might say. Where the fuck had he been last night? He felt the need stronger than ever to speak to someone whose mind he knew, who knew his own mind, who'd laugh at his jokes or at least recognize when he was joking.

He fell asleep and was awoken by a hand squeezing his shoulder and the conductor's voice saying, "Time to pretty up, sir. Next stop, Williamsburg."

Still yawning on the platform, Dalziel reached up and shook the man's hand.

"Bye-bye, Blackbird," he said.

"Now I got you!" exclaimed the conductor. "It's been an honor to have you aboard, Mr. Greenstreet. You keep chasing that falcon, you hear?"

Laughing, Dalziel turned away. The temperature was a pleasant change after the damp chilliness of New York. It was like a balmy English summer evening. And the pleasant surprises continued with his taxi driver. Taciturn but courteous, he drove with a painstaking attention to legality and safety that won Dalziel's heart and a large tip, which he examined doubtfully.

"It's all right, friend," said Dalziel. "I've been saving it up."

At the hotel he was processed with friendly efficiency. Quickly unpacked, he consulted his corporeal needs and decided what he'd like best after the long journey was to stretch his legs and inhale some fresh air. Always suspicious of any urge to exercise for its own sake, he thought he might combine it with a recce and asked the desk clerk for directions to Golden Grove.

The man was impressed. "Nice address," he said.

"Yes, I know, it's in the historic area," said Dalziel impatiently. "Can I walk there?"

"Reckon you'll have to," said the man glancing at his watch.

The force of this remark didn't strike Dalziel till after crossing a busy main road, he realized that ahead of him the buzz of traffic and the glare of street lights had vanished. Even more disturbing was the absence of tarmac from the road. There was lighting of a kind, but it was very dim. He began to wonder if he'd gone wrong. He knew from the movies what an American high-class neighborhood looked like— a sort of cross between Ilkley and Babylon—and this didn't begin to fit the bill. He drew some reassurance from the sight of other people strolling around and he accelerated to overtake a couple.

"Excuse me," he said.

They turned and he ceased to be reassured. The woman was wearing a long muslin dress and a mobcap, while the bearded man was dressed in knee britches and a leather tunic. They smiled at him with the instant effulgence of doorstep evangelists, and the man said, "How can we help you, stranger? I'm Caleb Fellowes and this is my wife, Mistress Edwina."

Dalziel took a step back. America, he knew from his reading of the British tabloids, was full of way-out religions and he was not about to be kidnapped by the loonies or moonies or whatever they called themselves.

"Nay, it's all right, I can find me own way," he said.

"Are you come late from England, sir?" inquired the woman. "What news of the tea tax? How fares King George?"

"Dead," said Dalziel. "But his missus is still going strong."

They looked at him blankly, then burst into laughter, which was a lot more reassuring than their welcoming smiles.

Fellowes said, "What is it you're looking for, friend?"

"Place called Golden Grove," said Dalziel, still uncertain.

"The Bellmain house? We're going that way. Why not walk along with us?"

He sounded so normal that Dalziel began to seek explanations other than religious nuttiness for the fancy dress.

"You going to a party?" he wondered. "Or is it a film, mebbe?"

"You really don't know? No wonder you looked like you'd seen a ghost. You're in Colonial Williamsburg, friend, where everything's like it was two hundred years ago, round the time of the Declaration of Independence."

"Does that mean I can get drunk for sixpence?" asked Dalziel.

"Hell no, more's the pity," said Fellowes, drawing an indignant snort from his wife.

"And you actually live here?"

"My family's lived here almost as long as there's been a *here*," said Fellowes proudly.

"How about the Bellmains?"

"The same, only they made more money. They had a big plantation down by the James River. Golden Grove it was called, which is how the house got its name. Golden Grove tobacco used to be one of the very best." He spoke with the nostalgia of a recent apostate.

"Plantation? Like with slaves and all that?"

"Surely. 'Bout the same time as back in England they were still shoving five-year-old boys up chimneys to clean them."

"Still do where I come from," said Dalziel. "A lot of these Bellmains, are there?"

"Nope. There's only Marilou left. And her kids of course, but they're English and I guess they've got their father's name."

"But there's a Mr. Bellmain, isn't there?"

"Her second husband. From the sound of it he ain't going to be around much longer."

"Cal!" said his wife reprovingly.

"Local custom, is it? Man taking the wife's name?" asked Dalziel.

"No. Could be she felt she didn't have much luck first time she changed it, so this time round she felt she'd keep a hold of it."

"Mebbe," said Dalziel. "Does she have to wear fancy dress too?"

"No," said the man smiling. "She doesn't work for the Foundation, but naturally the house has got to fit in. That's Golden Grove there."

It was larger and set farther back than most of the others, constructed of warm red brick and framed by trees. A solitary upstairs light shone behind a curtained window.

"You planning to call now?" asked Fellowes.

"No," said Dalziel. "I'll leave it till morning. It's a bit late. Good night. And thanks for your help."

He walked away. It was a lie of course. In his game, it didn't matter whether you called early or late as long as you were unexpected.

The truth was that for the first time, or mebbe the second, he didn't fancy the truth. What he did fancy was street lights and traffic, even New York style. He'd had his fill of the past. These eighteenth century streets with their absence of any noise but a burst of frenetic fiddle playing from a wooden tavern were far more disturbing than the darkest alleys of home.

Ahead the lights of cars passing along the boundary road signaled the return of the twentieth century. Behind . . . He glanced back and shuddered. It was like looking down the throat of Old Time. It was a dangerous business disturbing the past. That dark shape moving sideways at his glance to merge into the shadows, illusion? ghost? or a living presence watching in the night?

There was a time when he would have gone to find out.

Not tonight. Tomorrow would do. Tomorrow was another day. Who'd said that? Some tart in a movie. He remembered thinking it were a pretty daft thing to say and if some sod got paid cash for writing it, he should give up bobbying and sell his notebook to Metro Goldwyn Mayer.

Now it made sense. He began to walk even faster toward his hotel.

Toward tomorrow.

Thirty

"For as I draw closer and closer to the end, I travel in the circle, nearer and nearer to the beginning."

Sergeant Wield said, "You want your head looked."

Pascoe was taken aback. It had bothered him from the start, keeping Wield in the dark, even with the argument that it was for his own good. Now that all his cards were on Trimble's table, he saw no reason not to bring the sergeant up to date. While he hadn't expected fulsome thanks, he'd anticipated at least a gratified neutrality.

"Why so?" he said defensively. "Look, okay, perhaps I was silly to let Andy involve me in sneaking around. But now it's all in the open, there can be a real investigation without having to worry that maybe someone's trying to fix the results."

"I reckon you were better off sneaking," said Wield grimly. "Where've you been? It's not just results that get fixed, it's people."

This echoed his own earlier fears too closely to be comfortable.

"Openness is our best protection," he proclaimed.

"You've been pulling too many Christmas crackers," said Wield. "What I can't understand is why Fat Andy's got himself so het up. He knows the way things work."

"Loyalty to Wally Tallantire," said Pascoe. "I explained all that."

"So you did. Dalziel defending the dead. He'll be into table-rapping next."

This echo of Pottle's speculation about the Fat Man's motives was disturbing. Was he naive in accepting simple loyalty to a dead colleague as sufficient?

Anyway, it no longer mattered. Did it?

He got down to some work.

About five in the afternoon, there was a tap at the door and Stubbs came in.

"Hi," said Pascoe, smiling a welcome. "We never got that drink."

"No. Busy busy busy. You know how it is."

"Any chance this evening? They'll be open in an hour."

"Maybe." Stubbs was examining his reflection in the glass of a Chagall print. "Christ, this hard water plays hell with your hair."

He had something on his mind. He'd get round to it sooner or later.

Pascoe said, "You want the name of my barber?"

Stubbs turned his gaze on Pascoe's head, dropped it slowly to his chain store suit, and said, "Know how old you are? Same age as me, only a fortnight in it. I punched up your record on the screen."

"So?"

"So nothing. Maybe the older look's the way to get on round here."

"You've got to be inconspicuous," said Pascoe mildly.

"Like your boss? He wears a suit but he's about as inconspicuous as a rapist in a nunnery."

To say whatever he wanted to say, he needed to provoke a reaction.

Pascoe said, "How come you were looking at my record? That's supposed to be confidential."

"Not once you started sticking your nose into our business."

"Now, hold on," said Pascoe. "All right, so I might have got out of line a bit, but that's all sorted between me and Mr. Hiller now."

"Sorted for you maybe," said Stubbs. "Listen. I can't stand people who fart and run. Couple of things you ought to get straight about Geoff Hiller. First is, he's dead straight. Okay, he'd win no prizes in a charm school, though maybe he'd come out ahead of your Mr. Dalziel. But he doesn't work to orders. He got picked for this job because anyone who knows him knows he wouldn't try to cover up police incompetence."

"And if he found there was something more than police incompetence being covered up?"

"He wouldn't back off from that either," said Stubbs. "That's what I mean. You and your boss have gone creeping around behind Geoff's back. Now it's starting to look as if something really nasty might turn up, where are you? Safe in your pits while Geoff's out there in the open, taking the flak."

"What flak?"

"I don't know. But that's how I know it's coming. He's loyal to his troops. When the heavy shit starts flying he gets us out of the way. You've started something, you and that fat bastard, and I just wanted to be sure you knew what you'd done."

"Now hang about!" said Pascoe, genuinely provoked now. But Stubbs wasn't in the mood for hanging about. The door shut behind him with a bang.

"Shit," said Pascoe. He tried to argue with himself that whatever hole Hiller found himself in, he would have reached anyway, unless he hadn't managed to dig up what Dalziel had managed to dig up, in which case it was just as well the Fat Man had gone sneaking about. But still he felt guilty.

Finally he reached for the phone and dialed.

"Hello? I would like to speak to Lord Partridge, please. Tell him it's Detective Chief Inspector Pascoe."

There was a long pause. He pictured his lordship debating whether noble disdain or noblesse oblige was the more profitable reaction.

"Partridge here. How nice to hear from you, Mr. Pascoe. How can I help you?"

"You've heard about Miss Marsh?"

"Yes, indeed. Dreadfully sad. Still, time and tide wait for no one, not even Scottish nannies."

"But they do have considerable control over other natural forces. Conception, for instance. The pathologist's report states conclusively that she never had a child. Not even an abortion. Was never pregnant."

Now the pause felt as if it might last forever.

"Now what makes you think I might be interested in that rather esoteric piece of information, Mr. Pascoe?" said Partridge at last in a level voice.

"I recall you talking about your interest in law and order," said Pascoe. "I presume that Miss Marsh, in pursuit of both verisimilitude and profit, presented you with some form of medical bill. An abortion clinic, was it? Or did she go the whole hog and claim to have had the child? That would up the ante considerably. Now you, my lord, are not a simple man, ready to dole out cash on the evidence of a few figures on the back of a fag packet. You would need to see a properly receipted account, and in order to get that, Miss Marsh would have needed an accomplice, possibly a nurse or a clerical worker in the relevant medical establishment. Surely as a big law and order man, you want to see this person brought to justice?"

He could hear himself speaking in the measured reasonable voice Dalziel accused him of always using as his flights of fancy spiraled into the inane. He finished and waited for Partridge to shoot him back to earth with anger, amazement, threats of phoning the Chief Constable, petitioning Parliament, bringing back the cat. What the hell! It was worth it just to know that the old bugger knew that he knew. Also the realization that he'd been doling out cash all these years on the basis of a phantom pregnancy would probably haunt him forever!

He heard a sound at the other end of the line. The splutterings of inarticulate rage perhaps? It increased in volume. Now there was no mistaking it. Not rage, but laughter. And not the forced laughter of a man trying to put a good face on things, but the wholehearted laughter that comes from relief and genuine amusement.

"Mr. Pascoe, I thank you. It was a great kindness, in the midst of your busy life, to find time to ring me. Many thanks. If you're ever up this way again, do call in. We'll always be glad to see you. Good-bye now."

The phone went dead.

"Well, bugger me," said Pascoe.

There was a discreet cough from the doorway. It was Wield with a cardboard folder in his hands and a faint smile on his craggy features.

"Trouble?" he said.

"No. But that's the trouble," said Pascoe. Such antilogy required explication.

Wield listened, sighed, and said, "You can't leave it alone, can you?"

"If Partridge had got mad, maybe I could."

"But he sounded relieved? Well, he's got a problem off his hands, hasn't he? With Marsh's death, I mean."

"He knew that before I rang him. Maybe he knew it before anyone rang him."

Wield whistled and said, "Hold on. You start saying things like that without evidence and you really are in trouble."

"The description of Marsh's visitor fits," said Pascoe stubbornly.

"Only like Hiller's jacket," mocked Wield. "Tallish? Grayish hair? British warm? Quick glimpse from behind? It'd make a great lineup! In any case, if he killed her, the news that she'd conned him all these years, so he didn't need to kill her anyway, would hardly send him over the moon, would it?"

"You'd think not." Pascoe laughed. "Odd thing is, I quite like the old sod. I picked on him because he was the only target I had. As old Tory lords go, he's not so bad. I've been reading his autobiography. I reckon on the whole he does more good than harm, which is more than you can say about most ex-politicians."

"Knows how to blow his own trumpet, does he?" said Wield skeptically.

"Naturally. But, oddly enough, it's at its most muted when he mentions his charity work; you know, like he wants to publicize the charity, not himself. This Carlake Trust that's getting the royalties from the book, well, it seems he hands his House of Lords Attendance allowance straight over to them too. But he doesn't make a big deal of it, just mentions it in passing."

"Funny kind of thing for him to get involved with," mused Wield.

"Why so?"

"Nowt really, except that people like Partridge must get a lot of requests to sponsor charities and they usually pick on summat they've a personal link with, like cancer appeals if your missus dies of it, or heart if you've had an attack."

"So why should Partridge be so interested in an organization that runs homes for kids so badly handicapped their parents couldn't face bringing them up . . . ?"

The two policemen were looking at each other in wild surmise.

"When did he first get interested?" demanded Wield.

"Hang on," said Pascoe, turning pages. "If I remember right, Partridge was in almost from the start. It's his support that has built the Trust up into a national charity . . . here it is. 'When I first met Percival Carlake, he was running a single home, created from his family house near Dunfermline in Fife . . .' And that was, let me see, 1971. It fits! And they've now got over twenty homes all over the country, mainly due to Partridge's support."

"Conscience money?"

"More than money, Wieldy. Bloody hard work. Oh, that cunning woman! She fixes things with a mate in, say, Edinburgh, I bet it was Edinburgh, that's where she came from. All she plans to start with is to get a bit of pocket money, and a birth costs more than an abortion. Perhaps she's going to say it was a stillbirth, but her mate tells her about some other woman at the same clinic or hospital or whatever who's just had a dreadfully handicapped child. She cannot or won't look after it, and the kid's going off to the Carlake Home. Marsh sees a chance for a really long-term stranglehold on Partridge.

271

Saying she'd had a healthy kid and put it out to adoption was too risky. Partridge might have got too interested. Checking up would have been easy. But a child like this . . ."

"There'd still be records."

"Sure. Mother's name. Say she's called Smith. Marsh tells Partridge she used the name Smith to hide her shame. Gets all the forged receipts made out in the name Smith. And once Partridge accepts it, she's got him for life."

"So he starts taking an interest in Carlake's work to ease his conscience?" Wield frowned. "You'd think a man who was that bothered would have said, 'Stuff it,' and simply admitted to the kid. He was out of politics by then, wasn't he?"

"He still had Lady Jessica to worry about," said Pascoe.

"You think she knew?"

"The way she talked about Marsh, she knew something. Anyway, Wieldy, this is all speculation. I'll pass it on to Hiller, but it's a dead end for me, as you'll no doubt be relieved to hear."

"Not quite a dead end," said Wield.

Pascoe looked at the sergeant keenly. There was no gleaning anything from that fallow face, but his ear was finely attuned to the modes of his voice.

"In what particular respect?" he inquired.

"If you're right about Miss Marsh, it shows there's nowt much she'd not have done to earn a bit of extra bread," said Wield.

"What have you been up to, Wieldy? Don't tell me that you've forgotten to practice all that stuff you were preaching?"

"Not exactly. I just thought it might be interesting to get a look at the alumni (is that the word?) of Beddington College in 1976. This is it. See anything you fancy? I've underlined the name that caught my eye."

He put the open folder before Pascoe with a flourish of a head waiter presenting a menu.

Pascoe's eyes drifted slowly down the names till he arrived at the one with the red line beneath it.

"Well, well, well," he said. "Now this does look like a tasty little dish, though I'm not sure how much it will be to Andy Dalziel's taste. How are we fixed with America? Is it still yesterday over there, I wonder?"

"God knows," said Wield. "It could even be tomorrow."

PART
THE FOURTH

"Golden Grove"

Thirty-one

"I have sometimes sat alone . . .

listening, until I have made the

echoes out to be the echoes of all the

footsteps that are coming by and by

into our lives."

The morning sun through the window first warmed then woke the gaunt-faced man. He lay without moving, for until he moved, he could almost forget what he was and recall something of what he had been. His thoughts drifted like dust motes in the sunbeams, inconsequential, uncontrolled, touched by golden light for a moment, then gone.

The door opened. Marilou Bellmain said, "You're awake."

"Like Lazarus," he said, trying a smile.

"I heard Lazarus was reluctant."

"He can't have had a wife like you."

"I bet he didn't have your gift of the gab. You ready for breakfast?"

"I think I shall get up for it."

"You think that's wise?" she said. "Shouldn't you rest up a few days till you get your strength back?"

"All otherwise to me my thoughts portend," he said. "I want to get up while I still can. And besides, like Milton's Samson, I feel I may be getting a few visitors during the course of the day."

"Like who?" she said suspiciously.

"Like friends and neighbors dropping by to see how I am."

He pulled back the sheet and she came forward to help him saying, "I don't want people tiring you out."

"Hush, dear," he said. "At the first sign of fatigue, you may rush forward dragonlike to burn them off."

He looked at himself in the dressing table mirror and said sadly, "I'm like Samson at least in this. I've lost my hair."

"It'll grow again."

"Now they've stopped the treatment? Yes, there may be time to complete my Americanization with a crew cut. I'm sorry, I don't mean to upset you with my morbidity."

"I don't mean to let it show."

He put his thin arms around her comfortable waist. Once a slim elegant woman, she had thickened out as he had wasted away, as if by eating for two, she could keep them both alive.

He said, "Marilou, you're the best thing that ever happened to me. You more than make up for all the rest."

She looked at him seriously and said, "All? You can't mean that."

"I can't change it so I've got to add it up and balance it out. And I must admit my life looked like bankrupt stock till that day we bumped into each other in Mexico City. After that, you can't argue with the figures."

She stooped to him then and pressed her lips to his, no peck for an invalid but a full-blooded kiss. She said, "You want to get dressed as well as get up?"

"Certainly I do. Only whores and the Bourbons receive visitors *déshabillés*."

"These visitors again," she said. "You *are* expecting someone, aren't you?"

"Not exactly," he said slowly. "But I've felt for some time now that someone, somewhere, perhaps more than one, was on the way to see me. And they won't have to hang around too long, will they? Sorry again. But, Marilou, my darling, promise me this. Whoever comes asking for me today, let them in. Turn no one away. No one."

"If that's what you want," she said. "But just today. After today, I call the shots, okay?"

"Agreed," said James Westropp. "Now go and start breakfast."

"Sure you don't want a hand?"

"An English gent may on occasion allow a lady to take his clothes off, but putting them on he reserves to himself."

"Is that so? Well, this is America and we do things our own way here."

"Wrong," he said. "This is the capital city of the Colony of Virginia, preserved as it was when my great great great great grand something was your undoubted sovereign, so when I speak, you'd better jump."

"I'm jumping," she laughed, and went out.

And now James Westropp rose slowly, steadied himself against the bed, then opened the wardrobe door. Above the hanging rail there was a shelf. He reached his hand deep inside this, groped around for a moment, then withdrew it holding a shoe box.

Temporarily exhausted he sat down on the bed till he got his breath. Then he opened the box.

It contained a small automatic pistol, an old buff envelope, and an ormolu pillbox with a coat of arms on the lid. He shook it. It rattled. He glanced in his dressing table mirror and studied his wasted features.

"Coals to Newcastle," he murmured.

Then he stood up once more and began to dress himself for his visitors.

Less than two miles away Cissy Kohler stood under a shower and raised her face to the stinging jets. After three decades of English trickles, she had forgotten the fierce delight of a real American shower. She would have to take care not to become addicted. Already her skin was developing the pink puffiness which comes from too much exposure to hot water, but it was hard to step out of this burning stream which eased her tense muscles, misted up her scarred mind, and almost threatened to wash away the ingrained memory of those prison years.

She twisted the control to cold, gasped as the temperature dropped by forty degrees, and switched the flow off.

As she toweled herself vigorously, she took note for the first time that she was beginning to put on weight. She had no particular interest in food, merely ate what was put in front of her, but clearly what was being put in front of her now was much more likely to show in front of her than the rigid diet of Her Majesty's Prisons.

What was more interesting than the actual changes to her flesh and her skin was the fact that she had noticed them.

Was she experiencing the return of vanity? Could it really be that as this climactic confrontation approached after so many years, instead of trying to refine all she felt, all she had experienced, into clear unambiguous phrases, she was letting her energies be sidetracked into looking her best?

She turned to the long bathroom mirror. It was misted up and for a moment the pink figure she could see dimly through the vapor was the girl she had been the day before that endless yesterday. She reached forward with the towel and drew aside those misty curtains.

She took a long steady look at the picture revealed, then slipped into her bathrobe, and went out into the bedroom.

Jay Waggs was standing in the doorway.

"Hi, I knocked but guessed you couldn't hear me for the shower. Hey, you look almost happy. Is that a smile I see?"

"I was thinking, why look your best when your worst will get you by?"

"Yeah? I'll need time to work on that one. Meanwhile I've news for you. That cop, the one I hit. He's staying here, the same hotel. I saw him coming in to breakfast, then he got paged to the phone."

Cissy Kohler shrugged.

"So he's here. He's got no authority."

"We don't know that. We don't know who he's working for. He bothers me."

Cissy said, "He's the kind of man, if I'd hit him I guess he'd bother me too."

Waggs said, "If that wasn't so true, it'd be almost a joke. Ciss, you're very lively this morning. I knew this reunion scene was something you wanted, but I don't anticipate it being something to make you happy."

"What's happy?" said Kohler. "Don't be deceived, Jay. I'm ready, that's all."

"Good girl. First though, I think maybe I should talk to the fat guy, find out where he's coming from. I don't want him spoiling things."

"You're very brave, Jay," she said.

"No, I'm not. I'll wait till he's finished his phone call, then follow him back into breakfast. Cops don't like beating up on people in public, and besides, he doesn't look the kind of guy will spoil good food by fighting over it. You wait here for me. Half an hour at most. After all this time, half an hour's going to make no difference, is it?"

"No difference at all."

"Good girl."

He left. She locked the door, lit a cigarette, and thought about Jay. She felt he was delaying, not just because he had a reason for delaying, but also because now the moment was close, he felt a dragging reluctance to take the final step. She sensed this motive in him because despite her bravado that was the way she felt too. What she didn't know was why he should feel like that.

Curiosity about other people's motives was like concern for her appearance, an insidious growth to be quickly excised. She stubbed out her cigarette and got dressed. Her makeup took a little time because when she turned to her mirror, she found she was crying. The only way to stop the tears was to understand what they were for.

It wasn't too difficult. She was crying for the ghost of herself she had seen in the misted bathroom glass.

Once known, she was able to apply her makeup with steady hand, check that she could pass for living even in the dawn with the sun before her, and go out to lay her own ghost forever.

Thirty-two

"It doesn't need an interpreter to

explain the meaning of these creatures.

They have but one and it's Midnight,

Murder and Mischief."

"Hello?" bellowed Dalziel. "You there? What the hell kind of time is this to be ringing decent folk? I've not had me breakfast yet."

"Sorry," said Pascoe. "But I did try to ring last night. Twice. First time they said you'd not arrived, second, that you'd gone out for a *walk*."

"You could've left a message."

"And had you ringing me in the middle of the night again? No way," murmured Pascoe to Wield, covering the mouthpiece as he spoke. Wield, listening on an extension phone, grinned.

"Hello! You fallen off your perch? So what's so important it can't wait till a man's eaten?"

"Quite a lot. In fact I may amaze you."

Quickly Pascoe described his conversation with Mrs. Friedman and read out the letter from James Westropp. Then he told of his visit to Harrogate and the discovery of Miss Marsh's body and all the consequences thereof.

"Now, Wieldy put two and two together and got on to Beddington College . . ."

"Wieldy? So yon bugger's in the act now too, is he? And you let him loose near a school? Christ, one way or another he could scar the little buggers for life!"

Pascoe glanced at the sergeant and made an apologetic face.

Wield replied with a mildly obscene gesture with one finger.

Pascoe said, "Wait till you hear what he found out. You know who was a pupil at the school back in 1976 when Marsh went to visit Kohler in jail?"

"Ask me summat difficult," snorted Dalziel derisively. "Has to be young Philip Westropp. It's obvious. And Marsh thought, hello, I wonder if yon lass Kohler's in touch with her old boss, and if not, how much would she pay to be put in touch?"

Pascoe put his tongue out at the phone and said, "Yes, that's what we worked out. Though why Marsh should think it was worthwhile, I don't know. I mean, Kohler can't have had much money, and why should Marsh think she might be willing to pay anyway?"

"Christ, I'm away a couple of days and already their brains have turned to jelly," sighed Dalziel. "Whatever money Kohler had when they put her away was likely just to be sitting somewhere collecting interest. I mean, there's not much to spend it on where she was, is there? Could have been a tidy sum. Any road, Miss Marsh was a good Scot. Many a mickle maks a muckle. Basis of all good detective work too, as I've been trying to drum into you for years."

"But why should she think Kohler would want to get in touch?" said Pascoe obstinately.

"Because she knew a bloody sight more than she ever let on," growled Dalziel. "People like her always do. They watch, note, poke, pry, and then save everything up till they think it's worth something. So she never had a kid? Wasn't even pregnant? By gum, you've got to admire her nerve!"

"Have you?" said Pascoe. "The more I learn about her, the

worse she sounds. Listen, if you think she knew more about the Mickledore Hall business, I wonder if this gave her some kind of hold over Partridge? Obviously she fooled him about the baby, but I've not been able to understand why he let himself be squeezed for so much. I mean, according to my Welsh undertaker, the villages around Haysgarth are full of his beaming bastards, so why should another one bother him so much?"

Dalziel said, "We'll never know for sure now that you've been daft enough to tell him he's right off the hook, will we? But my guess is, it weren't Lord Thomas that Marsh said were the father, it was young Tommy, the son and heir."

"Good lord! It's a theory, but why . . . ?"

"She'd been at the boy ever since he were a nipper," said Dalziel. "That's how she got her jollies, I reckon. How do I know? Listen."

He described what he'd read in Kohler's "journal."

"So, 1970 he'd be nineteen, going up to university, getting out of her reach. Time to forget pleasure and look to profit. Mebbe the boy himself went to his dad and confessed all. I mean there were other kids to consider. So, confrontation, and she pulls this last cat out of the bag. Could be this is how this mate of hers first got involved, providing her with fake results for a pregnancy test. Once Partridge showed he was willing to pay to hush things up, it'd be all downhill. He was just protecting his lad to start with from the gutter press. Imagine what they'd have made of it! But once she conned Partridge into accepting this stuff about the handicapped child, he was hooked for life. The higher young Tommy got in his career, the greater her hold. Think what it would do to a Tory minister if it came out he'd let his handicapped bastard be looked after in a home for all those years! No use pleading ignorance. Even if his dad had kept it all from him, he'd still have to resign. It wouldn't help the government much either."

"So this is why Kohler got released, because Waggs was getting too close to the truth, or at least what everyone thought was the truth?"

"Very likely. Fix up another story with Marsh to explain the blood; reasonable doubt; off she goes; Waggs stops prying. Makes sense."

"Then we start prying, and next thing, Miss Marsh suffers heart block. Jesus."

"Come on, lad. Could be coincidence. No need to cry funny buggers till you see the reds of their eyes."

Pascoe said seriously, "Andy, that could be sooner than you think. One other thing I've not told you. We've just heard on the grapevine this morning, there's rumbles down in South Thames about an investigation into misuse of police funds through false expense claims. Geoff Hiller could be implicated."

He should have foreseen the fat man's joyful reaction.

"Eh? Adolf caught with his hand in the till? Well, he never got near one in a bar, that's for sure. Always had deep pockets, and short arms. Nay, lad, you've kept the best for last. This'll cheer me up all day!"

"No!" said Pascoe sharply. "You're missing the point. Look, whatever you feel personally about Mr. Hiller, I've come to the conclusion he's a good straight cop."

"What? Fell off your bike on the road to Damascus, did you? I know him, lad, and yon streak of pigeon drool's good for nowt except wiping up."

"Think what you will," snapped Pascoe. "All I know is he knows everything we know, and I don't see any signs he's ready to sweep it under the carpet. But I reckon unless he plays ball, he'll be off the inquiry and heading back south to answer these expense allegations in twenty-four hours."

Dalziel said, "He'll play ball," uncertainly.

"I don't think so. Andy, I don't know exactly what's going on but I do know if they're willing to gag Hiller, they won't have any qualms about fixing you."

Pascoe could almost feel the huge indifferent shrug down the transatlantic line.

"They'll need Super Glue," said Dalziel. "Take care, lad. You too, Wieldy."

The phone went dead. Wield said, "How'd he know I was listening?"

Pascoe said, "How does a hedgehog know it's spring?"

In the breakfast room, Dalziel studied the menu. There was something called grits. He shuddered, then placed an order for bacon and eggs, spelling out his specifications in the kind of voice pharaohs used for ordering their pyramids.

He had just set to when Jay Waggs arrived.

"Mind if I sit down?" he said, uncertain whether to be reassured by the Fat Man's lack of surprise.

"I'd rather have you in front of me than behind," said Dalziel.

"I'm sorry about that," said Waggs, taking a seat. "I really thought you were a burglar."

"Oh, aye? Did you aim good or were you just lucky?"

"Bit of both. I said I'm sorry. Can we forget it and talk?"

"I were brought up never to hit a man with my mouth full. So what is there to talk about, lad?"

"That's easy," said Waggs, relaxing as he moved into the familiar territory of negotiation. "I just want to know what you're playing at."

"Playing at? Tell you what," said Dalziel. "I'll show you mine if you show me yours."

Waggs was really into his role now. He took a napiform bun from the bread basket and, nibbling its nobble, said, "Deal."

"You first. You in this for family loyalty or just for the money?"

Waggs laughed as he replied, "Oh, I'm in it for family loyalty, you'd better believe me, Mr. Dalziel."

Dalziel washed a shovelful of bacon shards down with a torrent of coffee and said, "So how about these backers of yours, Hesperides, isn't it?"

"You're well informed. Yes, I've got backing. I couldn't have done without it, in more ways than one. Thing is, I'd sold these people another deal which turned out a real dog. I needed to talk fast to prevent them recouping their investment in the organ transplant market. So I let them in on what I said was the story of the century. They don't think so long-term, but when I whittled it down

287

to the book of the month and the film of the year, that got them hooked. It really is a great story, wouldn't you agree?"

"Not really," said Dalziel. "It's old stuff, and I know how it comes out. I helped write it, remember?"

"And that's why you're here? To make sure nothing gets changed? Then you'd better head back and tell your Mr. Sempernel he's picked the wrong country. We stopped covering up scandals while you people were still covering up piano legs."

"Oh, aye? Well, I'll tell old Pimpernel if you tell Scott Rampling," said Dalziel.

"Rampling? The CIA man? How do they fit into this?" said Waggs in what seemed like genuine surprise.

Dalziel didn't answer. He had just seen Linda Steele appear at the door of the breakfast room. She was wearing shorts and a T-shirt with the legend COPS NEED SUPPORT TOO undulating across her breasts. She saw him and her luscious lips stretched in a delighted smile. Then she blew him a kiss and disappeared.

"Very comfortably," he said.

He realized that as if influenced by some sympathetic magic he was fondling one of the turnip-shaped buns.

"What's this?" he asked.

"The muffin? It's, well, it's a muffin."

"Oh, aye? Ages since I had a muffin," said Dalziel taking a deep, sensuous bite.

Then, "Jesus Christ!" he spluttered through a cloud of crumbs. "It's not a bloody muffin. It's a bloody cake!"

He took a long draft of coffee. That was the trouble with this crazy country. Just when you thought you'd got it sussed out, you found yourself eating cake for breakfast.

He wasn't going to let himself be surprised again.

He said, "So what precisely is it that you reckon our Mr. Pimpernel, and I reckon your Mr. Rampling, are trying to hush up?"

Waggs laughed almost triumphantly.

"You don't give much away, do you? You want to be absolutely sure that I'm sure what it is we're talking about here. I'll be explicit. I'm a media man, Mr. Dalziel, and I know there's nothing more calculated to bring everyone from the press to Hollywood running with their tongues and their checkbooks hanging out than a story which involves a high-class sex murder, or the British Royal Family. So how could even a computer come up with anything better than the tale of a Royal who does the business on his lovely American wife, then fixes things so that his best friend who's been screwing her hangs for it?"

He finished and watched Dalziel's reaction closely.

The Fat Man drank some more coffee. There, it hadn't been so bad. Sometime, somewhere, someone had been bound to say it, and now it had been said, he could start dealing with it.

"So that's the gospel according to Kohler, is it?" he said.

"That's what Cissy tells me," said Waggs.

"I'd best talk to her then. Where's she at?"

"Upstairs in her room waiting for me."

"You're staying here? Wish I'd known last night, we could have got things straightened out then."

"Mr. Dalziel, I don't know there's much to straighten out . . ."

"You'd be surprised. Come on."

He rose with a suddenness that sent the table rocking toward Jay Waggs. The American shrugged resignedly and followed him into the elevator. They didn't speak till they came to a halt before Kohler's door.

Waggs tapped and said, "It's me, Ciss. Open up."

There was no reply. Waggs frowned, took a key out of his pocket, and unlocked the door.

The room was empty.

"So where's she gone?" asked Dalziel.

"I don't know."

"But you can guess? She's gone to see Westropp, hasn't she?"

"Probably. Shit. I told her to wait. I wanted to be there."

"Why? What's she going to do? Christ, you're not hoping there's going to be a big climax for your story with Kohler pulling a gun out and blowing Westropp away?"

Waggs said, "I doubt it'll come to that. She's got very mixed up feelings about this guy."

"Mixed feelings? About a man who set her lover up for the big drop? And kept her in jail for half a lifetime?"

For a moment Waggs looked puzzled, then he began to laugh.

"This really isn't a test, is it, Dalziel? You still haven't got it! I'm wasting time asking you questions. You don't know a thing! It was Jamie Westropp she was crazy about, Jamie Westropp she was screwing. Mickledore and her were never lovers. That was a story you Brits invented because it suited you, and Cissy went along with it because it suited *her*."

And now there was no way of not being surprised. It was always the obvious that hit you hardest. But being obvious didn't make it true.

He said, "I shouldn't be too quick to believe a crazy woman, Mr. Waggs."

"Crazy? Yeah, maybe she was for a while after the little girl drowned. That's what made it all possible, Mr. Dalziel. But what really made it work wasn't Cissy's craziness, it was your Mr. Tallantire being so hell-bent on pinning it on Mickledore, and your Mr. Sempernel not giving a fuck who got the blame so long as it wasn't your Right Royal James Westropp!"

He spoke with a passion and force which came of conviction. Or could it be of the desire to be convinced? Perhaps, thought Dalziel, he needs it carved on tablets of stone, which is the way I'll need it too before I accept that Wally was anyone's stooge.

He said, "So you reckon what got her out of jail was the news that Westropp was dying? Well, this is one reunion I don't want to miss."

"But you're going to," said Waggs. "This is family only, Mr. Dalziel. I reckon you'd just complicate matters. So why don't you hang on here?"

He had a gun in his hand. Dalziel looked at it in disbelief.

"You silly bugger," he said. "Here's me feeling all virtuous 'cos I'd not thumped you for thumping me, and now you've gone and made me have to thump you anyway."

Waggs had the puzzled look of one who knows from the movies that it's the guy with the gun who gets to do the threatening.

"Into the bathroom," he said.

"Nay, lad," said Dalziel kindly. "Gun's no use unless you're willing to use it. I reckon you used up your share of muscle when you biffed me yesterday morning. Not your style. Words is what a clever sod like you uses to get out of trouble. Stick to what you do best."

He moved gently toward Waggs who let the gun dangle limply as he said, "Okay, Dalziel, so you're right, words it is. All I'm asking . . ."

Dalziel hit him in the stomach, catching the gun as it fell toward the floor and stepping out of the way as Waggs followed it.

"Thing about me is I'm a naturally violent fellow," said Dalziel. "I can go on thumping all day."

He dragged the retching man into the bathroom, took the doorknob in both hands, braced his left foot against the door, and pulled.

There was some slight resistance before the screw gave way. He then pushed the spindle out onto the bedroom floor, went out, and slammed the door shut behind him.

He switched on the television. It was tuned locally and there was an item about some visiting Asian politician who was being put up at the Williamsburg Inn for a spot of R and R from his official schedule. The camera showed the streets of the historic area and they looked very different from Dalziel's first impression; broad and airy, lined with elegantly proportioned buildings and filled with a golden sunlight which seemed to flow from an older, less hectic age. Even the slow drifting tourists had the look of genuine time travelers come in search of the history which their cities had concreted over.

It was his history too, he acknowledged with a slight shock of recognition.

He went out to see what he could add to it.

Thirty-three

"I am going to see his ghost. It will be

his ghost—not him!"

The doorbell rang.

It was the same bell that had rung ever since the first house had been built on this site in 1741. Its tinny note was imprinted so deep in Marilou Bellmain's consciousness, it came close to being a genetic memory. Once during her marriage to Arthur Stamper she had caught an echo of that sound in the windblown decorations on Sheffield's civic Christmas tree, and that had been the moment when she knew she would leave him.

Through the porch outer door she saw a young black woman in shorts and a T-shirt, and she was ready with her little speech pointing out politely but firmly that this was not part of the Colonial Williamsburg public area when the woman said, "Mrs. Bellmain? Hi! My name's Linda Steele. I wonder, could I have a word with your husband?"

She would have said no if James hadn't been so positive about admitting visitors today. But that was no reason to let insurance salesmen or religious freaks across her doorstep.

She said, "What's your business, Miss Steele?"

"Just a social call. We've got some mutual friends in Washington and they said to be sure to look James up."

"Who's there, dear?" called Westropp from the sitting room.

He didn't trust her. She didn't resent the thought. He was quite right. She'd have put up a "Gone Fishing" sign if she thought she could have got away with it.

"Come on in," she said.

Westropp regarded the smiling black woman with interest.

"Forgive me if I don't get up," he said from the old hickory rocker which gave him the pleasure of movement without the effort. "But I need to conserve my resources."

"Hi," said the woman. "I'm Linda Steele. Scott Rampling said I should call."

"I see. Marilou, I wonder if we could have some coffee?"

Reluctantly his wife left.

"I saw Scott only the day before yesterday. He didn't mention you, Miss Steele."

She looked at him curiously. What all the fuss was about she did not know, but at last she was seeing who it was about. This man with his clear English voice whose tone, at once courteous and amused, still contained charm enough for vivid imagination to flesh him out into the sexy number he must once have been. Silent, he was simply a wreck. A wreck of a wreck. A refugee from a concentration camp with wrists so thin, you'd need a glass to read his number. She was here to save him hassle, was all she knew. Well, it shouldn't be a long job.

She said, "I guess I'm not important enough for Mr. Rampling to mention, sir. I gather things have developed since last you and he talked, and he got kind of anxious in case you might be bothered by anything."

He considered then said, "No. No, I don't think anything's bothering me. You can go back and tell him you found me happy as a sandboy."

He was definitely laughing at her but not maliciously. Rather he was inviting her to share the joke.

293

"I think Mr. Rampling's hoping to get to visit you himself," she said. "He's coming to Williamsburg in connection with Premier Ho's visit, you've probably read about it, and if he can make time, he says he'll call."

"If anyone can make time, it's Scott," smiled Westropp. "I wish he'd make some for me. Aren't you staying for coffee, my dear?"

She'd risen. This guy was at death's door, but in his own house he still called the shots. Outside was the place to protect his privacy.

She said, "I don't think so. Mr. Rampling said to be sure you didn't tire yourself out with visitors, so I'd best set a good example."

The door opened and Marilou came in with a tray.

"Aren't you staying?" she said.

"Thanks but no. I was just telling Mr. Bellmain that maybe he shouldn't be bothered by visitors for a while."

"You were?" said Marilou frostily. "Tell me, young woman, are you a doctor?"

"Only of philosophy," said Linda flashing her keyboard smile. "Have a nice day."

She let herself out and saw that she had made the right decision just in time.

Standing at the gate was Cissy Kohler.

She hurried down the path toward her and said pleasantly, "Hi, honey. It's Miss Kohler, isn't it? My name is Linda, Linda Steele. We haven't met but we've got a lot of friends in common. Mind if I stroll along with you a while?"

Cissy Kohler said, "Excuse me, but I have to go in."

"Save yourself the bother," said Linda. "I've just been talking to Mrs. Bellmain and she says her husband's too ill to see anyone. So why don't we take that walk and talk things over?"

She smiled as she spoke and took Kohler's arm with all the confidence of one who'd done all the training necessary in her profession, and more besides, because she belonged to that generation of women who know there's no such thing as a safe street.

What she didn't know, because there's only one way to find out, is that hours in the multi-gym are but a lightly taken breath alongside twenty-seven years in the slammer.

A finger jabbed at her throat, forcing the thyroid cartilage hard against her larynx. She choked, gasped, tried to gulp, but her epiglottis remained firmly closed, her knees buckled, she staggered forward against the picket fence and jack-knifed over it. At last some air was getting slowly, painfully to her lungs.

She partially straightened, turned her head, and through her tear-filled eyes saw the slight, middle-aged woman who'd so easily brushed her aside vanishing into the house.

"Cissy Kohler?" said Marilou. "Oh, my God."

"Yes," said Cissy. She screwed her eyes up and said, "I seem to recall you were kind to me. I don't think I ever thanked you."

"No. Well, it doesn't matter, I only . . . what do you want?"

"Tell me one thing. You're married to him, right? Were you making it with him that weekend at Mickledore Hall? Had it started then?"

"No!" cried Marilou. "I hardly knew him. It wasn't till we met in Mexico . . . but why am I telling you this?"

It wasn't altogether a rhetorical question. She truly found it hard to explain the effect this very ordinary looking woman was having on her. There was about her a kind of authority, the kind that comes from extraordinary experience—a trip to the moon, a descent into hell, a life out of time . . .

"I'd like to see Jamie," she said.

Jamie . . . ? No one called him Jamie. No one she knew.

She drew in a long breath. She was Marilou Bellmain of Williamsburg in the house that her family had built and lived in for more than two centuries. That was experience worth having too, that left its own mark of authority.

She said, "Miss Kohler, Cissy, you were my stepson's nanny; you may or may not have killed my husband's first wife; you were certainly responsible in some measure for the death of his daughter. What gives you the right to come into my house and make demands?"

Cissy Kohler said patiently, "Would you tell him I'm here, please?"

"I know you're here, Cissy," said Westropp.

He was on his feet, standing in the doorway, his fingers lightly touching the doorknob, otherwise unsupported. To Marilou Bellmain he looked marvelous, stronger, more alert than she had seen him in many long months.

Then she saw Cissy Kohler's face. Gone was the prison mask of patient blankness. In its place was a silent scream of shock and pain. Cissy hadn't seen this man for twenty-seven years. Her mind's eye was not so ingenuous as to let time stand still. It had grayed the black hair a little, lined the smooth brow, stooped the narrow shoulders, but the basic model had remained the same. This long sack of bones, this papier-mâché face beneath a bald and wrinkled dome, these eyes peering out like small creatures of the desert from some deep burrow, had nothing to do with that man.

For a moment Marilou saw her husband with the newcomer's eyes and saw also with relief that his gaze was fixed too firmly on Kohler's face to register the transfer of shock to her own.

"James, here's Cissy Kohler to see you," she heard herself saying briskly. "Miss Kohler, why don't you go through and I'll make us some coffee."

"We've got the coffee you made for our last visitor who decided not to stay, remember?" said Westropp. "Cissy, come and sit down."

The woman walked slowly through into the sitting room. She was back in control now.

Westropp closed the door firmly in his wife's face, mouthing, "Ten minutes."

They sat opposite each other, he in the rocker, she on a chaise longue. For a long while, neither spoke. It was not the silence of competitors, each hoping to force the other into a false move, but the silence of two people long accustomed to self-containment.

Finally he poured two cups of coffee.

She said, "I've dreamt of this moment many times over many years. Sometimes it ended with you making love to me, sometimes it ended with me killing you."

"And which dream did you enjoy most?" he asked courteously.

It was the delicately weighted irony which brought him back to life, like a fuzzy distorted image suddenly slipping into focus.

She said, "Hello, Jamie."

He said, "Hello, Cissy."

She said, "You answered my letter cruelly."

He said, "You wrote your letter threateningly."

She said, "All I wanted was . . . understanding."

"That's not how it read to me."

"I was out of practice letter writing."

"I was out of practice understanding."

"Don't you and . . . she understand each other then?"

"We love each other. That is how I have survived. When we met I was ready to give up on survival. Then this new chance came. And with it your letter. The future and the past together. It was no contest, Cissy."

"And no contest where I've been either. The past is all there is."

"But now you're out of there. The future has started for you."

"Not yet, Jamie. This is still the past."

He moistened his lips with the coffee. He was a strange color, almost yellow. She might have been talking to some ancient Oriental sage.

He said, "When I read about your release in the papers, I thought, she won't come here. But somehow I knew you would. That's why I decided to head for home."

"Because you wanted to hide?" she said.

"Why on earth should I want to hide? Because a hospital bed's no place for a man to receive visitors. In any case I'd always planned to come back here to die. Why have you come, Cissy?"

"Why did you think I would come?"

"Because I could see that, while for me there'd been twenty-seven years of forgetting, for you there's been twenty-seven years of remembering."

"What are you trying to say, Jamie?" she asked gently.

"That it's all so long ago and I'm dying and you're free. That I can only guess at what prison has done to you, Cissy, but it doesn't matter whether you've come here in search of revenge or of forgiveness. I freely forgive you if that's what you want, and a few more weeks will provide any revenge you imagine you need. So why not walk away now and start your new life and leave me to finish my old one?"

He couldn't tell if she were seriously considering the proposal or not. She was certainly considering something. And as presumably she had discounted making love as a real possibility, he had to guess that she was weighing up the alternative consummation of her dream.

She was carrying a large handbag. She opened it and put her hand inside. He slipped his right hand under the cushion of the rocker and felt the smooth butt of the little silver automatic.

Strange the motives for killing. Was she willing to take a life which a couple more weeks would bring to a close anyway? And was he willing to kill to protect such a life?

Another moment might tell.

The doorbell rang.

She took a handkerchief from her bag and blew her nose.

He drew his hand from beneath the cushion and lifted his coffee cup. His hand was trembling slightly, but no more than you'd expect in a dying man.

He could hear voices, Marilou's and a man's. The door opened and Marilou appeared.

She said, lightly, "You told me to wheel them in."

She was studying him with concern but also with the wry amusement she had always shown at what she called his nursery games. Her utter openness was what had drawn him to her in the first place. In a life full of watchfulness, it had been marvelous to be at last with someone whose motives were never concealed. His heart swelled with love for her and with self-disgust at the long deceit he had practiced on her. She must be spared knowledge of that. That alone would be worth killing, or dying for.

He smiled and said, "It's open house. You always said I needed to learn about good old southern hospitality."

Marilou stood aside and Westropp looked with interest at the figure who filled the doorway. He was fat, but it wasn't a blubbery fatness, more the redistribution of bulk you get in an aging wrestler whose muscles have lost their youthful elasticity but still retain much of their ancient strength. He had a head which would have seemed huge on shoulders less broad. What hair remained was cropped and grizzled, and the eyes which shone beneath the shaggy overhang of his brows were hard and unblinking.

They were fixed firmly on Cissy Kohler.

Westropp coughed dryly and said, "I don't think we've had the pleasure . . ."

"That's where you're wrong, Mr. Westropp, or do you prefer Bellmain? Except it weren't much of a pleasure. Nineteen sixty-three, Mickledore Hall. Superintendent Andrew Dalziel. Only I were just a young detective then."

"I'm afraid I don't remember you. Names didn't really register, except for Mr. Tallantire's. As for faces, well, I think we've all changed."

"Aye. Some things change. Some not."

He advanced into the room. Marilou moved quickly after him, as if fearing he purposed an assault, and stood behind her husband with her hands on his thin shoulders. But Dalziel halted when he reached the chaise and said, "Hello again, Miss Kohler. Nice to see you dry for a change."

She looked at him calmly and said, "What do you want?"

"The truth."

A ray of amusement touched her lips palely.

"You've taken your time," she said.

"You reckon? Took a day and a half as I recall back in sixty-three. Don't see why it should take more than a minute and a half now."

"For confirmation of my guilt, you mean?"

"You admit it then?"

"I never denied it, remember?" She looked toward Westropp. "Jamie, there hasn't been a day for twenty-seven years that I haven't thought about little Emily."

"Really?" said Westropp. "I won't lay claim to quite such a distinguished record."

The true test of the English upper classes is not the blueness of their blood but the coldness of their cut.

Westropp's was permafrost.

Dalziel saw something in Kohler freeze at its touch. But when she resumed speaking, her voice was at the same quiet monotone.

"The papers made it sound as if there was something deliberate in it, like throwing someone to the chasing wolves. That at least you must have known as absurd. Mr. Dalziel, you were there. Did I look as if I were trying to run? Where would I run to?"

She turned to him in appeal. She'd chosen the wrong court.

He said, "Oh, you were trying to get away right enough, luv. I saw you flip that canoe over like a matchbox in a bath."

And now the cracks began to show, as her face screwed up in an effort at memory and then came apart like a weakened dam as the memories poured through.

She said, "I just wanted to be somewhere quiet and think . . . and the children were so good . . . they fell asleep in the heat . . . and there was only me and the willow branches and the sunlight dappling through . . . and it was almost like I could hide in there forever. Then suddenly there was this voice. It bellowed my name, it seemed to come booming across the water like thunder. And I knew then there was nowhere to hide. I paddled out from under the trees. The voice called again. I could see the margin of the lake was lined with figures . . . black silhouettes like a frieze around an urn . . . and I couldn't face them . . ."

Now there were tears, flowing like the first in all those years. But the voice somehow remained quiet and even.

"You were right, Mr. Dalziel, I was trying to escape. Can you believe I forgot about the children? There was just me and the voice and this one figure above all at the end of the jetty, and the water. Cool, dark, deep. I went over and in. Then I remembered the children. I started searching . . . I could see nothing . . . I glimpsed something sinking, turning . . . I didn't know it was Pip, I just grabbed him and came up . . . the canoe was upside down, there was nowhere to put him while I dived for Emily . . . Pip was sputtering in my arms and trying to cry . . . the water erupted beside me and this man came up holding Emily, and for a moment I felt such joy, everything else was forgotten . . . then I saw her face . . . and I saw your face . . . it was you, wasn't it, Mr. Dalziel?"

"Oh, yes. It were me," said Dalziel.

She nodded. "I've often seen your face in my dreams," she said.

"It's the kiddie's face I remember," said Dalziel grimly.

The tears had stopped as suddenly as they'd begun.

She spoke again to Westropp.

"I've never remembered that properly before. There was a time in the beginning when I genuinely could remember almost nothing. Except that I needed no longer worry about making a decision. I was willing to write anything the police wanted me to write. There's a sort of selfishness in doing something for love, isn't there? But self doesn't come into it in the same way when what you're doing is expiation."

"Expiation?" echoed Westropp, mockery in his voice to hide his pain.

"That's right. I've learned all the long words. Remember you used to laugh at me, saying that Americans only used long words when short ones would do? Well, now I've had time to get me a proper English education."

"I wasn't commenting on your remarkable vocabulary, merely trying to catch your drift."

Dalziel was suddenly sick of both her soul-searching and his cold control.

He said, "Look, luv, we're both a bit short on time, him 'cos he's going to snuff it, me 'cos I want me lunch. So why not spit it out, whatever you've come here to say?"

They both turned to him, momentarily united in shock, and Marilou Bellmain who had not stirred these several minutes took an angry step forward.

The doorbell rang.

"Saved by the bell," said Dalziel.

Marilou shouldered past him and went into the entrance hall. They heard the front door open.

"Pip!" said Marilou. "I'm glad you've come." Then, her tone

modulating from genuine to formal welcome, "And John too. How nice."

"We met at the gate," said a young man's voice. "How's dad?"

"Fine. He's got visitors so maybe you should . . ."

But her stepson had already moved by her into the doorway.

"Dad, hi . . ." he began. Then his eyes registered Dalziel and Kohler and the smile froze on his lips. "What the hell are you two doing here?"

Dalziel regarded him with interest. Seeing him in this context he was unmistakably Westropp's son, the same thin features, the same dark good looks.

He was also the young mugger Dalziel had knocked out in his New York hotel, the young CIA man who'd stolen Kohler's Bible.

But the surprises weren't finished.

"Pip, it's okay, calm down," said Westropp. "John, good to see you. You're looking well."

Behind Philip Westropp, Jay Waggs had appeared.

Kohler looked from him to Westropp and back again.

"*John?*" she said. "Who the hell are you? What's going on?"

Waggs said, "I would have told you before we came if you hadn't jumped the gun. I might even have caught up with you but I got sort of held up."

He smiled faintly at Dalziel who was scratching his ursine neck in the same way a cat starts washing itself to show the world it's not in the least surprised.

"So who am I? Hell, Ciss, you've dandled me in your arms! And I told you true, Mr. Dalziel, when I said I was mixed up in this business out of family loyalty. You got the wrong family, was all. That's right. I'm John Petersen, Pam Petersen's boy, and I've come to visit my poor sick stepdaddy in the hope that I may find out at last exactly who it was killed my dear dead mother."

Thirty-four

"In the day when all these things are

to be answered for, I summon you

and yours . . . to answer for them."

The least surprised person in the room seemed to be Cissy Kohler.

She nodded as if in confirmation of Waggs's statement and said, "You never felt like kin but you felt familiar."

"You took me in the park a few times," said Waggs. "I was five or six. I fell in love with you. Don't worry. I got over it when I decided it was really your fault when my mother dumped me and took off to England with stepdaddy here and the squalling brats."

"We left you because you'd just started school and it seemed silly to uproot you till I knew where my next posting would be," said Westropp. "I explained all that."

"So you did. A great explainer, my stepfather," said Waggs, addressing Dalziel.

"You've been in touch all these years?" said the Fat Man.

"No. Not directly. My Aunt Tessa who brought me up told me my mother had died in an accident and that my stepfather lived a

303

long long way away, but still sent money to help with my upbringing. I didn't find the truth till I was in my teens."

"And what was the truth?" asked Dalziel after a pause in which he assessed that the others were quite happy to leave him in the interrogator's chair till they collected their wits.

"Might as well ask, what was the time?" said Waggs. "That's one thing I learned in Hollywood. But back in Ann Arbor in the seventies, truth was that Mom had been murdered by Cissy here and some English creep. And the other English creep who took Mom away paid a bit of conscience money through a Washington lawyer."

"John, I thought this was settled between us long ago," said Westropp. "What's happened to change things? Do I gather you had something to do with getting Cissy released?"

"You could say that."

"But why . . . ?"

"Hang about," said Dalziel. "Me, I'm a tits-first man, everything in its proper order. What did you do when you found out this truth?"

He glared at Cissy Kohler as if defying her to deny that the truth had been found, but she made no effort to speak.

"I'd always been a bit wild. Now I had a reason, so I guess I did the whole mixed-up teenager bit. As well as all the usual stuff, I started using my old name, my real name, John Petersen instead of Jay Waggs. I must've been a real pain. I guess my aunt was glad to see me go to college. I messed about there, changing courses, trying anything and everything, not knowing what the hell I was doing. I found it useful having two names though, one backed up by a birth certificate, the other by the adoption documents my aunt and John Waggs took out on me. It meant you could put a bit of space between you and your screw-ups. There were times when I even acted as my own referee and credit reference!"

"So you were a right brainless young shit," said Dalziel. "And you decided to make contact with Westropp here so's you could tap him for a bit of money, right?"

"No!" exploded Waggs. "It wasn't like that. There was a car pileup. Aunt Tessa and old John got killed. I didn't realize how much I needed them. John was so laid-back, didn't give a fuck about anything I did as long as I didn't wreck the car. Ironic, huh? But I really liked him. No pressure. As for Aunt Tessa . . . You know, I used to call her mom till she told me what really happened, then I stopped. God, that must have hurt her. What a shitty thing to do. When I wake up in the night and start feeling rotten about things, that's always the first thing in my mind. I stopped calling her mom."

"Bloody hell!" said Dalziel. "No wonder you buggers don't win everything anymore. You've gone beyond contemplating your navels, you've got your heads stuck up your own arseholes."

Westropp said, "You're sure you're not from the Foreign Office, Mr. Dalziel? I can confirm John's statement. His motive in contacting me wasn't financial. Not the first time anyway."

He glanced at his stepson and raised what would have been a quizzical eyebrow if the chemotherapy had left him any hair. Beneath his ocherous pallor there were hectic streaks, like dawn in a monsoon sky. Marilou was watching him, her face taut with concern.

Waggs said, "I just felt a need . . . Anyway, I went to the Washington lawyer and told him I wanted to get in touch with my stepfather. At best I expected an address in Singapore or somewhere. When I found he was living down the road, so to speak, all tucked up nice and cozy with a new wife, I felt really angry. Stupid, huh? But he said he'd like to meet me, so I came. And it was okay. Not great, but okay. And they'd brought Pip back from school in England ready to start college over here, so I got a half brother out of it. And that was okay too."

He glanced at Philip affectionately and the younger man's grim expression relaxed for an instant.

Dalziel said, "Okay, let's skip to when it stopped being okay."

Waggs said, "You're the detective," challengingly. But also delayingly. He likes Pip, thought Dalziel. The lad's presence bothers him. He doesn't want to bad-mouth his father in front of him.

He said, "I don't know how, but I reckon the exchange of letters between Miss Kohler and Mr. Westropp had summat to do with it."

"What the devil do you know about that?" demanded Westropp.

"I know Miss Marsh tried to sell your American lawyer's address to Kohler and likely got sent off with a flea in her ear. But then you got to thinking, didn't you, lass? And you sweet-talked Daphne Bush into getting the address from Beddington College somehow, then posting a letter to your old boss. But when his reply came, Bush decided not to show it to you, out of selfishness perhaps, or mebbe out of love. Then you quarreled, and she did show it, and said some pretty nasty things. And you killed her . . ."

"It was an accident," said Cissy Kohler. "She fell. No one was going to believe me, and in any case I didn't care, so I said nothing . . . How do you know all this?"

"I've read the letter, lass. Oh, yes, it's true. Did you think it got buried with Daphne? But I haven't seen the letter you wrote to him. What happened to that, Mr. Westropp?"

"I don't know. I tore it up, I expect, burned it . . . I really can't remember. Does it matter?"

"Oh, yes, I think it matters," said Dalziel, looking at Waggs.

"Jesus, you really get off on this Great Detective thing, don't you?" said Waggs. "Yes, I've got it. My stepdaddy's right. Money didn't come into things at first, but later . . . I came down here a couple of years back when the Hesperides guys were leaning on me hard. I wanted a loan to buy them off. But that was the weekend you got really sick, remember? You were rushed to the hospital and I had to act all filial. Funny thing was I felt really concerned. I got the job of putting some things together to bring on after you, while your real family sat by your bedside. It was like I had a license to poke around, so I poked. Do I need an excuse? I could say I was looking for some mementos of my mother. I certainly found one. Cissy's letter. It was creased and faded and it wasn't exactly coherent, but I got its drift. First, you and your pretty young nanny had been screwing around behind my mother's back. And second, and this really blew my mind, she reckoned it was you that blasted her in the gun room at Mickledore Hall!"

He paused, for breath, for dramatic effect, it didn't matter.

All heads were turned to Westropp. Even Marilou had released

306

his shoulders and taken a step to one side as if she needed to see his face.

He said, "And if you believed what the letter said, dear boy, why have I been such an unconscionable time in dying?"

Waggs said, "Good question. My first impulse was to head down to the hospital and rip the truth out of you, but when I got there you were already being ripped open by professionals. By the time you were well enough for me to take over, I'd done some thinking. What had I got? The hysterical outpourings of a woman banged up for life in a Brit jail. For all I knew she could be sending letters to the King of Siam. I needed to see for myself just how mad or sane she was. But how the hell could I get near her? Then God moved in a mysterious way."

He glanced at Dalziel and said, "It was like I told you this morning. I got so preoccupied with my stepdaddy I forgot to hide and the heavies from Hesperides picked me up. You've got to go with what you've got. I heard myself selling them the story. It was sheer desperation at first, but then I began to convince myself. I needed to make it sound like I really had the inside track, but I didn't want to bring my mother into it, so I claimed I was Cissy's kin. And they bought it! And the way it's panned out so far has kept them happy they'll get a good return on their investment. I've kept them off my back by persuading them we need to wait to see how it all turns out. That's the nature of the story, isn't it? That's what's going to stop the kids from rustling their popcorn or screwing in the drive-ins. I mean, look at us here. No one's leaving till they see the credits roll. So here's your big scene, stepdaddy. How're you going to play it?"

It was all-eyes-on-Westropp time again. Dalziel found himself thinking, this really would make a great movie. Then he thought, Jesus! Keep your hand on your wallet while that young man's around!

Westropp looked like a man who'd dried in every sense. The eyes in that shriveled face drifted round the expectant gazes of his audience, touching but never engaging each in turn. Finally they came to focus on the telephone and there they stayed.

It's going to ring, thought Dalziel. Before I count three.
One . . . two . . . three . . .
Shit, thought Dalziel.
The telephone rang.

Thirty-five

"It has been kept from her, and I hope will always be kept from her. It is known only to myself and to one other who may be trusted."

It was Marilou Bellmain who picked up the receiver.

"Hello? Look, can you . . . ?"

Whoever was ringing clearly couldn't. Beaten back by a superior weight of words, she fell silent, listened, then said to her husband, "It's Scott Rampling. He says it's imperative he talks with you."

"In that case," said Westropp.

He took the phone, looked apologetically around as though a pleasant preprandial drink had been interrupted, and said, "Would you mind . . . ?"

Waggs looked as if he would very much. Pip too, but Dalziel made for the door, saying, "Okay by me, squire. I'm busting for a pee anyway. Upstairs, is it, luv?"

309

Without waiting for Marilou's answer, he went out into the hallway and ran lightly up the stairs.

The first room he looked in was the toilet. He went on to the next door. A bedroom. By the bed, a telephone.

Carefully he picked it up, put his hand over the mouthpiece and pressed the receiver to his ear.

A moment passed, then Westropp said, "All right, Scott. What is it?"

"I gather you've got company," said Rampling's voice. "They still there?"

"My guests have kindly stepped outside for a moment," said Westropp. "How can I help you, Scott?"

"I want to know what's going on? You know the Kohler woman kept a diary? In code in a Bible, for God's sake! Well, I've got it and it makes interesting reading. She thinks she's been protecting you."

"So?"

"So nothing. So it's not like they said. So I got to thinking, what is it like?"

Westropp said gently, "Scott, these are old, unhappy far-off things and battles long ago. My advice is, let them rest."

"I tried," protested Rampling. "I've had my people on it."

"That girl, you mean?" Westropp laughed. "Oh, Scott, you always wanted things all ways. I can just imagine it. Sempernel or someone like him warning you that trouble was on its way and asking you to clean it up. You saying, *sure thing*, but thinking maybe if it's something *they* want cleared up, it might be interesting to let it run and see what it's all about. Getting poor Mr. Dalziel to do your dirty work for you! Oh, Scott, you're so devious, you sometimes fool yourself."

"Dying's making you real sassy, James. I'm in your town at the moment to make some slant-eyed sonofabitch think he's important enough to need protection. I'll call by later to find out what's really been happening. Meanwhile my advice is, get those people out of there. Guy in your condition shouldn't be entertaining visitors."

"Your solicitude is almost unbearable," said Westropp. "Do try to keep calm, there's a good chap. As the French aristo said on his way to the guillotine, this is no time to be losing your head. Sorry. I realize in your case the image is rather crass, but you know what I mean. À *bientôt!*"

He put the phone down. In the bedroom Dalziel replaced his almost simultaneously, went out of the bedroom into the bathroom, pulled the chain, and ran lightly down the stairs.

The others were standing around like job applicants waiting for one of them to be called back into the interview room.

Waggs caught his eye and raised an eyebrow. He at least suspected a nonurinary motive.

Dalziel said, "That's better out than in."

"Truth, you mean?"

"I'd not bet your pension on it. A word in your ear?"

He glanced around. Marilou was standing close to the sitting room door, staring hard at it as if hoping to penetrate the woodwork by will alone. Philip stood by her, his young face pale and anxious. Cissy Kohler had lit a cigarette and was leaning against the wall, face blank, eyes unblinking, even the smoke from her narrow cigarette hanging still in the air before her.

Dalziel took Waggs's arm and pushed him through a door into the kitchen.

"So where's all this taking us?" he asked.

"That's an odd question for a cop."

"Oh, aye? Why's that?"

"I thought you guys just went along with the facts."

"There's facts and facts," said Dalziel.

"How so? I thought a fact was a fact was a fact."

"Sometimes they're like bits of china. You piece them together and you've got a bowl that'll hold water. Other times they're like bits of chocolate. You chew 'em up, and all you've got is shit."

"Jee-suss! You know what, Dalziel? Inside you, there's a poet trying to get out. In fact from the size of you, I'd say a whole anthology. Jee-suss!"

The second divine invocation was at suddenly finding himself translated to a higher sphere, which was to say, the top of the electric stove.

Dalziel said, "I ought to turn this thing on and see if I can boil some sense into you. You want to know if he killed your mother? What good'll that do you? All you do is give Philip a murderer for a father and Marilou a murderer for a husband."

"And Cissy?" cried Waggs who didn't lack courage. "Don't I give her something too? Something she deserves? Listen, she's lost a life because of all this. Nothing that can happen to any of the rest of us can come close to that. She wants to see the guy she gave that life up for before he dies. She wants to hear something from him that might help her think it was even just a fraction worthwhile. She deserves that chance, doesn't she?"

"Why?" said Dalziel. "She's got three deaths on her hands. In my book, that's at least two too many for second chances. Did they all three deserve to die? Your mother? That little lass? Daphne Bush? So what's that leave her deserving except what she got?"

But he didn't sound all that convincing, not even to himself.

He turned and went back into the hallway. The others were still there. He went toward the sitting room door, but Marilou Bellmain barred his way.

"He will call us back in when he's finished his phone call," she said.

"Missus, he finished long since," said Dalziel, easing her aside. Philip looked for a moment as if he might get chivalrous, but Dalziel gave him a look that would have stopped a horse let alone a knight and opened the door.

Westropp lay back in his rocker, his eyes closed, looking more like something the Egyptologists had just peeled the bandage off than a living being.

Marilou went to him and took his hands. Now the eyes opened like a lizard's on a rock. "There you all are," he said. "I'm sorry but I don't think I can go on with this just now. Another time, perhaps. Yes, another time would be nice. But before you go, an apology. Hopelessly inadequate, but what else can I offer? To you, Pip. To you, John. It was an accident, believe me. I may have sometimes wished your mother harm, but I never purposed it. And to you, Cissy, what can I say? Except that the events of that dreadful weekend, especially Emily's death, deprived me of the power of rational thought and action just as they must have deprived you, otherwise how could either of us have stood aside and let poor dear Mick die? I'm sorry for all the . . . misunderstanding. Aren't words inadequate, particularly when you've had a classical education? Now if you don't mind, I'd like a little time with Marilou."

Cissy Kohler was drawing in huge breaths as if air was going to be rationed.

"Is this *it*?" she managed to gulp out. "Is this all I get?"

"It's all there is," said Westropp. "Sometimes it is better to travel hopelessly than arrive. I know that too, believe me."

She took a step toward him, fumbling with the clasp of her handbag. Dalziel caught her in his arms, spun her round, and pushed her through the doorway. Screened by his own bulk from the others, he dipped his hand into her bag, took out the small revolver he found there, and slipped it into his left-hand pocket.

He turned and called, "Mrs. Bellmain."

Marilou looked toward him impatiently and he said, "Cissy's not too well."

It was the first time he had brought himself to call her Cissy.

Marilou looked unhappily from Jay Waggs to her husband who said, "I'll be all right, dear. Don't be long."

She went out into the hall and Dalziel reentered the room.

Waggs took a step toward the man in the rocking chair but there was no menace in the move. Rather he seemed to want a closer look.

He said, "I've been around the entertainment industry too long not to recognize the smell of bullshit."

"You say so?" said Westropp. "John, believe me, when I say I'm sorry . . ."

"Yeah, yeah, I gotta see that Cissy's okay. But this isn't the end, stepdaddy. There's a lot of mileage in this yet."

He turned and pushed past Dalziel.

"Poor John," said Westropp. "For a man who makes a living out of selling ideas, his forecasts seem sadly off the mark."

"At least he's worried about that woman out there," growled Dalziel.

313

Westropp shrugged, shoulder bones moving like sticks in a sack. Then he turned his attention to his son.

"Pip," he said. "We've never been as close as I could have wished. I lost too much of your childhood, but I had to send you away to school till I finally settled down with Marilou . . ."

His son said, "Dad, please, it's okay, forget it . . ." His face was soft with grief. He leaned over Westropp as if to kiss him but the sick man turned his head away and patted his shoulder and in that moment Dalziel saw how distasteful the memory of his dead wife was still to him.

Philip straightened up. Westropp said, "We'll talk later. Ask Marilou if she'd mind not coming in till Mr. Dalziel comes out."

The young man turned away, looked at Dalziel as if about to say something, but left without speaking.

"Funny," said Dalziel.

"What?"

"Lot of men would make more of a live son than a dead daughter."

"Well, well. A Moralist perchance appears, led, heaven knows how, to this poor sod. You are a father perhaps yourself to know so much about these relationships?"

"No, but I know enough to guess that it's the lad who's the real poor sod here," growled Dalziel. "I'd put money it was your missus insisted he should come back from yon school in England to live with you."

He saw he'd hit home and he pressed on, "Been working long for Rampling, has he?"

"I'm sorry?"

"Didn't you know he was one of that lot? Breaking and entering hotel bedrooms a speciality. Well, not really. He weren't much good at it. Only did it, I daresay, 'cos he got told the bugger whose bedroom it was might be a threat to his dear old dad."

"Your room, you mean? That was Pip? Well, well." Westropp frowned, then said, "But this is a diversion. I have little time for such things. You want something from me, I assume?"

"The truth."

"Indeed? And perhaps you will perform me one or two little services in return?"

"Such as?"

"Always leave the bathroom as you'd like to find it. That was one of my old nanny's maxims. It's tidying up time for me. For a start, perhaps you could dispose of this."

He produced a little automatic pistol from beneath his cushions. Dalziel took it gingerly, checked the safety was on, tried to put it in his left pocket, found it full of gun already, and transferred it to the right.

"Keeps me well balanced," he said. "Like you."

"You think so?"

"Man has to be well balanced to live what you've lived through without cracking. Or completely cracked to start with."

"Now, that's not for me to say. All I know is that the greatest obstacle to human progress is our capacity for bearing things. Ah, as the heart grows older, It will come to such sights colder By and by, nor spare a sigh . . ."

It was, Dalziel guessed, a poem. Pascoe used the same funny voice when he slid into poetry too. But his face was never striated with pain and weariness like Westropp's.

"You want me to call a quack?" he asked.

"No, thank you. I have my medication." He opened his hand to show a tiny pillbox. The lid snapped up at the touch of his finger. He took out a green and black capsule and examined it quizzically.

"Sometimes coals are needed in Newcastle after all," he said. "Catch."

He tossed the box to Dalziel who plucked it from the air and examined the coat of arms.

"It's all right. I didn't nick it from Windsor. It's mine by right of inheritance."

"Worth a bob or two."

"Probably. Keep it. Souvenir."

"I don't need to be reminded."

"No, you don't, do you? Interesting that. Keep it anyway. You said you'd help tidy up. Let's press on. There's not much time."

"I thought you had weeks."

"Not weeks of control. Weeks of growing pain, increasing help-lessness. No, thank you. I prefer to do my own tidying."

"With my help?"

"That's right. But the task is not onerous. What precisely you are doing here, Mr. Dalziel, I don't pretend to know, and I have not time to find out. I suspect your motives and your function go far beyond anything which can be called simply official. But you will, I am sure, make an impressive messenger. And you need have no fear of maltreatment, for the message is good."

"Oh, aye? I hope it's short too."

"Tell them . . ."

"Who's them?" interrupted Dalziel.

"Don't worry. You'll have no difficulty identifying them. Tell them that when last you saw me, I was in full possession of my faculties and you found my assurances of tidiness convincing."

Dalziel thought a moment then shook his head and said, "No."

"No? Is it perhaps too long for you? Shall I write it down?"

"Funny," growled Dalziel. "What you say about possession of your faculties, I'll need a lot more evidence of that. Like the truth, for instance. Let's stop farting about. Did you kill your missus or not?"

"Did *I* kill *her*?" mused Westropp. "You speak as if killing is a single act of a single person upon another single person."

"Stop pissing around!" said Dalziel angrily. "There's a woman out there needs to know what happened."

Westropp gave a thin knowing smile.

"*She* needs to know or *you* need to know, Superintendent? Whose peace of mind is it you're worried about?"

Even arrows that strike home cannot divert the charging buffalo.

"She was your mistress. You were lovers. You owe her something!"

Westropp shook his head.

"If I do, it's beyond payment. What's best for her to know? For all these years, I've believed her guilty, Dalziel. Not necessarily as charged, but guilty nonetheless. And I still think it. You don't do things like that to yourself unless you're guilty!"

"Or obsessed."

"Guilt. Obsession. Bedfellows, when you get down to it. As I suspect you know. Do you understand women, Dalziel? I don't. Or men either, I suspect. I had a wife who turned out a whore. Well, I could live with that. It's an old tradition of the upper classes. Anything goes as long as you don't frighten the horses. I didn't even mind too much when Mick got in on the act. But it ruined our friendship. He despised me for not minding! Dear old Mick. Strange man. But he paid, of course. You see, Pam didn't just want his lily white body, she turned obsessional, she wanted . . . everything! Me, I bedded little Cissy from time to time. She was young, she was attractive, she was there. But damn me, if she didn't turn obsessional too! Why am I telling you all this, Dalziel?"

"Because I remind you of your mother," said Dalziel. "Also because you're afraid if you tell your wife, she might not be obsessional enough to go on loving you. So go on. The gist. That's all I want. The gist."

"And if I don't care to?"

"Then I'll mebbe shake you till that little bit of Newcastle coal falls out of your pocket, and have a word with your missus and your quack, and make sure you fall off your perch legally, naturally, and very slowly."

Westropp regarded him closely and said, "Oh, Dalziel, I wonder, what really is your own particular obsession?"

"Beer," said Dalziel. "I'm parched for a decent pint, so the sooner I get done here, the sooner I'll get back to Yorkshire. Are you sitting comfortably? Then why don't you begin?"

PART
THE FIFTH

"Golden Boy"

Thirty-six

"I do hope there will be no oniony and tobaccoey smotherings in the form of embracings all round, going on in the streets."

Everything ends, and everything starts again. Justice returns, Saturn rules okay, and the firstborn son of the new Golden Age is already dropping out of the skies on his way down to earth.

In other words, Dalziel was flying home.

Preferring people to clouds, he'd asked for a seat on the aisle from which he studied those around him in hope of booking the same kind of free ride through Heathrow officialdom as he'd got in New York. A nun with five-o'clock shadow held his attention for a while, but when he saw her pour three Irish miniatures into one glass and down them in three sips, he acknowledged that such instinctive Trinitarianism could not be affected, and followed her good example with single malt.

At Heathrow he found he needn't have worried. As he came out of the tunnel from the plane, a young woman in the kind of smart black and white clothing which stops just short of being a uniform approached him, smiling, and said, "Superintendent Dalziel? Your Mr. Sempernel says he'd be grateful for a word. If you'd come with me . . ."

"Oh, aye? What about passport control and my luggage?"

"That'll all be taken care of," she assured him.

"Well that's big of my Mr. Sempernel. Lead on, lass."

She might, of course, be leading him to a curtained car and a quick trip to the Tower, but so what? They'd need a bloody big ax.

They soon moved away from the hoi polloi and came to a halt outside an unmarked door in a corridor with the cushioned hush of a good hotel.

"I'll let Mr. Sempernel know you've arrived. He shouldn't be too long," said the girl, opening the door.

"Thanks, luv," said Dalziel stepping inside. "Bloody hell!"

He had cause for astonishment. Sitting in a deep armchair, drinking coffee from a china cup, was Peter Pascoe.

"Hello, sir. Good flight?" said Pascoe.

"Fair," said Dalziel looking round the room. It was thickly carpeted, newly decorated, and furnished with several huge armchairs, an old oak coffee table, and a sideboard on which a percolator bubbled alongside a silver tray, bright with bottles.

"Don't tell me," said Dalziel. "You've flogged your ring to Sempernel and he's set you up as his toy boy."

"I'm glad to see travel hasn't spoilt your native charm," said Pascoe. "I came to meet you, got paged in the arrivals area, and told that you'd be brought along here. It's a sight better than down there, believe me."

"I believe you," said Dalziel, looking out of the window. He could see out across the runways but could hear very little. Soundproofing like this must really cost. He doubted if it was on offer to the poor sods under the flight paths.

"How did they know you were meeting me? In fact, how the hell did *you* know you were meeting me?"

"Mr. Trimble set it up. Somehow he'd found out what plane

you'd be on and he seemed to think it would be a nice gesture if I was here to meet you. Also I was able to kill two birds with one stone."

"Oh, aye? And who was the other lucky chicken?"

"Mr. Hiller. You were wrong about him by the way. He didn't back down. Now he's been suspended, pending inquiries into expense claims. His team are tidying up in Yorkshire, so he needed a lift to the Smoke."

"Good God. I thought Sempernel's toy boy were the lowest a man could get, but Adolf's chauffeur! Well, thank God we've seen the back of him."

"You're not being fair!" protested Pascoe. "What he's done took guts. And probity."

"Oh, aye? Had a heart-to-heart about his motives as you drove down, did you?"

"As a matter of fact, we didn't. Mr. Hiller made it quite clear he didn't want to talk about the affair. For my sake, I suspect."

"Christ, he's got you feeling grateful too! So what did you talk about?"

Pascoe hesitated then said, "Well, you were mentioned, actually. In fact, Mr. Hiller asked me to give you a message."

"What's that then? Love and kisses? Or a bit of pious moralizing?"

"No. More like advice, sort of." Pascoe took a deep breath. "He said to ask Andy Dalziel if he'd ever thought of sticking his head up his arse and shitting some sense into it. End of message."

Dalziel looked at him in astonishment. Then he began to laugh.

"He said that? Well, mebbe I have misjudged him after all and there's summat more than cold tea trickling through his veins. Talking of which . . ."

He examined the bottles, selected the Highland Park, and poured a Trinitarian measure.

"So how have things turned out up there?" he asked.

"I'm not sure. I get a sense of everything being wound down. The inquest on Marsh passed without any fuss. Natural causes. I don't think anyone will be sent to replace Hiller. Stubbs says that there'll probably be an inconclusive report along the lines of administrative errors compounded by Kohler's own emotional trauma. She knew what Mickledore had done but wasn't actively involved, sort of thing. So he stays guilty and she gets pardoned, but there's not enough public sympathy to keep the story running as she did let the little girl drown and she definitely killed Daphne Bush. So that looks like that, all neat and tidy. Except for you . . ."

He looked at the Fat Man expectantly.

"Me? Aye, I could still rock the boat if I took a fancy."

"But you don't?" said Pascoe doubtingly.

"As long as no one chucks dirt at Wally Tallantire, I'll be happy," said Dalziel. "Something bothering you, lad? You look like you've found a spider in your glass."

"You mean you're willing to let things slide? After all you said about Geoff Hiller?" Pascoe shook his head in bewilderment. "Didn't you find out anything in the States? From what you said . . . Didn't you even catch up with Kohler?"

"Oh, aye, I managed that. She were pretty elusive but in the end we were able to sit down and have a nice quiet chat. Well, at least it started quiet."

Dalziel smiled reminiscently. He had seen Kohler once more after he left the Bellmain house.

Waggs had taken her back to the hotel and that was where he found them, sitting on the bar terrace overlooking the car park. He sat beside them. The waiter came. That's one thing he liked about America. You could often get a waiter without recourse to threat or bribe.

He ordered Scotch for himself, pointed at the others' almost empty glasses, and said, "Again."

"So what's the word, Dalziel?" said Waggs. "Stiff upper lips and imperial solidarity?"

"Stiff? Aye, that's the word. Stiff," said Dalziel.

"As in *stiff*?"

"I doubt he'll see the day out. It's been a strain."

"Is that a medical opinion? Or a police opinion?" said Waggs.

"It's an opinion. How're you feeling, lass?"

Cissy Kohler said quietly, "I stopped feeling long ago. It's not a habit I want to get back into. Not after today."

"So why'd you come? What's it all been about?"

"Jay told me he was dying. I thought, sooner or later I'll get out of here and if he's dead, I'll never understand anything. No, that's not quite true. I thought, this is maybe my last chance to *want* to get out of here. It's wanting that's important. I'd been inside all those years. I felt I ought to have a last try at making sense of it. I think I may have been wrong."

"Shouldn't let it worry you, luv," said Dalziel comfortably. "I've been on the outside all that time and it doesn't make much sense to me either."

"Jesus! You do counseling too, do you?" sneered Waggs.

"Sort of. So the two of you set out to get back here before Westropp died in the hope of . . . what? Hearing some truth that'd set you free? So how's it worked out?"

"I'll maybe tell you that when I hear the truth," said Waggs.

"I'll give you it," said Dalziel. "Only it's not clear-cut. Pam Westropp died. Who killed her? Everybody, including herself. It was an accident, it was suicide, and likely there was a bit of murder in there too. Mickledore tried to tidy things up. Altruistic? Mebbe. But there's a lot of self-interest there too. It's his house. He's been banging the dead woman and if that gets out, his rich dad-in-law to be will definitely scupper his wedding plans. Only, his tidying-up's too good, especially when he gets help from someone willing to take the whole thing on herself. But just how far would you have gone, Miss Kohler, if Emily hadn't drowned? Even your motive's not clear-cut, is it?"

"Come on, Dalziel!" said Waggs. "You're just making smoke for the Brit Establishment. We're going to get this thing out in the open . . ."

"Not with Cissy's help, you're not," said Dalziel glancing at the woman whose blank face confirmed his assertion. "I doubt if you really want to, anyway. Man'ud need to be a real shit to want to make a blockbuster movie out of his ma's murder. Particularly if he weren't all that sure how he really felt about her anyway. I mean, she did dump you so's she could take off with her new family . . ."

Waggs was on his feet, his face flushed.

"I don't have to listen to this crap . . ."

"That's right, lad," agreed Dalziel. "In your situation I'd be much keener to spend time thinking up my next story for your mates in L.A. Like the Arabian Nights, isn't it? A story a day keeps the heavy mob away. In fact, I hope the golden tongue's well oiled just now. There's two burly gents just got out of a car and it's either love at first sight or they're looking for someone."

Waggs peered over the terrace rail. At the far side of the car park two men were standing, one pointing toward their table. Now they began to move purposefully forward.

"Ciss, I'll be in touch," said Waggs.

Dalziel watched him hurry away and said, "He's not a bad lad, but not really cut out for this avenging angel stuff."

"Is he really in trouble?" asked Kohler anxiously.

"From the minute he was born. Don't worry too much. He's had the practice dodging it. What'll you do now?"

"Concerned, are you?" she laughed shortly. "I got the impression you fancied yourself as a bit of an avenging angel too, Mr. Dalziel."

"Like I say, nowt's clear-cut. We all got conned a bit that weekend, but it was you who got stuck with the bill."

"You're forgetting Mick. And Pam. And little Em. I'm still alive. At least I think I am."

"So what'll you do?"

"Who knows? Collect my compensation, settle down somewhere, grow a tree, hang myself from it."

For a second Dalziel was alarmed. He examined her closely, this woman he had chased across an ocean in the certainty of her guilt. He knew there was no way he could have tholed what she'd put up with these long years. He'd have either broken the cell door to get out or broken his neck in his efforts to do so.

That thought reassured him almost as much as the level

unblinking way in which her gaze held his. There was a strength here which his own strength, though so different, responded to.

He said, "Make it an oak, luv. Give yourself a bit of time to think."

A hand touched his shoulder. He looked up and realized he'd frightened Waggs unnecessarily. The two men from the car park had arrived and, close up, his newly educated eye fixed them as more likely to be Rampling's "guys" than Hesperides heavies.

"You Dalziel?" said the taller of the two not discourteously.

"I'm not sure, not till I know who you are, sonny."

"Come on," said the shorter man aggressively. "Of course it's Dalziel. Do you see any other fat ugly slobs out here?"

"Now, where'd you get a description like that, I wonder?" said Dalziel reflectively.

"Pardon me, sir," said the courteous one, "but Mr. Rampling would like a word."

"He can have two if he likes. Can't you see I'm busy?"

"Jesus Christ. These Anglos really piss me off," said the short man. "Listen, fella, just move your big fat butt off that chair and come with us, okay?"

"You really sure you want me to stand up?" asked Dalziel.

"What's that? A threat?" sneered the man.

"Please, Harry," said his friend.

"Fuck please. This guy's beginning to believe his own publicity. What are you going to do, friend? Roll over me with your belly? Or maybe you've got a concealed weapon in there?"

"Nay, lad," said Dalziel smiling as he rose. "The only hidden weapons I've got are these."

And thrusting his hands into his jacket pockets, he brought them out with a gun clasped in each.

"You should've been there," said Dalziel reminiscently. "I felt like John Wayne. Them two buggers went diving for cover just like you see in the movies! There was chairs and tables scattering everywhere! One of them, the hardcase, he vaulted clear over the terrace rail and landed on top of a car. Broke his arm in two places. Didn't do the car much good either. And the other was trying to pull a gun out, only it got snagged on his jacket and he couldn't get it loose. I thought he was going to end up shooting himself in the balls!"

"You could have got killed," protested Pascoe. "What were you doing all this while?"

"Doing? Nowt. Except laugh. I near on fell out of my chair laughing. And after a bit, I realized she were laughing too. Not just a smile or a giggle, but a real good laugh, the kind you just can't stop. She got serious again before we parted, but. She said, I don't blame him for getting married. Outside, you've got to forget, or you go mad, I'm getting to see that now. But was he worth it, Mr. Dalziel? Did he ever feel enough for me to make it even for one moment worth it? And I told her, yes, he was worth it. I told her he'd asked me to give her his pillbox because the coat of arms on it was his only excuse for the lousy way he'd acted. I told her how after he got his skull together again, he'd wanted to come forward put everything straight, only because of who he was, his family connections and such, they pressured him and persuaded him and threatened him till he didn't know what to do. So he did nothing, and he regretted it for the rest of his days, which was why he was so cold seeming toward her when she got in touch. It was pure guilt."

"And you think that's the truth?"

"No," said Dalziel. "Load of bollocks. I think he were a right shit. Like all on 'em. Right shits. Talking of which, where's Pimpernel? I bet the bugger's going through my case! I hope he doesn't crease my shirts. I spent a long time packing them shirts."

He poured himself another drink and was halfway through it when the door opened and a tall gray-haired man came in with an apologetic smile creasing his canine features.

"Mr. Dalziel, so sorry you've been kept waiting. It's just that when I heard you were coming back after seeing poor dear James Westropp, I just had to take this chance of talking with you. He was a dear friend, a dear old friend, and I've been meaning to visit him for ages but kept on putting it off, you know how it is, pressure of work. And now he's gone. Sit down, let me fill your glass. Tell me all about him, poor dear James. Did he mention me at all?"

"As a matter of fact he did, sir," said Dalziel. "He sent you a message."

Pascoe, recalling the message he'd just passed on from Hiller, closed his eyes, and inwardly groaned.

"What did he say?"

"He said if I ever saw you to say he'd kept the faith to the end, and he'd left things tidy. He wanted you to know that, sir. I thought it must be something to do with his old school song or something."

"That's right, Mr. Dalziel. His old school. Our old school. I'm touched, deeply touched. I thank you with all my heart."

"My pleasure, sir," said Dalziel, in tones vibrant with sincerity. "My very real pleasure."

Sempernel regarded him speculatively for a long moment then visibly relaxed.

"So tell me, Superintendent," he said in a voice which stayed just this side of patronizing. "This was your first trip to America? What do you think of it?"

Dalziel thought for a while, then said with saloon bar judiciousness, "Well, what I think is, it'll be right lovely when they finish it."

Thirty-seven

"But it's not my business. My work is

my business. See my saw! I call it my

Little Guillotine. La, la, la; La, la,

la! And off his head comes!"

They drove up the A1 in silence, if Dalziel's snoring could be called silence. This was the Great North Road, or had been before modern traffic made it necessary for roads to miss the townships they once had joined. Hatfield they passed, where Elizabeth the First heard of her accession, and Hitchin, where George Chapman translated Homer into English and John Keats into the realms of gold; Biggleswade where the Romans, driving their own road north, forded a river and founded a town; Norman Cross, near which a bronze eagle broods over the memory of eighteen hundred of Napoleon's dead, not on a field of battle but in a British prison camp; then into what had been Rutland before it was destroyed by little men whose power outstripped their vision by a Scotch mile; and now began the long flat acres of Lincolnshire, and the road ran by Stamford, once the busy capital of the Fens and later badly damaged during the Wars of the Roses; and Grantham, where God said, "let Newton be," and there was light, though in a later century the same town ushered in some of the country's most twilit years . . .

All this and more Pascoe mused upon, uncertain whether such cycles of human grossness and greatness should be a cause of hope or of despair, till the road began to drift westward toward Newark in whose castle, King John, the reluctant signator of that first faint assertion of civil liberties, Magna Carta, died.

Pascoe slowed down. Instantly the Fat Man was awake.

"We stopping? Grand. I could murder a pint."

"Actually I was wondering if you'd mind a short diversion. It's Ellie. She got so worried about her mother, she booked her into the Lincolnshire Hospital for some tests. She went in yesterday and I know Ellie's going to be down there today, and as it's only a dozen or so miles out of our way, I wondered . . ."

"It's your car, lad. The Lincolnshire? That wouldn't be the Lincolnshire *Independent* Hospital, would it? By gum, that'll mean a kneecapping at least when they get to hear about it back at the Trotsky Fan Club!"

Pascoe smiled wanly and wondered if this were such a good idea.

The diversion east proved to be rather farther than twelve miles but Dalziel offered no comment. In the hospital car park, he scratched himself comprehensively, yawned, and said, "They'll have a bar here, I expect."

"I very much doubt it," said Pascoe.

"You're joking! What's the point of being independent?"

"I'm sure you'll get a coffee."

"Nay, I'll drink nowt in these places unless it's been brewed or distilled. More germs than a midden."

They walked together through the serried ranks of cars.

Pascoe said, "Look, sir I still don't get it. You and Sempernel cooing at each other like a pair of randy turtledoves, what the hell was that really about? And don't give me that crap about searching your case. They could have done that easy enough without letting you loose on the Highland Park!"

"So your brain's not gone altogether maggoty since I left you? Good," approved Dalziel. "So what did they get that they couldn't have got any other way?"

Pascoe thought, then said, "Nothing, except you and me together talking . . . Good God, are you saying that Sempernel was listening to us?"

"Aye, lad. And he'll likely carry on listening for a bit which is the reason I'm talking to you now. I can't be falling asleep all the time to make sure you don't start asking daft questions."

This was even harder to take in.

"The car? You think they've bugged my car? Come on!"

"Why not? Whose idea was it for you to drive down to the Smoke with Adolf and back with me?"

"Mr. Trimble's."

"But where did he get it from? Who was it told him which plane I was flying on for instance?"

"But what the hell did they want to hear?" demanded Pascoe.

Dalziel grinned lupinely.

"Exactly what they heard was what they *wanted* to hear."

"You mean . . ." Pascoe's mind raced round a maze of meanings but always found himself forced back to its center. Dalziel was watching him impatiently like an old-fashioned pedagogue. If he'd had a cane, he would have been swishing it encouragingly against his calf.

"You mean all that about Westropp killing his wife, and the Establishment cover-up, wasn't true?"

"That's right. Like a henhouse floor, all a load of crap."

"Then who did . . . ?"

"Mickledore, of course. Who else? And for exactly the reasons that Wally worked out. Poor Cissy almost caught him in the act. He knew about her and Westropp, so he thought quick and invented this cover-up tale. She was so besotted, she bought it. Whether she'd have gone on buying it if it hadn't been for the little girl, Christ knows. But by the time she got her mind together she was months into her sentence and all she wanted to do was blot out that night at Mickledore Hall."

Pascoe shook his head not in denial but to clear it.

"But this is fine, this was what you wanted to prove, more or less. Okay, Kohler got the dirty end of the stick but she grabbed hold of it with both hands and wouldn't let go, so it's no one's fault. And if Mickledore really was guilty, then Wally was right. Where's the problem?"

Dalziel now shook his head too, but not for clarity.

"The maggots are back, lad. You're not taking drugs, are you?"

Pascoe, whose doctor had prescribed a mild tranquilizer which Pottle had approved, was shocked for a second into thinking Dalziel knew about it. The Fat Man's medical philosophy could be reduced to two propositions: men who made money out of putting people on drugs should be called pushers not doctors; and, anyone going to see a psychiatrist needed his head looked. But it was surely too soon for even his spy system to have spotted Pascoe's visits to Pottle? Therefore he was still being prompted to say why what looked like the end of a problem wasn't . . .

He said, "If the Establishment cover-up wasn't to make sure Westropp didn't get done for topping his wife, there has to be another reason, right?"

"Not quite brain-dead then? You're getting there. Now you only need to answer the last question. What is it that's had buggers like Sempernel and his mob running round like blue-arsed flies for twenty-seven years? What was it that made it worthwhile topping Mavis Marsh and probably poor old Wally himself, just so the boat wouldn't be rocked? What was it they were afraid might really come out if there was too much deep digging?"

"Apart from the Partridge business, you mean?"

"Aye. That came later. That gave Waggs the leverage to get Kohler out. He told her that Westropp was dying and that made her so keen to get to see him, she told Waggs about catching Marsh giving young Tommy a blow job. Once they realized Waggs knew about the alleged baby too, they got worried the whole story might come out, either because he kept digging or through Marsh herself.

They knew she'd be very susceptible if the tabloids got a hint of it and came round waving huge checks."

"She didn't need it," said Pascoe. "Do you know how much she left? A quarter of a million! God knows what other little scams she had going."

"And all this lot started when Pip Westropp turned up at Beddington College and Marsh thought she saw a way to get her hands on whatever Kohler had got stashed away in the bank. She were greedy as a guppy, that one, but clever with it. You say Partridge laughed when he heard this handicapped kid had nothing to do with either Marsh or his son? It would be a load off his conscience, assuming he's got one. But the funny buggers must have been furious to realize that they'd been jerked around for years by a little old Scots nanny! I bet they wished they'd canceled her pass years ago!"

"Yes, but why did they decide to kill her now, after all those years?"

"I reckon they'd thought they could rely on her keeping her mouth shut for her own sake. She seemed to be cooperating all along the line. When Waggs confronted her with Cissy's story, she probably contacted Partridge who passed it on the funny buggers. Waggs had enough sense to protect his back so they offered him a deal. Go along with Marsh's original story about the blood, which had never come up at the trial, remember? Cissy would be let loose under safeguards, the Partridge scandal would be kept quiet, and hopefully Westropp would be long dead before she got anywhere near him."

"So why kill Marsh now?" persisted Pascoe.

"You came along, lad," said Dalziel. "Sticking you neb in. Asking questions, looking at photos. That was probably the turning point, when they heard her asking you to look at the photo that linked her and Pip Westropp."

"They heard . . . ?"

"You don't imagine the place isn't bugged? And once this naughty nanny starts dropping little hints to a clever copper, well, someone's got to go. Lucky it wasn't you, lad. Except you still knew nowt, whereas they were beginning to wonder just how much Nanny Marsh really did know."

About what? wondered Pascoe desperately.

What could be worse than having a peripheral member of the royal family suspected of killing his wife?

"Got there yet?" asked Dalziel, telepathic as always. "Think of the year 1963."

"Got it," said Pascoe. "It was Westropp who shot Kennedy."

It was meant as a joke, in rather poor taste perhaps, but they were the kind Dalziel usually liked. But, incredibly, absurdly, far from being amused, the Fat Man was nodding encouragement.

"Warm," he said. "You're getting warm. January sixty-three, Philby dropped out of sight in Beirut, turned up in Moscow in July. In the autumn, the funny buggers fingered Antony Blunt's collar for the first time. Him they did a deal with. Why? Mainly because he helped clean the pictures at Buck House or something! So how do you think they were going to react if . . ."

". . . if Westropp, if a Royal, turned out to be another communist agent. Bloody hell!"

"Well done, Peter. But it's been like squeezing Eskimo Nell out of a nuns' chorus. You'll need to be sharper than that if you're going to be Queen of the May."

In fact Dalziel's lofty reproof came close to equivocation. True, he had worked it out, but only after a series of nods and winks which made his own hints to Pascoe look like leaves from the Sibyl.

Westropp was eager, almost desperate to talk. It was, Dalziel decided later, the deathbed confession he was scared he might make to Marilou. So when Dalziel said, "You weren't just one of our spooks, you were a bloody commie spy too!" his wasted face had contorted in a congratulatory grin which wouldn't have been out of place in a horror film.

"And they knew about it back in 1963?"

"They were very suspicious, though of course they simply didn't want to believe it, which helped. I think it was Tony Blunt who gave them the positive confirmation. Oddly, it was Scott Rampling who first came right out with it. No royalist inhibitions, you see. You know, James, he said. It wouldn't surprise me one little bit if you didn't turn out to be one of these Cambridge commies too. I smiled and said, Indeed? And what would you do about it, assuming it were true? He said, Hell, if I got the proof, I'd do nothing. I could use it to jerk you and that bunch of amateurs you work for any which way I like, couldn't I? He was right, that was the only professional response, but fortunately he didn't get anything like proof till it was far too late. Loquacity is the American disease. Didn't he imagine that my friends would give me something to shut him up with?"

"So what did the funny buggers do with you after Mickledore Hall?" asked Dalziel.

"They whisked me away out of sight. They'd have done that anyway. It's a knee-jerk damage limitation exercise when someone in my position looks like they might get too much publicity. I was in no state to resist, not after Emily's death. It was clear that they didn't give a damn what had really happened, they weren't even particularly interested whether or not I'd actually murdered Pam, they just wanted to be sure I came across as the sympathetic figure, the betrayed friend, widowed husband, bereaved father. They knew about me and Cissy of course. In a way, what I know now was her lunatic act of loyalty worked out to her benefit . . ."

"Benefit!" exclaimed Dalziel.

"Indeed. As Mickledore's mistress, she was safe, well, fairly safe. If she'd been tempted to broadcast that she was mine, I fear that other measures might have been taken to silence her. It wasn't till after the trial and poor Mick's execution that they came to me and put it bluntly—no pun—that I was a Russian agent. I, of course, cooperated fully—I had surprisingly little to tell them—but when they suggested they should put me back on station and work me as a double double, I took off. I'd had enough, you see."

"That'd not please them."

"How true," said Westropp. "Had I met with, or even put myself within reach of, a simple accident in the years that followed, there'd have been few regrets. But though life was a pretty gray thing to me then, gray is a color a man can live with, so I kept on the move, until one day in Mexico City I ran into Marilou, and suddenly there was color in my grayness once more. Since my undergraduate days, I have been a devious bastard, Mr. Dalziel. It was part of my job description, it eventually became part of my being. You cannot imagine the joy I got, and still get, from Marilou's utter openness. I had no right to marry her, I had no resource not to marry her."

"And you came to settle here? Bit exposed, weren't you? Like a turkey taking refuge in a butcher's shop just before Christmas. Especially if Rampling had sussed you out way back."

"On the contrary, Scott was my main reason for being so willing to settle here," said Westropp gleefully. "He was by now powerful enough to offer protection."

"For old times' sake?" said Dalziel skeptically.

"Of course not. Because I had it in my power to undermine him."

Dalziel thought a moment then said, "You mean this thing your foreign mates gave you to shut him up with? Something to blackmail him with, it must have been. Christ, I've put men with cleaner hands than your lot away for life!"

"Do I detect a note of disapproval? Of what, precisely?" said Westropp.

"Of someone like you betraying his country for a start," exclaimed the Fat Man. "I can thole most things, but not a traitor, especially not one with your fancy background."

"It was my background that first got me thinking about the condition of the West, Mr. Dalziel. If patriotism is the last refuge of a scoundrel, perhaps treason is the first resort of an honest man. Take a look out of the window. This town is preserved the way it is because the Americans want to honor their past and their ancestors who fought for their freedoms. My ancestors back in England called these people traitors too."

"Oh, aye? You reckon a hundred years from now folk'll be paying money to gawk at the bed you died in, do you?"

Westropp laughed and said, "You really should have gone into the Diplomatic, Dalziel! I'll tell you what. I had planned to let Rampling off my little hook when I died. I've made him executor of my will and intended that he should find my little prophylaxis among my effects. But having discovered today for the first time how far he has inveigled Pip into his ranks, I begin to wonder if Scott deserves such consideration."

"You knew the lad worked for the CIA then?"

"Yes. It amused me to think this was the last stage in his Americanization, but I am not amused to learn how far Scott has got him involved in my affairs."

"I'd say it were likely the lad volunteered to get involved, 'cos he were worried in case I meant any harm to you," said Dalziel.

"A touching picture. Perhaps you're right. So I'll tell you what. As you seem to fancy yourself as a moral arbiter, I'll pass this on to you and leave you to decide what to do with it."

"And he handed me this old buff envelope," said Dalziel.

"What was in it?" demanded Pascoe impatiently.

"A photo. Remember all the talk about the man without a head during the Profumo thing? I think that poor old Partridge were one of them who had to get his doctor to check his tackle with a slide rule to prove it weren't him in the picture. Well, I don't know if it's the same picture that Westropp had, but this one had a head, and it showed young Scott Rampling looking very proud of himself, not without cause, and being much admired by a select audience, with one or two faces showing which suggest it were taken at one of Stephen Ward's little get-togethers. Now this 'ud mean that not only was Rampling an enthusiastic orgiast but also he didn't mind doing it in a circle which included a Russian KGB officer. The Yanks are about as hypocritical as us when it comes to sex, and even more neurotic when it comes to security. If that photo got loose and Rampling was identified, he'd not get elected as town dogcatcher!"

"So what did you do with this photo? Give it to Rampling?"

"I thought about it when I finally got to see him. But he were so bloody rude—told me I was a foreign alien and he could have me deported—that I thought, stuff it! Let the bugger sweat. I can't abide bad manners, you know that, Peter."

"Of course. Does that mean you've still got it?"

"Want a peep, do you, lad?" said Dalziel lasciviously. "It would just give you an inferiority complex and by the sound of it, you've got enough bother in the bonking department already. Nay, I tore it up and stuck it in a litter bin at Washington airport."

"Oh," said Pascoe, feeling this was a little bathetic.

Dalziel laughed and said, "But first of all, there was this fax machine. You pay your money, just like a telephone. There was a directory. I thumbed through it. You've really got to admire them Yanks. There was this number for the White House. When they talk about open government, they really mean it. So I thought, why not? Rampling was very young on the photo. Mebbe no one will recognize his face. And if they recognize any other bit of him, then it'll be a real test of patriotic zeal, won't it? So I paid my money and I faxed it to the White House."

Pascoe let out a snort of incredulous laughter which made a couple of distant nurses look round in alarm.

He said, "It's really good having you back, sir."

"Nay, don't go sentimental on me," said Dalziel in surprise. "Hadn't you best be getting off to see that lass of thine? Can't put it off forever."

"I don't want to put it off at all," said Pascoe spiritedly. "What about you? Where will you be?"

"Oh, I'll mooch around. Give us your car key in case I just want to sit out here. Don't rush. No hurry. Give Ellie my best. And the kiddie. I bought her something. A musical banana. Is she musical at all?"

"Not so's you'd notice."

"Good. It makes a bloody awful noise."

"I'm sure she'll love it." Pascoe took a few steps, hesitated, came back. "Sir, if this is all true, then you'd better really take care. You don't want to end up like Geoff Hiller."

"Suspended? Not much chance of that," said Dalziel grimly. "Suspended's what you get for knowing fuck all. Knowing what we know gets you what Mavis Marsh got. I'll take care, lad. You too. Only reason I told you any of this is so you can forget all of it. Now bugger off and see if you can bang some sense into that wife of thine."

It wasn't the most helpful advice he'd ever received from the Fat Man, however you took it. On the other hand, he hadn't worked out any viable alternative course of action.

He introduced himself to a receptionist who directed him to a waiting room. Through the glass door panel he saw Ellie deep in conversation with a white-coated doctor. Rose was straddling a chair back, looking bored. He pushed open the door.

It was Rose who spotted him first.

"Daddy!" she screamed. Fell off the chair. Bounced. Thought about crying. Decided that tears were not appropriate to the circumstance. And came running toward him, arms stretched wide.

He caught her up and swung her round, then folded her tight to his chest. Ellie had turned and was looking at him. Her face was set in her serious controlled expression, but when she saw her husband, she decided that tears were quite appropriate. He had time to register, thankfully, that these were not tears of grief before he had her in his arms too, with Rosie crushed and protesting between them.

"She's okay, Peter. She's old and arthritic and her blood pressure's terrible, but she's okay! Ninety percent of this forgetfulness is probably caused by her medication, and the other ten percent by worry. They're going to try her on other drugs and monitor the side effects. Pete, it's like having her back from the dead, like I've called her out of the tomb!"

"That's great. And what an endorsement for private medicine, eh?" he mocked.

"It just goes to show what a mess those Tory bastards have got the NHS into," she responded fiercely, then saw he was laughing at her, and laughed too.

"Can we see her?" he asked.

"I was just on my way to bring the car round to pick her up," said Ellie.

"She's not staying in then?"

"What? Do you know what these places charge per night? It's bloody extortionate!" exclaimed Ellie, her old antipathies fully reactivated. "They'll want to monitor her progress but I can fetch her back to outpatients for that. Now tell me how you've been, Peter. I mean really. You're looking pale. That fat bastard working the guts out of you with me out of the way, is he?"

There would come a time to tell her about his sessions with Pottle, but not here, not now.

"The fat bastard is at this moment sitting outside in my car," he said. "You'd better say hello and ask him yourself."

They walked across the car park together, Rose swinging happily between them, chattering away in a seamless monologue which bound them like a current of electricity. Pascoe led them confidently to where he had parked, then slowed into uncertainty.

"Where's the car, Daddy?" asked Rose.

"It's there . . . I think . . . Between that green van and . . ."

But it wasn't. The space was empty. Except for his overnight grip, which had been neatly deposited between the white lines.

"The bugger's stolen my car!" exclaimed Pascoe.

"In that case," said Ellie, "you'd better come back with us and spend the night."

Thus casually are armistices offered.

"All right."

And thus casually accepted.

Rose had broken free and run to the bag. The top half was unzipped and she pulled something out. It looked like a plastic boomerang, pimpled in purple and gleaming with gold.

"Good God," said Ellie. "I'm away for a few days and you're into appliances!"

"What is it, Daddy?" asked his daughter.

"I've no . . . hang on! Of course. It's for you, love. It's a present from Uncle Andy."

"I might have known," said Ellie.

"It's lovely," said the little girl examining the garish object closely. "But what's it for?"

Pascoe said gravely, "I do not doubt that, like Columbus, Uncle Andy has brought back much that is strange and exotic from the New World, but nothing to equal this. You are holding a musical banana without which, I believe, no American home is complete. You blow into it. But be careful before you accept such a rare gift. It may change civilization as we know it."

Rose nodded, as if registering the full implications of the warning, and examined the strange object with a grave fearlessness that reminded Pascoe so much of her mother that he felt tears prickle his eyes.

Then, dauntless, the banana to her lips she set, and blew.

Dalziel had been right.

It made a bloody awful noise.

Thirty-eight

"It is a far far better rest that I go to

than I have ever known."

The door jammed on a pile of junk mail and uncanceled papers, and there was a taint of decay on the dank air.

As Dalziel squeezed his belly over the threshold, one of his favorite precepts fluttered batlike into his mind.

A man got the welcome he deserved.

He shook the thought from his head. What the fuck had he expected? The kind of old-fashioned thriller ending yon bugger Stamper might have scripted, with a fire burning in the grate, a stew bubbling on the stove, and Linda Steele, hotter than both, lying open-legged across his bed?

He went into the kitchen.

On the table was a dusty cardboard box, unearthed from the junk room just before his departure, and half a pork pie with a fungus fuzzed bite out of it. Gingerly he picked it up, opened the back door, and lobbed the pulsating pie into his wheelie bin.

Then he sat down at the table and stared at the cardboard box.

Outside a cloud passed and a shaft of pale sunlight fell through the open door across the vinyl tiles.

Slowly, heliotropically, Dalziel's head turned.

And he saw again Mickledore bursting out of the library and pausing for a moment as he too looked toward freedom and the sunlit doorway, before turning to the stairs.

A choice had been made, that much Dalziel had registered, but he'd been a young detective then, ambitious and eager, well able to put one and one together to make three, but not yet aware how much more important it was to put halves and quarters and thirds together till you got one.

So he'd gone in pursuit, and only fractionally registered as odd that Mickledore had turned at bay not in his own but in James Westropp's dressing room.

Fractions.

He had no thought of anything except the brightness of his own future under Tallantire's patronage as he advanced, equally indifferent to both the clothing and the abuse which Mickledore hurled at him. Nor did the speed with which the man calmed down at his first touch strike him as anything other than part of that smoothing of the way which the divine crossing sweeper had ordained for him lately. Having to fetch the little girl's body up from the lake bottom had been a hiccup in that progress, but they had the bitch who'd done it safely stowed in a car outside, and this condescending, self-inflated prat was soon going to join her.

That task accomplished, he had rejoined Tallantire on the terrace.

"Nicely done, lad. You've handled yourself well all through this, and it'll not be forgotten. I reckon we could be into the big black headlines tomorrow."

"I'd not be so sure, sir," warned Dalziel. "There's plenty as'll want to put the mufflers on this one, double wrapped."

"You reckon? You could be right, Andy. Mind you, it wouldn't surprise me if there'd been a serious leak, and the press and telly boys knew I'd be bringing someone in this afternoon," said Tallantire, his eyelid drooping in the hint of a wink. "Now, I'm off. You tidy things up here. It'll be good practice for you. But don't worry. I'll see you get your share of the credit. And I'll make sure the buggers know the circus is coming to town!"

A few moments later the little procession took off with bells sounding and lights flashing.

Grinning, Dalziel went back into the house, thinking nothing of fractions, nothing of anything except short-term celebration and long-term promotion.

What took him back into Westropp's room he did not know. This was not the kind of tidying up that Tallantire meant. This should have been left to the labor of housekeeper or butler, man-servant or maidservant. Perhaps it was because something about the very idea of servants got up his nose that he found himself hanging up the clothes Mickledore had dragged from the wardrobe. Or perhaps after all his mind was already developing its sensitivity to fractions.

But his mind stuck at whole numbers when he noticed the faint flecks of color, gray and brown, on the cuffs of the soiled dress shirt which had fallen from the linen basket. He sniffed at the flecks, convinced himself they had no smell, looked further in hope of finding nothing, found instead a handkerchief, crumpled now but with folds that suggested it had adorned a breast pocket, and marked with streaks of what might have been oil. Such streaks as you might get if you rubbed the cloth along the barrel of a newly cleaned gun.

He turned to the wardrobe. The dark cloth of the dinner jacket showed nothing around the cuffs, though of course darkness would be no protection against a paraffin test.

It was all guesswork, not even that, for he refused to let his mind make such dangerous guesses. It was not as if there were anything of real substance here, anything solid . . . then his fingers had felt the shape of the key in the jacket pocket.

No reason why Westropp shouldn't have such a key. It was a common enough design. Of course, if it turned out it was almost exactly the same as the gun room key, yet wouldn't open the lock . . .

Only one way to find out. If he wanted to find out.

Slowly he stood upright.

Behind him a voice said, "Excuse me, but there is a situation downstairs which I think you should deal with."

It was Gilchrist the butler, his voice despite everything still pitched at exactly that level of courteous neutrality which placed policemen somewhere between tradesmen and gamekeepers.

Leaving Gilchrist looking in distaste at the untidy room, Dalziel descended to the hallway. It was at once clear that Tallantire's leak had been too successful, and if the main circus was opening in town, a substantial sideshow was developing here. The Partridge family, en route to their car, had been ambushed on the terrace by a media mob and beaten an inglorious retreat to the library. Here, with curtains drawn to deter prying cameras, in the vigorous language of both the stable and the hustings Dalziel was commanded to *do* something.

It took an hour of threats, lies, and promises to persuade the journalists that there was nowt for their circulation here and they were missing the real story back in town where even now Ralph Mickledore was being paraded through the streets in a gilded cage.

After that, the grounds had to be combed to make sure that a guerrilla force hadn't been left behind, before Partridge would expose his family to the open air.

As he watched the politician's car disappear, the phone rang.

It was a CID colleague.

"Andy, you still there? You want to get your arse back here, else you'll miss the party. The Black Bull. Wally's treat. He said to make sure you knew. Right little golden boy, aren't you?"

"Things went okay, did they?" asked Dalziel.

"Like a bomb. Press and telly boys everywhere, and the Chief Constable crapping himself with rage and wanting to know who'd tipped 'em off. But Wally handled it all beautifully. I reckon he's going to come out of this like a cross between Sherlock Holmes and Bobby Charlton."

Suddenly the key weighed like a rock in Dalziel's pocket.

He put the phone down and slowly, reluctantly, he went back upstairs. Feeling like a man who drops his wife's favorite ornament, and closes his eyes and opens them again, hoping against hope that the scatter of fragments will somehow not be there, he pushed open Westropp's door.

For a glorious moment he thought it had worked. The room was perfectly tidy and when he looked in the wardrobe, it was Mother Hubbard bare. But Yorkshire detectives are not allowed to wake up and find it has all been a dream. He ran downstairs, calling Gilchrist's name.

The butler appeared, radiating disapproval.

"Westropp's clothes, what's happened to them?"

"*Mister* Westropp, understandably, will not be returning to the house," said Gilchrist icily. "We have been asked to pack his things and send them to his London apartment."

"They can't have gone already?"

"Certainly not, sir," said Gilchrist, scandalized into according him a courtesy title. "We would not deliver a gentleman's clothes unlaundered."

"You mean you're doing it *now*? You're doing it *here*?"

Gilchrist obviously felt Dalziel's dismay was caused by the shock of learning that a butler had so demeaned his great office.

"Normally the maids would see to it," he said defensively, "but they are both . . . indisposed. Besides, Mrs. Gilchrist and myself are both happy to keep our minds and hands occupied in these tragic times. And though I say it myself, Mrs. Gilchrist is the best starcher of a gentleman's shirt that I know, and I am still able to sponge and press a suit till it looks like new."

It occurred to him to wonder why he was talking thus intimately to a policeman.

"There isn't a problem with the clothes, is there?"

Dalziel thought.

He thought of the brown flecks on the cuffs which could have been gravy, and the key in his pocket which could be Westropp's latch key. He thought of Kohler's confession, and Wally's unchanging certainty that Mickledore was his man. He thought of banner headlines and TV pictures and golden boys. He thought of the built-in safeguards of the English jury system and of the mystery man,

Sempernel, who had appeared like a ghost and said very little before vanishing into the thin air he seemed to have emerged from in the first place.

He thought of the party getting under way in the Black Bull.

He said, "No problem."

And of course there hadn't been. Not then. Not now. Just a slight rearrangement of the facts.

Had Mickledore drugged Westropp? Perhaps a little something in his brandy to make sure he fell asleep as soon as his head hit the pillow and didn't awake when Mick entered his dressing room, slipped out of his shirt and jacket and into Westropp's before heading for his rendezvous in the gun room. Entering as the stable clock gathered its strength for the midnight chime. Pamela sitting there, glowering, resentful, uncertain how this meeting was going to go, uncertain too what her lover was doing as with practiced ease he slipped the cartridges into the shotgun. Then the first note struck. His finger on the trigger. She probably never heard the second. Now the wire round the vise, the gun wiped with Westropp's handkerchief, Pam's hands pressed around the barrel, the note culled from the longer note with which she summoned him to this fatal meeting, dropped onto the table. And by the time the twelfth stroke was sounding, he was stepping out of the door.

And running into Cissy Kohler.

You had to admire a man who could think on his feet and Mickledore now proved he could do that.

First thought must have been to say he'd just found Pam and she'd killed herself. But he couldn't afford to raise a general alarm yet. Others, less overwrought than Kohler, might wonder why he was wearing a dinner jacket and dress shirt both manifestly far too small for him. He had to get back to Westropp's room to change. Wearing his friend's clothes had been both personal protection and a failsafe. He didn't intend to frame Westropp unless it was absolutely necessary. But now his fail-safe proved perfect for ensuring Cissy Kohler's silence, as he used his knowledge of her love for Westropp to make her his accomplice.

Later when he muddied the waters even further by letting himself be found trying to cover up the suicide, he must have thought he was home and free. Then, in the face of Tallantire's persistent skepticism and after Emily's death, having Cissy as his accomplice suddenly turned difficult. But not yet deadly. In the end surely she would tell what she thought of as the truth? And surely these bumbling policemen would come upon the evidence he had planted against Westropp?

But just in case they hadn't . . .

So he fled from the library like the unmasked killer at the end of a Golden Age murder mystery, and let himself be caught at bay in the place where he could hurl the evidence of his innocence at the feet of his pursuer.

Who had seen it, and understood it, and for reasons he had never dared to understand, turned away.

It would be wrong to say that Dalziel's conscience had been agitated by Mickledore's execution all these years. The memory of the drowned girl had been a greater troubler of his sleep. Grown men, after all, were usually guilty of *something,* and if they weren't, it was more luck than virtue. In any case, a wise cop lets the courts resolve his doubts. It's when judges change their minds that old wounds get inflamed.

But now he knew he was right, had always been right, and would always be right whatever any judge might say. It was surprising how little satisfaction it gave him. For now he had other questions to bring a little color to his white nights.

In his pursuit of justice, Tallantire had used Cissy just as ruthlessly as either Westropp or Mickledore. Okay, so she'd been a willing victim, but weren't cops supposed to protect victims, even willing ones?

Was a guilty man's death worth an innocent woman's life? And how much difference would it have made to his own actions if he'd thought of Cissy as innocent all those years ago?

He opened the cardboard box on the table. It was full of old keys, the useless accumulation of years. He stared at but did not touch the one on the top, the one he'd been looking at the night before he went to America. The marks of a file were clearly visible on its teeth.

This was the key Mickledore had used in his charade outside the gun room; the key whose existence Tallantire had deduced and whose absence he had explained by pressurizing Cissy into saying she'd thrown it into the lake; the key Mick had planted in Westropp's pocket to point the plodding police in the wrong direction.

What would Tallantire have done if Dalziel had given him the key?

Probably the same, which was why he hadn't bothered. It was his first command decision. Where the buck stops, there stop I.

And now it was history and therefore junk. There was only one place for junk. He picked up the box, took it out into the yard, and dumped the lot into his wheelie bin. Then he headed upstairs to unpack.

As he passed through the hall he noticed among all the old papers and mail an envelope with his bank logos on it. It was hand addressed which caught his attention. He tore it open. Inside was a computer printout and a note from the manager.

This confirms you now own two thousand pounds of shares in Glencora Distillery. I've just heard that Inkerstamm have taken them over which means you actually own five thousand pounds worth. Are you lucky or just a crook? Don't tell me!

God *is* good, thought Dalziel. I bet He even does plumbing on Sundays.

He ran lightly upstairs, and paused in his bedroom doorway.

God was very good indeed, or maybe just an old-fashioned thriller writer.

"Hi," said Linda Steele. "Hope you don't mind me stretching out, but I just landed a couple of hours back and I'm well and truly bushed."

"I can see that," said Dalziel thoughtfully. "You here on business?"

"Funny business, you mean? No, I'm out of that. Full time hack, is me. I got to thinking, if a little gray-haired lady twice my age can walk through me like a cobweb, what's a real heavy going to do?"

"So you decided to start the rest of your life by visiting me?"

He didn't try to keep the doubt out of his voice. Never look a gift horse in the teeth, his old mam, who liked her maxims mixed, used to say. But when a gift horse had such perfect teeth, and every-thing else, as Linda Steele, it was hard for an old cop not to start looking.

"You got a problem with that, Andy?" she asked.

"Mebbe," he said. Meaning, several. He wasn't much given to self-analysis. That was for poofs, wimps, and men with degrees. But when he did turn his eye inward, it was with the same brutal clarity of vision that he brought to bear on the outer world. He looked now and found uncertainty. How the hell could he credit that a lass like this would travel six thousand miles out of lust for a fat, balding, boozy, middle-aged bobby? No way!

Happily his doubt was a purely intellectual matter and had no channel of communication with his appetites. Even as his inner eye weighed his own attractions to the last scruple, his outer eye was totting up Linda's, and he felt his y-fronts taking the strain.

He said, "Rampling give you a leaving present, did he?"

She laughed and said, "Okay, Andy. I can see there's no fooling you. Never was. So here's the bottom line. I wanted out, that's true enough. But in that line of work, you don't just hand in your notice and walk away. Not if you want to be able to walk, that is. You part friends. I saw Rampling personally. He said, okay, if I didn't see my future with the company, that was my business. But he'd esteem it a personal favor if I could contrive to run into you and check what you got up to, who you were talking to, since you got back home."

"And you said yes."

"People like me always say yes to people like Scott Rampling," she said seriously.

"So you *are* here on business."

"Yeah, but I wasn't lying, Andy," she said. "The only *reason* I'm here on business is because I was going to be here in the first place. I told Rampling I was planning to try my luck in the UK, meaning I wanted to put a whole ocean between his boot and my sweet butt.

That's when he started talking about favors. What I hadn't told him was I was going to look you up in any case."

"Because of my bonny blue eyes, you mean?" said Dalziel cynically.

"No. Because I felt I'd like to be close to someone who did know how to say no to someone like Scott Rampling," she said.

He looked down at her assessingly. The doubts were still there, but so was the pressure in his groin. Her gaze seemed to take in both.

She said, "That's it, Andy. That's the best I can do. If it's not enough . . ."

"Nay, lass," he said, holding up a forbidding hand as she made to slip off the bed. "It strikes me, as long as you're still connected to that lot, mebbe before you left, you remembered to collect my expenses?"

She relaxed and smiled wickedly.

"Do you take American Express?" she asked.

"That'll do nicely," said Andrew Dalziel.

Thirty-nine

"I carry about with me not a scrap of writing openly referring to it. This is a secret service altogether. My credentials, entries and memoranda, are all comprehended in the one line, 'Recalled to Life,' which may mean anything."

So in the end it had been neither the best of crimes nor the worst of crimes, just another murder, ending nothing except a life.

The death of James Westropp's first wife hardly troubled his thoughts at all as he died in the arms of his second. Perhaps indeed for the first time he dimly acknowledged that, once the massive shock of events at Mickledore Hall had faded, he had been not unrelieved to have an excuse at last to back away from the tiresome trade of treachery. He had offered a defense to Dalziel, but to tell the truth he had long been perplexed to recall why he'd decided to betray his country at a time when it was a much nicer place to live than it had since become, when he felt no inclination to betray it at all.

He opened his eyes one last time to see the candid, loving, grieving face of Marilou, and suddenly knew that his silence on this subject which he'd always thought of as protective, was in fact the greatest betrayal of all. He opened his mouth to speak, but his life, so eager to escape, darted out, and his body had to be satisfied with the more general atonement of at last providing some genuine Hanoverian dust to mingle with the honored remains of Williamsburg's patriotic martyrs.

It was a quiet funeral.

Westropp's family was represented, firstly, by his son, Philip (later to distinguish himself as a CIA operative specializing in destabilizing friendly regimes to keep them grateful); and, secondly, by a tasteful wreath of red and white roses, beribboned in blue, delivered via the British Embassy with an unsigned card inscribed *In One's Thoughts At This Sad Time.*

Marilou's family was represented by her son, but not her daughter. To tell the truth, William was there only because he could fit it in as a legitimate expense en route to New York to try to interest his American publisher in *The Golden Age of Murder.* The book was completely free of any reference to Mickledore Hall, though the final chapter on the Chester Races case still opened with the words, *It was the best of crimes, it was the worst of crimes,* proving that in the desperate quest for publication, a writer will sacrifice anything except a nice turn of phrase.

Scott Rampling was there too. For years he had misused his authority by having Westropp's phone calls monitored and mail opened in the hope of getting a pointer to the whereabouts of the telltale photo. Now, finding himself appointed as executor to Westropp's will, he was able to go through all the man's papers with a fine-tooth comb. Nothing. Just when he was considering himself totally safe, a Presidential aide tossed the photo onto his desk and said, "Thought you might like a look at that, Scott."

He could not speak, his bowels felt loose, his bladder painfully full.

Then the man went on. "Came over the fax a while back. Probably some joker, but we've shown it around and one or two people have a feeling there's something familiar about the guy with the tackle. Could be worthwhile getting your people to check it out."

"I'll put someone on it," said Rampling.

Shortly after this he began to wear spectacles and grow a mustache, and fellow members of his exclusive Washington sports club noticed that he no longer took his daily sauna and cold plunge.

Jay Waggs did not attend the funeral, nor send any flowers. A man whose muddled upbringing had left him permanently confused about his own motives and emotions, he had surprised in himself a fondness for Cissy Kohler which made him reluctant to subject her to the indignities of creative journalism. Yet, in the absence of her cooperation, there was no other way of giving Hesperides anything like their due, so he had retired to Canada till such time as his fertile mind would come up with an even more amazing story to placate his predators.

As for Cissy herself, she waited till the last black car crawled away before approaching the grave.

She was here, not because of what she felt but because of what she hoped she might feel. There had been a moment when she fumbled in her bag before Dalziel pushed her from the room, which might have provided the cathartic climax she was seeking, but even now she wasn't sure if she would have pulled out the gun or her handkerchief.

The coffin was still visible beneath the obsequial scatter of earth. It was plain oak with dull brass handles. She nodded approvingly. An unostentatious man, Jamie would have wanted no more.

Then the nod changed to a wild shaking as she tried to dislodge this complacent assumption of knowledge. What the hell did she know about his likes and dislikes? What did she know about anything! She had loved with the total passion of first love. She had given herself without stint and without question, and because he had accepted the gift with such delight, she had assumed a commitment as complete as her own.

But it hadn't all been naive self-deception. When she ran into Mickledore as he came out of the gun room and glimpsed behind him the bleeding body and staring eyes of her rival, it hadn't been simply the hyperegotism of love which caused her unhesitating acceptance of his assertion, "Cissy, it's terrible . . . Jamie's killed Pam . . . He did it for you!"

She had known it was true, because this was what she and Jamie had planned to do.

No. Not *planned*. That was too precise, too cold a word for what had passed between them as, drifting in those deliciously warm shallows left by the receding tide of ecstasy, she had whispered, "If I died now, I'd be truly happy." He laughed and said, "It's not dying yourself that brings true happiness, Cissy. It's having the strength to will the death of others if they stand in your way."

"I don't know if I've got that kind of strength."

"Few people have. And few of those are willing to use it."

"Are you one of the few, Jamie?" she asked, sensing a meaning, a commitment.

"Oh, yes," he said pulling her to him and caressing her so that she felt the distant tide begin to surge back once more. "I've got strength enough for both of us."

He had been talking about Pam—what else?—and from that moment she had been warmed by the certainty that, one way or another, this sole obstacle to their permanent happiness would be removed.

Now it had happened. The bloody reality of the removal almost overwhelmed her, but strength returned as Mickledore urged the danger Jamie was in and told her of his own efforts to make the death look like suicide. If mere friendship could make a man act so nobly, how much further should love be able to go?

She had wanted to go in with him to Jamie, but he insisted this would be madness. Any hint now of a connection closer than employer and servant could be fatal. She had paddled out to the island with the children and hidden there under the shading willows till she heard her name booming like gunfire across the shining waters and knew she was being summoned to betray her lover.

After Emily's death, everything changed. Now she knew that there could be no limits to what she must do to protect Jamie, and at the same time she knew there could be no reward. It had taken a whole afternoon to work out precisely what it was the police superintendent wanted her to say. Every form of confession she made, he painstakingly copied out, then read it to her and asked if it was true. Each time she answered, "Yes," he tossed it aside and told her it was worthless. "What do you want me to say?" she screamed at him finally. "The truth. That you were Mickledore's mistress, that you and he planned and carried out the murder together, that there was a false key which you threw in the lake . . ."

"Yes yes yes!" she cried, sobbing with relief. "That's true. That's true. I'll write it!"

That Mickledore should be willing to die for his friend, and that Jamie should have allowed him to die, was no problem. He had betrayed his friendship by sleeping with Pam and this sacrifice was a fitting atonement. Hers was the harsher penalty, the longer pain, and she had no will to move to free herself till Jamie should give her a sign that enough was enough, the account was balanced.

Madly, she had weakened when she learned that Pip was at Beddington College. It seemed like a sign, not strong enough to make her pay for the help offered by that monstrous woman, but enough to make her turn to Daphne Bush, hinting promises she had no intention of keeping.

Jamie's letter had destroyed hope and with it, incidentally, Daphne's life. More guilt, more years. She had sunk beneath them once again, this time with no intention of ever resurfacing.

And then had come Jay with the news that Jamie was dying. Suddenly she had known that unless she saw him before he died, this life-in-death was all she would ever know.

Now she had seen him and what had altered?

She heard the sound of an engine and looked up to see that the small bulldozer employed to push the earth back into the grave had

357

emerged from behind the chapel. It paused as the driver spotted her. She also saw she was not alone.

Philip Westropp was walking toward her. Somber-suited, somber-faced, with a Bible clutched in his left hand, he could have been a young preacher come to offer comfort.

"I guessed you'd be here," he said.

"I didn't want to cause any embarrassment."

"All those years, and *you* don't want to embarrass *us*?"

"None of you harmed me. I harmed myself. Pip, about Emily, I was, I am, I always will be, so so sorry . . ."

"That's okay. Water under the . . . it was a long time ago." He smiled faintly. "When I first understood what had happened, I used to fantasize that you saved me because I was your favorite."

She shook her head.

"*You* saved *me*," she said. "It was dark down there. Dim shapes and waving weeds. I just grabbed. If there hadn't been anything to grab at, I think I would never have come up."

"Are you glad you did?"

"For your sake, of course. For my own? I can't say."

"What will you do?"

"Is this official?"

"It can be if you like."

"Then the answer is, I don't know. But I'll do it quietly, that's for sure. What about you? Do you really work for the CIA?"

"Why not? It's in the blood, so to speak."

"But you're British . . ."

"I was born here, remember? Mom was American. And I renounced any claim I had to dual nationality way back. I prefer the American Way."

"Because it's better?"

"Because it could be," he said. "You can cure sickness, you can't resurrect a corpse."

The image seemed to remind them where they were. They looked down into the grave in silence for a while.

"Did you really *know him*?" asked Philip.

"No," she said, surprised. "Didn't you?"

"No. There was always something . . . a barrier . . ."

Cissy dug into her purse.

"This was his," she said, proffering the pillbox. "Would you like it?"

"No," he said without hesitation.

"Okay."

She opened her fingers and the crested box fell into the grave.

"Good-bye, Pip," she said.

"Good-bye. Oh, this is yours, I think," he added, handing over the Bible. "We have no use for it."

She took it, opened it, read her mother's inscription with a faint smile.

"Me neither," she said, tossing it into the grave alongside the glittering pillbox.

Then she beckoned the waiting bulldozer to advance, turned, and walked swiftly away.